JOHN 3:16

NANCY MOSER

Tyndale House Publishers, Inc., Carol Stream, Illinois

Visit Tyndale's exciting Web site at www.tyndale.com

Check out the latest about Nancy Moser at www.nancymoser.com

TYNDALE and Tyndale's quill logo are registered trademarks of Tyndale House Publishers, Inc.

John 3:16

Designed by Jessie McGrath

Published in association with the literary agency of Sterling Lord Literistic, Inc., 65 Bleecker Street, New York, NY 10012.

Scripture quotations are taken from the *Holy Bible*, New Living Translation, copyright © 1996, 2004, 2007 by Tyndale House Foundation. Used by permission of Tyndale House Publishers, Inc., Carol Stream, Illinois 60188. All rights reserved.

Library of Congress Cataloging-in-Publication Data

Moser, Nancy.
   John 3:16 / Nancy Moser.
      p. cm.
     ISBN-13: 978-1-4143-2054-0 (pbk.)
     ISBN-10: 1-4143-2054-X (pbk.)
  1. Bible. N.T. John—Influence—Fiction. I. Title. II. Title: John three sixteen.
  PS3563.O88417J65 2008
  813'.54—dc22   2008021735

Printed in the United States of America

14   13   12   11   10   09   08
7   6   5   4   3   2   1

To Katy McKenna Raymond.

I prayed for a friend like the Katie I'd left behind.
And then I met you. . . .
May you be all-the-way happy.

ONE

The elevator doors opened. Maya Morano stepped out, nearly overwhelmed by a single thought: *The world is mine.*

"Morning, Ms. Morano," the receptionist said. "Congratulations on your award Friday night."

Triumph sang an aria in her soul. She wanted to pump her arm and shout, "Yes!" like an NBA player after a perfect three-pointer, but she knew better than to let loose. Reining herself in to a proper corporate humility, she gave a slight nod and said, "Thanks." There was a time and a place. . . .

She spotted her boss chatting with another employee outside an office nearby. She paused in the reception area, pretending to need something from her briefcase. But as she opened it, she mishandled the case.

It fell with a thud. Files scattered everywhere. Her ploy to get attention had succeeded—far beyond her wildest dreams.

"Why am I such a klutz?" she said, a little louder than necessary. She didn't have to fake her reaction. The embarrassment that turned her cheeks pink was all too real.

"Let me help," the receptionist said.

"Thanks," she said out loud, but inside she was thinking, *No! Not you* . . .

Maya sensed her boss approaching. She looked up, offering him the smile that had been so instrumental in earning Friday's award. "Good morning, sir. If you don't mind, I thought I'd work from here this morning." She waved her arms above the mess on the floor. "I do like to spread out."

"I've heard of employees wanting a bigger office, but this—" he knelt beside her to help—"is taking that urge to new heights." He winked. "I think we can do better than this."

Game. Set. Match.

She gathered her things with the help of her boss and the receptionist, then saw they had an audience. Other workers had noticed. She could see what they were thinking by the looks in their eyes.

Being on the receiving end of envy was very satisfying.

| | | | | | | | | |

Maya leaned the Top Seller award plaque against the wall of her cubicle. She hoped it was a temporary measure. An award like this should be hung on the wall of a proper office, not tucked away in an anonymous, gray-paneled cubicle, *leaning.*

Soon. The boss indicated you deserved a real office. Be patient.

She set her briefcase under the desk and shoved it out of the way with a kick of her foot, nearly toppling the trash can. She sighed. She really was a klutz. But she was working on it, getting better. Every day she got closer to being the person she wanted to be. With a quarter turn of her chair, she focused her attention on her computer screen. With a touch of her cursor, it came to life. Today's schedule glowed multicolored: green tabs for inter-office meetings, orange tabs for prospective client meetings, blue tabs for personal appointments, and red tabs for any HTDs—her personal shorthand for Hate To Dos.

She needed that code, her own warning system, stern orders to herself that on this day, at this particular time, she had to do something she disliked. The content of HTDs varied but usually involved babying some existing clients who needed reassurance that the office equipment they'd ordered from her was right for them and that Maya had given them *the* best price. She hated this part of her job. She was lousy at pasting on a smile, pretending to care. "Service after the sale" may have made a grand motto for the company, but in reality it was tedious work that Maya believed took time and energy away from getting that next big sale.

A coworker peered over the cubicle. "Hey, Maya. I would say congrats on the award, but both you and I know . . ."

"Leave me alone, Brian."

"You'd like that, wouldn't you?"

Another coworker approached. "Congratulations, Maya. Way to go on the award."

Brian shook his head and walked away.

"What's with him?" Susan asked.

Maya shrugged. "I don't know. Sour grapes, maybe?" Then she put a hand on the award, hoping Susan would bite.

She did. "Is that it? Let me see."

Maya held it close to her face like a game show cutie showing off a prize. She did *not* let Susan touch it. "Work hard, and you too can get one of these someday," she teased.

"Fat chance," Susan said. "I turned forty today. You young-sters have too much spring in your step for me to catch up."

Young? Hardly. At thirty-three, Maya felt the years rushing by.

A delivery person appeared, carrying a bunch of balloons. "I'm looking for Susan Bates?"

At the sound of her name, Susan looked up. "Hey, that's me." She took the balloons. "Thanks."

3

Maya examined the silvery globes bobbing above Susan's head. They were kind of hokey, but nice, in a weird sort of way. "Who're they from? Look at the card," Maya said.

"Doesn't seem to be one," Susan replied.

4

"Well, enjoy the gift from your secret admirer. Meanwhile, we'd better get back to work."

"Work. On my birthday." Susan looked at the balloons wistfully, then sighed. "I don't know where you come up with your clients, Maya, but if you have any extra, send a few my way, all right?"

Not in this lifetime.

Susan headed back to her work space. A few seconds later Maya overheard their boss say, "Happy birthday, Susan."

"Thank you, sir. People are being so nice. Joyce brought a cake. It's in the break room. Make sure you get a piece."

"I'll do that."

During the exchange, Maya set the award aside, flipped open a file, fanned a few papers out on the work surface, and picked up a pen. She leaned forward over the work, jotted some random numbers on the margins of a page, then moved her calculator close, adding something to anything as she waited.

"Busy at work, I see," her boss said, on cue.

She pushed her chair back and tossed the pen on the desk. "Always." She pointed at her daily schedule glowing on the monitor. "I'm clearing up the backlog so that I can visit a client who has some issues about some damage on his last order. I know he should just call claims to handle it, but—"

"But you want to give him personal service."

Not really. If he hadn't insisted on the meeting I wouldn't be going. But since I'm going, he's going to be eating out of my hand before I'm through with him.

"That's commendable, Maya. That's the way we do things here at Efficient."

"I aim to please." *You. I aim to please you.*

"It's not just about sales. I wish more salespeople realized that."

"Yes, sir."

"Carry on." He walked away.

Maya looked at her award. Her boss was wrong. It was all about sales.   5

Her future depended on sales.

| | | | | | | | | | | |

If I never have to hire another teenager . . .

Velvet Cotton leaned back in her chair, rubbed her eyes, then stretched until her spine popped. She'd already interviewed five students, and none of them were qualified. Considering the positions she was trying to fill were concessions workers, it was a pitiful situation. Although she hadn't given the five contenders math tests, she doubted any of them could count out change without having an idiot machine tell them how much to give back. And even then she wouldn't bet on them managing it well.

No. That was mean. There were plenty of good kids out there. Maybe if she was a better boss, a more patient person, she might be able to get more out of them. After all, any college kid who could program a computer, work a cell phone, or record a TV show had more talent than she did. Teaching them how to say, "May I help you?" with a smile and inspiring them to show up for work in the first place were doable goals—if she kept her attitude in check.

Velvet needed three more workers for Saturday's football game. But so far . . .

The task threatened to overwhelm her. She barely had the energy to get up to fetch the next applicant, so she broke her own internal code for professional courtesy and yelled, "Next!"

An employer's worst nightmare appeared in the opened door,

a twentysomething with a hoop piercing in her nose, a tattoo of a rose on her forearm, and a swath of gray hair sweeping around her face.

"Hey," the applicant said from the doorway.

Brilliant. "Have a seat."

To her credit the girl was dressed in something besides jeans. She wore a long gathered skirt with contrasting bands of patterned fabric, Birkenstocks, and a voile peasant blouse. Not that far from Velvet's style of choice: anything vintage, anything that screamed "bohemian."

The girl handed over her application, and Velvet took a quick look to see if there were any obvious red flags beyond the body piercing with—she glanced at the first name—Lianne. Before she could examine the résumé in detail, the girl spoke up.

"I don't know why I'm applying for this job. I hate football. In fact, I hate all sports. Why waste all that energy chasing a ball around a field when you could be doing something productive?"

It was an odd way to start an interview, and a bizarre way to get a job—although Velvet shared the girl's views, to a degree. But it certainly got her attention. "If that's your attitude, then why are you here?"

Lianne crossed her legs. "Karma, I guess. I was looking through the *Daily Nebraskan* and saw an ad for the job."

That didn't explain—

"At first I read it wrong. It said 'concessions worker' and I thought it had something to do with the law—you know, maybe arbitration or mediation. Something interesting."

Velvet laughed. "Trust me, this job can be interesting. Dealing with hungry customers often utilizes mediation of the most serious sort. But I'm still not sure why you're here."

"I didn't realize I'd read it wrong until I saw that this office was attached to the stadium. And then I figured a job's a job, and I need the money, so . . ." She shrugged. "Here I am."

Teaching this one to smile while helping a customer might stretch even Velvet's capabilities, but she was desperate. She looked again at the girl's application. Lianne . . . Lianne Skala.

"Skala?"

"It's Czech. Means 'strong as a rock.'" She shrugged again. "Whatever."

It may have been Czech, but Velvet was more interested in the fact that it was unusual. A rare name. One Velvet hadn't heard in over twenty years.

She checked Lianne's address. It was an apartment a few miles south of campus. But where was she *from*? In a college town most of the kids were from somewhere else. "Are you a student?"

"Sociology. Sophomore, though I'm old enough to be graduated."

"You're from . . . ?"

"Here. Born here. Live here. Hopefully won't die here."

Velvet's heart skipped as an assortment of details converged. *No, it couldn't be.*

The girl spoke. "You're shaking your head. So does that mean I crashed and burned? Or do I get the job? Whatever."

The job was the furthest thing from Velvet's mind.

Lianne leaned forward, resting her hands on the edge of Velvet's desk. "I know I've probably blown it, saying all the wrong things. I always do. But you need to know I am a hard worker. I show up and I do what needs to be done, which is more than most morons I've worked with can say." She pushed away from the desk. "No offense, but selling junk food is a no-brainer. I can handle the job. I promise."

Velvet's mind swam. She had one more fact to check. She needed to find out Lianne's birthday, yet age was not something she could ask about; that whole antidiscrimination thing regarding race, age, creed, etc.

She had an idea. "May I have your driver's license, please?"

"For . . . ?"

"It's procedure. We make a copy when people apply."

Lianne looked skeptical but dug a license from her floppy crocheted bag.

8

Velvet restrained herself from looking at it. She would wait until the girl was gone. She made a copy and returned it. "Well, then. I'll get back to you about the position."

Lianne rose. "But you need someone for Saturday, right? That's what your ad said. Saturday is just five days away."

Velvet got her point. "I'll call by tomorrow."

"Cool."

Maybe.

Maybe not.

As soon as Lianne left, Velvet drew the copy of the license front and center. She braced herself, not sure whether she wanted the date to match or not. Her uncertainty was surprising. It had been twenty-three years.

She looked down. Twenty-three years, two months, and twelve days.

Her hands covered her mouth. "No."

Yes.

| | | | | | | | | | |

Lianne had been the last applicant. Objectively, the girl had as little or as much going for her as the other applicants. As the girl had said, selling junk food wasn't brain surgery. It wasn't a question of capability. Velvet could choose the three she needed from the applicants and get by.

The question was, should she choose this particular girl?

Lianne.

Lianne Skala.

A hometown girl.

A girl with a unique streak of gray hair framing her face.

Not so unique.

Velvet crossed her office to a grouping of photos on the wall. Faces looked back at her: football players from her past, coaches, administrators. There, in a photo on the right-hand edge, was the one she was looking for. She removed it from its nail and stared.

At herself. Twenty years younger, smiling at the camera, a sweep of gray hair framing her face.

She pulled the photo to her chest and endured a wave of panic rushing up her spine. To have seen that same streak of hair in this girl—proof that, in spite of decisions made back then and the circumstances created since, they were cut from the same cloth.

Lianne had mentioned karma had brought her here. Today. To apply for the job. Velvet didn't believe in karma any more than she believed in divine intervention, or signs, or predestination, or fate, or . . . or much of anything. Life just *was*. Things just happened.

Yet the fact remained: Lianne had walked into Velvet's office. No one else's office. Velvet's office.

It hardly seemed a coincidence.

Lianne, born on the same day as the child Velvet had given up for adoption, as the daughter she'd not seen since the day they'd both left the hospital. Lianne, looking enough like her younger self to be her double. No, that wasn't coincidence.

Punishment. That's what it was. Further punishment for her own ignorant, rash stupidity.

More than twenty years ago, Velvet had messed up her life. And because of that, she knew she deserved every trial, every slice of suffering, every price—no matter how steep and unpayable— that she'd endured ever since.

Including this.

Yet rather than run from it, Velvet did what she always did. She embraced it.

She returned to her desk, found Lianne's application, and dialed the phone.

10 "You got the job," she told the girl and ended the call with the details of where and when to show up for the first day of work.

Now she just had to figure out what came next in this dance of . . . what had Lianne called it? . . . karma.

She put her head in her hands and cried.

| | | | | | | | | | |

Peter McLean sat on the plaid couch in his apartment, his feet on the coffee table, a copy of *Cross-cultural Sociology in Today's World* open on his lap. Chapters one and two were assigned for Wednesday's class. He just couldn't wrap his head around them. Turning on the TV sounded much more appealing. Maybe changing his major wasn't such a good idea. Not that the textbooks for his old agribusiness major would have been any more riveting.

He felt stupid for not being able to get into any textbook that came his way. Peter wasn't a kid anymore—and this wasn't his freshman year. Shouldn't he be able to grasp big ideas, big concepts, and even big words by now? Shouldn't he find his classes interesting and inspiring? This was real life he was working toward. Shouldn't he feel more grown-up about it?

Peter looked up when he heard whistling in the exterior hall. His roommate, William, never whistled. It had to be Lianne.

Lianne never bored him like his textbooks did. Excited him, challenged him, and even scared him more than he would ever admit. But bored him? Never.

Making her usual grand entrance, she burst through the front door without knocking.

She didn't say anything, just plopped onto the couch beside him, slammed his book shut, swung her legs over his, and lay down, taking possession of the couch. And him.

"So?" Peter asked. "Did you get the negotiations job?"

She wiggled her feet, a sign she wanted him to remove her sandals. Which he did. "Actually, it wasn't that kind of concessions work. It's food concessions. For football games."

Peter tried unsuccessfully not to laugh. Only Lianne could have made such an assumption. Lianne saw everything a half step off square from the rest of humankind. Whether that made her less or more than anyone else, he hadn't fully discovered yet. But it sure made her intriguing. Unlike him, she was wild and wonderful, always doing the unexpected.

She swatted at him but missed. "Stop laughing. It was an honest mistake. And I applied anyway. I might even get the job. So there."

"You? Selling pop and hot dogs? At a football game? Have you ever even seen a football game?"

"I don't need to know football to hand someone a burger and change." She snuggled lower, adjusting a couch pillow under her head. "I didn't know about the negotiating kind of concessions either, but that didn't stop me from wanting to apply for that job. I can learn anything. Do anything. I am *woman*."

"Yes, you are." He began to massage her feet. He admired her zest for life as well as her confidence. Nothing fazed her.

Most everything fazed him. He felt so stupid sometimes. In fact, half the time he opened his mouth, he heard stuff his father used to say pop out. Which freaked him out every bit as much as it freaked Lianne. Better to keep quiet and soothe his lady's feet.

She closed her eyes. "Mmm. Never stop that."

He could handle that. His constant goal was to make her happy, to have her smile at him and kiss him and . . . Peter hadn't had much experience with women. Living on a farm and going

11

to a small-town high school hadn't offered him many opportunities. It felt like people were watching him back home, no matter where he went. But now, here at college, it was like he was free for the very first time. And with Lianne . . . he was free to be hers—body, mind, and soul.

But was she his?

He wasn't sure.

They'd met last semester in an art history course—an elective for both of them. At the time he'd still been going after his agribusiness degree, learning how to run the family farm. Lianne was studying to become a world-class social worker—preferably in some far-off land that had poor plumbing, tropical diseases, and big societal needs. Making money wasn't as high on Lianne's priority list as it was for most people. Peter wished he could feel that way about life. Sometimes he wanted to break free. To experiment. But the expectations of his parents held rein over him, possessed him, propelled him, pursued—

A blast of some punk rock ballad shrieked its way through Lianne's handbag.

"Your purse is ringing," Peter said.

"Tell it to call back. I'm comfortable."

He reached over her legs and retrieved the bag. "Take it. It might be destiny calling."

She rolled her eyes but dug the phone out and answered. "You got me."

Lianne gave few clues as to who was calling. Her one-word answers of "Okay," "Sure," "Cool," and "Bye" were too generic to be informative.

Once finished, she flipped her phone shut and dumped her purse back on the table. "Where were we? Oh. Yes. Feet. Never stopping."

Peter resumed his foot massage. "Who was that?"

"My new boss."

"You got the job?"

"Looks like."

He shoved her legs away and sat upright. "Awesome. Congratulations."

Though she was sprawled across the couch, totally relaxed as usual, she still smiled.

And crooked a finger at him.

"Let's celebrate."

He could handle that. . . .

| | | | | | | | | | |

Lianne brought him a glass of water. "Guilt is for idiots, McLean," she said.

He patted the space beside him on the couch. "A lifetime of being told not to have sex before marriage hangs over me. Hovering. Threatening to crash down on me."

"It's wrong for your parents to hold you to that. You're an adult now. A baby adult, maybe. But an adult just the same."

She loved holding her older-woman status against him. But three years wasn't that big a deal.

"I don't feel like an adult. I feel clueless."

"Yeah. I know that feeling." She nodded. "Sounds like an adult to me."

He pushed her silver streak behind her ear. "You always make me feel better."

She smiled. "I know."

"Not like that!" He grinned at her. "That's not what I meant— or not just like that. You always make me feel better about life. You make me believe there's stuff out there waiting for me. Stuff I'd miss without you."

She pulled back in order to see him fully. "That's the nicest thing you've ever said to me, McLean."

"I mean it." He took her under his arm, and she settled in as if she belonged there. He couldn't believe how amazing it felt to hold someone he loved and have that person hold him. "I've led a boring life. I had it good as a kid. Good parents on a good farm. Got through school okay, too."

"I know—big man on campus and all that. But?"

"But . . . I'm expected to go to college, get a degree, and go back to the farm like I never left. To carry it on, just like my dad and his dad before him."

"And you're supposed to marry a nice local girl, go to church on Sunday, and have 2.5 children."

"Yeah. Like that. Like some Gomer out of a sixties sitcom. Though my mom would probably prefer even more grandkids. She keeps telling me we've got that big ol' farmhouse to fill."

She pulled out of his embrace a second time. "You know I'm not what your parents want for you, McLean."

"No. But you're what I want for me," he said.

"Awww." She gave him a big, smacking kiss. "Style points for that one. Still, your parents aren't going to like me tomorrow. And I'm pretty sure I won't like them."

"They're good people. Give them a chance."

"I will. But I can't be who I'm not. Before we got serious, I told you I'm no churchgoing Lutheran farm girl. I warned you."

He traced the edge of her knee. "You did. You warned me. It was one of the things that made you irresistible."

She narrowed her eyes and stared at him in a way that always made him feel warm inside, like he was melting. There was something about Lianne that drew him in like a moth to a flame. He let himself fall further into the fire now.

Lianne groaned. "You are so . . . so . . ."

He couldn't let that one go by without a challenge. "Perfect for you?"

She answered with a kiss.

| | | | | | | | | | | |

Roman Paulson sat in the bleachers and closed his eyes, imagining a sea of red all around him.

On Saturday this stadium would be just that: a sea of red. Eighty thousand people dressed in the color of the Nebraska football team. Wearing red was not a requirement for entry, but the local culture meant it was near enough to being a law. Anyone coming in sporting another color was given a second look, their loyalty to team and state in question.

Being in the stadium was electric—even today during a simple practice. His dream was finally within his grasp. He'd left work early to be here. The advantage of being the sales manager at Efficient Office Machines was that he could do such things. Yet with his son's first starting game coming up Saturday—being high in the corporate ladder or not—he couldn't concentrate on work any better than a clerk in the mail room.

Roman's best friend, AJ, bumped against him, shoulder to shoulder. "Hey, proud papa. Keep your head in the game."

Roman opened his eyes and let the dreams of a glorious victory transform into the reality of a daily practice. No crowd, no cheers, no marching band. Just the sound of pads hitting pads and the shouts of coaches drilling the plays.

"I've waited a lifetime for this," Roman whispered.

"Five more days and our Billy will have his day on the turf—his first start."

Five more days. What was that compared to a lifetime of preparation?

AJ pulled his XXL T-shirt away from his chest a few times to get some air moving. It might have been September, but summer held on fast. "I remember you and me teaching Billy how to hold a football. The thing was as big as he was. And now . . . the way he runs with that ball . . . I'm so proud you'd think he was *my* son." He slapped Roman on the upper arm. "Should have been my son if only you hadn't wooed Trudy away from me."

"It didn't take much," Roman said.

"So you'd like to believe."

"So I know. The better man won. Me." It was their usual banter. Roman knew AJ didn't take offense.

And it was the truth. Roman had indeed won AJ's college sweetheart away. He'd been glad about it—because he'd loved Trudy madly—but a part of him always felt guilty too, because after losing out on their love triangle, AJ had settled for someone far lower on the great-woman pole than Trudy. She'd been a woman who had no tolerance for AJ's humor or the fact the two couples lived next to each other. Roman hadn't been too keen on that last detail either—at first. But as the years passed, and the love he and Trudy shared deepened, he quit worrying about having an ex-boyfriend next door. All he remembered was that AJ was his best friend. *Until death do us part.*

AJ's wife never got used to it. After eight years of marriage, she'd moved on.

Soon after, Trudy had also moved on. But not because she'd felt the need to find herself. A heart defect that had silently been a part of her since birth made itself known, invaded their lives, and all too soon, took Trudy away from him.

He'd never felt whole since. But he'd had a son to raise, so he'd gotten on with the business of living. He'd made a good job of it, he thought, even though he still missed Trudy with every breath, every heartbeat. And AJ was a part of his parenting success.

The friendship between the two men had intensified due to their common grief and anger at the world. Without children of his own, AJ had become a second father to Roman's seven-year-old son, Billy. AJ was the unassuming good old boy to Roman's driven stage-father routine. Two fathers. No mothers.

No women to speak of.

Roman had dated a few times since his wife's death, but no one could match the spirit and inner loveliness of Trudy. She had been the spark to his fire, the wind to his sails, the . . .

The love of his life.

Surprisingly, AJ had dated a lot. Hardly the handsome lothario type, more down-home than uptown, AJ always had a bevy of women who wanted to date him. He'd succumbed to many, but none for long, until a couple of years ago when he'd suddenly left the dating scene behind. He never would talk about it much, but Roman guessed some date had accidentally (or not so accidentally) made a bad comment about AJ's growing paunch and receding hairline. AJ's offhand remarks about women these days made Roman think something along those lines had given AJ second thoughts about the entire process. In Roman's experience, men could be every bit as vain as women—and their egos even more delicate.

"Hut!"

The ball was hiked and the quarterback executed a smooth handoff to Billy, who sped around the right side, sloughing off defenders, juking left, then right, gaining nine yards.

"Good one, Billy!" Roman yelled as AJ let out a holler.

Billy looked up at them, and even with the helmet, Roman could see the smile that continued to melt his papa-heart.

Roman had often wondered what he, as a father, would have done if this plan to bring up a football star hadn't worked out as planned.

Thankfully, that wasn't an issue. Billy had been a fine running back in high school, fine enough for Nebraska to come calling, offering him a scholarship. Roman often wished Lincoln were a smaller town so everywhere he went people would know him and ask about his son, a star football player for the Huskers. Lacking that, Roman managed to bring up the subject in most venues. He knew it was bragging, but he couldn't help himself. His son was an amazing kid.

If people didn't like it? They could move to another state.

This coming Saturday, after two years in the program, after working himself up from third string, Billy was going to start the game. Roman had aspirations he would be another Heisman trophy winner like Mike Rozier or Johnny Rodgers. The tradition and legacy were firmly established. His son was ready to slip into those same running shoes. If his buttons were threatened by bursting now . . .

Roman let his gaze rise from the green of the field to the sky. It was a brilliant blue with white clouds offering the occasional blessed shade. Once again his thoughts turned to Saturday, when thousands of red and white balloons would be released upon the first Nebraska score—the first Paulson score. He always found the balloons mesmerizing. The majority rose quickly above the stadium, yet there were always a few that offered an interesting side step as a current of wind took hold. Roman would follow the stragglers until they found a point of release and sped skyward as though the heavens had drawn in a breath.

Heavens. Trudy. He and his wife had never had a chance to discuss plans for their grown-up son. Yet Roman was certain she would approve of the path he'd set for Billy. Trudy loved college football. They'd met as students at a Nebraska game. If only she could see him now. See Billy. Sit in the bleachers next to Roman. Hold his hand, lean her cheek against his shoulder . . . He could easily remember the feel of her hair against his lips.

Billy broke through his tackles and sped toward the end zone. Roman and AJ stood and cheered—even though Billy didn't run full-out the entire way. After all, this was only practice.

Saturday was the real thing. Saturday was *every*thing.

| | | | | | | | | | |

Roman and AJ walked past a concessions stand, empty except for a lone woman with a clipboard. A special woman. Roman took a step toward her. "Make sure you have plenty of Runzas for the game Saturday, Velvet."

She took up her pen as though she would take notes at his command. "How many shall I put you down for? Ten? Twelve?"

"Three each should do it."

"Unless we're losing," AJ added. "We eat more under stress."

"Then let's hope for a loss."

"Watch it, lady." Roman walked to the counter and gave her a smile. He enjoyed teasing Velvet. They'd met two years previous during Billy's freshman year. Billy didn't play that first year— being redshirted so he could play when his body was more mature and finely tuned—but Roman had still come to every home game. He'd met Velvet Cotton at the first one, her unlikely name as eccentric as her massive mane of gray hair and her no-nonsense talk. They'd been friends ever since, though they had little in common other than she was the concessions manager and he was a concessions eater. Not even Nebraska football was common ground, because despite her position, Velvet disliked football and all things Husker. Roman had asked her about it—why she would want to spend time with him when he lived football and worshiped all things Husker—and she'd responded, "Sue me. I'm a masochist."

He'd tried to prod more out of her but had gotten nowhere. But he liked her style. And so they'd continued their strange relationship, as it was, illogical or no.

Responding to her hope for a loss, Roman crooked a finger toward her. She dutifully leaned forward. "Don't ever talk about losses, Velvet," he said. "You know Billy's starting for the first time Saturday. They can't lose."

She laughed and stood upright. "They can't lose because Billy's the greatest player who's ever lived, or they can't lose because you'd die on the spot if they dared?"

"Both," Roman and AJ said at the same time.

She pulled a box of cups from under the counter and checked its contents. "Then I retract my statement. I will sacrifice a few Runza sales for the sake of your pride."

"I appreciate it."

"I appreciate it, too," AJ said. "He's too heavy to haul back to the car."

She made a notation on the clipboard, then pointed at a stack of boxes on a shelf. "Get me that top one, will you, Roman?"

He went behind the counter and pulled down a box of paper napkins, placing it on the counter.

"So," Velvet said, "aren't we due for another outing?"

Roman noticed her choice of words. They never called their time together *dates*. It wasn't that kind of a relationship. But when *had* they last seen each other? Two weeks? "I'm game if you are," he said. "Wednesday? Dinner?"

"You're on."

The two men walked away. "I still don't understand why you two see each other—or what you see in each other," AJ said. "From what you tell me you never really get beyond small talk."

Roman tried to put it into words. "We're more than friends, but less than . . . I let her be in whatever iffy mood she's in, and she does the same for me. We don't have to pretend or be *on*. We understand each other."

"A feat, I'm sure."

"Hey, it works, so back off, bucko."

"Fine," AJ said. "For the moment. But I reserve the right to razz you and harass you at a later date. If warranted."

As if Roman could stop him.

| | | | | | | | | | |

Roman and AJ stood outside the door to the team locker room waiting for Billy to exit. Others waited for their players, an impromptu society of well-wishers.

The door opened and the boys streamed out. They were far less formidable without their shoulder pads, but many still outweighed Roman by a hundred pounds—of muscle. Billy was third out. His face lit up when he saw Roman and AJ. They took turns pulling him into a manly hug with the requisite pat on the back. Roman snuck a peck to his son's ear. Then he slid his arm around Billy's shoulders and they headed for the parking lot. "So? How does it feel to be a football star?"

"The game's Saturday, Dad."

"You got two touchdowns today."

"Against our own players. Saturday . . . it'll be different."

"It'll be awesome," Roman said.

"I hope so."

Roman couldn't tolerate any doubts. "None of that. You've worked hard for this. You've earned your starting position. It will be great."

"I know. You're right. I admit that when I'm on the field—" he looked at his father, his eyes serious—"it feels amazing. Like I'm doing what I'm supposed to be doing. What I've been building toward, my entire life."

Roman drew his son's head toward his until they touched.

| | | | | | | | | | |

The restaurant near campus was nearly full, but nothing like Saturday, when it would be swarming with fans. The decor was pure Husker-mania with banners and pennants and signed posters of past football heroes on the wall. Roman edged his way through the crowd to the hostess desk and said, "Three, please."

"Name?"

"Paulson."

22 A man with a protruding gut that revealed he liked to watch football, not play it, stepped toward Billy. "Hey, I recognize you. You're William Paulson, right?"

"Billy," Roman said.

"Uh, yeah. That's me," Billy said.

The man shook Billy's hand, then shouted out to those present, "We have William Paulson here! Number sixteen! Our best hope for a national championship."

The people at the tables applauded. A few stood to get a better look. The good preseason press Billy had received paid off. Someone started chanting, "Go Big Red! Go Big Red!" until the entire place rocked.

A grandmother type who was waiting for a table kissed Billy's cheeks as if he were her own boy child. A couple of men slapped him on the back and wanted to shake his hand.

"This is my dad and our best friend," Billy said.

The greetings were expanded to Roman and AJ. Roman filed the moment away for later reliving. It was everything he'd ever hoped for.

Big Belly told the hostess, "We're up next on your list, but give these three our table. We can't have our best hope waiting like a nobody."

The hostess made a notation, winked at Billy, then said, "If you'll follow me, your table's ready."

Once they were seated, and the newest onslaught of well-wishers left the table, Billy leaned toward the two men in his life and said, "Send me to heaven now. It doesn't get any better than this."

Roman agreed completely.

| | | | | | | | | | |

They were just finishing their steaks when Roman asked his son, "When are you coming to dinner this week?"

"I can't," Billy said, sitting back in his chair with a satisfied grunt. "Not this week."

23

Roman couldn't help but voice his disappointment. "You couldn't last week or the week before. I bet you've only been over two or three times all summer."

"Sorry. I had that lawn job and then practice started, and . . . and this week I have something every night." He looked at AJ, and some kind of acknowledgment passed between them.

What was going on?

"What kind of something?" Roman asked.

"Just stuff I committed to. I'll come next week."

Roman was saddened to see how their once-a-week visits had diminished the past year or so. When he'd first started college, Billy had often brought his friends over to hang out. Recently, more often than not, he had something going that kept him away.

Roman's disappointment overflowed. "It's always something."

"I can't help it, Dad. I've made promises. Commitments."

"You've made a promise to me." He felt bad for being so harsh and straightened his unused spoon so it was perpendicular to the edge of the table. "Come on, Billy. How about Thursday?"

"I . . ." Another look to AJ. "I can't."

"Lay off, Roman," AJ said. "The boy has a busy life, you know."

I don't know, but apparently you do.

Roman pushed his plate toward the center of the table. "I don't mean to complain, but it feels like I'm in the middle of a conspiracy against me; like you two have something planned, and I'm not invited, and . . . and I don't like the feeling."

"It's not a conspiracy, Dad." He looked down at the table. "On Thursday I have this picnic thing I have to go to. For charity.

Some kids I'm mentoring with a few friends. We're taking them for a picnic and swimming, and in a few weeks they're even going to get to go to a Nebraska football game."

"Who's *we*? Who's taking them to this picnic?" *And why am I not invited?*

Billy hesitated and once again glanced at AJ. "Church. I'm doing it through church."

Roman fell back against his chair. "Since when are you still involved in church? I thought we discussed that ages ago."

"We did. And I know the whole church thing made you nervous back then—"

"Still makes me nervous. I thought you stopped going to church."

Billy sighed. He looked like he wanted to be anywhere else. "I stopped telling you about me going to church. But I still go."

AJ defended him. "Back off, Rome. Since when is church a bad thing?"

"Since my son became obsessed with it." His insides churned in a way he hated. His relationship with Billy had always been good. They were best buds, chums, friends. But lately . . . it killed him to see Billy pull away. Especially because he suspected the culprit was an interfering coach who was butting in where he wasn't wanted.

"I'm not obsessed. I just got involved. Coach Rollins said that—"

Roman felt vindicated. "Your coach is making you go?"

"Not at all. But some of my teammates—"

"The coach should keep his faith to himself."

"He does. He doesn't preach at us. Nothing like that. But his faith is a part of him. We all see it. You can't talk to the man without seeing it. Feeling it."

"I know what you mean," AJ said. "Even when he gives an interview to the press, you can tell he's an honorable man, a good man. A godly man."

Roman objected. "A man can be good and honorable without being a Holy Roller." *Look at me, Billy. Look at me.*

"He's not like that," Billy said. "He just makes a guy want to be a better person, you know? Off the field as well as on."

"Sounds good," AJ said.

25

All Roman's frustration came tumbling out. "It sounds intrusive. Like I told you when you first started talking about this God stuff, I don't want you involved with people like that. People who offer false promises, who get you involved with a bunch of meaningless ceremony, with a God who doesn't . . ." He couldn't finish the sentence as intended. "I said it then, and I'll say it now: You have a father who loves you. You don't need another one in your coach, or God."

AJ laughed nervously. "That's pretty egotistical of you, Rome."

Probably. But Roman didn't take it back. He couldn't. "I told you I don't want church stuff to interfere with your life. With sports. Your future is football."

Billy rearranged his steak knife on his plate, setting it just so. "That's my present. My focus right now. But it's not my future— at least not forever. Not completely. John 3:16, Dad. That's my future. Our future."

John what? Roman had no idea what he was talking about.

The waitress came to the table and reached for their dirty plates. "Can I tempt you with some Death by Chocolate or Crazy Carrot Cake this evening?"

"No," Roman said, staring across the table at his son, pleading with him with his eyes. "Unfortunately, we're done here."

| | | | | | | | | | |

The ride back to Billy's apartment was made in silence. As was the trip to Roman's and AJ's homes—until Roman pulled into the driveway and turned off the car.

AJ put his hand on the door handle. "You really shouldn't be so hard—"

Roman pointed a finger at him. "Don't." He took a calming breath. "Please."

AJ kept his eyes locked on Roman, took in a breath, let it out, and took another one.

Roman mentally coaxed him. *Don't say anything. Not a thing, AJ. I don't want to discuss—*

AJ got out of the car, shoved his hands in his pockets, and started to walk away. Halfway across the lawn he turned. "Barring the gates of heaven is a hefty job, Roman. I hope your muscles are as strong as your ego."

Low blow.

| | | | | | | | ▶ | |

Roman tossed his keys on the table in the foyer and stormed to the kitchen. The door of the refrigerator was the next victim, as was the can of Coke, which dared to foam upon opening. He tossed it in the sink, where it gurgled and fizzed down the drain.

AJ's parting words returned to him, fresh and biting: *"Barring the gates of heaven is a hefty job, Roman. I hope your muscles are as strong as your ego."*

The kitchen table, which had the audacity to exist, seemed to mock him. Anger washed through him until he could hardly stand it. He swiped his hand across the surface, sweeping it clean of the morning newspaper, salt and pepper shakers, napkins, a coffee mug, and a plate and fork dirtied with egg yolk.

They fell to the ground with a satisfying crash.

"He's not yours; he's mine!"

Roman's words echoed in the sudden silence. He felt a shiver course up his spine.

I shouldn't have said that.

Yet how could he not say it? Billy was everything to him. Billy was the only thing that gave his life meaning and purpose. Sure, he had his work, but it was just work. And, yes, he had friends, but they had their own lives.

Billy was *his*. And the thought of his son being lured into a world of church and charity without Roman's knowledge and against his will—it was like getting slugged in the stomach.

27

The house was quiet. And empty. Too empty.

He never should have let Billy move out of the house. Yet everyone had said it was a good idea. They told him letting kids live in a dorm, and then an apartment, gave them the full college experience, helped them make friends, forced them to be tolerant and deal with problems and people issues. It helped them become independent.

Which is exactly what had happened.

And it had Roman's temper steaming at full boil.

Billy's newfound independence had made him defy his father's wishes. Over the last thirteen years Roman had carefully honed a plan for Billy's life, a plan which Billy was now ignoring.

Roman looked upon the litter of debris on the kitchen floor. It sickened him. The whole situation sickened him. The broken shards were like the debris of his shattered dreams, evidence of Billy's betrayal. And of God's greedy nature.

God—if he existed—had stolen Roman's wife from him.

No way was Roman letting God take his only son.

He left the mess where it had landed.

Turning his back on everything, he turned out the light and stomped off to bed.

| | | | | | | | | | |

After work, Maya pulled into the driveway and was surprised to see her husband's white pickup. It was still daylight. As a landscaper,

Sal used the daylight like a fisherman used the sea. Too soon the days would be short and the work would dry up for the winter.

She sneaked her compact car beside his and entered the house via the kitchen door. Sal was at the kitchen table arranging purple asters in a vase.

"For me?"

He reddened. "For Mama. She wants to see us as soon as we can get over there."

Agata Morano. The quintessential Italian mother-in-law: full of pasta and pester. And Salvatore was the quintessential Italian son: full of pamper and provision.

Maya set her briefcase on the floor by the coat tree. "Oh, Sal. Can't it wait? Or . . . or maybe you could go alone? I'm just not up to it." It's not that she didn't love her mother-in-law, but polite chitchat after a hard day at the office was not what she had in mind.

He cut off the end of an aster before slipping it into the vase. "I saw her alone last time. Tonight she specifically asked for both of us to come." He glanced up. "I've been thinking about asking *her* for the money."

Really? Maya perked up. "Your mother doesn't have that kind of money. Does she?"

"She might. Dad left her some."

She knew the concession Sal was making in offering to do this. And yet she wasn't sure it would be worth it. Not when the chance of success was so small. "Your mother barely gets by as it is. Besides, as her only son and daughter-in-law, we should probably be the ones giving her money, making *her* life easier."

A flower stopped in midair. "But I know she wants us to have a child as much as we do. Unless we keep trying the infertility treatments . . . We don't have the money for another one, Maya. You know that."

All too well.

He snipped another stem. "I'm sure she'd like to be a part of it, contribute something to the cause." He placed the last flower in the vase. "I just want a child. I want one now."

Maya's stomach clenched in a far-too-familiar degree of tension. This need they shared, this desire to conceive, consumed nearly every thought she had and far too many of their actions. They'd been disappointed twice already. To try again was her greatest desire—and also her greatest fear.

Practicality claimed its moment. "There's no guarantee more treatments will work, Sal. We've already spent twenty thousand with nothing to show for it, not to mention the mental and emotional cost of getting our hopes up each time only to fail. It's enough to break my heart."

"It'll happen. I know it." He pointed the clippers at her. "Don't get pessimistic on me, Maya Morano. God wants us to have a child. Period. Because of that, nothing will stop it from happening."

She was far less certain. If the past six years of trying was any indication, Maya was pretty sure Sal was reading God's intentions wrong. Way wrong.

He was waiting for her to say something, to yield to his pep talk. But she couldn't egg him on. It didn't do either of them any good. There wasn't much that did either of them any good anymore. Which was another problem.

He took her silence as dissension. "Super," he said. "With your kind of attitude nothing's going to happen."

She'd hurt him. Again. "Sal, I'm just trying to be realistic."

He picked up another flower. "Let me finish this. Mama is waiting."

As was *this* mama.

| | | | | | | | | | |

Agata met them at the door, catching them before they knocked. "Come; come in," she said.

Maya's defenses rose immediately. Not that Agata wasn't always welcoming, but her eagerness, and the fact Maya spotted the requisite cherry biscotti and coffeepot and cups already set on a tray in the tiny living room—there was a hint of desperation in the air.

They offered their hugs and received Agata's dual kiss to their cheeks. Sal received an additional cupped hand to his face. "I am so glad you have come."

It was too formal. Too arranged.

Instead of heading back to the kitchen to sit around the table while Agata puttered at the stove or sink, they were led to the gold couch. The piping along the cushion's edges was worn where the bend of the knee met fabric.

Agata sat in her usual place, the olive Queen Anne chair across from them, the table of coffee between. She made no move to serve, but sat with her feet on the floor, her hands playing with the edge of a flowered apron.

Sal adjusted a needlepoint pillow at his ribs. "Well then."

The easy conversation—as much a feature of this house as the bevy of throw rugs leading from here to there and the porcelain knickknacks holding court on every doilied surface—was absent. The gallery of family pictures looked down on them, their smiling faces covering their certain confusion.

Something was up. Something big.

Maya was about to take a napkin and place a biscotto on it—for she knew nothing pleased Agata more than an eating guest—when her mother-in-law lifted her hands from her apron for the briefest of moments, then let them fall as words spilled out. "I have lung cancer."

The room became a snapshot, a slice of time caught forever in Maya's mind. *Oh yes, this is what my mother-in-law's living room looked like the day she told us she had cancer.*

Sal was out of his seat, kneeling at his mother's side. He put his arms around her and hugged her like he thought his strength could hold the cancer at bay. "I'm so sorry. So, so sorry." Tears rolled down his cheeks, mirroring his mother's.

Maya tried breathing and was surprised when a breath allowed itself to be taken in and released. She felt frozen, like Lot's wife. A pillar of salt trapped in a living world. But even when freed from that paralysis, she didn't know what to say. She knew her first thoughts were probably not the best to put into words just yet: *What's the prognosis? How long do you have?*

Agata took Sal's hand in both of hers and looked into the eyes of her son. "I've already had tests. It's rather extensive. All those years living with your father's smoking, I guess."

That Eduardo Morano had died in a car accident even though he should have been the one to suffer lung cancer was an irony that didn't change a thing. His beloved wife had been left behind to pay the price for her husband's vice. Life was so unfair. Maya thought of her own childless state and immediately felt a twinge of guilt. Her troubles were dwarfed by what Agata was facing.

She searched for the right words. What came out of her mouth finally was, "What can we do to help?"

"I go in for my first round of treatment tomorrow."

"So soon?" Maya asked. Yet time . . . time was always of the essence in these things. All things, really. . . .

"The doctor thinks it's best."

Maya's eyes met her husband's, saw what was implied, then looked back to Agata.

"I'll take you," Sal said.

"I'll go too," Maya said.

"No, Maya. I appreciate the offer more than I can say, but I don't want to make a big production of it. But, Sal, I *was* hoping you would come with me." She reached for the coffee and began to pour. "Maya, take a biscotto, dear."

Maya took a napkin and placed a biscotto on it. As she waited for her coffee, her mind ticked along its ingrained track. An un-gracious thought intruded.

So much for asking her for money.

Stop it! she told herself firmly.

And yet the need to have a grandchild *now*, to give this woman some bit of happiness, just in case . . .

Maya had to get pregnant. Had to.

| | | | | | | | | | |

Sal drove a fist into his pillow before placing his head in the in-dentation. Although he had done so every night of the seven years they'd been married, tonight's punch seemed to possess an extra dose of force.

Maya lay on her side facing him and waited. Once under the covers he turned his head in her direction and held out a hand, palm up. "We need to pray. About Mama."

They didn't pray every night—at least not together—but Maya *did* pray. Quite often. *Make me a mother, make me a mother* was a prayer she said so often she wondered if God was getting tired of hearing her.

A lot of good it had done. She kept thinking there was some magic word, some stance or way of praying that would assure her God would hear and give her the answer she wanted. She'd tried most of them: sitting, standing, shouting, whispering, begging . . .

In her deepest, most secret core, she sometimes wondered if there was a God out there to listen at all.

But her questions about prayer could not be answered to-night. Tonight, to please her husband, she took his hand and let him reach out to the Almighty for them both.

TWO

The wicked think, "God isn't watching us!
He has closed his eyes
and won't even see what we do!"

PSALM 10:11

Velvet purely hated mornings.

She had perfected the act of walking out to get the paper without opening her eyes but for a quick glance to the first of the stoop's steps. Her bare feet knew the way.

She cracked her eyes open enough to give herself a destination—three feet onto the grass, to the left of the driveway—then made a beeline for it. She shuffled back inside. The early morning air already dripped of humidity and the promise of a scorcher. As a child she'd always associated September with sweaters and falling leaves. As an adult, she held on to the promise of cooler days. Besides, football games shouldn't be played in the heat, but with a chill in the air. She loved it when the weather let hot chocolate sales soar.

Velvet tossed the paper onto the scruffy, overstuffed chair that owned the space where a dinette table should have lived. She was not a table sort of person, preferring a chair that was wide enough and cushy enough to pull her feet into. A small table to the right was big enough to hold a mug or a glass, but otherwise Velvet was quite content to eat with a plate or bowl in her lap. She poured herself a mug of chai, chose a carton of blueberry yogurt from the fridge, held a spoon in her mouth for safekeeping, and retired to the chair.

She opened the newspaper's front page on her lap and removed the lid from the yogurt, licking the foil liner clean. She'd just begun to stir the yogurt when—

Velvet set the yogurt aside and drew the paper close. In a teaser across the top of the front page was a picture of John Gillingham.

Her John Gillingham.

Next to his picture was the heading, "Best-selling Preacher Holds Local Book Signing."

Preacher? Best-selling?

John was an author?

And he was in town.

Velvet suffered a shiver. This was too creepy. First Lianne. And now John. It was as though her past—which up until now had possessed the good manners to remain in her past—had suddenly decided to step forward and demand attention.

She opened the paper to page three, where she found a larger picture. He looked good. Great, in fact. Velvet's hand strayed to her hair, now completely gray. Did she look older than her forty-two years? Although the newspaper photo was in black and white, it looked as though John's hair still held more brunette than salt and pepper. It was, of course, far shorter than the messy mane he'd had in college. Hers hadn't been any better back then: a mass of permed corkscrew curls. And bangs that reached a room a good two seconds before the rest of her.

But his smile . . . He still had a way of making her feel as if he had a glorious secret—one she'd obviously sought out and shared. Their romance had been explosive, in good ways and bad, so that now she had a hard time reconciling a preacher John with the rebellious John who'd won her heart.

Among other things.

She'd told him the news when she'd found out she was pregnant. He'd shrugged it off, saying he'd pay for an abortion. He'd even go with her to the appointment if she wanted him to.

Velvet's answer had been absolutely clear: Thanks but no thanks.

Until that moment in her life, Velvet had not had any reason to think much about abortion. It sounded like a good idea, a permanent solution to a sticky problem. But when it was *her* choice to make . . . she couldn't do it.

Not that time anyway.

And so she'd had the baby and given her up for adoption to a local childless couple with a Czech last name.

The Skalas had been nice people who were desperate to love a baby. They offered to send her pictures as the child grew up, but Velvet thought it best their contact stop at the hospital door. She asked that they not tell the baby *her* name, and she, in turn, had not asked what they planned to name the girl.

Lianne. It was a pretty name, a little exotic yet old-fashioned. Twenty-three years after the fact, Velvet approved.

The article about John said he lived in San Diego and spent much of his time giving inspirational seminars. He'd even been on TV a few times. It was not surprising she'd never seen him. For Velvet, TV was a means to watch the weather forecast and movies, the older the better. And since he was into the God-Jesus stuff, Velvet wasn't interested in hearing his message—old flame or no old flame.

The article mentioned John's book: *My Mistakes and Other Leaps of Faith.*

Mistakes? Her radar screamed.

Had he considered their relationship a mistake? their baby

a mistake? Was all of that mentioned in the book? How could such a book *not* mention a love affair that ended badly and with the birth of an illegitimate child?

She had to find out.

The book signing was at two. . . .

| | | | | | | | | | |

Roman turned over and looked at the clock: 7:16.

He was late.

He rolled out of bed and stumbled into the bathroom, catching a glimpse of himself in the mirror. He looked as bad as he felt. He had not slept well, fighting variations of the spiritual battle against his son and God. They were conspired against him, against all his hard work to plan how Billy's life should play out.

Not his *life*. Roman wasn't that presumptuous. Just his football career, which would lead to a good life, with good possibilities, and—hopefully—grand outcomes. To achieve that, Billy had to stay focused. And getting involved with God and church and charity and the needs of others . . . it fragmented that focus.

That Billy had continued on this path even after knowing Roman's wishes only added to his anguish. Billy had been his obedient son for so many years. To have to share him now . . . Roman wouldn't give up without a fight.

He got dressed quickly, knowing AJ would be over any minute to carpool to work—

Roman heard a knock at the kitchen door on the floor below. He ran a comb through his hair, grabbed his electric shaver, and headed down.

When he entered the kitchen, he found AJ with his face pressed to the door's glass. His eyes were scanning the debris on the floor.

Oops.

Roman sidestepped a pool of salt and opened the door. "Don't ask." He went to the automatic coffeemaker—which *hadn't* overslept—and filled a travel mug to the brim.

AJ stopped at the foot of the mess. "What's with the war zone?"

Roman put a lid on the mug. "I was mad last night. Sue me."

"Mad at me?"

"Among others."

AJ poured coffee into his own travel mug. "I'm sorry if I hurt your feelings with the ego comment, but we've been friends forever. Amigos, blokes, compadres. Neither snow nor rain nor heat nor gloom of night—"

"That's the post office."

"I'm male. Get it? Mail? Male?"

In spite of his determination to remain stoic, Roman smiled.

AJ took a banana from the counter and started peeling. "Don't be mad at Billy's good deeds. Most dads would kill to have a kid who thought of someone besides himself. He's got a kind heart. That's a good thing."

Roman got a blueberry muffin from the bread box. "And I am glad of it. I just want him to concentrate on football."

"And spend his free time with you."

Roman shrugged. "I repeat: sue me." He grabbed his briefcase and keys and headed for the door.

AJ pulled it shut behind them. "He's not abandoning you by doing church stuff; he's expanding his life."

Roman pointed his key fob at the car. It beeped a greeting, flashed its lights once, and unlocked the doors. "Billy did it on the sly. *That's* what bugs me."

"You're the one who made it impossible for him to do it any other way."

Sometimes AJ's full knowledge was annoying. They both got in. "Isn't a child supposed to obey his parents? parent?"

37

AJ put on his seat belt, his banana half-unfurled. "A more powerful Father figure urged him to be a part of these events. Try as you like, you are *a* father, Roman, but not *the* Father."

AJ's mention of God caused Roman to pause before putting the key in the ignition. "Since when did you get all come-to-Jesus about things?"

"I'm just saying what most people believe, what most people know even if they don't choose to acknowledge it. There *is* a God, Roman. Whether we like to believe it or not."

Not. "My point remains; Billy doesn't need any father but me. And I won't—"

"He's twenty years old. Old enough to make his own choices."

A truth which made Roman all the more angry. He turned the ignition. The car sprang to life at his command.

| | | | | | | | | | |

Roman knew he should have been using his computer for work, but he couldn't help himself. He alternated between the Web sites of Husker Countdown and Big Red Fever, reading everything about Saturday's game and the upcoming season. Billy was mentioned often, especially on the community discussion boards. Roman particularly liked the last one he'd read: "William Paulson could be our savior. I'm looking for him to inspire the rest of the team to—"

"His name's Billy!"

"Mr. Paulson?"

Brian Adams stood in the doorway to his office. Roman flipped off his computer screen. He'd gotten after his workers for using their computers in non-work-related ways. "What can I help you with, Brian?"

The young man stepped closer to the desk, but in a tentative way, far different from his usual go-to-guy manner. "I need to talk to you about something." He glanced toward the door. "It's somewhat delicate."

Hmm. "Have a seat."

"May I close . . . ?"

"Certainly."

Brian closed the door and sat in the leather guest chair. He leaned his arms on the padded rests and clasped his hands above his lap. "I really hate to bring this up; I know it will probably make me look horrible, and I normally wouldn't—"

"Just say it."

"You know the award Maya Morano won on Friday night?"

"The Top Seller award."

"She shouldn't have won it."

Ah. Jealousy. "I assure you, the accounting department did an accurate count of everyone's earnings and—"

"She stole my clients."

Roman jerked back an inch. The accusation didn't make sense. Maya Morano was a good employee, always working hard, always attentive. He didn't know what to say.

Brian added detail. "She got her sales by taking mine, taking my clients away from me."

Roman felt his inner tension ease a bit. Brian sounded like a little kid who'd lost a toy to a playmate. "Clients are free to buy from anyone they—"

"I agree. But when a salesperson contacts my clients and woos them away . . ." He pushed his glasses into place. "It's not kosher. If she worked for another company, everyone might consider it a part of doing business, but to take clients from someone within her own company? That's not ethical. Is it?"

The playmate analogy faded away. This sounded serious. "I'm sure there's an explanation." He hoped there was an explanation. A good one.

"There's more. She offered kickbacks. I know that's not ethical.

And I know in one case she virtually bribed a city official to get them to order from us. Her."

Roman inwardly sighed, the joys of the morning fully shattered. This could get nasty. "You have proof?"

"I do. Back in my office."

"Why didn't you come forward before we gave Maya the award?"

"I didn't have the proof until yesterday." He took hold of the armrests and pushed himself straighter in the chair. "I know this looks like I'm mad because I didn't win. It's not that. I'm not one of the company's top sellers. I know that. I'm working to become one of the top sellers. But I can't get ahead if someone within the company is working against me, or working . . . illegally."

Roman did not like that word. Not just for Maya's sake but for his own. As the sales manager, Roman was in charge of ten salespeople, with their emphasis on selling to government agencies. But there was a protocol for such work. Hoops to jump through and red tape to navigate.

But he also knew there were ways around the hoop and under the tape—ways he had perfected at Efficient and . . . before. Ways that, in the hands of someone with fewer skills and finesse, could be botched. Noticed.

Documented.

Speaking of . . . "Well then," Roman said, "I suppose I need to see the documentation."

Brian was quick to rise. "I'll be right back."

Roman disliked his eagerness but understood it. It wasn't every day a mediocre salesperson had the chance to bring down a top seller.

Roman knew.

Firsthand.

He looked at the poster that hung on the wall directly across from him: *Unless you're the lead dog, the view never changes.* Long ago he'd taken the sentiment to heart and had worked hard, done things to make certain he was in a position of power—with its perks. He hadn't done it for himself. He'd had a son to raise, a son who needed football camps, gym memberships, special shoes and equipment, and fees for extra leagues and tournaments, not to mention the cost of Roman attending all the games.

Brian reentered Roman's office, out of breath. A bit too excited, he tripped over his own feet as he traversed the distance between door and desk but managed to hand over a manila folder. "Here. Here it is."

Roman was not eager to see. He didn't want Maya to be guilty.

He noticed the index tab on the folder had been innocuously titled: *SALES INFO*. Thus named, it was a file Brian could have in his desk, or even on his desk, without raising any red flags. At least the man had been discreet.

Brian returned to the chair. "You'll see on the top sheet I've made a list of clients and—"

Roman didn't open the file but offered Brian a supportive smile. "Let me take a look at the information." *Alone.*

Brian looked as confused as a child who'd been told Santa wasn't going to listen to his wish list. "But I would be happy to walk you through—"

"I think it's best if I view the information with a fresh eye. If I have any questions, I'll be sure to call you." He suffered a sudden fear. "You haven't shared this information with anyone else, have you?"

"No. I didn't want people to think . . ."

That you were doing it out of jealous envy?

"I wanted to be sure. I wanted to handle it right. Correctly."

"Good for you." *And perhaps good for me.* Roman clasped his hands on the file. "I want to thank you for your diligence on the part of the company. I'll get back to you."

When Brian's countenance fell, his glasses slipped lower on his nose. He rose from the chair and pushed the glasses into place simultaneously. Reluctantly. "Uh . . . thanks for your time, Mr. Paulson."

"No problem."

Big problem.

When Brian left the office, he closed Roman's door. It was not Roman's policy to go through the day with a closed door, and yet . . .

He did not correct the error.

Which, he feared, was the core of the issue at hand.

Roman was proud of the way he pushed his salespeople to achieve. He even remembered a few one-on-one meetings he'd had with Maya Morano when she was struggling to get the hang of the job. There'd been something familiar about the woman's desperation, her need to get in control of her life, her need to achieve certain goals and earn, earn, earn. She was so eager to do well.

Reluctantly he remembered digging beyond his normal bag of helpful hints and straying into a few how-to areas that stretched the limit of propriety. She had looked at him wide-eyed and said, "You can do that?"

He remembered immediately regretting he had taken her down that road. Just because he'd gotten away with such things was no reason to draw Maya into it. And yet, to his own disgrace, he hadn't backpedaled and said, "Never mind. Don't do it that way, Maya. You're better than that. You just stick to what you've been doing and you'll be fine." Instead, in answer to her question he'd said, "You can do that—if you're careful."

If Maya had followed his suggestions but hadn't been careful . . .

One plus one equaled . . .

A mess.

Roman opened the file. It was clear Brian had given careful time and thought to his presentation. It was a presentation that could bring down a colleague.

Suddenly, the full breadth of Roman's memories assaulted him.

43

"No!" he whispered.

He'd kept his guilt at bay for years. He couldn't let it gain access now. He just couldn't. With dogged determination he shoved the memories back into his past.

Where they belonged.

| | | | | | | | | | |

Roman shut Brian's file folder and sighed. His worst fears were realized—and had the potential to become full-fledged nightmares.

Brian had made his case succinctly and with all the proper corroboration. It was so well done a stranger to the business could follow the chain of Maya's mistakes.

And she'd made many.

Roman had been much more adept.

Maya's inability to be a keen manipulator, a slick juggler, and a sneaky player had been her demise.

There was only one thing he could do.

| | | | | | | | | | |

"How about this?"

Bob, the maintenance man, held Maya's award plaque on the wall of her cubicle, right next to the entrance—where everyone couldn't help but see it first thing. She knew it was a bit cocky to be so particular about where it was hung, but she'd never won anything before. Didn't she have a right to be proud?

"Perfect," she said. "Or maybe a couple inches higher?"

He raised the plaque just as Maya's intercom buzzed. "The boss wants to see you, Maya. As soon as possible."

Maya caught Bob's eyes, which confirmed that the tone of the message was as heavy as she'd thought. Missing was the usual "When you have time." Or even, "The boss wants to see you," without the ASAP spelled out to its fullest intensity.

Maybe he wants to give me the larger office he mentioned.

An odd knot in her stomach told her this would not be the subject discussed.

Yet she'd just won a top sales award. She was the star of the moment. She was being silly, reading nuances into a simple request for her presence.

Maya rose and felt the muscles in her legs beg to differ.

Should she bring anything? She grabbed a yellow pad and pen.

"Good luck," Bob said as she left.

Oh dear. Oh dear. Oh dear.

| | | | | | | | | | |

Maya knew.

It wasn't anything blatant. She hadn't knocked on the doorjamb of Mr. Paulson's office and received a growl for her efforts. Not at all.

She'd found him with his chair turned toward the window, deep in thought. Upon hearing her, he turned around. He was polite. Almost too polite. "Please come in, Maya. Sit."

Her feet moved. Somehow. She took a seat, letting her skirt slide against the leather until she could feel the solidity of the chair's back. If only he would smile. The world would return to normal if he smiled.

Mr. Paulson picked up a pen, made it teeter-totter back and forth a few times, then set it down. He straightened the edges of some papers, making them fall into line.

And she knew—she knew that her desire for her own office was not the issue at hand.

Surely, not . . . No, he couldn't. . . . He wouldn't. . . .

"Well then. Maya."

She swallowed and forced her lips into a smile. "Sir?"

"I . . ." He needed a fresh breath to continue. "I am very concerned about some allegations that came to my attention this morning."

Her stomach knotted. "Excuse me?"

"It seems you have crossed the line in your quest to obtain new clients—at the expense of your colleagues."

Her stomach did a backflip, and she sat up straighter to give it room. Her gut response was to remind him that he had been the one to give her hints about creative ways to get new clients. Didn't he remember?

Somehow she knew none of that mattered right now. She'd blown it. She wasn't sure how, but the jig was up. "I worked hard for my clients, Mr. Paulson. If someone chose to order from me over someone else, that's their decision."

He nodded once. "I agree. And by my position I am the first to stress sales and productivity."

Exactly.

But then he looked away, choosing the sight of a marble paperweight over her eyes.

So much was being left unsaid, unclaimed. At that moment, with Mr. Paulson's simple and seemingly innocuous act of looking away, Maya realized he'd distanced himself from her. She was in this alone. Mr. Paulson would not be coming to her defense.

He cleared his throat as if checking himself. "I stress sales unless *you* approached clients and wooed them away from one of your coworkers."

Oh.

"The CEO and company directors relate to hard numbers,

but—" Maya caught a glimpse of pity in his eyes—"there is a right way and a wrong way to do business. Especially when the client is a government agency. What may be acceptable for most businesses, isn't . . ." He sighed, as if the whole thing made him tired. "Our policies were stated plainly when you were hired." His eyes changed, softened. "You're a smart woman, Maya. Very capable."

"I try to be, sir. Very hard. And I'm sorry if I overstepped—"

"I'm afraid we're going to have to let you go."

All breath left her.

"There are right ways to do things, and . . ."

And the ways you taught me! You. You taught me.

"Also, I'm afraid you'll have to return your award. Your sales were . . . were ill-gotten. They cannot be commended." He stood. "I'm sorry, Maya. You had a lot of potential."

But . . . but . . .

But nothing. It was over.

| | | | | | | | | | |

The door of the stairwell clanged shut behind her. Maya stood behind it, out of sight of its small window. Once the echo of the door fell away, she listened for feet on the stairs below or above.

All she could hear was the rasp of her own breathing.

She was beyond stunned. Fired? Her? By Mr. Paulson, the man who taught her everything she knew?

She leaned against the wall and cushioned her lower back with her hands. The concrete block was cold and hard. Immovable.

Hiding in a stairwell. It was absurd. Maya used to take the long way around the inner office so she could see—and be seen—by as many people as possible. Now, to have slipped from Mr. Paulson's office through the nearest exit door . . . it was beyond humiliating.

Maybe if she kept going down the stairs . . .

She stepped forward and looked down the center of the stairwell. The railing snaked round and round. Was there an exterior exit, so she could go out to her car and drive away and never have to face—?

My keys. My purse. My briefcase. They're in my office.

Not her office. Her cubicle. A cubicle that seemed miles away and only accessible by traveling through a gauntlet of her fellow employees.

Would Mr. Paulson tell everyone? Was he telling them now? And why did he suddenly call her on it? He'd mentioned allegations "coming to his attention."

Brian. It had to be his doing. Brian had complained, had forced Mr. Paulson's hand.

She physically cringed. Brian, her coworkers, her competitors—they'd love this. Too much.

Yet facing it sooner was better than later. Sooner, before the office grapevine was in full swing and she was strangled by it.

What choice did she have?

She put her hands on the panic bar of the door, lowered her head, and closed her eyes. *Please . . .*

| | | | | | | | | |

They know.

It was a certainty. Not by anything they said, but by the way her coworkers looked away. Embarrassed. Satisfied. Ashamed.

For her? Or of her?

Maya kept her eyes straight ahead and walked quickly but without a hint of the panic that sizzled through her nerves longing for a quick getaway.

She was nearly there when Susan stepped out of her cubicle and blocked her way. "I'm so sorry, Maya."

Birthday balloons bobbed over the top of Susan's cubicle as if they wanted to eavesdrop.

"Thanks." *Thanks?* It was a stupid thing to say, but Maya couldn't think of a better response.

Susan extended a hand to touch her arm. "I wish you the best. What are you going to do now?"

Maya couldn't meet her gaze but instead she looked past her to the assortment of birthday cards and banners Susan had posted on the outside of her cubicle for all to see: *Happy 40th! Birthday Greetings. Over the Hill.*

Nothing remarkable, except . . . for a red banner that was oddly blank.

A red sign with nothing on it? Why would Susan tack up a blank banner?

Whatever. Maya had more important things to worry about. "I've really got to go," she said.

Maya slipped into her space and in the span of a minute collected her personal belongings. There weren't that many. A lot of people had plants and pictures and cutesy things in their cubicles, but not Maya. She was all for lean and clean. Besides, she didn't have any children to decorate her space with photos and cute scribbled drawings. Now, with the loss of her job, would she ever have a child?

She took one final look at the sales award. Mr. Paulson had told her to leave it behind.

She put it in her briefcase. It's not like they could reuse it. And she had earned it. If he didn't appreciate her methods, that was his problem. Besides, her methods had been inspired by his methods.

Talk about two-faced.

Maya got to the elevator and pressed the button. And again. And again. Her eyes locked on the down arrow above the door. *Come on. Come on.*

Just a few more sec—

Brian appeared at her side. "Sorry it had to turn out this way, Maya," he said. His smirk was very unsorry.

She looked back at the arrow. "I bet you are."

The elevator came and took her away.

| | | | | | | | | | |

Roman raked his fingers through his hair.

Maya Morano had just left. He'd just fired her. The guilty firing the guilty.

"What choice did I have?" he whispered.

None. Only by letting her go could he put an end to it. If only he could be assured the entire situation would fade away, with both sides scarred but able to recover and move on. Roman was very willing to let it go—for everybody's sake. Nothing good came from wallowing in past mistakes.

Past consequences.

But then there was Brian. The victim. Would Maya's firing satisfy him? Would it spur him to be stronger, work harder, and be wiser?

Roman knew in such a crisis human nature dictated two alternatives. Either the victim let the inequities of life run them over until they surrendered to the pain of being duped or bettered. Or they spread the word of their suffering and took measures to gain justice—as Brian had done.

If a worker can't ebb and flow with the realities of business, they shouldn't be in business.

It was an old rationalization that ignored the weaker worker, the person who practically begged to be one-upped by peers, the worker who buckled under pressure instead of rising above it.

Roman pressed his fingers against his eyes, not wanting to remember, yet knowing he could never forget.

If only things had been handled better back then. He'd never intended for it to turn out so badly. That he'd never been directly connected didn't mean he hadn't suffered for it.

Roman slapped his desk, refusing to feel the pain yet again. "No."

Now. Now was all that mattered.

Roman might be able to impact *this* situation. This crisis. These two people.

He picked up the phone.

| | | | | | | | | | |

"You wanted to see me, sir?"

"Have a seat." Roman smiled—but not too much—needing to interweave charm with a stern and somber decorum that would assure Brian the matter was handled. *Fini.* End of story. "I wanted you to know I have taken steps to rectify the situation with Ms. Morano."

"I know. I saw her cleaning out her desk."

Brian's smug comment confirmed he was the sort of victim who didn't falter, who fought back. All in all, a relief. But was it too late to initiate damage control?

"Brian, I want to ask you a favor."

The man hesitated, wary. "What?"

"I would like you to keep the details surrounding Maya's firing to yourself. The fact she won the award, plus mishandled government contracts . . . it would not be advantageous for the company if word got—"

"Oh."

With that one word, Roman knew all was lost. "Others already know the details?"

Brian picked a piece of lint from his pants. "A few."

"A few?"

He sighed deeply. "Most. Most know."

A moan escaped as Roman sat back in his chair. If the office was abuzz, it was only a matter of time before the higher-ups knew all about it and came calling. Asking for answers, making Roman relive other times. Making Roman accountable.

In their eyes the bottom line was that Maya was his subordinate. Under his charge. His responsibility.

Things couldn't get any worse.

Could they?

| | | | | | | | | | |

"Dude, you need to calm down. It'll be fine."

Peter kept pacing, shaking his head, and checking his watch. "I never should have arranged it. My parents will hate Lianne, and she'll hate them. It's gonna be a disaster."

"Man, I hate it when you do that—just assume the worst." Peter's roommate, William, sat on the couch eating a huge bowl of microwave popcorn. The entire apartment smelled of it. His girlfriend, Carrie, sat beside him, looking concerned.

"Didn't I tell you not to do this?" Carrie said. "I know you like Lianne, but . . . why are you asking for trouble by bringing your folks into the equation? Your parents are gonna think Lianne's from another planet."

"A friendly planet," Peter pointed out.

"Way friendly," Carrie agreed.

"Too friendly," William added. "They're gonna look at Lianne and imagine you two doing the wild thing on the couch."

"I'm not talking about this with you, man."

Suddenly William's eyes grew wide. "She's not pregnant, is she? That's not the reason you're introducing her to your parents, is it?"

"No, she's not pregnant." He didn't think she was. Though

it wouldn't be impossible. They weren't careful. Since sex wasn't something he'd anticipated before meeting Lianne, he hadn't been prepared for it. In a lot of ways. Besides, she was the one with the experience, so he figured she was on the pill or something. He probably should have asked. In fact, he'd ask her the next time he saw her. He loved her, so he should protect her. Man, he'd been an unthinking jerk . . . again.

"You didn't do it . . . ?" William extended his arms to encompass the apartment.

"No, no," Peter lied. "When you and I got the apartment last year, we agreed: no overnight guests." Technically, Lianne had never stayed overnight. William was gone plenty of evenings, so it was easy for her to be outta there by the time he got home.

William went back to eating. "The only reason I got this apartment with you was because I trusted you. You know how hard it is to find a decent roommate."

Now he felt bad. They *had* made a pact. Last fall they'd met at church and discovered they were both fed up with their old roommates. Getting an apartment together had seemed inevitable. They'd had no issues between them until Lianne had come into the picture.

Carrie popped one kernel of popcorn in her mouth, then said, "Look, the more we discuss this, the more likely it is to get messy. Let's get back to the problem at hand. Are you and Lianne going out to dinner with your folks?"

"My parents wanted to, but I didn't want them to spend that much time with . . . I mean I told them I had a lot of studying to do. We're going to the Dairy Store on campus. They like the homemade ice cream." He got an idea. "Wanna come?"

They looked at each other. "You want us to come along? What? You want us to be buffers?"

"No, of course . . ." He gave in to the truth. "Yes. I need buffers. Lots of buffers. Come on, guys. Help me out here."

William made noises like a squawking chicken. "Better watch out for that yellow streak—it doesn't go with your outfit."

Then there was a knock on the door.

The three friends froze. "Lianne's not here yet," Peter whispered.

"Maybe that's her," Carrie said.

"She never knocks. It's them." He realized the way he'd said *them* sounded as though his parents were space aliens or creatures from the Black Lagoon. Or worse . . .

But that was wrong. They were who they'd always been. He was the one who'd changed.

Carrie stood and took a step toward the door. "Do you want me—?"

"No, I'll do it." He wiped his sweaty palms on his jeans and opened the door. His parents greeted him with big hugs and bigger smiles.

"What took you so long, kid? We were afraid you weren't home," his dad said.

His mother swiped lipstick from the place she'd kissed his cheek. "We're so happy to see you. And excited to meet—" She turned toward Carrie and her eyes glowed with appreciation. "Lianne! It's so nice to meet you!" Peter's mom gave the girl a monster hug. "You are a beauty, my dear. What lovely eyes. Hazel eyes run in our family too. And yours have the loveliest gold flecks in—"

"Mom!"

His mother kept her arm around Carrie's shoulder but looked at him. "She does have beautiful eyes, Peter. Don't you think so?"

"Yes. I mean, no. I mean . . . Mom, that isn't Lianne."

His mother's hand fell to her side.

Carrie smiled awkwardly. "I'm Carrie, Mrs. McLean." She moved to William, putting her arm around his waist. "It's a pleasure to meet you. I'm William's girlfriend."

53

Peter's father extended his hand for Carrie to shake. "Sorry 'bout that. Nice to meet you, Carrie." He nodded at William. "You have good taste, kid."

Peter's mother put her hands on her hips. "So where's yours? your girlfriend?"

As if she'd been lurking in the hall awaiting the perfect moment to make an entrance, Lianne swung the door wide and stepped into the apartment. "Sorry I'm—" She was brought up short. "Oh. Really late. Oops."

Peter's parents went mute. They stared at Lianne . . . and turned to stone.

There was much to stare at. She wore one of her skirts of many colors, but this one had little bells tied to it so she jingled when she moved. Her gauze top had slid off one shoulder, revealing her rose tattoo, *and* that she was braless. As far as Peter knew, his mother had never left her bedroom without a bra. He didn't want to think about it. Lianne's attitude was, "I look good. Why should I bind my body into submission?" Peter had totally agreed. But now he realized this was yet another area of disagreement between the two women.

Lianne's accessories, as usual, were flashy. She wore orange beaded flip-flops and glittering earrings that skimmed her shoulders. Multiple earrings in each lobe. A toe ring or two. Fingernails painted purple. And of course the tiny gold hoop through the piercing in her nose.

Peter's parents had probably never seen anything like her back home, even on television. They had satellite TV, but they mostly watched the History Channel and HGTV. They'd given up on network TV because they thought it had gotten too racy.

Lianne studied Peter's gawking parents. So did he. It was clear they weren't able to speak just yet. Peter's heart sank. Before he could think of the right thing to say to smooth out this meeting, Lianne walked directly to him. She wrapped her arms around his neck and kissed his cheek with a loud *ummwah*. That done, she stood there, joined at his hip, daring his parents to argue with her right to be there.

Peter's face felt like it would burn away. Everyone but Lianne looked in his direction. Waiting. He cleared his throat. "Mom, Dad, this is Lianne Skala. My girlfriend."

She said, "Nice to meet you, Mom. Dad."

His parents merely nodded. And Peter caught his mother looking longingly at Carrie. His dad was staring at the piercing in Lianne's nose.

Suddenly he wanted to leave the apartment. Maybe if they were all on neutral ground, this would be easier. Peter took a step toward the door. "I've been looking forward to introducing you all. I know you're going to love Lianne once you get to know her. Would anybody like to go out for ice cream?"

"Great," Lianne said. "Lately I'm hungry all the time. And the Dairy Store has awesome pumpkin ice cream."

Lianne went out the door first, then Peter's mother. His father followed, shaking his head ever so slightly as he passed Peter.

Peter turned to William and Carrie. "Please come?"

They looked at each other. A silent communication passed between them. "We can't. Carrie has to go to work in a half hour."

She held up her right hand. "Honest." She lowered it when Peter glared at her. "Sorry."

"You'd better get going," William said softly. "The door to the lion's den is hanging wide open. Say a prayer."

Peter's dad called from the bottom of the stairs. "Peter?"

His voice sounded desperate and had a come-save-us-from-your-painted-hussy tone.

"Coming."

"We'll pray for you too," Carrie said with a wave.

"Thanks," he said and meant it. Peter would take whatever help he could get.

| | | | | | | | | | |

They rode in his parents' car because Peter's ancient clunker wasn't big enough for four—and was an embarrassment to look at, inside and out. It might have gotten him from point A to B, but it looked like it was about to fall apart. When it did finally die, he certainly didn't want his parents inside.

His parents' SUV had tons of bells and whistles and was meticulous, right down to the six cup holders, the GPS, and the Bose stereo system. *A clean vehicle represents a clean heart* was a mantra he'd heard again and again as he grew up. The entire McLean farm was just as spotless. Everything in its place and kept in fine maintenance.

The first thing he'd done when he left home was become a slob. It felt fabulous.

Actually, this rolling palace on wheels was his mother's vehicle. His dad drove a pickup. "How do you like your new SUV, Mom?"

"I love it. I'm looking forward to snow to see how it handles the country roads in the winter."

"The thing's a gas guzzler, isn't it?" Lianne asked. "What kind of mileage do you get?"

Silence. Then Peter's father answered, "It gets in the high teens. That's considered excellent for an SUV."

"But not as good as most cars. Why don't you have a car instead?"

Peter's mother looked over the seat at Lianne. "Because in the country we get snowdrifts in the winter, the plows don't always get out to our place before we need to drive somewhere, and the secondary roads are gravel. We need a vehicle that's higher off the ground than a car so we don't get stranded."

Peter tried to think of a way out of this conversation but came up blank.

"What kind of car do you drive?" his father asked Lianne.

"A small compact, though I mostly use public transit. I'd love to get one of those hybrids, but I don't have the cash. But a lot of times I take the bus or ride my bike. Or walk. I think walking is a lost art."

57

Art! Peter changed the subject. "Lianne and I met in an art history class. She's getting a minor in art."

"But my major is sociology," Lianne said. "I think art and sociology are intertwined, as art brings out the best in societies and lets people find true expression and release."

"Oh," his mother said. "How do you plan to make a living?"

"I'll figure it out when I get there. I always do." Lianne smiled.

Peter's mother cleared her throat. Remembering that sound all too well from the aftermaths of various childhood disasters, Peter swallowed. He tried again to think of something useful to say.

None too soon they reached the Dairy Store and parked. Peter nearly flew out of the car. Ice cream would be a good diversion. It would be hard to talk while they were eating. That was a good thing. And maybe if they ate fast, they could get home before things really fell apart.

When they entered the store, Peter and his parents stood back from the counter to look over the list of flavors. Lianne marched right up and said, "I want a double dip: pumpkin and chocolate peanut butter."

"Is that all?" the clerk asked.

Lianne looked behind at the others. "Next?"

Although Peter wasn't ready, he stepped forward and made a choice. "Vanilla, please. One scoop."

"Vanilla?" Lianne asked. "And only one scoop? Bor-ing. Take a walk on the wild side—at least try chocolate."

At that moment Peter's mother and father came up to the counter. "We'll each have vanilla cones. One scoop."

It was a snub, plain and simple.

"Suit yourself," Lianne said. Then she stepped aside as if assuming Peter's dad would pay for it all. Which he did.

How could so much innuendo and drama come out of getting something as innocent as ice cream?

Once they were served, they went outside and Lianne sat on a bench under a huge oak tree. Her tongue blended the two flavors.

Peter looked away and was glad she hadn't had her tongue pierced too. She'd talked about doing it. . . .

His mother sat on the far end of the bench, leaving the men to stand.

After a minute of eating, his father said, "You mentioned studying sociology and art. What do you plan to do after graduation?"

"I'm going into the Peace Corps, I think. I'll work with people and create something amazing and unique. Art will be our common ground. I love what I do." She dipped her finger in her ice cream and licked it off.

Peter's mother paused eating a moment and looked into the lush trees overhead. Peter could almost see her struggle for words.

"Actually," she said, "we're not that different from you, Lianne. We love what we do too. Farming is all about creating something amazing and unique—and helping people."

Peter could have kissed her. It meant a lot to see his mom trying to find common ground with Lianne.

Lianne considered this a moment, then smiled mischievously. "What if people won't buy what you create?"

Uh-oh.

Peter's father took over. "They have to. What we create, what we grow, is necessary for survival. Without the food we harvest, people would starve. People need it. They don't need art or people with a degree telling them how their society should work so it fits into some textbook mold of utopia."

"Dad, a lot of people consider the farming life a kind of utopia," Peter offered.

"Then they've never tried it," his father snapped. "It's hard work—honest work, but hard work."

"Absolutely," Lianne agreed. "Agrarian living is often quite primitive. A lot of my fieldwork will be with agrarian societies. I hope to save them by introducing other options. I plan to make their lives better. And as far as art? Without art the soul would starve."

"But they'll starve faster without food," Peter's dad said.

"And without God their soul would starve," Peter's mother said.

"Oh, I'm not doing that kind of social work. I don't believe in it. I think God constrains the soul."

Peter's parents gawked—also Peter's reaction. How had they moved from a discussion of art to farming to God?

He jumped in, hoping to soothe the moment. "Lianne didn't mean it like that," he said. "She just meant—"

"I did mean it like that," Lianne said. "Take your son, here. When I first met him, he was afraid of life, too afraid to even take a breath without looking up at the heavens for approval. How can a person live like that? He had to find himself, but it was tough. He was trying to be what you wanted him to be, not what he—"

Peter put a hand on her arm, trying to stop her words. "Lianne. Don't. I'm cool with it. Everybody has to make their own way to adulthood. Just because I had doubts about my major—"

"You have doubts about being a farmer?" his father asked him.

His mother chimed in. "We've always talked about you taking over the farm someday. It's your heritage."

Peter felt like he'd been hit with a hot poker. "I do want to be a farmer."

Lianne crossed her legs and sat back, looking as calm and comfortable as a cat in sunlight. "No, you don't."

"Yes, I do. I think. But—"

"That's not what you told me," Lianne said, licking her ice cream.

No. That wasn't what he'd told her. But when he was around her, black was white and the earth was flat. "I . . . I've just been thinking about my future, that's all. I'm twenty years old. Isn't it normal to flip-flop a bit?"

Lianne licked her cone full round. "I admire Peter for seeing the light and changing his major to sociology. No one needs another business major, seeking profit above all—"

Peter's father stopped eating. "You changed your major?"

"I—"

"When did you do that?" his mother asked.

If only they'd driven *his* car, he would have left them all to duke it out. "Just this semester. I thought about it all summer. Lianne and I had a lot of long talks and I—"

"So you've wasted two years of college? Is that what you're telling us?" his father asked. "I'll tell you the waste—changing your major from agribusiness to sociology. That will do you no good, Peter. And if this girl—"

He had to come between them. It wasn't Lianne's fault. Not completely. "Maybe I will want to take over the farm. But . . . I just want to try a few new things. I want to be sure." His father looked angry, and his mother looked sad. "Don't look at me that way. I'm finally realizing what a sheltered life I led back home. There's so much of the world I never imagined, so much I never experienced—"

"You can say that again," Lianne said.

He was appalled to feel himself blush. "I want to be sure that I know what I want. Not because it's expected of me, but because it's what I love to do. God gives us gifts, and he expects us to use them. Before I commit to you and that life, I want to make sure it's what I'm supposed to do. Haven't you always taught me that God has a unique purpose for everyone's life, for my life, and the trick is to find out what it is?"

61

"Of course, Peter," his mother said. "But everything in your life points to you being a farmer. You're good at it."

"How do I know I'm not better at something else? I don't. Because I've never tried anything else."

His father crossed his arms. "So, what are you wanting to try? Basket weaving? Tribal dancing?"

"Hey, don't knock it until you've tried it," Lianne said. "I'd be happy to give you lessons."

Peter stopped breathing. No one talked back to his father. No one. His dad had a temper and a worldview that pretty much stuck to the straight and narrow he'd always known.

His father walked over to the bench. Slowly. He took his wife's cone, and his own, walked to a trash receptacle and deposited them inside. Then he held out his hand for his wife's. She rose from the bench and took his arm. "If you'll excuse us. Nice meeting you, Lianne. Peter? We love you, Son. Keep in touch."

Then they walked away.

Peter didn't know what to do. His parents' approval had always been the measuring stick of every act, every choice.

Had been.

Until Lianne.

She leaned back on the bench, stretched her legs out into the sidewalk, and bit her cone. "Well, that was interesting."

Interesting?

Peter threw his cone into the trash and stood above her. He could feel his blood pumping through his body. "Why did you talk to my parents that way?"

"Because I could see you shrinking back into being a little kid again, right in front of my eyes. You need to learn to stand up for yourself."

Maybe so, but . . . how could she be so rude? His parents were good people, caring people—people he loved, who loved him. Even though he didn't always agree with them, that didn't mean he'd ever wanted them to be treated badly. "What right do you have to cause trouble between us?"

"From what I saw, there has always been trouble between you. They acted like you weren't allowed to have an independent thought in your head. Your dad, especially. It was like he thought he had the right to direct your every move. I wasn't even mad—just worried for you. He was acting like a dictator. He was the one who was rude. I simply shined a spotlight on it."

"But I wasn't ready to shine a spotlight on it. I just wanted to skim through this visit and send them off happy. I wasn't ready to tell them anything."

She dipped her finger into the pool of ice cream in the bottom of the cone. "At the rate you're going, you'd be graduated, married to your nice Christian farm girl, and on your fourth kid before you'd find the nerve to tell them this isn't the life for you."

He was going to protest. But then it hit him. She was right. Yet an important point remained. "It wasn't your place to say it. I needed to be the one to confront them."

"Somebody had to say it. And I could see it wasn't going to be you."

"But you said it so . . . bluntly, so . . ."

"Truthfully? Openly?" She pushed the last of the cone into her mouth and talked around it. "Truth and openness. You should try them sometime, McLean." She patted the bench. "Now, come sit beside me and let's enjoy the rest of the afternoon."

She was unbelievable. Her gumption and zest for living that

he had found so bright and appealing this morning had turned to ashes and pain this afternoon. Right now, the whole day felt tarnished and repulsive. But he wasn't sure if it was Lianne or himself who'd made it so.

He felt like crying. Before he could lose it, he turned and walked away.

"McLean? Come back here."

He kept walking.

| | | | | | | | | | | |

Peter rushed into his apartment and immediately locked the door behind him. Only then did he realize William was sitting in the living room, reading a textbook.

"Hey." He flopped down on the couch, grabbed the TV remote, and switched on the sports channel. Both guys watched the screen—anything to avoid looking at each other.

"Someone chasing you?" William finally asked.

"No. Maybe. Lianne. I mean, no one's chasing me, but I left her at the ice cream place and I don't want her barging . . ." He sank deeper into the comforting embrace of the couch and wished he had the energy to get up and grab a bag of chips. "It was horrible. A disaster of epic proportions."

"I *thought* I felt the earth move."

"Yeah. Earthquake Lianne. Or maybe that was my dad. Not sure which. But the earth was trembling, either way."

"I wouldn't doubt it."

Peter leaned his head on the cushions, closed his eyes, and rubbed the space between them to try to soothe the pain there. If he could have gotten away with curling up in a corner of the living room and shutting the world out for a week, he would have. "She drove them away."

"They left?"

"Yeah. As fast as they could go. Just threw their ice cream cones away and left." But it was more than that. "She hurt them."

"What did she say?"

"How do I know? I was getting pulled from both sides. I felt like the rope in a tug-of-war." He sighed. Oddly, he couldn't remember any one thing, just an overall feeling of disaster. "She's just so sure of herself. She insulted them, their life, the life they want for me. She offered to teach my dad to weave baskets. And I think she told him she could show him some tribal dances."

"Ouch."

"Yeah. Ouch." Peter sat up to face his friend. "My parents aren't perfect. They're old-fashioned and controlling, but they love me. And they mean well. It's just that they've only seen one possible path for my life. I know I should be more assertive in telling them how I feel about taking over the farm. But they're good people—God-fearing people. And . . . and . . ."

"You love them."

"Yeah. I do. I want them to be proud of me."

William closed his textbook, then set it on the coffee table. "Maybe you need to ask yourself if Lianne will ever be the sort of girl to make them proud. Or to make you proud. And ask yourself what you want to do if the answer is no."

"Oh, don't start lecturing me, man."

"I'm not. I'm merely asking you to think things through. Up until now your hormones have done the talking. But hormones aren't love. Love is something more, and it involves everything about a person—and that includes how they relate to your family."

"Are you in love with Carrie?"

"I don't know. I think I could be. I'm better when she's around. Can you say that about Lianne?"

Peter didn't answer out loud; but he knew the answer was sometimes, not always. He'd changed since she'd come into his life. The last few months . . . she made him question everything. She confused him and messed with his mind.

William continued. "What I don't like seeing is how she made you stray from who you are, your moral roots. She tempted you."

"'The spirit is willing, but the body is weak.'"

William punched Peter's shoulder. "See? You know the danger in it."

"But if Lianne is wrong for me, why do I feel so drawn to her?"

"Free will," William said. "He wants *us* to choose. But God didn't abandon you when you decided to hook up with Lianne, and he won't let you be tempted beyond what you can bear. He always provides a way out. Whether you take it?" He shrugged. "Your call, dude."

Peter thought back to the first time he and Lianne had slept together. Had it been the right thing to do? Had he thought about it or just given in to his hormones? He knew the answer to that question. Feeling good had won out over everything else.

He rested his hand over his eyes, wishing he could hit the Delete key and wipe out the memory. "So now what? I can't undo what I've done."

"Tell God you're sorry. God doesn't turn his back on you just because you screwed up. You've gotta remember Jesus took the rap for all our mistakes, stupid and otherwise. You didn't shock him by your sin. He's seen worse. You know he'll forgive you, no matter what you've done."

He knew.

What William said was at the core of how Peter was raised. Confession led to forgiveness—thanks to Jesus' sacrifice. He got it.

"So?" William asked.

"I'm . . . thinking."

William stood and headed to his room. "Don't just think. Pray. Be with him."

When William's door clicked shut, Peter found himself alone—alone with his messed-up life. Mistake after mistake after mistake surrounded him like a swarm of pesky gnats.

I'm sorry, I'm sorry, I'm sorry. I knew better. I really did.

With his admission, he felt the swarm of disquiet in his gut dissipate and a calmness settle in. He felt the presence of a living God settle into his soul.

William was right. God was with him, always with him. Why did he have such a hard time remembering that?

Because I've tried so hard to ignore him.

It was an awful truth. When his namesake, the disciple Peter, was doing wrong, going against what he knew was right, he didn't like the idea that God was anywhere close. Seeing. Grieving. Being disappointed in him. He'd denied God in his shame and fear.

It appeared he hadn't learned anything from his namesake. He'd made the same mistakes, and then some.

Talk about stupid and immature.

He drew in a cleansing breath, then let it out, wishing that doing the right thing would come as easily as the breath he'd just taken. He put his head in his hands.

God? I'm listening. Help me.

And though the guilty feelings lingered, he knew deep down the past was taken care of and there was hope in his future. He was forgiven. Jesus had died for his sins, and the burden Peter carried was lifted.

His soul was safe.

But his relationship with the woman in his life?

Somehow, Lianne would be harder to face.

He looked at the door and thanked God she hadn't followed him home.

He'd had enough for one day.

| | | | | | | | | | |

Velvet stood outside the bookstore and walked up and back, up and back in front of the windows. A sign proclaimed, "Signing today! John Gillingham, author of the best-selling book *My Mistakes and Other Leaps of Faith.*"

The sign, instead of luring her inside, kept her pacing outside.

He's here. He's actually here. After all these years.

Would he recognize her? By his picture she could see he had aged well. But had she? Her reflection in the store window was definitely that of a fortysomething woman. She had never worried much about hiding her age. Although she wasn't one of those annoying women who made comments about their wrinkles like they were welcome friends and evidence of a life well lived, she wasn't obsessed with looking thirty anymore. As long as she didn't look fifty.

She stopped pacing and looked at her gray hair. Maybe she should have dyed it.

No. That would have been ridiculous. Overreacting. Overcompensating. Overeverything.

She started to pass the entry yet again, when a man going inside held the door for her.

No, no. I don't want to go in.

He still held it open. Unless she wanted to be rude she had no choice.

"Thanks." She went through the door.

| | | | | | | | | | |

A clerk offered Velvet one of John's books. "Would you like to take a look?" she asked. "The author is here today and will sign it for you."

She nodded her thanks. A customer standing at the back of the line for an autograph pointed at Velvet's copy. "It's really good," he said. "Very honest. Moving."

"You've already read it?"

He displayed the copy he carried. "This one's for my mother. She always told me, 'Admit your mistakes, Johnny. God sees them anyway.'" He shrugged. "Gillingham's books helped me do that."

Another woman came toward the line, book in hand. The man said to Velvet, "Come on. You'll lose your place."

Velvet stepped into line.

To see John Gillingham.

The father of her child.

| | | | | | | | | | |

Why am I still here? I should leave. Just step out of line.

And yet Velvet didn't leave. She stood there and listened to the other people in line chatting about John and his book. Not everyone had read it, but many had and were getting another copy as a gift. She'd heard that word of mouth sold books, but today she witnessed the phenomenon in action. And the camaraderie of John's readers—it was as though they'd known each other their entire lives, chatting and openly sharing anecdotes of their own mistakes.

Divorce, job issues, family issues . . . The line in front of her was composed of people representing all seven deadly sins: lust, gluttony, greed, sloth, anger, envy, and pride. That all these people were admitting their deepest secrets—to strangers—was amazing.

"We seem to have our own little support group going here," Velvet said.

A red-haired woman clutched John's book to her chest. "Yet some of us aren't sharing." She eyed Velvet.

"Me? You want me to share my mistakes?"

"Only if you have any," said an elderly man wearing a beret. He'd admitted causing friction with his siblings over an inheritance.

Velvet glanced at the exit. She never should have come. These people were not of her world. They were deep into admitting mistakes, bringing them out in the open for all to see, while Velvet was intent on keeping hers safely packed away in an unmarked box. Taped shut and tied with rope.

Then why are you here?

The core of her mistake sat a short twenty feet away.

I can't do this. I shouldn't do this. Why am I doing this?

She pressed the book into the hands of the beret man. "I'm sorry. I have to leave. I never should have come."

The first man who'd talked to her took her arm. "Hey, don't go."

"We didn't mean to chase you off."

"You don't have to share. You don't—"

Velvet shook away from her captor's grip. "Let me go!"

She'd spoken too loudly, getting the attention of all those in line—and all those at the book signing table.

John looked in her direction.

Their eyes met.

And Velvet ran to the door.

| | | | | | | | | | | | |

Velvet fumbled for her car keys, muttering to herself, "I shouldn't have come, I shouldn't have come, I shouldn't—"

"Velvet!"

Her heart stopped. She froze, then reluctantly allowed her eyes to find him.

He'd run out of the store and was crossing the parking lot to her car.

To her.

"John, no. Go back." She saw a gaggle of people filling the entryway, watching the show. Beret, Redhead, Johnny, and all the others who had been in line. She nodded toward them. "They're watching. They want you inside. You have a signing to—"

He reached her, out of breath. He kept his back toward the store. "I don't care about a signing. I care about seeing you. I came here to see you."

She dropped her keys. He beat her to them and pressed them into her hands.

"Velvet. You are the one person I wanted to see. I am so glad you came here today. I hope it means you want to see me too."

Skin touched skin—and remembered. And wanted more.

More? There could be no more. His coming here was her punishment. Which begged the question: why had she voluntarily sought him out?

She pulled her hand away though she knew it wanted to linger. "I came to appease my curiosity. That's all it was. I saw an ad in the paper about the signing. I merely came to . . . to see if you were old and ugly yet."

He laughed. "And?"

"Not yet." *Not hardly. Not ever.*

"I'm so glad you haven't lost your humor, Velvet. It's one of the things I loved about you."

One of the things? As if there were more?

Her heart and mind warred with each other. Emotions crossed swords with logic. And anger. And a well-seasoned grudge.

The door to the store opened and a suited woman said, "Mr. Gillingham? Are you coming back?"

"Yes, yes," he said. "I'll be right there." He turned back to Velvet. "I have something tonight, an event, but . . . let me take you out to dinner tomorrow night. I'm leaving the day after that—Thursday, early afternoon. Flying home."

"Which is . . . San Diego?"

"That's right."

A world away. Good. And dinner—she wasn't sure about that. And then she remembered Roman. "I can't do dinner. I . . . I have a date."

"So you're not married?"

"I wouldn't be going on a date if I were married, would I?"

He laughed again. "No, I suppose not. If dinner is out, how about breakfast Thursday morning? Waffles. I remember how much you loved waffles. Surely you aren't occupied with another date for breakfast."

She opened her mouth to say no, but instead heard herself saying, "No waffles. But coffee. I will do coffee."

Crow's feet—deeper than her own—appeared around his eyes when he smiled. "You name the time and place."

"The Coffee Palace on Randolph. Seven sharp."

He leaned forward and kissed her cheek. "I'll be there." Then he ran back to the store, into the arms of his adoring public.

She missed him already.

Which made her a traitor.

To herself.

| | | | | | | | | | |

After the humiliation of being fired, Maya couldn't go home and risk seeing Sal. He often came and went throughout the day, stopping home in between landscaping jobs, and was usually home for lunch. To save money. For the next in vitro procedure so they could get pregnant.

To kill time, Maya made a pass through the mall, though she left quickly. She'd always been frugal, but it wasn't fun shopping when she didn't have *any* money to spend. No job. No money. No joy in a new purse or pair of shoes, even if they were on sale.

She ended up at the library. Wandering through the stacks usually made her feel complete; the knowledge and creativity within the books was hers for the taking. Actually, she could blame books for intensifying her desire to have a child. She loved romance novels where the girl caught the guy and lived happily ever after. Although kids were never mentioned—coming after the final *THE END*—at least in Maya's imagination they were implied, the luscious frosting to the marriage cake.

She'd married her own romantic hero, and they lived in the cute little bungalow of her imagination. The setting was in place, the actors ready to be cued for their proper roles of mommy and daddy. If only . . .

But today, Maya wasn't sure she was up for another novel. Maybe a history book or self-help? She could certainly use the latter.

While she was making up her mind, a mother came in the front door with an adorable toddler on her hip. She chanted to him in a singsong rhythm as they walked: "We're going to story time; we're going to story time." As she talked, the boy took hold of her chin as if studying exactly how this talking thing worked.

Before Maya had made a cognizant decision, she found herself following them to the juvenile section.

The mother held the swinging gate open for her, but Maya shook her head and retreated to the edge of the adult section that overlooked half-size bookshelves delineating the children's space. She picked up a book on travel to China and pretended to read.

An open space carpeted with a pattern of green and orange polka dots was filled with children and even some babies sitting on their mothers' knees. A librarian dressed in a pink and yellow sundress clapped her hands together, getting the children's attention.

"How are you today?"

"Fine!"

"Are you ready to hear a story?"

"Yes!"

She began reading, facing the pages outward so the kids could see the pictures. They sat enrapt, transported into storybook land.

The librarian turned a page. "See the rabbit and how it jumps so high?"

Maya blinked. *What rabbit?* The page was plain red. Blank but for the color.

The librarian leaned forward. "And who's this behind the bush?"

"A bear!" a child said.

What bush? What bear? Maya looked at the mothers to see if they thought the librarian was as wacky as Maya thought. But the mothers nodded and smiled, seeing the rabbit. Seeing the bear behind the bush.

All Maya saw was a red page.

The librarian turned the next page. "See the bear jump, jump, jump. Hear the bear go *Grrrr.*"

The new page showed a bear jumping.

What was going on? This was the second blank of red Maya had seen today. First, Susan's birthday banner, and now, the page in the children's book.

The mother of the little boy looked in her direction. Her forehead furrowed. She held her son a little tighter.

It probably did look strange. A woman standing on the edge of the children's section, *not* reading anything. Looking confused. Crazed.

The mother was still staring, as if she feared Maya would steal her son.

What an intriguing idea.

What?

When Maya realized the horrible direction of her thoughts, she rushed away.

What was wrong with her?

74

| | | | | | | | | |

When Maya drove up, Sal was unloading geraniums from his truck. "You're home early," he said. He wiped his hands on his jeans. "Did you take time off to come with us to the hospital?"

Hospital. Agata's first cancer treatment.

Instead of telling him that was the *last* thing she felt like doing, instead of telling him she was home early because she'd been fired . . . "I thought you could use the support."

He kissed her cheek. "You are some kind of woman, Maya Morano."

What kind was yet to be determined.

| | | | | | | | | |

Sleep did not come easily that night. They'd been late getting home from the hospital, as Sal had insisted on taking his mother home and staying most of the evening to make sure she didn't need anything. Agata had done very well, and Maya had been relieved that the focus on her illness had distracted her family from any odd vibes Maya may have been sending out. Only once did Agata ask, "Is something wrong, dear?"

No. Not a thing.

Not *a* thing. *Every*thing.

Maya could have told Sal the truth once they got home, but he was so exhausted and stressed about his mother she couldn't do it.

And so, added to the guilt and shame of the firing was her

current lie of omission. One more weight, balanced precariously upon her head.

Sal turned toward her in bed, momentarily opening his eyes. He reached through the moonlight and stroked her head. "I really appreciate all you did today, being there for Mama and me. But you need to get some sleep. You have work in the morning."

75

She closed her eyes rather than answer.

THREE

*Obviously, I'm not trying to win
the approval of people, but of God.
If pleasing people were my goal,
I would not be Christ's servant.*

GALATIANS 1:10

Now what?

Maya left the house.

To go to work.

The only problem was, she had no job. She had no work.

She used to dream about having a free day to run errands, shop, or get her hair done. For her last birthday, she'd splurged by getting a pedicure, a manicure, *and* a facial. A successful businesswoman could afford such perks. Deserved such perks. A disgraced has-been could not. And did not.

So what did she deserve?

She couldn't go there. Her ego was too raw.

So. Where could she go?

Then she knew. There was one place in the world that fed her and expected nothing in return.

| | | | | | | | | | |

"Here for another baby fix, Maya?"

As if I could help myself. Maya pointed through the nursery window at the five newborns. Five miracles. Five yeses to their parents' prayers. "Busy night last night, Betty?"

"Crazy," the nurse said. "And two more in labor."

The nurse inside the nursery saw Maya and waved. She spread her arms across the babies, symbolically asking which baby Maya wanted to see close up. All the nurses knew her and accepted her need to visit babies that weren't hers. She used to come occasionally, but of late had been coming once or twice a week.

Maya pointed to the middle child, a little girl with rosy cheeks.

The nurse wheeled her closer to the window. *Hi, my name is Miranda,* said the sign on the bassinet.

Maya pressed her fingers to the glass wishing she could touch . . . hold . . . have.

Betty put a hand on Maya's arm. "It will happen, Maya. When the time's right. I've never seen anyone more determined to be a mother."

"Determination doesn't make babies."

The nurse smiled. "Don't give up."

Maya looked back to baby Miranda. The sign announcing her name had oddly been replaced with a red sign. A blank red sign.

She rubbed her eyes.

"Are you okay?" Betty asked.

Maya looked at the bassinet again. *Hi, my name is Miranda.*

"I'm fine," Maya told Betty.

But she wasn't.

| | | | | | | | | | |

Roman took the elevator up to three—the executive floor. *So this is what going to the gallows feels like.*

Surely he was exaggerating. Surely Mr. Moore merely wanted an update. Surely Roman's superior didn't know, couldn't know, anything about Roman's own ethical shortcuts. It was too long ago. He'd gotten this far, gotten this job, without anyone knowing.

Surely it wouldn't come back to bite him now.

He smiled at Mr. Moore's receptionist as if nothing was amiss. After all these years and climbing this far, he knew that a man who acted confident gained the confidence of others.

Most of the time.

"He'll see you now," the receptionist said. "Go right in."

Mr. Moore stood when Roman entered and extended his hand to shake. Two good signs.

Once they were settled in their respective places, Mr. Moore opened a file. At first Roman worried it was Brian's file, but he quickly squelched that fear because he knew that file was safely tucked away in his own—

"I have a copy here of a file created by Brian Adams, one of your salesmen."

The cretin made a copy. "Yes, I'm aware of it." Roman decided to take the offensive. "It's very unfortunate that a woman with Maya's potential achieved success in ways . . . well, in ways we do not condone."

"Indeed," Mr. Moore said. "In response, you have . . .?"

"I have let her go."

He nodded once. "Good. We must lose the chaff in order to keep the wheat."

Was Roman the wheat? At the moment he didn't feel like the wheat. One gust of wind and he'd blow away.

His uncertainty was fed when Mr. Moore closed the file with a little too much deliberation. He avoided Roman's gaze a moment, and when he looked up, his eyes revealed a hint of regret.

"Of course there is the issue of supervision, Roman. And the Top Seller award. How could Ms. Morano conduct business as she did without your knowledge, and why wasn't it caught in time to prevent the embarrassment of the award? It does not look good. We do not look good."

And the unspoken, "You do not look good."

"I am very sorry, Mr. Moore. I truly think it was simply a case of an ambitious woman stretching the limits."

"So you don't see an indication of similar practices with the other employees?"

"No, no. Not at all. But please know I intend to do some checking to make sure nothing like this is happening with the others. Though I am fairly positive—"

"You must be fully positive."

"I will be. I will do everything in my power to uphold the reputation of this company." He hated sounding like a sound bite, saying all the right things. Yet not knowing Mr. Moore any better than he did, formal was good. Formal was safe.

Mr. Moore stood. "Let me know if you find any more of such actions—past or present."

Roman swallowed. "I'll do my best."

| | | | | | | | | | |

Roman was not in the mood to go to dinner with Velvet Cotton, and yet . . . if anyone could make him forget his troubles, even momentarily, it was Velvet.

Where some women were high maintenance, requiring phone calls, attention, and effort, Velvet was no maintenance. He'd never met a woman who needed less, needed him less, and—if he read her correctly—needed anybody less.

Besides having no need for people, Velvet seemed to have no particular liking for the beast. That she worked in a job where she had to deal with hundreds, if not thousands, was ironic and something she had never explained.

Not that he'd ever asked.

Velvet seemed the perfect type to do research in the basement of some library or work as a late-night stocker in a grocery store. Or maybe be a writer holed up in an attic, pounding away at a keyboard. Do not disturb.

But as far as Roman knew, Velvet had worked in the sports concessions department for the University of Nebraska since she was in college, twenty-some years ago. She'd risen to the top of the department. No hot dog, peanut, pop, or piece of pizza passed hands without her knowledge.

Or her care.

Yet the term *care* didn't seem to fit Velvet. Her manner was abrupt and a bit contemptuous, as though she would just as soon bite you as speak to you. She had made it clear to Roman that when they went out to dinner she never (not ever) wanted to eat anything that resembled the food sold at a sporting event. Roman was okay with that, though he might have liked to take her for pizza once in a while.

Velvet was an enigma, and it would have been confusing if he'd wanted to dissect her. Which he didn't.

Tonight they were going to China Treasure. Roman didn't have to ask if it was okay with Velvet. She'd made *that* very clear too. "Just choose. Thems that pay get to pick."

Which was another reason she was low maintenance. Whatever Roman felt like doing or eating was fine by her, and she preferred he not waste time with the technicality of him asking for, or her offering, an opinion. "I'm game" was her motto.

And she was. It didn't matter whether he bought tickets to see *Les Misérables* or Kenny G, some Chinese dance troupe or an evening of Mozart. She accompanied him without protest. Or complaint.

Or approbation.

Velvet was the mistress of the understatement. When Roman

---

would ask, "How did you like the concert?" she would say, "It was nice," which could mean she loved it or thought it was just above mediocre. Or she would say, "Eh. So-so," which spanned the balance of the negative options. This had bothered Roman at first, but he soon got over it. Her middle-of-the-road way of responding took the pressure off him to be *on* in her presence. With Velvet he could just *be*.

And tonight, after the upheaval going on at work, just being was all he could manage.

| | | | | | | | | | |

Velvet was not in the mood to go to dinner with Roman Paulson, and yet . . . if anyone could make her forget her troubles, even momentarily, it was Roman.

Where some men were high maintenance, requiring phone calls, attention, and effort, Roman was no maintenance. She'd never met a man who needed less, needed her less, and—if she read him correctly—needed anybody less.

Anybody except his son, Billy.

The devotion that man had for the boy was admirable, if not a bit obsessive. Roman's identity was so finely interwoven with Billy's . . . it wasn't healthy.

Yet who was she to define *healthy*?

The waiter handed them menus. "Hi, my name's John and—"

"John?" Velvet said. "I'm being inundated with Johns lately."

"How so?" Roman asked.

"It's nothing. Just a coincidence."

She handed the menu back to the waiter and reeled off her list of wants. "I want egg drop soup, cashew chicken with fried rice, an order of crab Rangoon, and some hot tea."

"You didn't even open your menu," Roman said, still looking.

82

"I knows what I likes and likes what I knows."

Roman closed his menu. "What she said."

"Are you acquiescing to my tastes, Mr. Paulson?"

"Actually, yes. I'm not in the mood for choices."

"Bad day at work?"

"I don't want to talk about it."

So what else was new? Yet it was fine with her. With Lianne and John back in her life she wasn't in a sharing mood. Not that she or Roman ever did much of that. When they were together they were both pros at living in the moment and leaving everything else behind.

She thought of a subject that *was* fair game. "Is Billy nervous about Saturday?"

"Excited. He's just excited."

Something about the intensity in Roman's words made her ask, "Is that the truth or wishful thinking?"

"I want him to do well."

"Duh."

"So much depends on this first game. The rest of the games depend on how he plays Saturday. But if he lets himself get distracted then . . ."

"Is something distracting him?"

The tea came in a pot and the waiter poured it into two handleless cups. Roman didn't answer until he'd had a sip. "He's going to church."

"Whatever for?"

"It's one of the coaches' fault. During his freshman year Billy got caught up in a Jesus frenzy brought on by this one coach, overstepping his bounds. I told him God and football don't mix. It's like those stupid people who hold up the John 3:16 signs at games. Last year there was a guy across the field from me who held up a sign every single game." He shook his head. "Stupid, stupid, stupid."

Velvet had seen signs like that and had always wondered about them. "What's that sign stuff about anyway?"

"It's from the Bible."

"I know *that*," she said. She wasn't ignorant. "But why spout Bible stuff at a football game? It's not like anyone's carrying their Bible with them."

"Exactly. And it's not like anyone's going to remember what it says so they can look it up later."

Velvet paused. "You remembered."

Roman sipped his tea and shrugged. "But I can guarantee you I have never, ever looked it up. You won't catch me falling for the Bible or church or praise-the-Lord glory-glory talk or praying, expecting an answer."

His vehemence made her curious. "Been there, done that?"

Roman shrugged. "I warned Billy to leave it alone. I told him believing in God and letting a church get their hooks into him would do him no good and only disappoint him, but—"

"But he did it anyway?"

"I feel like I'm losing him."

She wanted to say, "You're not" but couldn't. She and Roman shared a distrust and distaste for all things religious. Both had gone through enough sorrow and distress to realize believing in God—believing in anything beyond themselves—wasn't going to do any good, so why bother?

Back in college she and John had shared the same distrust of religion. They'd had rousing discussions about the power of the individual, the utter distrust organized religion deserved, and the illogic of throwing one's loyalty to an invisible being that may or may not care one way or the other. They'd been united in their worship of self.

But now . . . obviously John had changed camps. Big time.

"Velvet?"

She blinked herself back to the here and now. "Sorry."

"You're distracted."

It was a statement, not a request for information. Yes, she was distracted, but she couldn't talk to Roman about Lianne or John. They were a part of her past, the past she never talked about. The past no one knew.

85

"I'm just . . ." She was going to say *tired* but noticed he was also distracted, staring vaguely across the restaurant. "Speaking of . . ."

"Sorry." He made an effort to look at her, his face troubled. "Do you ever have the feeling something just isn't right?"

"Sure."

"There's stuff going on at work, but it's more than that."

"You're just nervous about Billy's first start."

He shook his head. "It's more than that too. It's *other* than that." He put his fists on his gut. "It's something to do with Billy, but I'm not sure what it is. Like something's going to happen."

"Good or bad?"

"I'm not sure."

Velvet thought of her coffee date tomorrow with John. And Lianne's first day of training. Yes indeed, something was going to happen, all right. Good or bad.

"This isn't like us," she said. "Brooding. Worrying." *Sharing.*

"I don't like it," he said.

"Then let's talk about something safe."

"Like what?"

"Politics? The economy? Which movie stars are divorcing, having babies, or pumping their own gas?"

"What?"

She acted aghast. "I am appalled at your lack of education and knowledge of current events, Mr. Paulson. You are obviously not up-to-date on the latest movie star magazines. They show actual pictures of stars shopping for groceries, buying shoes, walking in the park, and yes, even pumping their own gas." She put a hand to her chest, feigning deep emotion. "It's quite . . . inspirational."

"I had no idea."

"Get with it, man. You are way out of the loop."

Their soup came and blessed small talk reigned once again.

| | | | | | | | | | |

After leaving the hospital nursery, Maya wasted the rest of her day doing nothing and next to nothing. If someone had asked how she had spent her time, she would have been hard-pressed to account for it. Or for her thoughts. In that regard nothing had been accomplished, nothing resolved, and no new plan of action entertained. Time had passed. Period.

When enough time had passed that she could go home, she was surprised to find Sal changed from his work clothes into nice khakis and a green polo shirt. "Finally," he said when she came in the house.

"What—?"

"Your parents' place? For dinner? Your sister's birthday?"

She dumped her purse on the floor, closed her eyes, and sighed. *No. Not tonight.* Forced family frivolity was not on her emotional schedule. One-on-one the Castilla family could be tolerated, but en masse they often made her feel the need to gasp for air, like wearing a wool blanket on a hot day.

Sal picked up her purse. "We need to get going. You know what a stickler your parents are about punctuality."

That was the least of it.

| | | | | | | | | | |

Her sister Marcela met them at the door. "Warning, warning," she whispered.

"What's wrong?" Maya asked.

"Father and Mother are on the warpath. Apparently their nemesis was awarded their grant money."

"Grant money for what?" Sal asked.

"Money for fame, fortune, and fruitfulness, silly." Marcela winked. "Remember, we Castillas must produce and prosper at all times."

So Maya had been told. Repeatedly.

She steeled herself and entered the kitchen of the family home. The kitchen had changed drastically since Maya's childhood. Gone were the 1920s cupboards and old appliances. In their place were cabinets of deep cherry and appliances of stainless steel. The wooden countertops had surrendered to a slab of black speckled granite. An island had been added with seating along the back. It was a lovely renovation, and Maya did not begrudge her parents the improvements, but in the way of most children returning to the family home, she secretly longed for the kitchen of her youth to remain intact, a sacred shrine, never to be defaced or changed.

Maya's mother called the renovation "the kitchen Ptolemy built" because it was her parents' book on an Egyptian king named Ptolemy that had paid for it. It was the only major improvement they'd made to the house over a lifetime. With three daughters and income that vacillated according to the whims of grants and publishers, there had rarely been money for large improvements. And her parents were not savers. Whatever they earned went toward immediate needs—and historical research.

The room buzzed with family. Swarmed with them. Besides her parents bustling around the stove and counter, there was Marcela's husband, teenage son, and daughter, and the birthday girl, Marta, with her spouse and three children—and an additional baby on the way.

Maya and Sal's entering the room by themselves always made her self-conscious and apologetic. *Sorry we're it.*

There were greetings all around, though hugs were absent. The Castillas did not hug. Sal's family were big huggers—coming and going hugs were mandatory, and a few embraces interspersed throughout any gathering were to be expected, accepted, and returned. This close contact had taken some getting used to on Maya's part, as had the Castillas' *lack* of contact for Sal.

The decibel level of the two families was similar. Both sides liked to talk—and hear themselves talk. Tonight Maya was glad for it. For on this particular evening she was quite willing to let the rest of them fill any and all silences. The quicker she and Sal could eat and be gone the better.

Maya took a seat at the island and let the conversation spin around her, creating threads that wove her into a smothering shroud. Everyone spoke of their work: Marta was a chemist for a medical research group and her husband owned three hotels and was expanding by two in nearby Omaha. Marcela taught speech and drama at the University of Nebraska and her husband was a banker.

Sal worked with his hands. Outside. Mowing other people's lawns and planting daisies.

And Maya . . .

She thought back to last Friday when her family had attended the award ceremony. They'd been so proud of her. At the time she'd felt she had finally arrived, finally counted for something.

But now . . .

She shivered at the implications.

Once the food was ready the group moved to the dining room and took their usual places. Maya could not remember the seating ever being formally assigned, but she had always sat on her father's left with her two sisters across the table from her. For years she had been the one-person, sitting in the space meant for two (the extra chair pulled into the corner) which had somehow solidified—or ignited—her feeling that she was separate from the rest, certainly separate from Marta and Marcela, who had always been chummy and chatty, often leaving Maya on the outside looking in. Maya would have liked to attribute this to the close proximity of her sisters' ages, but since she herself was the middle daughter, and since Marcela was four years older and Marta four younger, that logic was moot. Maya was the odd duck in the middle. Always had been. Always would be.

With the addition of five grandchildren and three spouses, table leaves had been permanently added, as had inherited chairs from Grandmother Castilla's dining room set. Yet oddly, the original Castillas took the chairs belonging to the original set, and the newcomers sat in the hand-me-downs. Another act of subtle distinction that just *was*.

Grace was repeated in unison before the vast bowls of food were passed. Her mother wasted no time inducing the discussion to flow on her terms. "We must bring you up to date, Maya. We did *not* get the Pellar Grant for our continued Egyptian studies."

"It was stolen from us," Father said.

"Fran Madison got the money," Marcela added.

"Fran Madison couldn't research her way out of an encyclopedia," Mother said.

"An out-of-date encyclopedia," Father added.

"You'd been so positive about getting it," Maya said. "So hopeful."

"We were no match for Fran's underhanded ways. She made promises to the board she will never be able to keep."

Mother shook her head and passed the green beans. "She's always been unethical. Pushing her way in, grabbing what wasn't hers. Being greedy."

Maya fumbled the serving spoon, sending three beans across the table into Marcela's lap.

"Sorry," Maya said.

"No problem." Marcela popped the beans into her mouth.

"Try one over here, Aunt Maya," her thirteen-year-old nephew said.

"Enough, Brian," his mother said.

Brian. Her coworker's name was Brian. . . .

"Someone should stop that Fran woman," Marta said. "If she's finding success through dishonest methods . . ."

Father poured gravy on his mashed potatoes. "Your mother and I have talked about it, but we can't very well complain lest we risk the good graces of the board—and beyond. It would seem petty and unprofessional."

"Isn't being unethical unprofessional?" Sal asked.

"Absolutely," Father said. "Fran needs to be punished; we're just not sure how it should be done."

"She will be punished," Mother said. "People like that get what's coming to them. Eventually."

"Actually, not always," Marcela said.

Maya's stomach was in knots. She tried to think of a way to change the subject but it seemed her entire life was off-limits as subject matter. She looked at the clock on the buffet. Time was moving far too slowly.

Mother patted her lips with a napkin. "So, Marta, how's our grandchild-to-be coming along?"

Marta patted her expanding middle, which could be seen above the table. She beamed. "Would you like to know whether it's a boy or a girl?"

There was affirmation all around. Marta already had two girls and a boy.

She took her husband's hand. "You tell them."

"It's a boy."

"Two and two; how perfect," Marcela said. "I've always been glad I had one of each."

Leaving me with none of each.

Her mother's attention turned in Maya's direction and she braced herself. "And how goes the baby front for you, dear? Two failures . . ."

She cringed at the horrible, horrible term. "We hope to try one more time," Maya said. She looked to Sal, who avoided her gaze by slicing into his roast beef.

"You can only try one more time," Marta said. "Isn't that right? They only let you do the infertility treatments three times?"

Reluctantly, she nodded. That *was* the norm. But she'd get Dr. Ruffin to do it a fourth time. A fifth. She would not give up.

"There *are* other alternatives, you know," Marcela said.

Father's eyebrows rose. "Such as?"

"Adoption."

Jose Castilla blinked twice. "Taking someone else's child—a child who might have come from questionable stock . . ." He shook his head. "It's far too hit-and-miss. You might get a child who isn't quite right, or ugly, or hooked on some illegal drug their mother took while she was pregnant."

Maya shivered. Marcela spoke for her. "It's not as bad as all that, Father. Lots of important people were adopted."

Father sat back in his chair and folded his arms across his chest. "Name one."

Marcela looked around the table, clearly seeking help.

"Edgar Allen Poe," her husband said.

Marcela raised her hand. "'Once upon a midnight dreary, while I pondered, weak and weary . . .'" Her excitement waned. "I can't remember any more of it."

Her husband added, "'Quoth the Raven, "Nevermore."'"

"Faith Hill is adopted," Brian said.

"Some of those figure skaters too," Marta said. "Scott Hamilton and those Carruthers siblings."

Their father shook his head. "An author of the macabre, a

country singer, and people who fling themselves in the air. That is not strong confirmation."

Marcela wasn't through. "I think Nancy Reagan was adopted. And maybe Nelson Mandela? I'm not sure about that last one. But Moses was adopted. I believe his credentials are solid."

Before their parents could respond, Marta's ten-year-old said, "My friend Joey is adopted."

Marcela jumped on it. "And I bet he's a smart boy. A good boy."

He shook his head. "He can't write cursive at all and he eats his boogers."

Well then . . .

Maya took a sip of water, wishing her need to escape would subside but knowing it wouldn't. It never did. "We're doing everything we can to get pregnant, really we are. But—" she risked a look at Sal—"maybe God has other plans for us."

All movement stopped. Having children was a given. You grew up, went to college, got married, and had children. So be it, as per the Castillas.

"Oops!" Marta's two-year-old spilled her milk.

In the ensuing scramble the subject was dropped.

Maya knew she had been given a reprieve—but not a pardon. Never a pardon.

| | | | | | | | | | |

Maya sat on the couch in front of the TV and out of habit looked around for her laptop. She was the queen of multitasking. She never *just* watched TV but usually worked on her computer from the couch, or worked on the sweater she was knitting her father for Christmas, or paid bills. Without a job the laptop was unnecessary and the bills depressed her. She pulled out the knitting.

Sal sat in his leather recliner, but before he turned on the set . . . "Although I'm not usually on your parents' side, I kind of agree with them about the adoption issue. The whole fear of getting a crack baby or one with medical problems is valid."

Maya was stunned. "Do you also agree with my father's fear of getting an ugly baby?"

93

Sal shrugged. "That *was* kind of petty. But the rest of it . . ."

"I didn't know you were against adoption."

"I guess we've never talked about it. We always thought one of the fertility procedures would work."

They have to.

Sal searched for the remote. "Your parents' disapproval centers around genes—the Castilla genes." His voice turned sarcastic. "Genes that carry your parents' profound intelligence and talents—as if my genes have no impact. An adopted child will definitely be at a disadvantage in that household. I should know."

"Sal!" But she knew what he meant. Her husband had gone through a lot to be accepted—even minimally—by her parents.

"We wouldn't know what we'd get with an adopted child," he said.

"Do we know what we'll get with a blood child?" she asked. "There are plenty of children born to brilliant parents who fail and founder, and plenty of adopted children who flourish. My parents don't have a case, Sal. There is no basis in their reasoning."

"Reason or not, it's what they believe."

Maya straightened the magazines on the coffee table. "I thought about asking them for the ten thousand for the third procedure."

He found the remote in the seat cushion. "They certainly have more money than my mother has."

"But since they didn't get the grant they were counting on, I couldn't do it. They don't have much in savings. Mother has told me as much."

He tapped the remote against his thigh, looking at her. "That's not the real reason, is it?"

Maya wasn't sure what he was getting at.

"You don't want them to know that we don't have the money, that we don't earn enough."

"No, that's not it." Her voice didn't sound as convincing as she'd hoped. Would she ever get over the need to make her parents proud?

"You want their approval even more than a baby, don't you?"

"No!" This time she was more adamant. "I . . . I want a baby more than anything. I'd do anything . . ."

She'd already done plenty.

"It's good you want to please them, Maya, but I'm not sure it's possible." Sal leaned back in the recliner, causing the footrest to pop into place. "And unlike you, I *know* God wants us to have a child. I keep telling him we need a baby. Soon."

Sal was *telling* God what to do? That didn't sound right.

Telling. Asking.

Begging.

What did semantics matter? Right now they were in limbo—and she was weary and worn-out.

"Turn on the TV," she said. "Surely something good is on."

Good as in something mindless and distracting.

| | | | | | | | | | |

Peter put his choir folder back in its slot. Another tenor slapped him on the back. "Good to have you with us again, Peter. You have a good, blending voice." He leaned closer, confidentially. "A trait a few of the other tenors could work on."

Peter knew the voices he referred to. That was the problem with volunteer church choirs: you didn't have to be a good singer to join, and the mix of good and mediocre tried his nerves. And ears. He worked hard on not letting his voice stick out. Blending in was definitely the way to go.

"See you Sunday?" the man asked.

"Hopefully." It was all the commitment Peter could make. He hadn't been to church in months. Something always came up, keeping him away. Someone. Even when William and Carrie asked him to go . . . the lure of time with Lianne overshadowed their invitation.

The choir director came up to him, all smiles. "So good to have you back, Peter."

"Good to be back." He offered no explanation.

She pulled a notebook of music from the shelf and held it between them. "In honor of your return, I have a favor to ask."

He was wary. "What is it?"

"Could you drop this music folder off to Agata Morano? She's started cancer treatment and isn't feeling up to par. I told her I'd bring the music by. Since you live near her . . ."

He liked Agata. "Sure. No problem."

Peter left the church, calling out good-bye to his choir friends as they went to their cars. He congratulated himself on successfully avoiding Lianne all day. He was still upset about how she'd treated his parents, uncomfortable about being set between them and confused about what to do next. But the main reason he'd avoided her was because he was a coward. He despised confrontation and went to great lengths to avoid it. As a child he'd always been quick to guess what his parents wanted and was good at reading their moods. During the few times he'd gotten in trouble, they'd found him hiding in the barn or at his special place down by the creek. Lianne teased him about being a people pleaser. He didn't argue with her. Nor did he think it was such a bad thing.

But sometimes it did make life difficult. Like today. . . . Because Lianne knew his schedule, he'd skipped all his classes and had hung out in the stacks of the library, his back to the wall, checking out anyone who came close. He'd kept his cell phone off, unwilling to risk turning it on only to find a dozen messages, tempting him to make contact. Insisting he make contact. When evening rolled around, he'd avoided his apartment by coming to the weekly dinner at church and then to choir practice. Church was one place Lianne would never—

"You can't avoid me forever, you know."

At the sound of Lianne's voice, at the sight of her leaning against his car, Peter felt his heart fall into the pit of his stomach. "Sorry," he said, getting out his key. "I've been busy."

"Busy hiding from me."

He didn't deny it.

She'd positioned herself in front of the driver's door and wouldn't move aside.

He sighed dramatically. "If you don't mind? I have an errand to run for the choir director." He displayed the music as Exhibit A.

"Super. I'll come along." She opened the driver's door, climbed over the seat, and settled into the passenger seat.

He had no idea what to do. She was so sure of herself, so sure of him, so sure he'd forgiven her and was ready to move on. Suddenly being predictable was disgusting.

"Are we going or what?" she asked.

He leaned down to look at her, his breathing heavy. "Get out of the car, Lianne. This is my errand. I don't want a passenger."

She sang a line from a Rolling Stones classic. "'You can't always get what you want . . .'"

"Lianne. Come on. Give me a break."

She put her seat belt on. "I'm not getting out, McLean. So you might as well get in and drive."

Lianne, the immovable force, meet Peter, the compliant weakling.

Yet he couldn't see that he had much choice. He got in and

started the car. "I have nothing to say to you," he said, not because it was true but because he didn't know *what* to say.

"Look, McLean, I'm sorry if I told the truth yesterday, and that you and your parents couldn't handle it."

He snickered. "Is that supposed to be an apology?" He pulled out of the parking lot.

"If you want me to say I was wrong for being honest, I won't. The truth is always right."

"Ever hear of discretion? tact?"

"Never embraced either one of them," she said. "In case you haven't noticed."

Cute.

She flipped on the radio, changing from his favorite country station to the hard rock station she preferred. Yet Peter was grateful for the music.

Luckily, Agata's house wasn't far. He pulled up in front and shut off the car. "Wait here."

She ignored him and got out.

Peter scrambled out of the car and spoke to her over its roof. She was driving him crazy. "I'll just be a minute. She's an old woman, Lianne. She has cancer. She—"

"Then she could use a little cheering up." She strode up the front walk.

Peter dropped the notebook. The rings popped open and music started to flutter and escape. "Lianne!" he whispered after her.

Too late. She was at the door, ringing the bell.

Ignoring any order to the music, Peter gathered it to his chest and ran to catch up, reaching the door just as Agata opened it. The woman saw Lianne first and looked puzzled, but as soon as she saw Peter, her face softened.

"Peter. How nice to see you."

"I brought music from choir," he said with it splayed awkwardly. "I dropped it."

"Well, come on in and we'll get it organized again." She held the door wide. Her voice sounded hoarser than usual. Was it because of the cancer? "And what's your name, young lady?"

"Lianne Skala." Lianne shook Agata's hand.

"Are you a new member of choir?"

"Heavens no. I'm Peter's girlfriend." She went inside. "He's mad at me and I'm trying to make up but he's not cooperating."

"Lianne!"

"Well, it's true, isn't it?" She plucked a porcelain cardinal from Agata's coffee table. "This is pretty."

"Thank you."

Peter sat on the couch and let go of the music. "We won't bother you long, Mrs. Morano. I'll just get this music put back together and—"

"It's Agata, Peter. We're choirmates. And don't hurry yourself. I could use the company."

"See?" Lianne said. Her orange skirt and red top were a stark contrast to the muted gold couch.

Agata settled into a chair, the only concession to her age and disease a slight moan and a short burst of coughing. "How was choir practice tonight? I hate to miss it. Especially if you're back singing with us again, Peter. We missed you."

"Thanks."

"He doesn't go to church anymore," Lianne said.

Peter fumbled a copy of "Many Gifts, One Spirit" to the floor. "That's not true. I . . . I've just been busy."

"With me," Lianne said. "He's been busy with me."

"Maybe you could come with him," Agata said.

Lianne slapped a hand on the armrest and laughed. "I don't think so. God and I are not on speaking terms anymore."

Anymore? It was the first time Peter had heard Lianne imply she'd ever had any level of faith.

Agata shook her head. "God hasn't moved. He hasn't changed. So that means you're the culprit. What changed *you*?"

Lianne cocked her head to the side, giving Agata an appraising look. "I like you. You say what's on your mind."

"Not exactly," Agata said. "My mind plays tricks on me. But I do say what's on my heart. Now tell me what happened."

Lianne stood and strolled to the mantel. She ran a finger along its beveled edge. "You have cancer."

"Lianne!"

"Cut it out, McLean. Quit jumping on me for saying what's on my mind. Agata and I are having a conversation here. I think she can handle my questions."

He looked to Agata and she gave him a little nod. If only he'd locked Lianne in the car . . .

Lianne took a fresh breath, then said again, "You have cancer."

"I do."

"Are you angry about it?"

"I'm not pleased. But mad? No. I'm not mad. God has his reasons."

Lianne tossed her hands in the air. "He has a reason to give a person cancer? I don't think so. There's no reason. Ever. No way."

"But there are reasons, far beyond our understanding," Agata said. "'He will not let you stumble; the one who watches over you will not slumber.'"

"Cancer sounds like a big stumble to me. A nosedive."

Agata continued. "Every life has struggles and trials. But even those have purpose."

Lianne laughed. "To make us crazy?"

"To make us turn to him." She looked at Peter. "Would you two like some iced tea and raisin bars?"

"No thanks." He stood, hoping Lianne would take the hint. "We really have to be going."

"I'd love a raisin bar," Lianne said. Her glare challenged Peter. She returned to the couch and sat as if firmly rooted.

Peter sat too, then rose again when Agata started to struggle to her feet. "You sit, Agata. Tell me where they are and I'll get them."

"In the tin on the counter, Peter. And bring some napkins from the table."

He went on his errand but kept an ear toward the conversation in the living room. Why couldn't Lianne shut up? You didn't quiz people who had cancer. You said hopeful things that would cheer them up.

Lianne was talking again. "I've had plenty of hard times in my life, and I handled them fine, on my own, without getting God involved in any way whatsoever."

"I'm sure God helped you, even if you don't give him credit."

Peter reentered the room with the bars and napkins. He held them in front of Agata, who waved them off. Lianne took two.

"I'm sure God *didn't* help me. I handled everything on my own—in spite of his interference."

"I'm afraid you'll need to explain yourself, my dear."

Lianne pressed a finger into the top of her raisin bar, as if making certain a wayward raisin did not break its surface. "I'm adopted."

Peter was stunned. She'd never mentioned that before. "Why didn't you tell me?" he asked.

"Why didn't my parents tell *me*? I only found out way late. Too late."

"I'm sorry, Lianne," Agata said. "But I'm sure your parents had their reasons."

"Selfish reasons. They didn't want to share me with anyone else. They didn't want me to contact my birth parents."

"Have you?" Peter asked. "Contacted them?"

"I haven't looked."

"Have you asked your parents questions?"

She snickered.

"You haven't spoken with them about it?" Agata asked.

Lianne cleared her throat. "We don't speak at all anymore."

"That sounds a bit harsh," Agata said. "Are they good parents—otherwise?"

"As good as most. But for them to keep this secret from me, to pretend they're my real parents . . ."

"They are your real parents. They love you, they take care of you, they encourage you."

"They lied to me." She set the raisin bar aside and sighed. "And that's one reason—of many—why I don't need God. I don't need another father figure in my life. He abandoned me too, all those years. Answer me this: why does he let bad things happen?" She looked to Peter, then to Agata.

"I don't know," Agata said.

Lianne applauded. "Bravo! That's the most honest answer I've ever heard." She pressed her palms against her skirt. "All *I* know is that when I'm a mother, I'm going to be honest with my kids, right from the start. I'm going to be strong. And I'm not going to get so caught up in my own life and troubles that I let bad things happen and . . ." She stopped and placed her hands over her abdomen.

It was an odd gesture. A protective gesture.

No. She's just doing that to make a point, not because . . .

"Are you pregnant, my dear?" Agata asked.

Before Peter could get over the bluntness of the question, Lianne answered. "Yes. Yes, I am." She looked directly at Peter. "Surprise. Daddy."

| | | | | | | | | | |

Peter wasn't sure what was said after Lianne's big announcement, or exactly how they'd managed to get back to his car. In the short time since they'd been inside at Agata's, it had grown dark.

In so many ways.

In the moment after they pulled away from the curb, she said, "So? Are you happy with my news?"

He applied the brake too hard and they both lunged forward. "Happy?"

A car honked behind them, and he reminded himself to be more careful.

He was a little late being careful.

"No, I'm not happy. I'm twenty years old; I still have two years of college left. I'm having trouble figuring out my own life, much less having to figure out what to do with a baby. With this news . . . my life is over before it's even started."

Her voice turned huffy. "You don't have to marry me, McLean. And I don't have to have this baby."

He hated that his first reaction to both statements was—

"You're relieved I said that, aren't you?" she asked.

"Not exactly, but—"

"Stop the car!"

"Lianne."

"Stop the car right here. I'll walk the rest of the way home."

"But it's dark out there."

"It's mighty dark in here too." She put her hand on the door handle. "Either you stop the car, or I jump out while it's moving."

He pulled over and she got out. She slammed the door and rushed down the sidewalk, her orange skirt a waving flag. A warning flag? Maybe he should leave now, just drive away and be done with it. Pretend it never happened. Start over fresh.

A dog barked from the porch of the house nearby, breaking through his thoughts, making Peter accept the moment as real. Like it or not.

He crept along, following Lianne in the car. She stopped and turned on him, her arms wrapped around her body. "Get away!" she screamed.

A couple sitting on their front porch stood. The man walked to the edge of the front steps. "Is he bothering you, miss?"

His accusation startled Peter. He wasn't a stalker or a bad guy. He was just—

"Yes, he's bothering me," Lianne said. "Completely and absolutely. Will you walk me home, please?"

"Certainly," the man said.

The wife said, "Should I call the police?"

Police?

Lianne glared at Peter. "That won't be necessary. Will it?"

None of this was real. It couldn't be.

"Will it?" she repeated.

Peter shook his head and drove away.

What a mess. What a total, horrible, stinking mess.

FOUR

The plan came to her in the middle of the night.

Upon waking, Maya thought—far too briefly—about discounting it, but to her own shame did the opposite.

She got out of bed, changed into jeans, moved into the doorway of the master bathroom, and watched Sal shave.

As hoped, he noticed and stopped shaving. "Aren't you going to be late?"

The lie escaped with distressing ease. "I got permission to work from home."

His left eyebrow rose. "Since when?"

An inner voice reminded her she could still stop the lie but she clamped a hand over its words and answered her husband. "Since today."

"Why didn't you tell me?"

Oh what a tangled web we weave when first we practice to deceive. Ignoring the newest mental warning she made a little *ta-da* motion. "Surprise!"

Sal looked skeptical. "Are they letting all the salespeople work from home?"

She backed into the bedroom, needing escape. *No more questions. Please.* "Want some eggs?"

"Sure."

Maya hated to cook, but if making breakfast a few days a week would facilitate her being able to stay home instead of wandering around town, she'd become a top chef.

| | | | | | | | | | |

Maya sat on the couch with her computer in her lap. She logged on to her e-mail and braced herself.

There was nothing from anyone at work—except an e-mail sent just minutes before from her friend Susan.

That one e-mail was enough.

There's a reporter snooping around. Your name was mentioned.

Susan

Reporter? What would a reporter want with . . . "No. No, no. No!"

Maya e-mailed back:

Call me at home when you can talk.

She sat, staring at Susan's message. Getting fired was bad enough, but to have a reporter get involved? Surely this wasn't about her. Maybe her name had been mentioned because the reporter wanted to talk about her award.

Her ill-gotten award.

The words of her family intruded; it didn't matter that they'd been talking about someone else: *"She's always been unethical.*

Pushing her way in, grabbing what wasn't hers. Being greedy. . . . If she's finding success through dishonest methods . . . People like that get what's coming to them. Eventually."

Maya defended herself out loud. "But I was working hard, working harder than the rest. If Brian couldn't keep his own clients . . ."

107

The empty house did not reply.

Thankfully.

The phone rang, startling her. She picked it up before the second ring. "Yes?"

"Hi." Susan's voice was hesitant, far different from her usual zesty greeting.

"What's going on? Tell me everything."

Susan's voice was hushed, as if she was trying to keep it from being heard beyond her cubicle. "A reporter came by and asked to talk to the boss. Mr. Paulson was in a meeting—still is, I think—but as soon as he gets free . . . The reporter's already talked to Brian and he's been smiling ever since. Grinning, actually. Like he's really pleased with himself."

Maya closed her computer with a sharp click and shoved it onto the couch. "What did Brian tell him?"

"I don't know. Unbelievably, he won't say anything but, 'You'll see soon enough.'"

"What am I going to do?" Maya asked.

"The bigger question is, what *did* you do, Maya? I know what they say, but I can't believe you purposely took Brian's clients and . . . well, did you do what they say?"

Maya's first instinct was to say, "No. Of course not." But Susan was a friend. One of her few friends.

"I . . . I may have been a bit too aggressive."

Silence.

Maya wandered toward the front window. A white delivery van drove by with a red sign painted on the side. It was blank.

"I did it for the baby, Susan. To get money for another procedure. They're really expensive, and Sal and I are already tens of thousands in debt, and . . . you know how much we want a child."

108 Silence again.

This was ridiculous. "Surely, you understand. Besides, you dislike Brian as much as I do. He's always been a hook-or-crook kind of guy and—"

"So you did steal his clients?"

"*Steal* is too harsh a word. I simply talked to them, cajoled them, gave them a better deal."

Maya could hear Susan's breathing over the phone. "Did you . . . I mean, we're friends, so I would hope you wouldn't—"

"Did I talk to any of your clients? No."

Susan's voice turned to a whisper. "I gotta go."

The line went dead.

As did her future.

| | | | | | | | | | |

Maya sat on the couch, her shoulders slumped, the phone dangling from a limp hand in her lap. The world was against her, crashing around her, threatening to destroy her.

Susan's call had been bad enough, but within minutes of Susan hanging up on her, the phone had rung again.

Hoping her former coworker was calling back, Maya had answered it quickly. "Hey, Susan, I—"

"Sorry," the caller said. "This isn't Susan. My name is Ross Bredloe. I'm a reporter for the *Daily News* and I'm doing a piece on some unethical behavior at your company. I would like to ask you a few—"

"No comment," Maya barked.

"I haven't even asked you a question yet."

"No comment." Her heart was in her throat. *Just hang up! Hang up!*

"Ms. Morano, is that truly how you want me to quote you? 'No comment' is the response of the guilty."

Although she'd never made that connection, more often than not, it was probably true.

"Come on, ma'am. If you don't let me hear your side of the story, then I'll be forced to write it using the sources I've already talked to."

"Who have you talked to?"

"Your boss. A few coworkers. I prefer not to name names at this time. Ten minutes. That's all I'm asking for."

Although she wasn't sure she could make her side of things sound acceptable, she knew without her input there was *no* chance she would come off as anything but a conniving villain. Maybe she could appeal to the reader who would sympathize with her intense desire to have a child.

It was her only hope.

"When?" she asked.

"How about ten thirty? Can you meet at the coffee shop on Randolph?"

"Fine, fine." She thought of something. "How will I know you?"

"I'll know you. I saw a photo of you accepting some award."

Oh. That.

| | | | | | | | | | |

Roman came back from his meeting to find a note about a *Daily News* reporter on his desk. His assistant had added an ominous notation on the message line: *RE: Maya.*

The paper had heard about Maya's firing? It was none of their business; it was an internal affair.

Brian.

There was no other explanation. Vindictive, on-a-roll Brian must have called the paper. Could he fire Brian for arrogance?

Roman looked at the time on the message. It was forty-five minutes old. Maybe if he made the reporter wait long enough, the guy would leave.

His intercom buzzed. "There's that reporter here to see you, Mr. Paulson."

Never mind.

"Send him in."

An athletic-looking man in his early thirties entered and made a beeline for Roman's desk, his hand outstretched. He introduced himself, then said, "Thank you for seeing me, Mr. Paulson."

Roman would make it short and sweet. Quick and over. "What's on your mind, Mr. Bredloe?"

"Unethical employees."

Although he'd known the reporter had come about Maya, to hear it stated so plainly, so unmercifully . . . If only he could rewind the last minute he would have found some excuse to send the reporter away. The next best alternative was to feign ignorance. "I'm afraid you'll have to be more specific."

Bredloe crossed his legs. "Is the name Maya Morano specific enough?"

Roman stood. "I'm afraid I have nothing to say, Mr. Bredloe. Situations with our employees are private and—"

"You mean situations that culminate with firings due to un-ethical behavior?"

Roman's thoughts flashed to the back-against-the-wall interviews he'd seen on shows like *60 Minutes.* He'd always enjoyed seeing the guilty party squirm.

Until now.

"I don't like your attitude, Mr. Bredloe."

"Simply getting to the point. We're both busy men, yes? Both men who are interested in truth and fairness. And logic. When something's illogical it stirs my curiosity."

I'd like to stir you. "I think it would be best if you leave."

"As you wish," Bredloe said. He uncrossed his legs but made no move to get up. "Yet I think the business community would be interested in how a woman who won the Top Seller award last week is fired this week."

111

Roman took a few steps toward the door. "I don't know who you've been talking to . . ." Actually, he knew exactly whom Bredloe had been talking to.

"I have my sources."

"Then you don't need me." Roman stood next to the door. "You can see yourself out."

| | | | | | | | | | |

Brian appeared in the doorway to Roman's office. "You wanted to see me?"

"Sit. Now. But close the door first."

Brian did as he was told. Roman was glad to see he'd turned a whiter shade of pale. The man deserved to suffer a bit.

"I just had a visit from Ross Bredloe."

Brian's mouth opened slightly.

"Do you have anything to say about that?"

"I . . . I . . . he wasn't supposed to contact *you.*"

"Meaning he *was* supposed to contact someone else?"

"Well, yes."

"Names, please."

"Maya."

Roman felt a headache coming on. "She was fired. Isn't that enough?"

Brian looked at his hands in his lap. "Ross is a friend. He heard me talking about what Maya did and how she did it. He's a reporter for the business section. The story was his type of story. So he came over here today to talk to me and . . ."

"And who else?"

"Just a couple other salesmen."

"Maya took their customers too?"

"No, just mine. But they had information about what was going on."

"Hearsay."

"What?"

"They had information from you, from your point of view."

"Well, yeah."

"I told you not to spread this around, Brian. I told you to keep it quiet."

"But that was after . . ."

Oh. So that's how it was. "After you'd already blabbed it around?"

To his credit, Brian's pale had turned green. "Pretty much."

Roman wanted to wash his hands of the entire thing. If only that were possible. "Go on. Get out of here."

He didn't need to ask Brian twice.

| | | | | | | | | | | |

William gathered his car keys from the bowl on top of the TV. He glanced at Peter, sitting on the couch. "Don't you have class?"

Peter didn't need to look at his watch. He knew he was late—had been late all day because he'd skipped them all. Again. "I'm taking a day off."

"How come?"

"Stuff." He didn't want to go into it, especially with William.

William stood there a moment, as though studying him. "Since you're not going to class, want to come with me? I'm going to a picnic with some orphanage kids. It's through church and—"

"No thanks. I'm good here."

"You don't look very good."

Peter shrugged. And William left.

After the disastrous meeting between Lianne and his parents . . . after her announcement about the baby . . .

His baby.

His mind was consumed. Lianne would never fit in with his family. His life. His future.

And the baby . . .

He knew his mother longed to be a grandma. Someday. Not today. Not yet. Not like this.

Peter looked at his cell phone on the coffee table. Lianne hadn't called. He hadn't called her. The silence was preferable over conversation. What could be discussed?

Solutions could be discussed, should be discussed.

"You don't have to marry me."

Lianne's words had filled him with relief. He did *not* want to marry her. Which brought to mind all the conversations he'd had with William and Carrie about waiting for sex and making sure he was fully committed.

I'm fully committed now.

Physically. Morally. But what about emotionally? Or financially? He attended college on a scholarship. He worked hard every summer so he didn't have to work a job during the school year. It was a luxury that would be erased if they married.

And they had to marry. He couldn't leave Lianne to handle parenthood alone. Lianne, a single mother? It was not a pretty thought. And she'd be very alone. From what she'd said at Agata's, she was estranged from her parents. He'd never asked whether they were paying for college. Would they refuse to pay now that a baby was on the way? Or would Lianne not even tell them, drop out of school, and raise the baby on her own?

Her other words returned to him: *"I don't have to have this baby."*

Abortion?

Peter had never had to think much about abortion before. When he heard women talk about wanting the choice to do it or not do it, he'd agreed with them. It only seemed fair. It was their body and all that.

And yet . . . it was more than *their* body. The baby in Lianne's womb was . . . a baby. Even at this early stage. He'd seen pictures. There was no denying it.

He thought of a quote his parents had often spouted at him. It was from the book of Jeremiah: *I knew you before I formed you in your mother's womb. Before you were born I set you apart.*

His parents had repeated it to prove to Peter that he had a purpose—from his conception, from before his conception. God had a plan for his life.

So . . .

He sat upright. "God has a plan for this baby's life."

The words rang in his ears. He said them again. "God has a plan for this baby's life. My baby's life."

He couldn't let Lianne kill it.

Peter reached for the phone and punched in her number. As it rang he asked himself why Lianne wasn't on his speed dial.

She would be from now on.

"This is Lianne. You got me. Leave a message."

Peter was put on the spot. If this were a movie, he'd leave a message saying, "I love you, Lianne." But this was real life and he wasn't sure he did love her. Or that she loved him. The most important thing was that she not do anything to hurt the baby. Yet exactly like a movie, he hoped things would work out happily in the end.

"Hey, this is Peter. . . . Don't do anything. We'll work this out, Lianne. We will. Call me."

He flipped the phone shut.

And prepared to wait.

│ │ │ │ │ │ │ │ │ │

As Velvet opened the door to the coffee shop, her muscles tensed to flee. *I shouldn't be meeting him* clashed with *I want to see him.*

Before the door could swing shut behind her, she heard her name. "Velvet."

John stood by a table in the corner, waving at her.

In spite of her reluctance, she felt a twinge of excitement—which was absurd. Surely she didn't still have feelings for him.

He held out her chair, something he had never done as a college student. She sat, and he helped her move forward. "What did you do?" she said. "Take a how-to-be-a-gentleman class?"

He looked taken aback. "I guess I grew up."

She regretted her flippancy. "Sorry. That was a rude thing to say. Apparently I need a how-to-be-a-lady class." She hung the strap of her purse on the back of the chair. "Truth is, I'm nervous."

"Me too."

"You? Surely not. You're used to speaking in public, mingling with strangers. You're . . . almost famous."

He sighed. "'Rather than love, than money, than fame, give me truth.'"

"Gillingham?"

He smiled. "Thoreau." He wiped a spot on the table with a napkin. "Whatever fame I have happened since I knew you, Velvet. To you, with you, I'm a kid again. Awkward, insecure." He looked out the window. "I was so wrong back then. I was arrogant, cocky, and a know-it-all. An ignorant know-it-all, the worst kind."

"You weren't that bad." She was being kind. *Actually . . .*

"I was bad. Very bad. If I'd been a decent person I never would have run out on you when you told me you were pregnant. I was wrong and I'm sorry."

Velvet was made speechless. She wasn't sure what she had

expected him to say, but an apology . . . She'd assumed John had appeared in her life to complicate things and further her punishment, not to be nice. Of all things. "I . . . I . . . I need coffee."

John took her order, went to the counter, and brought back the beverages along with two muffins. "This one's poppy seed, this one banana nut. Choose."

"I choose half and half."

"Good idea." He took a knife and split them top to bottom.

She grinned. "Actually, I was hoping I'd get the top half and you could have the bottom."

"I never imagined greed to be one of your vices."

"It was just a thought."

They ate a few bites in silence. Velvet didn't know what to say next. John had skipped the small talk and had spanned two decades in a few sentences. Was it her turn?

Yet the current difference in who they'd become and what they'd accomplished kept her silent. John had become somebody. He was known. He was a name. Velvet was still working in the concessions department where she'd worked when the two of them had first met. They'd had no contact between then and now. Life had gone on.

Overcome with nerves Velvet blurted out, "What do you want from me, John?"

He gave her a laugh. "Right to the point?"

"I lost what little subtlety I possessed aeons ago. I don't have time for it."

"Your life is that busy?"

"Actually, no. But I still can't stand tiptoeing around. Maybe it's because I'm no good at it. It's no longer a part of my nature."

"It was never your nature, Velvet." He sipped his coffee. "I do miss the streak." He made a sweeping motion from the top of his face to the jawline.

"What can I say? The gray took over and had its way with me. Time marches on."

He nodded, his face turning serious. "Which is exactly why I'm here. Time. Marching. Us getting older. I need to collect the stray ends of my life and tie them together in a nice neat bow."

Velvet felt an inner knot cinch tight. She crossed her arms. "So I'm a stray end?"

He reddened. "Sorry. My words trivialized what shouldn't be trivialized." He reached across the table and put a hand on hers. "You were important to me, Velvet. But I let you go and I'm sor—"

She pulled her hand away. "If I remember correctly, it was you who did the going. It was me who was left behind."

"Point taken."

Velvet thought of his newest book. "Am I a chapter in your book? a mistake?"

He blew on his coffee, clearly stalling. "I did change your name—to protect the innocent."

It was a relief, but . . . "I was hardly innocent. You were a big-shot football star, and I went after you like a pirate in search of gold."

He smiled. "I was hardly gold."

She shrugged. "Silver then."

"Tarnished silver."

She pressed her fingers against her temples. "Enough of this English class symbolism, John. Such talk taxed my brain in school, and it still does. Here's the truth: I wanted you, I got you, I got pregnant, you left, and I gave the baby away. End of story."

If only . . .

"And they lived happily ever after?"

Happy was no longer an option. Not after all she'd done.

Velvet broke off a piece of a muffin. "I'm happy enough, I

guess. As far as I know there's no measurement to happy." Actually, on a ten-point scale she'd pin herself hovering at a mediocre five. Or lower.

"A nephew of mine once exclaimed, 'I'm happy—all the way.'"

All-the-way happy. What a concept.

John smashed a muffin crumb with his finger, then licked it away. "Happiness, all the way—that's one reason I wrote the book. One day I realized I'd never been all-the-way happy and decided the only way I could ever come close was to purge the mistakes of my past—confess them, understand them, forgive them—and move forward."

"So the book is your therapy?"

"Pretty much."

"Do I need to read it to discover what you think about our mistake, or will you give me a Cliff's Notes version?"

He laughed, shaking his head. "You certainly know how to put me on the spot."

She sat back in her chair, feeling quite pleased with herself. He wasn't some big shot. Not with her he wasn't. He was just John. "So? Tell me your great revelation—about us."

"I . . ." He took a fresh breath. "I want to find our child."

Velvet was glad she had a chair for support. "You can't. She was adopted."

"She? It was a girl?"

Oops. "Yes."

His smile was that of a satisfied father. Daddy. "A little girl."

"Not so little anymore. She's twenty-three. She'd be twenty-three."

He shook the satisfaction away. "Of course. I'm late, so very late."

You could say that.

"Surely you know who adopted her or where I can find her."

As a matter of fact . . . The idea that they could drive to Lianne's apartment in a matter of minutes made her shiver.

"Are you in contact with her adoptive parents?"

"No. Never. I know very little about her upbringing."

"Little? What do you know?"

If only she'd said she didn't know anything. "Her parents were from here, in Lincoln. But I don't know if they moved while she was growing up, or anything else."

"You seem defensive, Velvet. As if you know more but don't want me to—"

More? He didn't know the half of it. No one did.

Meeting with him had been a bad idea. She couldn't pick and choose what parts of her past she wanted to embrace and what parts she wanted to banish. If she gave John and Lianne access, the rest of it might rush through the breach in her fortification. And she couldn't let that happen. She couldn't survive remembering all that. And so . . . it was accept all her past or none of it.

Velvet chose the latter. She stood. "You can't be gone this long and then come back and want to insert yourself into our—into my life. You say writing the book helped you move on, then move on. Alone. Without us."

Velvet grabbed her purse and headed out the door.

| | | | | | | | | | |

Maya opened the door to the coffee shop but immediately had to stand aside as a woman stormed out, clearly upset. It wasn't hard to see whom she'd been sitting with, as a lone man stood by a table containing two coffees and two half-eaten muffins. He looked around, embarrassed, then sat down.

Otherwise, the coffee shop was full of the usual: couples chatting over cups of espresso and singles sipping sugar-free, nonfat mocha lattes, working on their laptops or reading a book. Other than the spurned man, only one person was sitting alone doing nothing, looking toward her expectantly. When their eyes met, the man stood. "Maya?"

She nodded.

"Ross Bredloe." He held out a hand and she shook it. "Can I get you something?"

She shook her head and sat at the table. Maya realized she hadn't spoken. But she was afraid to speak. Afraid to hear Ross's questions. Afraid she wouldn't be able to come up with decent answers that wouldn't completely condemn her.

He sipped his coffee and took out a small spiral notebook and pencil. "So," he said, offering her a smile.

She decided to say what she'd come to say. "I want you to drop the story, Mr. Bredloe. It's not that interesting. People lose jobs every day. It's not news."

"People don't win awards one week and lose their job the next. That's interesting. That's news."

"It's personal. More personal than anyone could know."

His face showed a keener interest. "Tell me about it. Tell me your side."

She regretted saying anything, even coming in the first place.

He pushed his coffee toward the center of the table. "Why don't you tell me why you think you were fired."

A tricky one. "Because I disappointed my boss."

The corner of Ross's mouth lifted. "Can you be a bit more specific?"

Maya suddenly wished she had a cup of coffee or anything else to occupy her hands. She tried clasping them on top of the table but ended up sitting on them. "I am—I was a very hard worker for the company. I was a top seller."

"Ah, yes. The award." Ross tapped the lead of his pencil into the pad. So far, he hadn't written down a thing. "I'm sure your husband was very proud. Or . . . are you married, Ms. Morano?"

That one she could answer. "Yes."

"Any children?"

Without warning Maya's composure left her. Logic and control fell away as if they were a discarded coat. What was left behind was bare and vulnerable. She began to sob. "I just want children. We need another procedure but they're expensive and we're already in debt for the first two that didn't work, and my family . . . Kids are mandatory. My sisters have five kids between them with another one on the way, and I feel like a total failure that I haven't been able to conceive and—"

She stopped talking, appalled at what she'd revealed. She pushed her chair out, making it skitter on the tile floor. "I have to go."

Ross extended his hand, touching her arm. "Please don't. The desire to have children—that's something our readers can relate to."

She hesitated. Was this a way out? a way to justify her actions? Would people understand she wasn't a bad person, just a woman driven to extreme means in her quest to become a mother?

Maya sat down. "I never wanted to have an outside job. I want to be a stay-at-home mom. But the job . . ."

"You were good at it."

"I seemed to be. I didn't mean to hurt anyone, but they taught me how to make the sale, how to get new customers." She caught herself before she mentioned the special help Mr. Paulson had given her. There was no need to bring him into this.

"You did as you were told."

Maya was relieved she could move on without mentioning him. "We were paid on commission. I came across companies and agencies who were looking for our product. I spoke with them. We hit it off. They bought from me."

"But they were the customers of your coworkers."

She expelled a breath, then looked to the door. She should have left when she'd had the chance. "I didn't force anyone to buy from me, Mr. Bredloe. I simply gave them the choice. I gave them the best deal."

"You undercut your coworkers."

"I gave the customer the best price."

"And earned yourself a Top Seller award along the way."

Her thoughts zeroed in on the bottom line, the one motivation people had to understand. "I earned myself another chance to become a mother. I'd do anything to have a baby. Anything."

When Ross's eyebrows rose, Maya realized her wording was too extreme.

"That didn't come out right."

"It came out fine. It came out honest," Ross said.

The bad feeling that had accosted her since their first hello moved close and tightened its grip. Maya was through. She stood again, this time determined to leave. "I'm done here, Mr. Bredloe. I really don't have any more to say except . . . please don't write this article. Leave it be. Leave my family be."

Their eyes met and Maya tried to read his gaze but found no certainty there. "Thanks for talking with me, Ms. Morano," he said.

She left the coffee shop with the bad feeling nipping at her heels.

| | | | | | | | | | |

The bad feeling took up residence.

Maya knew—she *knew*—the newspaper article about her firing, about her unethical behavior, would be printed. Whether Ross Bredloe spun the story to make her a sympathetic subject—desperate mother-to-be and all that—would not change the fact that everyone would know what she did.

Her family would know.

And Sal would know.

I have to tell him.

After leaving the coffee shop, Maya headed home. If Sal was there, she'd tell him right away. If he wasn't . . . she'd use the time to strengthen her nerve to do it when he arrived.

When she saw that Sal wasn't home, she felt the relief of a coward: *later* was always better than *now.*

As soon as Maya entered the house the phone rang. Her stomach rebelled. Was it Bredloe, wanting more information? Or some other reporter who wanted to jump on the story?

Her stomach relaxed when she saw the caller ID. It was her doctor—her gynecologist, Dr. Ruffin.

"Hi, Dr. Ruffin. I know you're probably wondering when we're going to schedule another procedure, and I want you to know we are really trying to dig up enough mon—"

"Maya, there's a problem."

Tell me about it.

"Did you hear me, Maya? There's a problem."

Another one? "What kind of problem?"

"There was a fire in the lab and—" she heard him take a breath— "and we can't do another procedure."

Can't? The word did not compute.

"I'm so sorry, Maya."

Sorry?

Sorry?

She was tired of the word, disgusted with it. In fact, she'd long ago decided to never accept its pathetic assault against the hopes she tried so hard to protect. There was always another chance. Another option. Another way. There had to be. "We'll just do it later. I'll get on the medicine after the lab is rebuilt. We can—"

"No, Maya."

"Why not? I'll do any—"

She heard him sigh. "Maya. Don't you remember? Your

condition . . . Remember me telling you that there was a limit to your chances? Unless there's been a miracle between then and now, there are no more chances. I'm so sorry. So, so sorry."

There was that word again. . . .

"If you and Sal come in tomorrow we could talk."

"There's nothing to talk about except the fact that I want my own child."

"I know, Maya. But sometimes that's just not poss—"

Maya slammed the receiver down. This wasn't happening. She'd lost her job during her attempt to earn enough money for a pregnancy procedure, and now there were no more chances. It was all for nothing.

"Nothing," she said aloud.

Suddenly, the thought of seeing Sal and warning him about the article, of telling him about losing her job . . . of telling him there would be no baby . . . ever . . .

Her entire treasury of hopes collided with the sorry facts—and didn't have a chance. They were outgunned, outmaneuvered, and outnumbered. It was a battle they could not win. Her hopes had kept her moving from moment to moment, had given her a reason to get up in the morning and the strength to endure all she had endured. Without them . . .

Maya ran upstairs and packed a bag.

| | | | | | | | | |

Maya surveyed the living room. Was she forgetting anything?

Not that she knew how long she'd be gone. A few days? Forever? What was here if she stayed? Pain, sorrow, humiliation, disgrace?

She didn't have time to ponder long. Sal would be home from work any min—

She heard a truck outside and ran to the window.

A blue truck drove by. Not Sal. Looking out the front of the house, she saw a red sign in her neighbor's yard across the street. A blank red sign.

Their house is for sale. That's a For Sale sign. I know—

The ringing of her cell phone interrupted her thoughts.

It was Sal.

"Hi, hon," she said. The normal tenor of her own voice surprised her. Had she been living a life of secrets for so long that she'd become good at it?

"Can you meet me at Mama's? She's been feeling poorly because of the treatment and needs us."

"Oh, Sal . . ." All artifice left her. She didn't want to go.

"Please, Maya? You know she'd do anything for you."

Agata *would* have done anything but certainly wouldn't after the newspaper article came out.

"Maya?"

Unable to fight another battle, she said, "Fine. I'm on my way."

It would be nice to say good-bye. She owed the woman that much.

As Maya pulled out of the driveway, she saw the For Sale sign in her neighbor's yard: a blue Realtor's sign complete with a logo, photo of the Realtor, and phone number.

Odd.

| | | | | | | | | | |

When she arrived at her mother-in-law's home, Maya saw Sal's truck parked out front. As were six other cars. The lights of the living room glowed and through the sheer curtains Maya could see people milling about.

Great. She was in no mood for a crowd. And Sal had said his mother wasn't feeling well . . . yet well enough to have a party?

The front door opened and Sal beckoned her in. He kissed

her cheek and took her purse. "Thanks for coming over. Mama's eager to see you."

Before Maya could wonder why, Agata called to her. "Maya. My dear girl." Agata sat in her chair near the couch. She extended a hand in Maya's direction.

Maya went to her. "How are you doing?" Maya asked.

"Better now that you're here." Agata patted the arm of an extra chair that had been added to the room. "Here. Sit by me."

Maya did as she was told. The knowledge that she was about to run away sat down with her, blocking her off from her mother-in-law. Yet no matter who might think they needed her, Maya couldn't stay. Her presence would only add to her family's pain. They had enough to worry about with Agata's cancer.

A dozen friends of her mother-in-law filled the room like a tide covering the shore, drawing back, then coming again in a different configuration. Sal found a place at her side. He offered her a smile, which she found difficult to return. *You wouldn't smile at me if you knew what kind of person I am, and that our hopes for a baby . . .*

Agata clapped her hands twice. "Friends? If you will?"

Everyone gathered close.

"I want to thank you for coming, and I want to thank my best friend, Mildred, for calling all of you. It was her idea to gather here today, to offer me support."

"And to pray for you," said a seventysomething in a red sweater. The woman extended her hands in front, palms up. "Toward that end, why don't we see what we can do. After all, God comes to all our meetings, so it's best he not feel left out."

The group adjusted themselves into a kind of circle, some moving chairs close, some standing, but all joining hands. Sal took Maya's hand on one side, and Agata took her other hand.

Surely they aren't going to pray out loud. . . .

Surely they were.

Everyone bowed their heads and one by one Agata's friends asked God for healing, strength, patience, comfort, care. . . . Some people's prayers were eloquent, but most were quite simple. There was a sprinkling of quiet murmurings of "Yes, Lord" and "Amen."

Out of the corner of her eye, Maya made note that not everyone prayed aloud. It was a huge relief. She wouldn't know what to say. It's not that she never prayed, but she knew she wasn't good at it. She was always afraid she would bumble and stumble even amid her own thoughts. A person didn't need to be a great orator, but surely God expected some level of prayer competence.

The prayers were offered without interruption like a finely orchestrated dialogue where each person knew their part. Maya silently prayed with them, wanting as much as anyone for Agata to beat the cancer. Yet, to her own horror, she often found her thoughts straying from Agata's illness to her own predicament, and she unwittingly hijacked the prayers of "Help her, Lord" or "Give her strength to get through this" for her own benefit.

Stealing other people's prayers for herself. How selfish was that?

Sal was one of the last to say something. "Lord God, take care of my mother as only you can. I'd like a miracle, if you have one handy. We'd all like to have her around for many more years."

"You bet," said a stocky man wearing suspenders.

Agata spoke last. "Father, I thank you for these wonderful people. I am loved by them and by you. I ask you to hear all our prayers, but please know I realize I'm in a no-lose situation. I live, I live. I die, I live. John 3:16. Amen."

"Hear, hear," Mildred said. Then she pointed toward the kitchen. "Let's eat. I've brought enough food for an army."

"Onward, Christian soldiers!" Suspenders said.

The group headed to the other room. Sal stood and said, "I'll get you some hot tea, all right, Mama?"

"That would be grand."

Suddenly Maya noticed that Agata looked spent. Frail. Why hadn't she noticed it before? She listened to the voices from the other room. Was it a good idea to have all these people around, even if they were praying? The woman obviously needed rest.

Agata still held Maya's hand captive. "Are you all right, dear?"

She's asking me *if I'm all right?* How did Maya's problems weigh against the threat of death? And yet Maya's desire for her own peace still overshadowed her mother-in-law's problems. How wonderful it would be to tell Agata about the tragedy at the doctor's, about the loss of her job, about the humiliation that was sure to come when the article was printed. Agata, above all people in the world, might understand and find some sort of way to comfort her. "Actually . . ."

But when Maya once again heard laughter and loud voices emanating from the kitchen, she chose to remain silent. "I'm supposed to be asking you that," she said, taking another stab at being the kind of person she ought to be.

"As I stated, I'm in a no-lose situation. John 3:16."

Maya wasn't completely clear on the significance of the Bible reference, but before she could ask, the group filtered back into the living room, their plates full and their conversation lively.

As the people pulsed around her, Maya's commitment to help Agata faded. Her thoughts returned to the suitcase in her car. It called to her, luring her.

Away.

Anywhere.

Away.

She'd be a good person later.

| | | | | | | | | | |

"Thank you so much for tonight, Maya," Sal said as they moved to their cars.

"She's got a great group of friends. They did it. I was just *there*." Kinda. Sorta.

He put an arm around her shoulders and kissed her hair. "Being *there* is the most important thing." He opened her car door for her. "I don't know what I'd do without you, *here*, with me. I need you so much." His smile—his most powerful weapon—confused everything and threatened to upend her entire plan of escape. "See you at home," he said.

Home? She couldn't go home. Could she? Although things might be okay tonight, what about tomorrow, or the next day, or the next?

Yet . . . how could she leave after hearing his kind words?

The decision was too much for her, and so she took the known alternative.

Even as her mind screamed, *Leave! Leave!* she drove home. Even as it nudged, *Tell him about the baby,* she parked in the driveway. Even as it tempted, *You could still drive away,* she turned off the car. And when her husband waited for her by the front walk, she got out and went to him. She took his hand. She went inside.

Sal closed the door behind her.

At that moment Maya realized she was a prisoner of everything that *had* made her life good.

And a frightened victim of all that threatened to blow it apart.

| | | | | | | | | | |

William tossed a grape into the air and caught it in his mouth. He spread his arms wide and grinned. "Hmm? Hmm? How do you like that?" The kids at his picnic table clapped and giggled.

William offered a by-your-leave gesture with his hand. He loved kids. They were so easy to please. This was the second time he'd attended a function with the First Hope Children's Home. It wouldn't be the last.

"That's not so hard," said a six-year-old named Barry. "My dad can do that."

Another boy shoved his arm. "You don't have a dad. You don't have a mom neither."

Barry's eyes flared. "Neither do you!"

The boys started shoving each other at the table. Somebody's foot kicked the little girl seated across from them.

"Hey!" she yelled.

William stood and downed the last of his cup of Kool-Aid with a dramatic *Uahhhh!* Then he said, "Who's ready to play some football?"

The ploy worked. All the kids at the table raised their hands. "Me! Me!"

He helped them throw the paper plates and cups into the trash barrel and grabbed two small footballs out of his backpack. He tossed one to Barry.

The boy looked at it suspiciously. "This is a baby football."

Although he didn't say it aloud, William knew regular-size footballs were too big for their small hands. He took the football back and held it like a trophy. "But this is a special football. This is the football I first played with. My dad used to play catch with me using this football."

"You have a dad and mom?" asked a girl who was wearing all pink.

"I have a dad. My mom died when I was seven."

"I'm seven," the girl said. "And I don't have either one."

William felt his chest tighten. It was hard for him to believe that none of these kids had any parents—or even foster families. But he couldn't let them dwell on that. Not today. He leaned down to the girl's level. "What's your name?"

"Tricia Ann."

He placed the second football into her hands. "Come on, Tricia Ann. Let me show you what my dad taught me."

He moved the group into an open field and showed the kids where to place their hands on the laces and how to throw from the shoulder. Then he divided them up into two groups of three. They got the hang of it and even managed a few spirals. The rhythm of each trio reminded him of how he used to throw the ball to his dad and AJ, back and forth, over and over. The hours they'd spent with him . . . He owed his entire football career to those two men—*the* men in his life.

William hated the tension that had sprung up between him and his dad. He'd tried so hard to keep things open between them. But his dad was so stubborn, so anti-God, and blamed the coach for all of it. Yet his dad would die if he knew it was AJ who'd caused the most recent bout of churchgoing. In fact, AJ was the one who'd encouraged him to choose his faith no matter what his dad said or did. "It comes down to this, Billy: you've got to choose *the* Father over your father."

"But he's my dad. He's done everything for me."

"I agree," AJ had said. "But that doesn't mean he can't be wrong. And in this case, he is." He'd put a hand on the back of William's neck and whispered, "God has big plans for you, kid. You have to make yourself available. Worry about pleasing God first."

"But what about Dad?"

"I'll take care of him."

And AJ had—for the most part. William still got grief for not spending as much time with his dad as he had in the past, and he felt a bit guilty about it, but the church stuff, combined with the football stuff, school stuff, and work during the summer . . . There was only so much time in a day.

If only his dad would see how God and faith had changed William's life for the better—had changed AJ's life too.

That was another one of their secrets. AJ had been William's first convert. After William had been moved by the coach's faith, and when his dad had first laid down the law about him becoming a Jesus freak, AJ had approached him one night as they were both leaving one of his dad's barbecues.

"Can we talk?"

"I'm not in the mood, AJ. One argument a night is all I can take."

AJ had glanced toward the house, as if checking to see if Roman was watching them. He'd kept his voice low. "I don't want to argue. I want to find out more about this faith stuff that's impressed you so much."

And so William had shared what he knew—what little he knew—about God and faith and Jesus. It was the first of many conversations they'd had about the subject—unfortunately, all on the sly, a secret from Roman. Eventually, AJ had been so moved by all of it that he'd dedicated his life to Jesus, right there in front of William. William would never forget that night, sitting across from each other in AJ's living room, their heads bowed, their hands clasped together, praying and crying and laughing. If only his dad could realize what he was missing. William prayed for his dad every day, but a part of him feared it would take something big for him to come around.

But the good news was that William had seen a change in AJ immediately. For one thing, he'd stopped sleeping around with every woman who came his way. And he and William went to church together when they could. AJ had even helped at the last First Hope event earlier that sum—

"Mine! Give it!"

William was pulled out of his memories and into a scuffle between Barry and Josh over one of the footballs. He ran over to break it up just as Barry slugged Josh in the stomach.

"Hey!" William pulled Barry away and knelt beside Josh. "Are you okay?"

"He hit me!"

"I know. I saw."

"Josh wasn't doing nothing, William," Tricia Ann said. "He was just getting his fingers set to throw it."

"He was taking forever," Barry said.

William made sure Josh was okay, then got the kids playing again—sans Barry. He took the boy to a picnic table and sat him down. "What's going on with you, Barry?"

A shrug.

"Uh-uh. A shrug doesn't cut it. Talk to me."

"I don't want to play football anymore."

"Okay, but that doesn't explain why you hit Josh."

"He said his dad played catch with him."

"Maybe that's true."

"He doesn't have a dad. None of us do."

Aah. William guessed the deeper problem. "Did your dad play ball with you?"

William could tell Barry wanted to say yes. . . . Instead he said, "I got nobody. Nobody cares about me. Nobody."

William's throat tightened. He hated to see these kids suffer, yet knew their suffering went far beyond his knowledge. He put a hand on Barry's back. "I care about you."

"No, you don't. You just came today because you had to." He looked over the picnic ground at the other groups of kids teamed with adults. "They all came because they had to. Because someone paid them to come."

"That's not true," William said. "Not at all. I'm not getting paid for being here."

Barry looked genuinely surprised. "You're not?"

William raised his right hand. "Not a penny. I came here today because I like kids and . . . and God's been good to me and I wanted to share some of that goodness, and—" he tried to think of something to make Barry laugh—"and because I really needed to perfect my grape-tossing routine in front of an audience."

Barry smiled. "You dropped one."

"But only one. I'm getting better." Barry wiggled on the picnic bench. It was time to move on. "Are you better now?"

Another shrug. But then he stood. "Can I go swimming now?"

"No more football?"

"Not today."

"I suppose you could do that. Do you have a suit?"

Barry pulled the waistband of his shorts down an inch, revealing a bright orange swimsuit.

"You came prepared."

"Mr. Blackmore told us to wear our suits under our clothes."

"Good idea. I'll bring you over to him right now, and he'll get you set up with the group that's swimming. Okay?"

"Okay."

William told the other kids he'd be right back and walked Barry over to First Hope's director, Nate Blackmore.

Nate tousled Barry's hair. "Sure, you can swim in the lake," Nate said to the boy. "But stay with the group who are wading, right over there. No farther, okay, Barry?"

Barry nodded. Then he stripped off his shorts, pulled off his shirt, shucked off his shoes, and ran toward the lake. Nate picked up his clothes, shaking his head. "That kid."

"He seems angry. Bitter."

"He has a right to be. His dad was a druggie, rarely around, and he never did marry Barry's mom—who died last year after the dad beat her up. The dad's in jail now."

"That's horrible. No kid should have to go through that."

"I agree with you there. We're waiting for a foster home to take him, but we need a family who really knows how to handle a kid with such a background." Nate called to another adult in the water. "I have another one for you, Grace. Barry's coming in." To William he said, "Thanks for bringing him over, William. We'll take over from here."

William looked back to the kids playing football. The rest of them were much easier to handle than Barry, so he should have felt relieved to be done with the troublemaker. But he wasn't.

135

"Hey, William, look at me!" Barry called from the lake. He fell back into the water, disappearing for a second before popping up with lots of splashing water.

"That's cool, Barry. But be careful," William called.

Tricia Ann came running up to him. "William, can we get an ice cream now?"

William turned to Nate. "Can they?"

"Over in the cooler. Help yourself."

William wished Barry had hung around a little longer. He would have loved to give the boy an ice cream.

| | | | | | | | | | |

After his hard day at work, Roman had wanted to spend his evening doing nothing or close to nothing. But AJ, being AJ, came over with brats, buns, and chips and suggested they watch TV.

Whatever.

The brats and chips had given way to an entire bag of Chips Ahoy! They watched a reality show about people stuck on an island, and Roman was content to let AJ do the commentary, stating which person he wanted to get kicked off, which player wasn't shouldering his proper burden, and who looked cute in pigtails and short shorts. It was mindless, which was just what Roman needed after fending off the reporter, dealing with Brian, and feeling guilty about Maya.

During an endless string of commercials, the phone rang.

AJ was closest. "I'll get it."

"If it's Billy, back from his stupid picnic, tell him to get over here to get some man food."

AJ nodded and answered the phone. His brow furrowed. "Just a minute." He handed the phone to Roman. "It's for you."

"Who is it?"

"It's for you."

Roman hoped his work hadn't followed him home. "Hello?"

"This is Saint Elizabeth hospital. Are you Roman Paulson?"

Roman sought AJ's eyes. They were dark with worry. "Yes," he said. "Is there something—?"

"Your son, William . . . There's been an accident."

Roman pushed the footrest out of the way and stood. "A car accident?"

AJ stood too. He shut off the TV.

"No. There was a swimming accident at a lake. Your son's here. We need you to come as—"

Roman hung up and grabbed his keys. "Let's go."

| | | | | | | | | | |

Roman and AJ burst through the ER doors, searching for anyone in authority.

A woman at a desk looked up. "May I help—?"

"Billy Paulson. My son. Where?"

She checked a roster. "William Paulson. Yes. Room three." She pointed.

Roman and AJ ran.

The door was open. A doctor and a nurse stood over Billy. They looked up when Roman came in. AJ stood in the doorway.

"I'm his father. How is he?"

"He nearly drowned," the doctor said. "An onlooker got him breathing again by administering CPR until the paramedics got there. We have him on oxygen and are monitoring his lungs and his heart and—"

He's alive! Roman rushed to Billy's side, taking his hand. "Billy? Son? Can you hear me?"

"He's in and out," the nurse said. She adjusted his oxygen mask. She stroked his hair away from his face. "He's a very brave young man."

137

"Brave?" AJ asked.

The doctor adjusted his stethoscope around his neck. "He saved a little boy from drowning. But then he got in trouble himself, and . . ." He looked down at Billy. "We're doing everything we can."

"He's still in danger?"

"I'm afraid so. The stress on the lungs and heart . . . He was under a few minutes before a group of men got him out. He's on the edge."

"The edge of . . . ?"

"Life."

The word fell upon the room, crashed onto the floor, sending sharp shards in every direction.

The doctor continued. "These next twenty-four hours are critical. One of our biggest fears is pneumonia settling in."

"Then stop it from settling in," Roman said. "You have to save him. You have to." He looked to AJ, his head bowed, his hands clasped at his chin, his eyes closed.

The doctor put a hand on Roman's shoulder. His eyes were sincere, and yet . . . they were *not* intense with confidence. "We'll do our best."

It was such a feeble word: *best.*

FIVE

I am suffering and in pain.
Rescue me, O God, by your saving power.*

PSALM 69:29

"Come on, Billy. Fight."

Roman sat at his son's bedside in the ICU. Eight hours earlier, as the doctor feared, Billy had contracted pneumonia. They
were giving him antibiotics, but to find just the right medicine they relied on trial and error. Hopefully, this first attempt
would work.

Billy looked so weak with the oxygen mask, the IV. . . .
Roman held his hand, wishing there were more he could do.

He'd gotten to know his son's hand very well these past hours.
Its back was smooth but for a small scar, evidence of a scrape
with a pine tree during a camping trip to Colorado when Billy
was twelve. The nails were ragged, the cuticles rough. And the
palm . . . Roman turned the hand over and cradled his son's
palm in his own. Intricate lines crisscrossed an unfathomable
maze. He traced Billy's lifeline from wrist to the crook of his
thumb. Its curve was deep.

Representing a long life?

Roman held his own hand next to his son's. "They're different," he whispered. This surprised him. As a father and son, sharing the same genes . . . shouldn't their hands be the same?

"Mmmm."

The hands were forgotten. Roman stood and leaned close. Billy's eyelids fluttered. He hadn't been awake since . . .

"Come on, Son. Open your eyes. It's Dad. I'm right here. Wake up."

After a few attempts, Billy opened his eyes.

"There you are! You're here! Good to see you."

It was hard for Billy to talk around the mask, but Roman didn't dare move it aside.

A nurse rushed in.

"He's awake," Roman told her.

"I see that." She calmly checked his pulse, acting as if what had just occurred was the most normal thing in the world. When Billy looked in her direction she said, "How you doing, Billy?"

He didn't answer, only stared like he was not quite *there* at all.

She patted his arm. "Let me take a listen." She put the stethoscope in her ears and listened to his chest. Her face was intent.

"Better?" Roman asked.

She offered a smile, but it seemed for Billy's benefit. "We'll just keep those antibiotics coming. Can I get you anything, young man?"

Billy shook his head. Barely.

Roman remained standing, wanting to make it easy for his son to see him. "Did you hear that? You're getting better."

With effort, Billy attempted to speak. "Boy . . ." It came out as a whisper.

"Boy?"

"Lake."

"The boy in the lake. You wonder how he is? He's fine. Just fine. You saved him. You're a hero."

"Goo—"

He slipped off to sleep.

You saved the boy, Billy; now save yourself. Don't leave me.

| | | | | | | | | | |

The door to the ICU opened and AJ stuck his head into the room. "My turn."

Roman looked at the clock. He'd been sitting at Billy's bedside four hours. Billy had not awakened other than the one time he'd asked about the boy and the lake.

Roman moved to the door and whispered to AJ as he passed, "I'll get some coffee and come right back."

"No hurry. Billy and I need a little talk."

Good luck on that. Immediately, Roman chastised himself for the sour attitude. Billy was doing his best. His body was fighting the infection, trying to get better. It had more important things to do than ease other people's worries.

Roman knew it was the exhaustion talking. But he couldn't give in to it. He had to be ready when Billy fully awakened and needed him.

He walked to the ICU waiting room, rubbing his face roughly to wake himself up. The room was full, and he sidestepped the people in chairs to make his way to the coffeemaker in the corner. He dumped two sugars in his Styrofoam cup, along with two creamers. Although he usually drank it black he didn't feel like dealing with anything remotely bitter.

"Excuse me?"

Roman turned around to find a gaggle of five men standing close. The younger ones were brawny, and the older one he'd met . . . somewhere.

"Yes?" Roman said.

"Hello, Mr. Paulson. I'm Coach Rollins from the team."

Ah. The offensive coach—in more ways than one. "You're the man who forced my boy to go against my wishes."

"I'm sorry, I don't—"

142

Roman leaned closer, not needing the entire waiting room to hear. "You're the man who preached that God bunkum at my kid and got him involved in church when I explicitly told him I was against it. And worse than that you got him involved in a church that held a picnic. *The* picnic."

"I'm sorry you feel that way, Mr. Paulson, but I assure you no one preached at anyone. The boys and the coaches get very close. Who we are as people comes out, and yes, I do believe in God and Jesus and going to church, but no one ever forced William to—"

"It's Billy. He likes to be called Billy."

The coach made a face. "Really? He asked us to call him William."

"It's true," said a linebacker-type with a shaved head.

Roman paused a second and put the kid in context. "You've been at my house."

"Yes, sir. Way back. Freshman year."

"Me, too," another kid said. "You make great ribs. Sir."

Another player nodded.

"Why haven't you boys come . . . ?" Roman let the question slide, not sure he wanted to know the answer. During Billy's first year in school, many of his teammates had come by for barbecues. But little by little they'd stopped. Billy always had an excuse for them, but seeing the same boys here, now, meant they were still close friends.

"We were at the picnic too, Mr. Paulson," the ribs kid said. "William was having such a good time with those kids."

"He was a kid-magnet," the linebacker said. "I saw him doing tricks for them at the picnic tables."

The third boy looked to the door and shoved his hands in his pockets. "William wasn't even swimming. Some other people were in charge of that. He was helping some kids play football, and I was nearby helping some other ones fly kites, when all of a sudden, I see William look to the lake, drop the ball, and go running. That's when I saw the kid flailing, in big trouble. William ran right into that water—shorts, shoes, and all. Everybody was screaming, but he was the first in."

Roman shook his head, not sure he wanted to hear. Not sure he could breathe, or that his heart was even beating.

The linebacker continued. "Others went in too, and William managed to hand the boy off to somebody and they carried him to shore, and . . ." His face crumpled.

The coach took over the story. "Everybody was concentrating on the little boy, giving him CPR, calling 911. But then, somebody looked out and saw a hand, William's hand. . . ." He swallowed. "His hand went down. Under the water."

The face of the third boy contorted as he fought back tears. "A bunch of us ran in but he'd sunk way under. We had to dive after him and—"

Coach Rollins put his hand on the back of the boy's neck. "But we got him. We pulled him out, and to shore."

"He was so heavy, with all his clothes. . . ." The linebacker covered his face with a hand and his friends gathered to comfort him. And commiserate.

Roman was torn. These boys had saved his son. Yet Billy wouldn't have been in the situation in the first place if they hadn't gotten him involved in church. Needing to be free of them, he said, "I have to get back."

"Tell William we're praying for him," the coach said.

Not in this lifetime.

| | | | | | | | | | | |

Roman paused at the ICU window and watched as AJ had an animated conversation with Billy.

It was an odd sight, seeing this overweight hunk of a man gesturing wildly when no one was listening. In the midst of a sentence, AJ noticed Roman at the window, made one last comment to Billy, and came to the door.

"What are you discussing like a crazy man in there?" Roman asked. "He can't hear you."

AJ shook his head. "Quit being so black-and-white, Roman. Yes, I was talking *to* Billy, or *at* Billy, if you will. And no, technically, he was not talking back, so in that respect, we were not discussing anything. But that doesn't mean he wasn't listening." He looked toward the bed. "Somehow."

"What were you saying to him?"

AJ shrugged. "Just stuff. Giving him a pep talk. Telling him what's going on. Telling him about all the people who are rooting for him." He hesitated, then added, "Praying for him."

As if that would do anything. The prayers of an entire church hadn't healed his wife. Even his own prayers hadn't helped Trudy live. Busywork—that's all prayer was. But if AJ and the others wanted to waste their time . . .

So be it.

| | | | | | | | | | | |

The phone rang—in Peter's hand. He'd fallen asleep on the couch and now awakened to find the apartment completely dark except for the glow of the phone's display. He'd been waiting for Lianne to return his call all day. And apparently, all night.

He answered. "Lianne?"

"No, Peter. It's Carrie."

This didn't make sense. Carrie never called *him*. He reached over the arm of the couch and turned on a lamp. The clock on the wall read 3:16.

A.M.?

His mind raced. Since the apartment was dark, was William asleep? Peter didn't remember him coming in.

145

"Carrie, yes, I'm here." He looked toward William's bedroom. The door was open. William always closed his door to sleep. "Is William with you?"

She began to sob. "No. He's . . . William's in the hospital. There was an accident."

Peter pushed himself to sitting. "A car—?"

"No. He was at a charity picnic. Kids were swimming. A child went under and William went in after him and . . ."

And? "Is he alive?"

"Barely. He drowned, Peter. He died. They had to bring him back to life. I was at work last night, so I didn't know anything about it. We weren't planning to see each other, so . . . I didn't even know. But I just got a call from Coach Rollins, who's at the hospital with him. Some of the players who were at the picnic are there too, waiting. . . . Oh, Peter . . ."

Peter tried to find his shoes. The coach and William's football buddies were at the hospital—and at the picnic? Peter shoved his guilt aside. Now was not the time. "What hospital?"

"Saint Elizabeth. I'm going there now. I should have been there with him, Peter. He'd asked me to come to the picnic with him but I had to work. I could have gotten off if I'd really wanted to, but I didn't, and . . ."

Peter heard William's parting words repeated in his memories. *"Since you're not going to class, want to come with me? I'm going to a picnic with some orphanage kids."* William had mentioned it was through church, but Peter hadn't let him finish his sentence. He'd been too absorbed in his own troubles with Lianne.

"Peter? Will you come get me?"

"I'm on my way."

| | | | | | | | | | |

146

"You can't see him. Family only."

"We're nearly family," Peter said. "I'm his roommate, and Carrie's his girlfriend."

"Sorry," the nurse said. "But I will show you to the waiting room."

Peter and Carrie held hands and followed the nurse. Others were there before them. "Who's here for William Paulson?" Carrie asked.

Most hands rose.

"How is he?" she asked an older man.

"The same. At least no one's told us anything new." The man looked to Peter, extending a hand. "Hi, I'm Nate Blackmore. I'm from First Hope Children's Home." He turned to the group nearby. "We were at the picnic with William."

Peter nodded a greeting. "I'm Peter, his roommate, and this is Carrie, his girlfriend."

"It's such a tragedy," Nate said. "The kids from the home were having a great time, playing ball, flying kites, swimming. . . . But then—"

A woman interrupted. "We had four adults in the water with them, watching them. And some of the other football players were helping. But . . ." She put a hand to her mouth. "William saved that little boy. Handed him off to another volunteer, but then, when we looked back for him . . ." She shook her head and blew her nose in a much-used tissue. "He saved the boy. William saved him."

"It sounds like William," Peter said. It wasn't just a polite thing to say, it was the truth. William was always helping people. And it wasn't just charity stuff.

One time Peter had come home and found William tutoring a couple of his teammates in math at the kitchen table. One of them was William's rival for the starting running-back position, who was on the verge of being kicked off the team if he didn't get his grades up. Peter had asked William about it afterward. "Why don't you just let him flunk out? That way you could take his place on the team."

147

"I don't want to get the position that way," William had said. "I want to earn it on the field."

Peter had been impressed by that and had wondered—even if only briefly—if he would have done as much. He'd only thought about it briefly because the answer was no. He would not have helped a rival. He would have let him sink or swim on his own.

The memory collided with reality. *Sink or swim?*

Peter shivered.

A man approached and introduced himself. "Hi. I'm AJ, a neighbor of the Paulsons. I've known Billy since he was a kid. He's like a son to me." He smiled at Carrie. "I didn't know Billy had a girlfriend." He took her small hands in his. "Glad to meet you, Carrie." He looked to Peter. "And you, Peter. Billy mentioned you. Said you were a good guy, salt of the earth. You're taking over your family's farm, is that right?"

An answer caught in Peter's throat. "Maybe."

"Good for you," AJ said. "Family farms are something to be proud of. Farmers working the earth keep the rest of us firmly rooted—and well fed."

Peter felt himself redden. AJ made it sound so noble. Peter wasn't noble, not at all. He was an ungrateful, stupid kid who didn't know what he was doing and was on the verge of blowing everything he'd spent twenty years setting in place. He cleared his throat and forced his thoughts back to William. "Have you seen him?"

"I'm spelling his dad. He's in ICU with Billy now."

"But I thought only family—"

"Today I'm officially an uncle." AJ shrugged.

Peter looked across the waiting room. There seemed to be two groups, one from the children's home and the guys sitting across the room with huge necks and muscles. Obviously football players.

A man sitting with the athletes approached. "Excuse me, I don't mean to intrude, but . . . are you Carrie?"

"I am. Coach Rollins?"

"Yes. I'm sorry we didn't call you earlier." He nodded at one of the players. "Joe was the one who mentioned you, mentioned we should call you."

At that moment a guy looked up and waved at Carrie. She waved back. "I'm just glad we're here now," she said.

The coach nodded to the boys sitting nearby, and they immediately stood and came close. "Just before you came in, we were talking. . . . We were just about to gather people up and pray for him." He smiled at the group from the children's home. "'For where two or three gather together as my followers, I am there among them.' Yes?"

"That's a super idea," AJ said. He held out his hands, and others quickly made a circle.

The prayers began. It had been a long time since Peter had prayed, and longer still since he'd prayed with a group, but the feeling of oneness and peace—of doing something worth anything—quickly overtook him and made him question why he'd been away so long. There was nothing like it. As one prayer was handed off to the next prayer, Peter smiled, visualizing a perfectly executed football play, as the players worked together toward a common goal, gobbling up the yards leading to . . .

Victory. He squeezed his eyes shut and did his part.

| | | | | | | | | | | ⊢

Maya sat at the kitchen table; the newspaper—remarkably devoid of any article from Ross Bredloe—lay before her, as did a cup of untouched coffee. One thought replayed itself: *Leave. Leave. Leave.* She'd been given a reprieve. But it wouldn't last. If the article wasn't in today's paper, it would be in tomorrow's. Or the next day's.

From her first waking moment she'd held hostage the thought of flight. And when Sal had left her to go to work . . .

There was nothing to stop her from going. Nothing. No one.

And yet, there she sat. Inconsequential, insignificant, incapable, an immovable blob. The coffee cup had more right to exist than she did. More purpose. More value. She brought it to her lips and was shocked to find it was cold.

Not even warm.

Cold.

The clock in the hall began chiming the hour. Maya waited to hear a long string of *bong*s at the end. She guessed it was probably eleven o'clock.

Bong. Bong.

She held her breath. *And . . . ?*

Was the clock broken?

She stood and found her muscles oddly stiff. She went into the hall and stared at the clock face. Two. Two o'clock.

No. That can't be right.

She rushed back to the kitchen, to the clock on the microwave. 2:01 glowed back at her in green numbers. It wasn't possible.

Needing yet another confirmation, Maya raced upstairs to their bedroom. 2:02.

She stood in the middle of the room, incredulous. She'd lost three hours.

What had she done during that time, sitting in the kitchen, staring at nothing? Thinking of nothing. Accomplishing nothing.

The truth of it scared her. She had always been a woman on top of her game, vibrant, vital, and with-it. To zone out like this . . .

"What's happening to me?"

You lost your job, a reporter is writing a scathing article ruining what little reputation you have left, you have no money for more fertility procedures, and the lab burned.

A bitter laugh escaped—which scared her more than the lost time. There was nothing funny about what was happening to her. Nothing.

Her thoughts leapfrogged over her list of woes and stopped on the last two. Getting pregnant. There had to be some way it could still happen. Maybe the doctor was wrong.

"I need a miracle."

Agata's friends had prayed for a miracle for *her.* Maybe . . .

Maya sank to her knees, clasping her hands beneath her chin. "God? Please make me a miracle. Give me a child. Somehow. Some way."

After a few moments of silence, she realized there was nothing more to say—certainly nothing that God hadn't heard from her before. And so far he hadn't done a thing to answer her prayers. What made her think he'd jump into action now?

The need to do *something* sparked a flame. There *was* something more she could do.

She got dressed.

| | | | | | | | | |

Maya leaned on the receptionist's counter. Loomed.

A young woman slid the glass partition aside. "May I help you?" There was a wariness in her voice.

"I need to see Dr. Ruffin." Extra emphasis: *need.*

"Do you have an appointment?"

"No. None. Not at all. But I need to see him. Now." She looked down and saw that she was gripping the edge of the counter. She forced herself to let go. Forced a smile. "Please. The name's Maya Morano."

151

The girl did not smile back. "Just a minute." She closed the partition, turned her back to Maya, and spoke with another worker who was seated at a computer screen. The woman glanced at Maya, then got up and left through a door leading to the examination rooms. Just the way she moved—deliberately but quickly—just the way the receptionist kept her back to Maya . . .

They're afraid of me.

Maya heard the clearing of a throat. She glanced behind and saw another woman in the waiting room, a magazine open on her lap, her eyes furtive, as if she too had been alerted to something amiss.

Was *she* that something amiss?

She needed to calm down and lose the antagonistic attitude.

But I have a right to be antagonistic. Because of this doctor's ineptitude in the lab my chance for a baby has been ruined.

Not ruined. It couldn't be totally ruined. That's why she was there. She had to find a solution. Everything had a solution, yes? Besides, she'd prayed for a miracle. God owed her a miracle on this, didn't he?

He doesn't owe you anything.

Doubt sped through her like a tremor. What was she doing there, demanding action when there was none to be taken? demanding things to be fair? demanding her own way? demanding special attention? demanding a miracle?

Or else.

Or else what?

Or else she'd find herself losing more and more hours to the nothingness of nothingness.

I have to leave.

She hurried toward the exit and had the door open when her name was called.

Dr. Ruffin stood in the doorway leading to the back. "Ms. Morano? Maya."

She felt like a fool. A crazed fool. "I'm sorry. I don't have an appointment. I don't need to see you. I don't know why I came. Just forget—"

He came toward her, his face calm, his eyes focused on hers. She'd seen that look in movies, in the doctor trying to pacify the crazed lunatic. "I will not forget you came, Maya. You need to see me. I have some time now. Please come in." He placed himself between Maya and the other woman in the waiting room, his arms extended toward the door leading to the back, inviting, urging.

She was tired of feeling crazed. She needed calm and peace. She accepted the invitation, hoping he would give her those things—and more.

He led her to a consultation room and indicated she should sit on the couch. It was the same couch she and Sal had sat on many times when they'd discussed their pregnancy options.

He took his usual place in the chair nearby. "So. You're upset." His voice was soothing, like cream being poured from a pitcher.

"I . . ." She didn't know what to say. She hadn't thought this out. She'd come on impulse, madly driven to make something happen *her* way. "I want a child."

It was an inane statement. A given. And yet it summed up everything.

"I know you do," he said. "And I'm so sorry the fire destroyed your chances—via that avenue. But as I said to you on the phone . . . there's always adoption."

She shook her head vehemently. "I want my own baby. I want—I need—a Castilla child."

He nodded once. "Your family."

"My family. The pressure there is . . ."

He nodded, then leaned back in his chair. "The pressure is un-fair. And obviously hurtful." The cream had suddenly curdled.

"Family is *so* important to them. That's why Sal and I really want—"

"I remember now. You've spoken of them before. To be hon-est I find their desire for a blood grandchild verging on egotisti-cal and prejudicial."

"Preju—?"

"I know their type. They don't believe a nonblood child, brought up in their family, is good enough. If you ask me, they are the ones who are not good enough."

Maya sat back against the cushions. She had never heard Dr. Ruffin talk like this.

He noticed her shock and took a deep breath. "I'm sorry if I sound brusque, but every day, all day, I deal with couples longing for a baby. Medical science has provided us with a myriad of op-tions. Yet in the end, we all have to accept that sometimes it just doesn't work. I don't know why. I don't know God's reasoning. But sometimes childlessness just *is*. And if—in the end—that is the case with you and Sal, then we'll have to deal with it. But for now, there are those options I mentioned. There is a chance to bring a child into your family, to love and nourish and adore. If your relatives declare the child tainted and unworthy, then . . . then I would tell them so long and nice knowing you."

The image of herself saying such things to her mother and father made Maya smile.

Dr. Ruffin smiled too. "You enjoy that image?"

"A little."

He reached forward and touched her knee. "If God wants you

to have a child we can get you a child. God never closes a door without opening a window."

Dr. Ruffin had mentioned God multiple times in this conversation. He'd never mentioned God before. Or maybe he had and Maya hadn't noticed.

He slapped his hands on his thighs and stood. "So? What do you think?"

She wasn't sure.

"Do you feel better?"

She took a moment to measure her emotions. She found them soothed and even hopeful. "Much better, actually. I'm sorry for coming in and scaring your staff like that. I didn't mean—"

"They'll recover. As will we, from the setback at the lab. We will carry on, you and I, yes?"

"Yes. We will carry on."

He opened the door of the conference room. "How did Sal take the news about the lab?"

He doesn't know yet. "He's sad, but I'll talk to him about all you've said. We'll discuss it."

"You do that. Call me anytime and I can go over the details of the new procedure or give you references for adoption."

Maya left the office feeling more substantial, more whole. She was not nothing. Nor was she inconsequential, insignificant, or incapable, because one way or another, she *would* become a mother. And that was the height of significance.

| | | | | | | | | | | |

"Hey, Roman? Third time I've called. What'd you do? Fall off the face of the earth? Call me."

Velvet flipped her cell phone shut. Although she and Roman didn't talk every day, they rarely went two days without speaking. And he was usually good about returning her calls.

Except today.

But she didn't have time to ponder it much. Not with a game tomorrow. Not with three new employees standing before her.

She slipped the phone into her pocket and turned back to her new charges, who were supposed to be reading the employee booklet she'd compiled over the years. She'd found that some trainees listened well, but others needed it in writing. Telling them what to do *and* showing them . . . it was best to cover all the bases.

But did this group understand the duties she'd already gone over? They were a mixed bag of three. One was a gangly kid who nodded constantly while he read, until she feared his head would nod right off his skinny neck. And the girl with Heidi braids had a permanent crease between her eyebrows as though the entire concept of filling a food order was beyond her ken.

And then there was Lianne. She hung back from the other two, the handbook tucked under her arm, her head cocked to the side. Chomping gum. Velvet hated people who chewed gum. Popped gum. Clicked gum.

As if she knew this, Lianne blew a bubble. It popped.

Velvet looked right at her. "In addition to the other directives, there will be no gum chewing. None."

Lianne pulled the booklet free. "Where does it say that?"

"Call it an addendum."

Lianne shrugged, spit it into her hand, and lobbed it into a trash can nearby.

Cocky kid.

Velvet tried to regain her focus. "This is probably a good time to go over the uniform. Page three."

Heidi tentatively raised her hand. "We have to wear a uniform? I don't have money for a uniform."

"Not that kind of uniform. You can wear jeans—no holes or tears—and some kind of Nebraska shirt. And tennis shoes."

"I don't own tennis shoes," Lianne said. There was disdain in her voice.

Velvet noticed her red flip-flops with a silk flower at the toe. "You don't need tennis shoes, per se, but you do need comfortable shoes." She would get in her own jab. "Shoes that cover your toes."

"So no sandals."

"No sandals."

"What if I wear socks with sandals?"

Velvet gave Lianne a slow gaze. "Are you testing me?"

"Just establishing the boundaries, that's all."

Velvet wondered how many times Lianne had tested her parents' boundaries, pushed them, or broken them completely. And how would *she* have handled such a child?

She didn't allow herself to answer that.

Suddenly, Lianne put her hand to her mouth, froze there a second, then bolted toward the women's restroom.

Those left behind looked after her, then at each other.

"If she's got the flu I don't want to work next to her, okay?" Heidi said.

"If she's got the flu, she shouldn't be handling food," Velvet said. The logistics of finding a worker to take Lianne's place rushed into her thoughts. And yet, if the girl was sick—if her daughter was sick—shouldn't she be compassionate? go after her?

It was obvious such an attribute did not come naturally, which was probably yet another indicator that she would have made a lousy mother.

Yet the nudge to go after her returned.

Forced compassion? Was such a thing even possible?

Her other employees stood there, waiting. Waiting for her to be a good person?

She gave in. "I'd better check on her. Be here tomorrow at

ten thirty sharp. If you have other questions, I'll answer them then."

Velvet headed to the restroom, feeling the slightest bit virtuous. She hoped if any celestial being was looking down on her, keeping score, she'd get at least a couple of brownie points.

There was only one stall door closed. Velvet heard retching noises. She waited for a break, then said, "Lianne? Are you all right?"

"Perfect. Thanks."

The toilet flushed, Lianne came out and headed to the sinks. She was pale.

"Don't look at me that way," she said.

"What way?"

She squirted foamy soap into her hands. "Like I have the plague."

"I'm just concerned about you." Velvet realized she'd rarely had the opportunity to say those words. To anyone. How pitiful was that?

"You're concerned about me working. Don't be."

"But if you're not well, you shouldn't—"

Lianne pulled two paper towels from the dispenser. "I'm well enough. I'm just pregnant."

Velvet didn't realize she was gawking until Lianne said, "Don't act like it's a big deal, or that it's never happened before. Being unmarried and pregnant isn't a scandal, you know. This isn't the fifties."

Or the eighties.

Lianne threw her paper towel in the trash. "Still want me to work for you?"

"Uh . . . of course. If you're up to it."

Lianne bared her teeth in front of the mirror and picked at something between them. "I won't let this pregnancy stop my life. I need to earn a living, same as everyone else."

"How far along are you? If you don't mind my asking?"

"Three months or so. Just told the father. Just had him abandon me."

She said it so matter-of-factly, as if she was daring Velvet to cross her. Memories of her own pregnant youth clashed with the odd fact that her daughter—that same baby—stood before her now. Velvet remembered the young John Gillingham's response to *her* news, his abandonment, and his apology received only yesterday.

"The father's probably in shock," Velvet said. "He may come around." Hopefully it wouldn't take twenty-three years.

Lianne shrugged and headed out of the restroom. "If he does he does. If he doesn't, I'll handle it alone."

"What do your parents think about it?" Velvet asked.

"I haven't told them."

"They need to know."

Lianne stopped in the stadium concourse. "I haven't even decided if I'm having it."

More déjà vu. Velvet had nearly aborted Lianne. She suddenly shivered at the idea that if she had, this young woman would not be standing before her.

Pregnant. Belligerent. Eccentric. Difficult. Needy.

"You don't approve of abortion?" Lianne asked.

Velvet was put on the spot, yet said, "I don't. In the end, it doesn't solve anything."

Lianne gave her an incredulous look. "Of course it does."

No, it doesn't. Trust me.

"Easy for you to say you're against it, for others to say as much. Until you're in my position, you have no idea the pressure—"

"I do have an idea," Velvet said. "I've been unwed and pregnant."

Lianne's head moved back an inch. "You?"

Why had she said that? It was a secret no one knew. No one.

It was too late now. "I was young once too. Impulsive. Romantic. Stupid."

Lianne laughed. "Slice right to the point, why don't you?"

"I will," Velvet said. "I always do."

Lianne moved aside to let a man pushing a delivery dolly pass.

"Hey, Velvet. Where do you want 'em?" he asked.

"Concessions Two, please. I'll be there in a minute."

"Will do."

She had to go. But she couldn't leave it like this. "I know what you're going through, Lianne. I *know*. And I considered abortion too. And now I realize a life's a life, no matter how inconvenient."

"What happened to your baby?" Lianne asked.

It was a loaded question. "I gave her up for adoption."

"Is she happy?"

"I think so."

"Do you ever want to find her? I mean, what if she wanted to find you? Would you be open to that? Because a lot of adopted kids aren't even told they are adopted, which is totally unfair."

Was she talking about herself? Hadn't the Skalas told her she was adopted? "Parents must have their reasons."

"Selfish reasons. A child has a right to know her roots."

Velvet wasn't sure she should ask the next question—to get it out in the open—but . . . "Are you adopted, Lianne?"

"I am."

"Your parents didn't tell you for a long time?"

"Didn't tell me until I found out. Only a few years ago. I nearly didn't find out at all. It's just . . ." She sighed. "I know now. I guess that's something."

Although Velvet had not chosen to be a part of her daughter's life, the fact Lianne hadn't even known of her existence . . . it hurt. "I'm so sorry, Lianne. But why didn't they tell you?"

"Beats me." She put her hands over her abdomen protectively. "If I choose to have this baby, I may raise it myself, or I may not. But either way I want to know what happens to it and how it's doing. My adoptive parents were wrong to not tell me, but I'm not too keen on my birth mother either. Or father. Didn't they ever wonder how I was? How could they abandon me like that?"

Velvet's mouth was dry. "Maybe they thought it was better—easier—not to know about you. To know and yet not be able to participate would have been hard."

"Hey, life's hard. Get over it." Lianne's eyes narrowed. "That's you, isn't it? You didn't have anything to do with your baby once you gave it up."

Velvet swallowed. "No, I didn't."

"But what if you suddenly had the chance to know her? to get involved in her life? Would you?"

"I—"

The delivery man approached. "Hey, Velvet, sorry to interrupt, but I need you to check this stuff in. I've got more deliveries to make."

"Sure, Ed. Sorry." She turned back to Lianne. "I have to go, but I think the short answer to your question is, I *would* be interested. Scared, but interested."

Lianne adjusted the waistband of her skirt. "I'll see you tomorrow. If you don't mind an occasional mad dash to the restroom, I'll be here."

And so will I.

| | | | | | | | | | |

Eeeeeeeeeeeeeee . . .

Roman sat upright, suddenly awake. A machine at the head of Billy's bed screamed. He looked at his son. Billy's eyes were closed. He was pale. Too pale.

Two nurses burst into the room.

"The machine," he said stupidly.

"You need to move aside, Mr. Paulson. Please."

He stepped back, giving them room. A doctor came in, and the nurses brought him up to date. He barked orders. Shots were given; the bed was made flat. The doctor started CPR, pressing Billy's chest while a nurse used a breathing bag over Billy's mouth to push in air.

"Nothing," the other nurse said, watching the machine.

They worked a short time longer; then the doctor said, "V-fib."

A machine was brought forward. The doctor took control of two paddles and the nurse squirted gel on them. When the machine buzzed its readiness, the doctor yelled, "Clear!" He pressed the paddles to Billy's chest.

A jolt of electricity raised Billy up off the bed. A scene Roman had watched a hundred times on TV and in the movies became all too real.

Come on, Billy. Come on. Come on. Come on.

"Again!" the doctor said.

Roman stared at the vitals monitor, willing it to show the *blip-blip* of a heartbeat.

But . . . nothing.

He grabbed the doorjamb and leaned against it. This had to work. Any second now the machine would show the heartbeat again. A happy ending. Like on TV. Like in the movies.

As the doctor and nurses continued their work, Roman found himself pulling away from the moment, as if watching it from afar. This wasn't really happening. It was a movie. It wasn't—

He felt a hand on his shoulder. "Roman? Oh no. What . . . ?" AJ stood beside him.

Roman didn't answer, didn't offer details. He couldn't bridge the distance he'd created.

He vaguely felt AJ's arm around his shoulder, pulling him

close. He felt AJ's breath skim his ear, heard his whispered words: "Please, God. Please, God, please . . ."

But then suddenly, amid the frenzy, the two nurses and the doctor froze.

They looked at each other as if affirming . . .

One nurse looked at the clock on the wall, then said quietly, "Time of death: 7:13."

What? Roman spiraled back to earth, to this hospital, to this room, to this moment.

One nurse looked at him, then the others.

Roman heard the doctor's intake of breath, saw his sorrowful eyes.

"No," Roman said. His head shook side to side, and he pulled away from AJ's arm, away from the room. "No. No. No!" He couldn't let the doctor say the words. Somehow, if he could keep the doctor from saying them, it would be all right.

"I'm so sorry," the doctor said.

The words fell upon him. Unable to bear their weight, Roman collapsed.

| | | | | | | | | | | |

"Who had the grande with a double shot?" Peter asked the crowd of William-supporters in the waiting room.

"That was me," a linebacker said.

Peter and Carrie passed out the spoils of their beverage run. The coffee in the waiting room was terrible so they'd volunteered to go to a proper coffeehouse.

They'd just dispensed the final cup when AJ came into the waiting room. "Sorry, AJ," Peter said. "We never got your order."

AJ didn't answer but stared ahead, blankly.

Something was wrong—terribly wrong. There was only one

thing that could cause a look like that. Peter's voice caught in his throat, not wanting to ask, but needing to. "What is it?"

For the first time, AJ blinked. He scanned the room. All eyes were on him. No one seemed to breathe.

"He's gone. He died. Billy is dead."

Responses of "What?" melded with "No!"

Carrie fell into Peter's arms. "No, Peter. It can't be true. William can't be dead."

She was right. It was impossible. They'd prayed. They'd all prayed together. Prayed hard. William couldn't be dead. God wouldn't do that.

But as Peter looked around the room at William's friends, sobbing, crying out, falling weak-kneed into chairs . . .

No. William couldn't be dead.

Yet somehow, some way, he was.

And the pain of that was unbearable.

SIX

I am counting on the Lord;
yes, I am counting on him.
I have put my hope in his word.
I long for the Lord
more than sentries long for the dawn.

PSALM 130:5-6

AJ unlocked the front door and went inside. He held the door open. "Coming?"

Roman saw him, but didn't see. Heard him, but didn't hear.

"Come on, guy. You're home."

The word made Roman blink. Home? No. There was no home anymore. No place like home . . . *There's no place like home. There's no place like home.*

AJ offered his hand. "Come inside. I'll help you get to bed."

Help me? Help? Me?

There was no one who could help him. He didn't exist anymore. He was not *there.* He was *not.*

AJ still waited, and Roman realized the only way to get him to go away was to enter this place and pretend . . . something. His brain told his feet to move, and they did—which surprised him. One in front of the other, over the threshold, into the house.

He heard the door click shut behind him. AJ took his arm. "Let me help you upstairs."

Roman's body rebelled at the thought of so much movement. He focused on the couch nearby. "There."

"The couch? Sure." AJ busied himself, paving a way between here and there. Roman's legs quivered, a warning they could only go so far, and might not even—

He fell upon the couch and let the weight of his body take him all the way downward. Somehow a pillow appeared under his head, his legs were lifted to the cushions, and a covering was placed over his body.

A shroud.

He closed his eyes against the world and let oblivion have its way with him.

| | | | | | | | | | |

"Hey, sleepyhead."

Maya grunted and reluctantly opened her eyes. Sal stood over her, fully dressed.

"In a few minutes I'm heading to work. There's rain in the forecast. I need to get the Connor house done."

She squinted her eyes to see the clock—9:15. She threw the covers off. "Why did you let me sleep in?"

"Sleep as long as you like. It's Saturday, silly. I just didn't want you to wake up and find me gone. You looked so peaceful, I hated to wake you at all. You tossed and turned all night."

She held out her hands to him. He pulled her to standing and into his arms, where he gave her a kiss. "Coffee's ready. If you hurry I'll make you an English muffin." He pushed her toward the bathroom. "*Fretta, fretta!* The weekend's a-wastin'."

Hurrying would not be easy. Sal was right. She hadn't slept until nearly 4 a.m. She'd been dogged by disbelief, sorrow, and panic regarding her lost hope for a baby, and she'd been harassed by guilt, shame, and fear regarding her firing and the upcoming article. In the midst of the nocturnal battle she was torn between staying and leaving. That she had eventually fallen asleep had sealed her fate.

For the night at least. Today was a new day, full of new battles and decisions—

Maya heard the front door open and the realities of the day came rushing in. She ran to the window. Sal wasn't leaving for work, was he? He'd mentioned break—

No! He was . . . he was getting the morning paper.

She ran downstairs, reaching the bottom step just as Sal came inside. He blinked. "What's wrong?"

She tried to force the panic into hiding. "I . . . I want to read it." She glanced toward the bedroom. "Upstairs."

He gave her a quizzical look, tapped the paper against her head, and said, "Too late. A muffin's already in the toaster."

"But—"

She heard the toaster pop.

Sal headed to the kitchen. "Butter or jam?"

Who cares? But she managed an answer. "Both," she said, following him. "Give me the paper."

He did as she asked, and she sat in her place and removed the rubber band. She chose the front section and quickly scanned the pages. *Nothing. Nothing.*

Sal gave her half an English muffin and sat across from her with his own half.

She moved on to the local section.

"You going to share?"

"Oh. Sorry." She pushed the sports section his way and went back to her search.

"Hey, what's that?" Sal pointed to the back of the paper in her hands.

She turned the paper over. And there it was: "Ethics Inquiry at Efficient Office Machines."

"Efficient? Your company?"

Of all the luck, to have it be on the one part of the section Sal could see.

The byline was Ross Bredloe's. This was it.

"Maya?"

"It's nothing."

"It said something about ethics. Is there trouble at work?"

She knew her face showcased her panic; she could feel the heat in her cheeks.

He reached across the table and took the paper away from her.

She sprang to her feet and snatched it back, placing it behind her back. "No, Sal. You can't read—"

The cordial banter of the morning was extinguished. There was no way out. If only she could replay the morning and . . .

And what? Sal would have seen the article eventually, one way or the other.

"Maya, what's going on?"

When tears threatened she let them loose. What did it matter now? Her world was coming to an end. "I made a mistake. I . . ." She shook her head, still incapable of letting it happen. "I can't tell you."

"Then hand me the paper."

She shook her head vehemently.

Sal let out a sigh. "Either I read it or you tell it. One way or the other I'm going to find out the truth."

Would it be better coming from her? She took the plunge. "I was fired."

His look was incredulous. "You just won a Top Seller award."

She sank into her chair, slipping the paper onto her lap, out of sight. "It's how I got the clients that's at issue." She hurried to explain the motive. Surely if he knew what was behind her actions . . . "We needed the money for another try at getting pregnant. The baby . . ."

"Maya . . . what did you do?"

"I didn't break the law. It wasn't as bad as that."

"Break the law?"

Why had she said that? "I just pushed. Too hard. That's all."

He wasn't buying it. "It said 'ethics.' You were unethical?"

"To some. One. Just one guy."

"You were unethical enough to get yourself fired?" He shoved his plate away. It bumped into his coffee, spilling it. "Out with it. All of it."

Maya looked to the now-cold muffin. It mocked her with its promise of a normal morning. Things would never be normal again.

"I'm waiting."

"I took the customers of one of my coworkers."

"You stole their business?"

"I . . ." She was too weary to couch her answer. "Yes, I guess I did—though at the time, it didn't seem as bad as it does now."

"How could you do that?"

"I was desperate. We needed money, so I—"

"Why didn't you just rob a bank? That would have gotten you money."

She didn't know what to say.

"If you were fired yesterday, why didn't you tell me last night?"

Oh dear. "Actually, I was fired Tuesday."

He did the math. "That was four days ago."

She shrugged.

His head shook back and forth in small movements. Then he said, "Your office didn't give you permission to work from home. You were already fired when you told me that."

"I was tired of finding something to do all day, away from home."

A bitter laugh escaped. "Four days. Four days of sneaking around and lying. To me."

"I wanted to tell you, but . . ." She remembered the news from Dr. Ruffin. Maybe if she told him about that he would feel sorry for her, sorry for them. Maybe that sorrow would override his anger. "There's something else I should tell—"

He pushed away from the table. "No. No more. I've had more than enough. You are not the woman I thought you were." He went to the back door and took his keys off the hook. "I need to think."

"Where are you going?"

The door shut behind him.

| | | | | | | | | | |

Maya sat at the kitchen table, staring at the English muffin. She couldn't believe what had just happened. An innocent weekend breakfast had transformed into a setting for accusation, confession, and abandonment.

If only I'd left yesterday. If only I hadn't been here when the newspaper came, when he read all about my . . . my . . .

Sin.

Maya blinked at the term. Sin? She never thought in such terms. *Sin* was a word used by obsessive religious fanatics. It applied to murderers, rapists, and other horrible, detestable people.

"I made a mistake."

Sin.

She had to go. She couldn't be there when Sal came home.

If he comes home.

She ran upstairs and put on jeans and a T-shirt. She drew her hair into a ponytail and ignored any thought of makeup. She put on her left shoe but couldn't find its mate.

She lifted the dust ruffle, looking for it. She spotted the shoe, but when she reached, she managed to push it just out of her grasp.

With a groan, she got to her hands and knees to retrieve it. "Not now. Please not—"

The doorbell rang.

Sal?

She grabbed the shoe to her chest and held her breath. Then it hit her. Sal wouldn't ring the doorbell. Who would be coming to her house on a Saturday morning? She tiptoed to the window. And gasped.

Her parents' ancient Volvo was parked in the driveway—behind her car.

She ducked behind the curtain. Her parents never stopped by unannounced. Not unless they had good reason.

Such as . . . reading a scathing article about their daughter? She might as well lie down and die right now. The judge, jury, and executioner had arrived.

The doorbell rang again, accompanied by the deep resonance of knocking. She heard the murmur of her parents talking to each other on the stoop below. *Go away, go away, go away.*

Then, the unthinkable.

The sound of a key in the door.

The door opening.

Her mother's voice: "Maya?"

"She's not here," her father said.

"Her car's here."

"But Sal's truck is gone."

"*Her* car is here. She is here. Maya?"

Maya looked longingly at the closet, but when she heard footfalls on the stairs, she knew that—save jumping out the window—she couldn't escape.

She took a deep breath and walked into the hall.

"Oh," her mother said, halfway up the stairs. "You *are* here. Why didn't you answer?"

Maya realized she was holding a shoe to her chest. She balanced herself against the wall and put it on. "I was getting dressed."

"Well, come down here. We want to talk to you."

Her parents descended the stairs and moved to the living room. Her mother took a place in the very center of the couch, and her father stood near the front door, motioning for Maya to sit in Sal's recliner.

The thought, *Hey, this is my house, don't tell me where to sit*, was quashed by their serious expressions, and even more so by the fact they were her parents and at age thirty-three she still did as she was told.

But then, as if on cue, her worst fear was revealed. Her father pulled a newspaper from the inside pocket of his jacket. He held it in the space between them. "What do you have to say about this?"

Maya knew there was absolutely nothing she could say that would be an acceptable explanation or appease her parents. They had the power. She . . .

She took a deep breath, then said, "I got nothing."

"That is not a proper answer," her mother said.

Maya shrugged and felt an absurd satisfaction in the tack she had taken, and even in her use of bad grammar. She was not up for another confession this morning or trying to prove she was worthy of their love. She simply could *not* do it.

Her father opened the folded paper to reference her shame. "It says you got fired on Tuesday. That means when you were at our house for dinner Wednesday, you had already lost your job."

She shrugged again.

"Why didn't you tell us?"

"It was Marta's birthday. And you were upset about not getting the grant."

Her mother pegged her index finger into her thigh. "Your omission was cowardly."

Maya took a breath, let it out, then said, "Why don't you just add that to my list of bad character traits."

"Don't be flippant," Father said. "It's extremely unbecoming." **173**

A small laugh escaped before Maya could press a hand against it.

Her mother shook her head. "You don't seem to be taking this very seriously."

I beg to differ. My life is ruined. Is that serious enough for you? Yet in spite of her thoughts, Maya found herself continuing with the blasé attitude. "What can I do? It's done."

"It's *done?*" Her father moved directly in front of her, holding the article as Exhibit A. "'Unethical.' Our daughter, unethical?"

"Don't worry, Dad. I'm married now. The Castilla name isn't mentioned, so your impeccable reputation is still intact." As soon as the words left her mouth, Maya wanted to grab them back.

Her father stared down at her. "How can you be so dismissive?"

"And disrespectful?" her mother asked. "What have we ever done to deserve such an attitude?"

Maya felt an unfamiliar anger rise, and with it, a foreign boldness. She pushed the article aside and stood, moving away from her father's presence. "You want to know what you've done? You've pressured Sal and me unmercifully to have a baby. You've made it clear that a baby is essential to our purpose and to finding any kind of respect or approval." She pressed her hands against her chest. "I can't get pregnant every time I want to, like Marta and Marcela. There's something wrong with my system. I'm flawed, all right? Do you get it? I'm broken!"

"You are not broken. You'll have a baby once that . . . that procedure takes hold."

Their reaction was typical. Everything was fixable and anything could be attained through logic, determination, and hard work.

"That procedure takes money," Maya said. "We're already in debt over twenty thousand." She pointed at the article. "I did *that* so I could give you a grandchild. So you would be proud of me."

174

"So this is our fault?" Mother asked.

"We never forced you to be so desperate that you'd do . . ." Her father scanned the article for something, then quoted, "'I'd do anything to have a baby. Anything.'"

Unfortunately, the quote was accurate. Maya lowered her chin to her chest and covered her face with a hand. Each minute was playing out worse than the last. If only she could make it all go away.

Her father continued. "The article makes you sound deranged, Maya. Like one of those crazies who steal other women's babies or—"

Suddenly, an inner timer went off. The meeting was over. Maya faced her father and grabbed chunks of her hair. "Crazies, you say? *You* made me crazy! All the pressure to have a child with the precious Castilla genes. I want a child to love and care for, but you . . . you want a child to be a trophy, an exhibit of your own greatness."

Her parents froze, dumbstruck. Staring.

Maya was in a daze, hardly believing the words that had just been hurled across the room had come from her mouth.

After a measure of moments that dripped with uneasy tension, her father said, "Come, Margaret. We're done here."

Without another word they left, leaving Maya standing alone.

What had just happened? She had never—ever—talked to her parents like that. It was as though another person had entered her body and taken over her thoughts.

She heard their car pull away, the tires screeching.

Away. Yes. Away.

It was her only choice.

| | | | | | | | | | |

The Castilla family lake cabin was not fancy—by anyone's standards. It didn't even have indoor plumbing, though her parents *had* fancied up the outhouse with a carpeted seat and painted walls.

It was a place of memories—pleasant memories—of weekends swinging over the water on a rope, lying on blow-up rafts, and fishing from the dock.

Today it was a place of escape.

The day was as overcast as Maya's mood. The first leaves of autumn sprinkled her car as she pulled up in front. She got her suitcase out of the trunk and used her key to open the door. The air was stuffy. The cabin wasn't used every weekend.

Thankfully.

Maya wasn't sure what she would have done if she had seen one of her sisters' cars in the drive.

She would have kept going.

Somewhere.

Away.

Maya surveyed the cabin. It hadn't changed much since she was a child—which was probably the reason it held such appeal. The cabin never changed. It was the keeper of all good things from her past. It took the responsibility very seriously and never forced her parents to fix the furnace or change the kitchen or redecorate in any way. It was the one place in the entire world where time stood still. There was no thought of the future there, only pleasant memories of the past eliciting a calming comfort in the present.

Yet Maya wasn't sure what to do here, alone. Voices and laughter were as much a part of this place as s'mores in the fire pit and games of pitch and canasta around the kitchen table.

Yet feeling as she did at that moment, there was only one thing *to* do.

She went into the red bedroom (as opposed to the master bedroom or the loft or the green bedroom) and pulled the red and white quilt back. She shucked off her shoes and got in bed.

She pulled the covers over her head, blocking out the light. Darkness was good. Darkness was what she deserved. Lots and lots of darkness.

| | | | | | | | | | |

Roman was roused from his dreams by a knocking on the door.

The memory *Billy is dead* rushed into his consciousness with fresh teeth, its strong arms pulling him down, down, down into the dark waters. . . .

The strength of that horrible monster prohibited him from reacting to the door. Barred him from it. *You cannot escape. You will drown here.*

But then he heard another knock and female sobs and a plaintive, "Please, please be home. . . ."

The young voice, crying . . .

Roman propelled himself upward and broke through the surface, into the air and the light. He struggled out of the afghan, nearly tripping when it got wound around his legs. "Coming," he told the door. His voice sounded foreign, as though it didn't quite belong in this moment. And he was rather surprised when his hand found the doorknob, was able to make it turn, and had the strength to pull the door open.

The girl was college-age and pretty. Wholesome. Yet her eyes were red and puffy, any makeup long gone.

"Are you William's father?"

Am I? Oh . . . yes. The words he managed to say aloud came out separately, as if one was not necessarily related to the other. "I. Am."

"I'm Carrie."

Roman did not possess the strength to scan his list of acquaintances to find a Carrie.

"Donigan?"

The conversation was too taxing, too difficult. He glanced over his shoulder at the couch. He shivered at the thought of the monster who lived there, and yet . . .

"I'm William's girlfriend. Was William's gir—" She began to cry again.

The sound and sight of her tears lifted the veil that had shrouded his senses. He cleared his throat, hoping his words would cooperate and string themselves together properly. "I . . . I didn't know Billy had a girl—" It was as much as he could manage. Vaguely, he realized his ignorance revealed too much.

"Can I come in, Mr. Paulson?"

In? Inside? Here? And yet Roman stepped aside. As she crossed the threshold, brushing his arm as she passed, he found himself made fully awake. *Awake* was an alien sensation, yet somehow familiar. Yes, he'd felt this awake before. Once.

Before.

His awakened eyes saw the girl as a tiny thing, only coming up to his shoulders. The too-long sleeves of her shirt were pulled halfway over her hands, which had formed fists over her mouth.

He wasn't sure what to do with her.

"Can I sit down?" she asked.

Yes. Sitting. "Of course," he said.

She perched by the window on the edge of an antique chair that no one ever used. Roman picked the afghan off the floor and tossed it in the recliner. He sat on the couch.

And waited.

"Can I have a tissue?" she finally asked.

He went to the bathroom and brought her the entire box. She used two, crammed their remains into the pocket of her jeans, then cradled the tissue box as if it were precious. "I still can't believe he's gone." Another sob threatened, but she managed to pull it back.

The murky world of the monster called to him, but Roman closed his eyes and tried to hang on to the moment that was *now*. "How long have you been—were you—Billy's girlfriend?"

"Three months, but it seemed like forever." Her voice caught. "What are we going to do without him?"

A surge of annoyance caused his blood to fully flow, his heart to fully beat, his lungs to fully breathe. *We?* Certainly she couldn't lump her short-lived college fling into the same category as his fatherhood?

"When's the . . . funeral?" she asked.

He stroked the couch cushion, assuring it—and being assured—that he would once again be its captive soon. "Monday afternoon," he said. Oddly, Roman couldn't remember what time. AJ had taken care of the arrangements.

She nodded. "I'll be there. We'll all be there."

The concept of *all* had little meaning. He just wanted her to leave.

Then stand, he told himself. Somehow, he complied. "Thanks for coming by, Cassie."

"Carrie. It's Carrie."

He took a step toward the door.

She did not move.

Roman felt panic slide into place. He didn't want to be rude, but . . . "If you don't mind I—"

"Today was supposed to be William's first game as a starter."

She might as well have hit Roman in the chest with a two-by-four. He staggered back to the couch. "It's Saturday," he said meekly.

She nodded. "The game's just starting."

I've got to go collided with *There's no reason to go.*

"William told me how much you supported his football. He said that without you he never would have become good enough to play college ball. He was so excited about starting. He wanted you to be proud of him."

Roman's throat tightened and once again threatened to strangle him.

"His first starting game . . . That's one reason I came today," Carrie said. "Today at the game I was supposed to hold up a sign William made."

A sign? She'd lost him.

"I can't do it. I can't go. I'm not sure I'll ever be able to go to a game again."

Not holding up a sign was like a tiny nick in the mountain of life. Roman was dealing with a deep, dark crevasse. He didn't have time for this. "Don't worry about it," he told her. "There are plenty of signs at the game."

"Not like this one."

He didn't want to ask but sensed she would never leave if he didn't. "Why?"

"I'll show you. It's in my car."

She went outside, and he mourned the extended time this was taking. Some stupid sign wasn't his problem. His eyes caught hold of the dead bolt. One flick and—

Too late. She came back in, carrying a rolled-up sign made of a vinyl-type fabric. She began to unroll it, face out, talking as she did. "William made it himself."

The sign was not large, perhaps two feet by three. And the words were nicely lettered. Bold. Easily readable. Yet what they said could have been Greek to Roman.

"'John 3:16'?"

"It was William's favorite."

Oh. Yeah. That.

Carrie explained further. "His favorite verse. From the Bible."

Which was exactly why Roman was through with this conversation. And though he *had* seen a man holding up such a sign at a game before, he wanted nothing to do with *this* sign, even if Billy had made it.

Carrie rambled on. "William and I were watching a baseball game last summer and we saw someone hold up a sign like this. That's what gave him the idea. It's *the* promise of the Bible. It has nothing to do with the game—not *that* game—but it affects every single person watching. To win the game of life you need to embrace what it says."

The girl talked too much. And Roman knew she wanted him to ask what the verse said, but he refused. Since Billy hadn't been able to get him to look it up, he couldn't—and wouldn't—give this stranger the satisfaction. Besides, he felt his visit to reality fading. The couch called. Oblivion beckoned.

She bit her lip. "Well . . . anyway . . . where else do you have eighty thousand people gathered together, facing each other?"

Marketing. It was always about marketing.

She rolled the sign back up. "William was so proud of this. He was probably as excited about me holding it up as he was about his first start."

Roman pressed his fingers against his forehead. He felt a headache coming on. And then the tears surprised him. He was not a crier, especially not in front of a woman. "I'm sorry, I really need . . ." Surely she could fill in the blank.

Thankfully, she moved toward the door. "I understand completely," she said. She set the sign against the wall next to the antique chair. "I feel horrible I can't fulfill his wish. Maybe someday. But in the meantime, I think you should have the sign.

William's sign. Next time you go to a game, you can hold it up knowing it was important to William. To Billy."

He wanted to argue with her, tell her there was no way he would ever hold up such a sign, but to do so would extend her time there, and he was already far past his limit. "Nice to meet you," he managed.

"Nice to meet you too, Mr. Paulson." Once on the stoop, she turned back to him and studied his face in a way that was almost embarrassing. "I really believed that William and I might have married one day. You would have been my father-in-law. You have a nice face. Strong. Determined. I like that."

He nodded once and closed the door.

Nice. Strong. Determined. These words did not compute. In fact, within one intake and exhale of breath, the past few minutes were swept away into a nether-land. A shadow-land.

Roman turned from the door and surveyed the room. It looked foreign to him, irrelevant and not quite real, like a set for a sitcom with all the correct accoutrements of daily living but none of the spark of real life.

He noticed the green light on his answering machine was blinking. Messages. He had messages.

They were of no interest to him.

He returned to the captivity of the couch.

| | | | | | | | | | |

Velvet's life on game days was frenetic. From the time she entered the stadium until she left, she was transported into another world totally separate from reality. In the stadium no one cared whether the stock market was up or down, the current war was being won or lost, or what movie star was sleeping with whom. The world on game day consisted of eighty thousand people from all walks of life, from big cities and small towns, all wearing red and white, all intent on two things: winning the game and having a great time doing it.

Velvet loved to see the fans streaming in, not just because their presence (and appetites) represented income, but because at the start of the day they were happy. All of them happy and full of hope and big dreams. The victory of the team was embraced as their own personal accomplishment to be celebrated, while a defeat was a joint failure to be mourned. She always hoped for victory because it made her life easier. Happy fans made happy customers. The surliness of a tense game spilled over at the food counter. And if it was close? Food sales suffered as people stayed in their seats. If it was a rout? They left early.

So far, so good. Although TV monitors had been added in the concourse, Velvet rarely looked at them. After all these years she still relied on the roar of the crowd to monitor the score. Nebraska was winning, yet it must have been close enough to keep the large crowds in the stands.

She kept an eye out for Roman. And AJ. They'd teased her about how many Runzas they'd eat today, yet so far, she hadn't seen them. There *was* the chance she had missed them as she'd made her rounds to all the concessions stations. As she walked from one to another, she got out her cell phone and called him. *Hey, Roman. Your Runzas are getting cold* was ready on her lips.

But Roman didn't answer. Again. Between his cell and his house she'd left half a dozen messages. This was not like Roman; not at all.

She reached the concessions stand where Lianne was working but pulled up short when she saw the man Lianne was helping. John. Her John.

She wasn't sure what to do. John didn't know the young woman helping him was his daughter. And Lianne didn't know the man she was helping was her father.

It would be okay. In a matter of seconds it would all fade into just another transact—

Lianne looked in her direction, her eyes showing recognition. "There. There's the person I need to ask about this."

Ask about what?

John turned toward her. He smiled. "My, my. Just the lady I also wanted to see."

Lianne looked a bit confused but added, "He wants to change a hundred, and I didn't know if I should."

"Change it," Velvet said, glad for the mundane distraction. She moved behind the counter, choosing her daughter's side over her lover's. She relished the buffer between them.

"Thanks," John said. "I never even thought about the need for smaller bills."

Lianne took his money, made the change, then went off to fill his order.

"I thought you were flying out Thursday, after the book signing," Velvet said quietly, so Lianne wouldn't hear.

"I was, but . . . I decided to stay. I would have called you yesterday but when my publisher found out I was staying over, they arranged another book signing last evening." His grin made him look twenty again. "Besides, I thought it would be fun to try to surprise you here." He spread his arms. "Surprise!"

She was not amused. She hated surprises of any kind. She liked to know what was going to happen, when, and how, and by whom. The moments she preferred were those she instigated.

John finished putting his change in his billfold and slipped it into a back pocket. "Actually, I was hoping we could go out after the game."

She went with her gut reaction. "I'm usually pretty busy for quite a while afterward, wrapping things up."

"I'll wait." His smile was so pleasant, so calm. It unnerved her.

Lianne brought his hot dog and Coke. "Here you go. Ketchup and mustard are on the counter against the wall."

Suddenly, John began to stare at Lianne. Then his eyes flitted to Velvet. Then back to Lianne.

Velvet's stomach grabbed. *Oh no. He sees!*

She had to get him out of there. Now. In order to get him to leave she said, "Fine. I'll meet you out front by the statue at five thirty."

He seemed not to hear.

She had to break the moment. "Hey, John, I'd love to chat, but I can't right now. Five thirty, all right?"

He nodded, but his eyes were on Lianne.

"My face turn green or something?" she asked him.

"No, no. Sorry. You just remind me of someone, that's all. I like your hair."

Then with a nod to them both, he took his food and walked away.

This is not good. Not good at all.

| | | | | | | | | | |

After John faded into the crowd of the stadium, Velvet tried not to think about him or about their meeting tonight. How would she respond when he made a comment about Lianne's gray streak of hair and her own—or rather, the one she used to have when she was Lianne's age?

What could she say? *Oh really? I never noticed* or *Lucky girl* or *Don't you know it's the latest fashion?*

Lame, lame, lame.

Velvet had trouble concentrating. She found herself repeating the same instructions twice, or asking a question and getting an answer but not hearing and having to ask it again.

All because of John.

And Lianne.

Why did they have to show up anyway? She wanted her life to go back to normal as soon as—

She saw a photo of Billy on the TV monitor and was pulled out of her pity party. She'd forgotten today was his first day to start. He must have been doing really great to get singled out on television. She left the counter and moved closer, wanting to tell Roman what was said about his son.

She heard the middle of it. One announcer was saying, "William Paulson was a budding running back, with the potential to be one of the greats."

The other announcer said, "He shall be sorely missed."

Missed? Was a budding running back?

The screen went back to the game. A man and his son stood nearby watching the coverage. Velvet stopped them as they moved to head back to their seats. "Excuse me? I only heard part of that. What did they say about William Paulson?"

"He died," the little boy said.

"He drowned saving a kid at a picnic."

Her heart stopped. "Drowned?"

The man nodded. "On Thursday. It was in all the papers yesterday and on the news."

"Dad? I want to get back to the game."

They walked off, leaving Velvet standing in the middle of the concourse. Dead. Billy dead. This didn't make any sense. Billy couldn't be dead. Roman would have called. Roman—

Roman!

"Ma'am? Are you okay?" an elderly man asked.

"Fine." She forced herself to move. "Thank you. I'm fine."

She started to walk to the left, then pivoted and walked to the right, then stopped again. Roman wasn't at the game. He was home. She had to leave. She had to see him. Now.

"Ms. Cotton?" One of her workers stood nearby, holding three hundreds. "We need change?"

But she couldn't leave. Not until after the game.

She was stuck.

186

| | | | | | | | | | |

Peter returned to his car and got in. He'd knocked on the door to Lianne's apartment but had gotten no answer. He wanted to see her. Needed to see her.

They hadn't talked since she'd got out of the car after their visit to Agata's Wednesday night. They hadn't talked about the baby at all. And now . . . with William's death . . .

Peter needed to talk to her. About everything. About nothing. He needed to feel her arms around him and have her hold him close and tell him everything would be okay.

Not that he could be certain Lianne would do that. Could do that. They hadn't been together through any crisis. Was she a compassionate person? Did she feel things deeply? He wasn't even sure she was a crier. If he was real about it, he doubted she was. Could a person who was so matter-of-fact about life, so blunt, feel true sorrow and be broken by it enough to cry and hug and need comfort?

Actually, the person he wanted to talk to about all this, the one he wanted to get comfort from, was William. How ironic was that? How stupid. How strange. Yet his thoughts kept returning to *I have to tell William. I have to talk to William.*

"Sick. I'm sick," he said aloud.

He was startled when a bicyclist passed his window. Should he just sit there and wait for her to come back from wherever she was? Should he go home to his empty apartment where he'd be confronted with all things William? He was in limbo, in no-man's-land, completely lost.

Suddenly, Peter noticed a Nebraska flag in a neighbor's yard.

The game! Today's Saturday!

He had a ticket for the game yet had never once thought of it. All week he and William had talked about his first start. Now, for Peter to have spaced it off so completely . . .

Death will do that.

"Lianne!" That's where she was.

Lianne was at the game, working her new job in concessions.

Peter took hold of the steering wheel and banged his head against his hands. "The game. The game."

The game went on without William. The world went on without William.

It wasn't fair. And it wasn't right.

But it was a fact.

Peter had no energy or will to go anywhere, to be anywhere but here. And so he settled in. To wait.

For something.

Or someone.

| | | | | | | | | | |

Peter woke up. It took him a moment to realize he was seated in his car. He rubbed his face hard, then turned toward a sound to his left.

Lianne was going into her building.

He called through the open window. "Lianne!"

She turned to him, but only for a moment. The door shut behind her.

Peter got out and rushed toward the entrance. She had to have heard him calling.

He caught up with her at her apartment door, the key in the lock.

"Lianne!"

"I thought that was you."

That's it? "I need to talk to you."

"I'm done talking."

"Not just about the baby. About William."

She opened the door and pulled her key out. "I heard about his death at the game. Bummer."

"Bummer?" He shook his head, incredulous. "That's all you can say?"

"I've got my own problems. In case you've forgotten."

Her coldness shocked him. Although she hadn't known William well, they'd talked. They'd even had a meal or two together when their paths crossed in the apartment. Most people, when hearing about the death of even a mere acquaintance, jumped on the connection—however vague—and reacted. Felt sorrow. Expressed sincere compassion.

But not Lianne?

She paused with the door unlocked. "Anything else?"

"We need to talk about our baby."

"My baby. Bye, Peter."

She went inside and shut the door, leaving him stunned. Again. He knocked. "Lianne! Talk to me."

No response.

He pounded. "Lianne!"

An elderly lady opened the door to the apartment across the hall. "Stop the racket, boy. She obviously doesn't want to talk to you. Which is no great loss, if you ask me. She's an odd one, that one is."

She shut her door. Peter found himself alone in the hall, surrounded by closed doors.

| | | | | | | | | | |

Roman. Roman. I have to get to Roman.

Velvet closed out the day's business on overdrive. And double

speed. One of her longtime workers kidded her. "Hot date tonight, Velvet?"

Only then did she remember John. John, waiting for her by
the statue. She was torn. If only she hadn't run into him. Yet she
couldn't blow him off, couldn't leave him standing there.

Her speed paid off and she finished her duties early, by ten after five. She'd told John she would meet him at five thirty. She
didn't want to not show up, yet her need to rush to Roman's
house . . .

Still uncertain what she should do, she left the stadium and
was relieved to see John already there, early.

He smiled as she approached; then his face clouded with concern. "What's wrong?"

She'd kept it in all afternoon. It felt good to say it out loud.
"During the game I found out that one of the players died. He
was the son of a good friend of mine and—"

"William . . . ?"

"Right. William Paulson. He was a great kid."

"A hero. He saved a child's life."

"Right now I'm worried about his father's life. I didn't know
about Billy; I didn't know. And for days I've been trying to call
Roman—just to talk. He didn't answer, and now I know why. I
feel awful. I should have been there for him. So I have to go to
him now and—"

He took her elbow. "Let's go."

She shook his touch away. "You can't go."

"Why not? I may be able to help. I'm a pastor, Velvet. Remember?"

To Roman that would not be a high credential. "My friend
doesn't believe in God."

"But God believes in him and is there for him." His voice
softened. "Let me help, Velvet. At least let me try."

She was too frazzled to argue.

| | | | | | | | | | |

Velvet knocked and rang the doorbell at the same time. She had to see Roman. Had to.

When the door opened, she barely recognized him. His eyes were red and puffy, his hair disheveled, his shoulders slumped. And he hadn't shaved—in days?

"Roman, I just heard. I'm—"

She saw his eyes move past her, to John. She angled her body so they could see each other. "This is John, an old college friend."

Roman did not react except to step back, allowing them in. He didn't wait to close the door, but left that job to them. He walked like a zombie to the couch, where an afghan lay in a pile. He sat. Velvet took the seat beside him. John found a place in a chair by the window.

Velvet put a hand upon Roman's back and willed a wave of sincere compassion to somehow be transferred through her touch. "Roman, I am so, so sorry."

"He's dead."

It was a statement made as though they weren't even present, as though he were reminding himself.

Velvet didn't know what she could say that would truly help. She had little experience dealing with grief.

John came toward them. He pulled the coffee table a few inches away from the couch and took a seat on it, facing Roman. "Tell me about William," he said.

Roman blinked and looked at John as if seeing him for the first time. "Billy. I loved him."

"He was your son."

"He played football."

"I bet you used to toss the ball around with him. In the front yard?"

Roman looked past John, out the front window. "We did it together."

"Did you play football in school?"

"I was never as good as Billy. He could catch and run. You should have seen him run."

"I love watching a good running back, juking in and out of the defense."

"He could do that. Turn on a dime. There was one time back in high school when he ran through five tackles for a touchdown."

"I would have loved to have seen that one."

Roman's face looked alive for the first time since they'd come. "I have it on tape. Do you want—?"

"I'd love to."

In a second Roman was on his feet, going to the TV cabinet. John turned to Velvet. "How about you make us some coffee?"

Okay . . .

She left the men alone and put the coffee on. She hung back at the edge of the kitchen, listening to them talk football. Listening to them bond.

Amazing. John had surprised her. As a preacher, she'd expected him to talk to Roman in Christian-ese, or at the very least with trite appeasements toward the grief-stricken: "Billy's in a better place" or the horrendous "It's God's will."

Baloney.

How could a God who supposedly loved his children take one of them who was so young, so full of promise, so good? How could that be anybody's will?

She was relieved John had ignored any phrases that meant well but caused pain. Getting Roman to talk about Billy, to revisit happy memories . . . it was genius. If John hadn't been there, what would *she* have said to help Roman?

Her mind was a distressing blank.

The coffeemaker sputtered its final offerings. She poured three mugs, putting milk and sugar in her own. Roman liked his black. She tried to remember if John had used anything in his coffee but didn't think so. She brought out a tray, adding a plate of Chips Ahoy! cookies from Roman's pantry. She carried it into the living room and placed it on the coffee table.

"Refreshments are served."

Without even looking up from the game on the screen, Roman took a cookie and bit it in half. "Now watch! Look at this one coming up."

She set his coffee nearby and handed John a mug. "It's black."

"Just the way I like it." He took a cookie and gave her a wink.

He'd moved his chair front and center and Roman had moved from the couch to his recliner. If she hadn't known better she would have thought it was a normal afternoon, watching football on TV.

She sat on the couch and let the two men in her life be men.

│ │ │ │ │ │ │ │ │ │

Roman showed them to the door. "Thanks for coming over." He kissed Velvet on the cheek, and when John held out his hand, Roman pulled him into an embrace. "It was nice meeting you, John. Come over anytime."

Anyone witnessing the parting would have thought they were best friends and never would have known one of them had just lost a son. Velvet wanted to say something about the funeral—that she'd see Roman there—but didn't dare break the mood.

She and John walked toward her car, but halfway there, the door reopened and Roman called out. "Thank you. Both of you. It . . . you . . ."

"You're welcome," she said.

Roman's face assumed a bit of the haggardness they'd seen

when they first arrived, as if the respite from his grief was fading. "You'll be at the funeral Monday then? First United."

"We'll be there," John said.

Roman nodded and closed the door.

"We?" Velvet asked him. "Don't you have to go home?"

"I've put my flight on hold."

"Why?" The question came out like an accusation.

"Because it seems I have business here."

She stopped him with a hand to his arm. "No, you don't. No business. Not with me, at least."

He looked at her eyes a moment, then said, "You're right. My business with you is hardly *least*." He continued toward her car.

Totally flummoxed at how to counter that, Velvet got in the car and put the key in the ignition. But then weariness took over. She glanced back to the house, wondering how Roman was faring, then back to John, wondering how *they* were faring, or if there even was a *they*. She allowed herself a sigh. "You were amazing. In there."

"Glad you think so."

"You surprised me."

"How so?"

"You weren't preachy-teachy at all. You weren't holier-than-thou."

"Was I supposed to be?"

"That's what I expected. I expected a sermon. Instead you talked football."

John ran a hand along the dash. "At times like these I remind myself of a quote I once heard: 'Preach the gospel. If necessary, use words.'"

The quote held power in its simplicity. It also made her wonder if her own faith might have been different if she'd come across more people who'd applied its wisdom to show, not tell. "I like that quotation."

"So do I. It's so . . . wise."

She smiled at their like-mindedness. "Apparently, so are you."

He gave her a smile. "Occasionally. Periodically. Finally, after years and years of being otherwise."

She turned on the car. "Although I hate to admit it, I'm glad you came along."

"Me too."

She pulled away from the curb.

"But," he said, "we still haven't had a chance to talk. A chance to discuss something that—"

Panic surged. Did he want to talk about Lianne? *Had* he seen their resemblance? Did he suspect? "No, John. Not now. I'm exhausted. I can't talk. Can we do it some other time?" *Like never.* She was completely torn between wanting to discuss everything and wanting him to go away and never discuss anything.

She felt him studying her but she kept her eyes on the road. Her exhaustion forced her choice: there could be no talking. She wanted him to leave her alone. Just *leave.* Out of sight, out of mind. She could handle Lianne. Actually, she never had to tell Lianne anything if she didn't want to. After the football season was over, Lianne would be out of a job and Velvet could fall back into the status quo.

John interrupted her thoughts. "I'm going to guest-preach at a church tomorrow morning. Two services. We could talk afterward."

She hadn't made herself clear, and it was apparent he was not reading her mind. "I'm not sure talking is such a good idea, John. Maybe we should just leave things alone."

"Alone?"

"Both of us have been fine all these years, without pushing the issue. Maybe we shouldn't . . ."

"Shouldn't give truth a chance?"

If only he realized the truth was best kept secret.

"Come on, Velvet. Let's do this thing. Talk it out. Tomorrow. After church."

Apparently he wasn't going anywhere until she gave in.

Tomorrow. It was a reprieve, however short-lived.

She had twenty-four hours to figure out what to tell him.

SEVEN

If you need wisdom, ask our generous God,
and he will give it to you.
He will not rebuke you for asking.
But when you ask him, be sure that your faith is in God alone.
Do not waver, for a person with divided loyalty
is as unsettled as a wave of the sea
that is blown and tossed by the wind.

JAMES 1:5-6

Without even opening her eyes, Maya squinted at the sun. Her mind tried to sort out the incongruity of this, until it finally gave up and her eyes opened.

She was at the cabin, in bed, with the morning sun streaming through the east window. Last night she'd been so eager to dive into the unconsciousness of sleep that she hadn't even closed the curtains.

Maya sat up and stretched until her muscles vibrated. She looked down and saw she was wearing jeans and a now-rumpled T-shirt, more evidence of the state of her one-track mind the night before.

She hung her feet over the side of the bed and spotted her shoes. At least she'd taken those off.

The air was cool, a relief from the previous heat. She hoped it would last the entire day.

Day.

What was she going to do with this day away from home? Would there be another day? And another—away?

Yet how could she go back? By now the entire city knew about her desperate deeds. After reading the article, those who didn't know her personally might exchange a few lines like "What an idiot" or "No one needs a baby that badly," while friends and family would shake their heads and say, "I can't believe she stooped to this. She should be ashamed of herself."

Disdain, contempt, disbelief, and shame. That's what lay waiting for her at home.

"And no baby," she said aloud. "No chance of a baby."

Suddenly, with a gasp for breath, the full implication of her own statements hit her with full force. No baby. There would never be a baby. Ever.

Although she'd heard the doctor's words it was as though she hadn't fully accepted them until now, until time and distance—and an attempt to sleep them away—had proved unrelenting. Facts were facts. She was never going to conceive her own child.

She spotted a teddy bear and box of blocks in the corner of the bedroom. Her nieces and nephews played here. This was a cabin meant for children.

Of which she had none.

She needed to get out—out in the open.

She donned her shoes and rushed outside, into the air, under the ripening morning sky. She walked down a flagstone path to the dock. The lake was so calm she could see when a fish came to the surface to snatch a dragonfly or bite of leaf. The sun had not reached this shore, but she could see its progress as a shimmer on the water headed toward her, ready to bathe her in the day.

What time was it? She had no idea but assumed it was early because no one was out and about, not even children eager for the water.

Children. Every thought, every memory brought them to mind. It was like being on a diet and always thinking of food. Thinking about what you could not have.

199

She sat at the end of the dock, dangling her feet over the side, keeping them just above the water. She heard a sound to her left. Their neighbor, Oscar Grady, was getting into his ancient baby blue rowboat. He spotted her and waved. She waved back. The fact he had not called out was another indication of the early hour. All lake dwellers knew that in its uncanny way, sound sped across water and intensified, making a soft sound audible and the most innocent shout obnoxious. Until residents acknowledged the need to make noise by popular consensus, early risers were respectful.

Oscar pushed away from his dock and rowed in her direction. Her muscles tensed, wanting to flee. She didn't feel up to chatting. She'd come here to be alone. But it was too late. She'd already sat down. There was no escaping without being rude. And she liked Oscar. Everyone liked Oscar. Everyone knew Oscar. The saying to new buyers was, "Oscar comes with the lake." He had lived here full-time since his wife died, spending his time in his workshop-garage, making lawn ornaments for sale: pink pigs, red windmills, and cutouts of women in polka-dot pantaloons bent over their weeding. Tacky stuff Maya's family disparaged. But Maya—although she would never buy anything for her own yard—appreciated his efforts, especially its intrinsic humor. To know the heart and character of Oscar Grady, you only had to look at his yard. He was a happy man.

And I'm an unhappy woman.

Oscar approached her dock, his boat creating smooth ripples in the water. "Haydeeho, Maya," he said quietly. "Long time no see."

"Hi, Oscar. Ditto."

He guided the rowboat close, letting the bumpers of the dock ease it alongside. He wore a green plaid shirt under an old-fashioned orange life preserver, along with a misshapen tan fishing hat with feathery lures sticking here and there like manly hatpins.

"Is Sal still sleeping?" he asked.

"I'm here alone," she said.

He beamed. "Then you're free to join me for an early morning boat ride. Might even catch us some breakfast. Hop in." He was already reaching for another life jacket in the bottom of the boat. "I always carry a spare. You never know who might want a ride."

She couldn't think of any way to refuse. Or any good reason.

The boat tipped and bobbled as she took Oscar's hand and got in, but the close proximity of the dock kept it from turning over. She put on her life vest and took a seat in the stern, facing him.

Using his oar, Oscar pushed away from the dock, and within a short minute he found a rhythm that let them glide through the still water. Although he was a gaunt man—Maya probably weighed more than he did—Oscar proved to have good strength in his wiry arms.

"Ain't it beautiful?" he said as they sped along the shore.

She nodded. "I can hardly wait until the leaves change color."

"Mmm," he said. "Autumn. My favorite time of year."

"Me too." Not wanting him to ask her questions, she grabbed the reins of the conversation. "How's the family?"

"Super-duper," he said. "Just got myself another grandchild."

Great. More children talk. "Congratulations. Boy or girl?"

"Mandy; she's four and has brown eyes that can melt this old man faster than a fire melts a marshmallow."

"Four?"

"Adopted," he said. "All my son's kids are adopted. Yuppers. Mandy makes three."

"Three? Adopted?"

He paused in the rowing. "You got something against adoption?"

"No, no, but—"

"'Cause Blake's adopted. And our two daughters. And me, when you get right down to it."

"I had no idea."

The oars took up the old rhythm. "Me and my Betty, we coulda had our own, but since I was adopted and saw the good in it, we decided it would be nice if we took in some kids that needed us. We got Blake when he was two, Cindy when she was eleven months, and Audrey when she was eight."

Maya was stunned—and yet why should she be? Lots of people were adopted.

"Yup, me and Betty coulda had our own, but Blake and Sandy—they tried and tried, but nothing happened. When life gives you lemons . . ."

He waited for her to finish the saying. "You make lemonade."

He smiled and shrugged. "But lemonade's still sour till you add sugar to it. Those three kids are pure sugar."

Maya looked toward shore, her mind reeling.

Oscar raised the oars and let the boat coast. "You look troubled, Maya. Confused."

She took a breath and then, without intending to, told him the truth. "I can't have children." She didn't tell him the details. She didn't need to. Those four words said it all.

His face softened with sympathy. "I'm mighty sorry."

Her eyes filled with tears. "Me too."

He took up the oars again. "Well, shoot, God musta had a reason for it. He don't do nothing without good reason."

All hint of tears left her. "I don't see any good reason for us not having our own—"

"Sure you do."

"No, I don't. I'd make a great mother. Sal would make a great father."

"I'm sure that's true. And you still can be—be a mother and a father."

"But we had our heart set on having—"

"Pooh. Nine months of morning sickness and swollen ankles, then pushing a baby out? That's not the end-all of being a mother, of quenching your thirst, of making lemonade. That's just getting the glass out on the counter. Parenting is loving the child in your arms. Holding it close. Seeing it grow. And all that starts after it's born. So what if someone else does the birthing part of it? You're the one who gets to make the lemonade. And the child will add plenty of sugar to make the whole thing sweet."

For the first time in a long time, Maya felt hopeful.

As they passed along the shore, she absently looked at the people's names posted on their docks: Ellison, Mach, Abbuhl . . .

And then a blank sign. A blank red sign.

She turned to Oscar. "Do you see that sign?" she asked, pointing toward the passing shore.

"Which one?"

"The red one. The blank one."

He stopped rowing and squinted his eyes against the sun. "Can't say as I do, but I can't see distance worth beans. Blank, you say?"

Never mind. The boat was past it now anyway. "I've been seeing blank red signs all over the place. Guess I'm going crazy."

"Who says?"

"It's not normal seeing signs."

"Who says?"

She realized he was talking about something more spiritual. "They're not that kind of sign, Oscar."

"Who says?"

Suddenly a fish jumped out of the water, not six feet away.

"Well, looky there. Breakfast. God does indeed provide."

203

| | | | | | | | | | |

Although Oscar had invited her for a fresh fish breakfast, Maya declined.

"I have to get home," she said as she helped him tie the boat to his dock.

He stood upright with a groan and nodded, as if understanding for the first time why she was at the cabin alone. "You do that. You go back to that handsome husband of yours and make him some lemonade."

She began to walk away, but Oscar had one more thing to say. "Remember something, Maya: God will give you wisdom every time you ask for it. So ask. All right?"

"I might just do that."

She went back to the cabin and paused at the door, looking at the place with fresh eyes. It was a family place. She knew that. She'd experienced that. It was her definition of family that had changed in the past hour, and with that expansion of thought came a new hope and determination.

I have to get home. Now.

She made quick work of the bed and was on her way in minutes. Pulling away, she spotted her cell phone in the car's console tray. She'd left it there all night.

Sal had called—four times. She listened to his messages, which were all variations on a theme: *Come home, Maya. Come home.*

She could do that. She would do that. Sal was waiting for her.

But so was humiliation and shame.

So be it. She had to face the mess she'd made. It wasn't going away.

Her car turned onto the highway, but her thoughts were on a roller coaster. She felt herself rising higher with the idea of adopting a child only to find herself hurtling downward when thoughts of her parents intruded.

How could she possibly please everybody?

She passed a billboard on her right. A red, blank billboard.

Okay. Enough of this. She expressed her frustrations to the car. "What is with these blank signs? Maybe I'm dumb, but I don't get it. Not at all."

Oscar's words came back to her: *"God will give you wisdom every time you ask for it. So ask."*

The idea that God would not deny her *this* prayer spurred her forward. She lowered her voice slightly, but its intensity remained. "Wisdom. I need it, Lord. Help me figure this thing out. I don't know what to do, and I feel the opposite of wise. So . . ." She decided to just say it plain. "God? Give me wisdom. A heaping double helping."

She laughed a bit at her wording, doubting that God had ever been offered a prayer with the word *heaping* in it. She said it again for emphasis: "Heaping, God. Heaping." Then added, "Please?"

A satisfied calm came over her. She didn't feel wiser, but she did feel like she'd done *something* toward a better end.

"I'm ready, Lord. Anytime."

She drove on.

Home.

| | | | | | | | | |

Velvet was well into her second cup of coffee and halfway through her second blueberry muffin when she noticed a trend.

The Sunday paper lay before her. As usual, she'd started on the front page, quickly skimmed over the war and destruction that thankfully seemed to be everywhere but here, and moved to the local articles—which were oddly filled with Johns.

According to the paper, John Stevens was badly hurt in a car accident.

205

John Markus was arrested for assault and battery.

John Severin, a city council member, voted no on a shopping center.

John Jalinsky made odd sculptures out of junk and was the bane of his neighborhood.

John Thompson was honored as an outstanding elementary school teacher.

John, John, John. Yes, it was a common name, but it seemed that a disproportionate number of newsworthy men owned the John moniker.

Including . . . her John, listed in an ad on page six announcing that he was preaching this morning at Christ Community Church. *Come join us!*

She shoved a stray crumb into her mouth. *I should go.*

Before she could talk herself out of it, she hurried to get dressed.

| | | | | | | | | | |

Velvet was late to church. By more than a few minutes, if she got right down to it. She was late by . . . decades? Had it been that long?

She knew it was true when she slid into a back pew and immediately received a mental image of patent leather Mary Janes and her grandmother by her side. Decades? It had been a lifetime.

The church was packed, with all eyes glued to John. With good reason. Not only was he a handsome man, he was a dynamic speaker. If he'd been speaking Russian or Turkish, the effect would have been the same. By the expectant stance of his body, the intensity of his face, the deep baritone of his voice, and the rhythm of his words the hearer assumed he was saying something important and worth hearing.

Not that he was overpowering like an old fire-and-brimstone preacher, yelling at the congregation to repent and be saved. He was more like a father or a favorite uncle, sharing his heart and life experience because he cared.

"Forgiveness is a busy intersection," he said. "We need to ask others to forgive us, we need to forgive others, we need to forgive ourselves, and we need to ask God to forgive us."

Fat chance. Forgiveness of any kind was not an option.

John continued. "The best news I can give you this morning is that God keeps the door open. Always. If we go to him feeling contrite, asking him to forgive us, he does. There is no lock, no line, no waiting list. Just him. He's waiting for us to step into his presence."

Velvet mentally shook her head. John was wrong. There *was* a door. A big one. Barred shut with chains and locks. Many locks.

John leaned on the podium, his voice soft. "Just go to him. Talk to him. Tell him everything, knowing that he loves you anyway. Jesus took the punishment for all our sins, past, present, and future—the punishment we deserve. The price has been paid. Our slates are wiped clean because of his sacrifice."

This time Velvet physically shook her head. No. Her slate was not clean and could never be clean. She'd done too much. Years ago she'd chosen her punishment: isolation from any intimate connection with anyone. Every day, every hour, she accepted it as her life sentence.

John sighed. "If you need further prodding, remember this: since God knows everything we've done or said, we might as well be honest with him and lay it all out. As bad as it is, offer it to him with a penitent heart." He turned his face toward heaven and opened his arms, palms up, in a stance of supplication. "And then . . . then he does the rest, cleansing us, giving us the blessed gift of grace and mercy and unconditional love. Hallelujah!"

The applause started as a smattering amid a few soft *amens*. But soon the entire congregation was on their feet, clapping and shouting.

Velvet couldn't remain seated—she couldn't be the only one—and so she too stood and clapped. But as she clapped, the joy of the room wrapped around her and through her, pushing its way in no matter how hard she tried to keep it away. Her breath turned into short gasps and her chest tightened.

What's going on?

The woman beside her in the pew took a step closer and wrapped an arm around her shoulders, giving her a squeeze.

Velvet began to cry.

Yet even as her thoughts sped to *What are you doing? Stop that!* a hidden part of her being embraced the tears as a watershed, a turning point, a defining moment.

Yes, let go. Please let go!

Suddenly, the choice she'd made aeons ago—forbidding herself to be close to anyone—seemed absurd and unnecessary, as though she'd told herself to never, ever enjoy chocolate or laughter or joy or any good thing even though no one had instructed her to make the sacrifice.

Sacrifice. Jesus had made the sacrifice—the ultimate sacrifice. For her.

Her punishment of isolation had been totally self-imposed. No one had forced it on her, condemned her to such a life. Her sins—though many—were paid in full. By Jesus, on the cross. John had said so.

And she believed him.

Someone started singing "Amazing Grace." The music fell upon her, reaching into every empty space, filling her to overflowing.

"I once was lost but now am found, was blind but now I see."

It was too much, but just enough.
Velvet slipped away and felt herself falling. . . .

| | | | | | | | | | |

She opened her eyes and saw John's face.
And others.
Velvet lay upon a pew, her purse and someone's jacket, her pillow. She immediately sat up, appalled. "Did I faint?"
"You slipped clean away," said the woman who'd shared a shoulder squeeze.
Most of the sanctuary was empty, but a few stragglers filed down the center aisle toward the back. Their faces were soft with concern and a few offered her supportive smiles.
"I never faint. I'm fine—embarrassed, but fine."
"Oh, don't be embarrassed," said a man wearing suspenders. "When the Spirit moves, he moves. It can be overwhelming."
Spirit? She knew what she'd felt, but . . . Spirit? What *was* the man talking about?
John took her hand. "Come on, people. Let me take her out for some fresh air."
The onlookers parted and she let herself be led into the foyer and beyond, out a side door, into the sunlight.
"Better?" John asked.
"Still feeling foolish but better, yes." She tried to look strong, sound strong. "Truly, I'm not a fainter, and I don't know why—"

"The man with the suspenders spoke the truth, Velvet. Al-though no one but you can say for certain, it could be you felt the Holy Spirit at work."

She took a step away from him and formed a time-out T with her hands. "Hold it there, preacher; I'm not one of your praise-the-Lord drama queens who faint and flail and speak gibberish."

"And I'm not a drama queen director. Or instigator. But the Holy Spirit was present in that room, Velvet. I know because I never planned on talking about forgiveness. Sometimes that hap-pens. I'm talking about one thing and God nudges me to take a detour. And it obviously was the right detour, because that's the subject people responded to. The Holy Spirit is the one who made the people jump to their feet and applaud. They weren't applauding for me but because God worked within them, mak-ing them feel him, making them know he exists." John stepped to a rosebush, cupped his hand around a full pink bloom, then leaned down to take a whiff. "It's the best part of my job."

"So this always happens?"

"Not at all. What happened today was not an orchestrated event. I said my piece, I shared my heart, and when it resonated with those who were listening, they let God in. My job was to nudge them through the door. He did the work."

He did the work in me?

John was watching her, studying her. "You felt something, yes?" he asked quietly.

Tears threatened, embarrassing her further. "When you were talking about forgiveness, I . . ." She forced herself to look right at him. "I've done wrong, John. To a lot of people, including myself. And I've done wrong to you." She glanced toward the church and saw a group of people at the doors, watching them, talking among themselves. Although she'd been on the verge of saying something—saying too much—she stopped and pointed in their direction. "They are probably waiting to ooh and aah over you and feed you ham loaf and Jell-O."

"They can wait."

So could she. The chance for release had been missed, the moment lost. Everything that had happened in the sanctuary took a step back and became like a dream, something she was unable to grasp—a dissipating mist. "I can't discuss this now," she told him. "Not here—if ever. Leave it alone, John. Leave me alone. Go home." She started walking again, toward her car.

He followed after her. "Does your reaction have something to do with the girl working concessions—the one with the gray streak framing her face?"

She kept walking, though if she'd had on different shoes . . .

Running would not have been out of the question.

| | | | | | | | | | | |

When Maya got back into town she did not go directly home. Instead she turned the car in the opposite direction. It took her a block to realize where she was heading.

"I suppose," she said to her subconscious, who had obviously made the decision. "One last time. To say good-bye."

She drove to the hospital and rode the elevator to the maternity floor. Would she ever be a patient on this floor? Was there *any* solution? Maya felt her thoughts colliding. *I'm getting confused again, God. Help me here. Wisdom? Remember me asking for wisdom?*

She reached the nursery window and spotted nurse Betty taking the vitals of a newborn. Maya waved.

Betty did not. She did not even smile. And as soon as she was finished with the baby, she exited the nursery.

Maya figured she was just involved with an infant and didn't have time to chat. She looked at the newborns anyway: two boys and a girl, all neatly swaddled and wearing little blue and pink cotton caps.

The hall door leading to the nursery area opened and Betty and another nurse came out.

"Hi there," Maya said. "Only three? A slow night, huh?"

The other woman, whose name tag read *Agnes*, spoke. "You have to leave."

Maya wasn't sure she had heard right. "Excuse me?"

Betty looked at the floor, then crossed her arms. "We can't have you coming around anymore, Maya. Looking at the babies, when you . . ."

Agnes picked up where Betty left off. "When you stated in the paper you would do anything to get a baby. Anything."

The newspaper article. "I didn't mean it literally," Maya said. "I would never steal—"

"You already did."

With that, Agnes moved to the double doors at the end of the hall. She opened one and held it.

Maya was being led out! Banished. She'd come to say good-bye to the babies, but not like this.

Not like this.

| | | | | | | | | | |

Maya drove aimlessly for over an hour. At every corner, humiliation dogged her to keep moving. She was mortified at being kicked out of the nursery. She wasn't a criminal. She would never steal a baby. Surely they knew that.

Yet as one block turned to two and then to three, her anger subsided. The nurses weren't to blame. It was their life's work to care for babies and keep them safe. Because of the article, Maya was a possible threat. They were only doing their job in keeping her away. Finally, the humiliation backed off, and the memory of

Sal's phone messages gained strength. *Come home, Maya. Come home.*

It was time. Home was the one place she could run to that would accept her, flaws and all. Yet as she turned in to their driveway, as she turned off the car, she felt her nerves turn on. Seeing Sal for the first time since he'd found out about her job fiasco, for the first time since he'd walked out needing to think, for the first time since she'd run away . . .

She said a quick prayer, hoping God would give her an instant answer. *Help me. Please help me.*

She gathered her purse and keys and exited the car. She tried to fortify herself with a mental pep talk. *Sal said, "Come home." He wants me home. In spite of everything, he wants me—*

She needn't have bothered, for at that moment Sal came out the front door to meet her.

He smiled.

He rushed toward the car.

He pulled her into his arms. "I'm so, so glad you're back, Maya. So glad."

She clung to him and sobbed into his shoulder, not realizing how much she needed him until she felt his embrace.

He pulled back and looked at her face, wiping a stray tear with his thumb. "Where were you? I called your parents, your sisters, your friends. . . ."

"I went to the cabin."

He nodded. "That's a good place."

To hide out.

Maya wondered if their neighbors were looking out their windows, thinking bad thoughts about her.

Thoughts she deserved.

She was glad to get inside, though once there, she and Sal stood awkwardly in the foyer, as though they were on a first date. "Well," he said.

Maya finished his thought. "Where do we go from here?"

Unfortunately, *here* was different for Sal than it was for Maya because he didn't know about Dr. Ruffin.

She took his hand and led him to the couch. "There's something I have to tell you." He looked wary but let himself be led. They sat, and then she took his hand in hers. She told him about the fire at the lab.

She expected him to react, to pull his hand away, to stand, or pace, or rake his fingers through his hair. She did not expect him to calmly nod, or to say, "That's that, then." He captured her eyes with his. "I'm so sorry, Maya. I know how much you wanted to have a child."

She stood and let out a huff of air. "'That's that'? That's all you can say?"

"You do have to admit that the whole thing has been pretty extreme. Sometimes it's felt like we're pushing it, stretching it." He looked at Maya. "I want a child as much as you, but all this . . ."

She remembered her morning conversation with Oscar. There *was* another option. She returned to the couch and took his hand once again. "Then . . . what about adoption?"

Sal shook his head. "Oh, Maya. I don't know." He blinked. "What brought that on?"

An early morning boat ride with a wise old man. She shrugged. "Just think about it, all right?"

He nodded, which was enough.

For now.

| | | | | | | | | | |

Peter opened the door to his apartment to find his parents in the hallway. "Mom! Dad. What are you—?"

His mother kissed his cheek and came in. "William's funeral is tomorrow. We had to come."

Yes, he supposed they did. Although Peter had barely met William's dad, William had been with Peter to the family farm many times. William had often made comments about how envious he was of Peter's family. "They love you wholly, Peter. Their love for you is not contingent on anything."

Peter wasn't sure about that. They loved him because he'd never tested their love. But now, with a huge test looming . . .

He was just closing the door when he heard Carrie's voice in the hall. "Peter!" She ran toward him. "I'm so glad to see you. I'm trying so hard to be strong, but—" He opened the door more fully to let her in. She stopped when she saw his parents. "Oh. I'm sorry."

"Carrie, you remember my parents."

His mother took Carrie's hand and squeezed it. "Your William was very brave, wasn't he?"

Carrie nodded and began to cry. Peter's mother pulled her close and comforted her.

Peter could have used a hug himself.

| | | | | | | | | | | |

Roman heard the front door open but didn't look up from the couch where he had lived for the past two days.

Friend or foe at the door? He didn't care. Nothing mattered. Ever could matter. Everything that *did* matter had died.

I'm so sorry. . . .

The doctor's words continued to haunt him, floating like a fog around his body, his mind, his soul. And yet . . . *Sorry?* What kind of inept, inconsequential, inadequate word was *sorry?* The doctor was sorry Billy died? Neither the word nor the sentiment held any depth and was as meaningless as saying "Sorry" when you accidentally bumped into someone, or forgot to gas up the family car, or were late for an appointment.

Sorry was insufficient compensation for the death of his son. His life. His reason for living. His hope. His future. His—

"Hey."

At the sound of AJ's voice, Roman pressed his face into the pillow. He did not open his eyes.

"Can I get you anything? I brought in your newspapers. You had a couple on the front porch."

Only a couple?

Suddenly, a laugh forced its way to the surface and, with its power, brought Roman to sitting. "You wonder if you can get me anything?"

AJ stuffed his hands in his jacket pockets. "It's been two days and I—"

Roman gasped dramatically. "Two whole days? It's been two whole days and you think I should be back to normal? Should we order a pizza? watch TV? maybe play a game of pool?"

AJ unwrapped the smaller of the two papers and started to open to a back page. "That's not what I meant, and you know it. It's just that there was an article in the paper yesterday about your company and the firing of that employee of yours, and I guess I thought you'd want to see it."

The reporter snooping around. The article about Maya. It all seemed to have happened in another life. "And why would you think that?"

"It's your job. Your company. Your name is mentioned."

Roman knew he should care, but he didn't. "Nothing matters, AJ. Don't you get that? Nothing that I ever did, or will do, matters."

"Don't say that."

"What do you want me to say? That I was a good father? That any small portion of my life has had any meaning?"

"You *were* a good father. Billy was the man he was because of you."

Roman laughed. "Because of me pushing Billy into sports he joined the Huskers, came in contact with a misguided coach who got him involved in church, a church that made him go to the picnic that killed him. If I'd left him alone, maybe he would have been some computer geek or trombone player or science nerd. Maybe he'd be alive."

"He was good at football. It was a gift."

"One he should have returned."

"God's gifts can't be returned."

Roman stared at his friend. Where had he come up with that piece of idiocy?

"Don't look at me that way." AJ sat on the edge of the recliner, making it dip precariously toward the floor. "Think about it. If a person's really good at something, has some inborn talent, then it must mean it was in him all along. From birth. It must mean that God gave it to him and—"

Roman pressed his palms against his ears. "Stop!" When he saw that AJ had stopped speaking, he let his hands drop. "Who are you? What happened to my rational, feet-planted-firmly-on-the-ground AJ?"

"If you really want to know . . . he's new and improved."

It sounded like a sound bite, a line someone would say after attending a change-your-life seminar. Whatever AJ had to say, Roman didn't want to hear it. He punched a pillow and stretched out on the couch. The cushions remembered him and welcomed him back. "If you don't mind, I'm tired." He attempted to get the afghan untangled so he could use it again.

But AJ sprang to his feet and yanked the afghan away. "Don't you want to know how I'm new and improved?"

Roman closed his eyes. "Not really."

"No wonder Billy stopped bringing his friends around. It's not very rewarding spending time with a brick wall." AJ drilled the afghan onto Roman's legs.

The door slammed.

Roman felt a twinge of regret, but it was soon replaced with the thought, *Good riddance.*

| | | | | | | | | | |

Roman sat on the couch and stared at the newspapers AJ had brought in. Saturday and Sunday editions. AJ had mentioned an article about Maya's firing. The reporter had obviously gone ahead and written it, even without Roman's cooperation. The stupid clod.

Roman picked up the smaller Saturday paper and scanned through it. There it was: "Ethics Inquiry at Efficient Office Machines." He read the article, which made Maya sound out of her mind, on the edge of desperation: *"I'd do anything to have a baby. Anything."*

I'd do anything to have my son back.

Unfortunately for them both, *anything* did not exist.

He crumpled the paper and tossed it across the room.

| | | | | | | | | | |

Drive faster. Please. . . .

Peter's muscles were taut. He was ready to jump from the moving car. Dinner with his parents and Carrie had started out well enough and had even been nice, talking about William and what a great guy he'd been. Nice until his mother had gotten it in her head that Carrie would make him the perfect girlfriend.

He'd seen it in her eyes right before the waitress had asked if anyone wanted dessert. One minute Peter was enduring chitchat about school and the farm and then suddenly his mother cocked her head to one side, took a good hard look at Carrie, then Peter, then Carrie again. "You two are good friends, aren't you?"

Subtle as a brick, Mom.

He couldn't remember how he or Carrie had responded, but he did remember saying, "It's too bad Lianne can't be here today. She wanted to spend more time with both of you."

Which, of course, had stopped all conversation.

Lies did that.

He could tell Carrie was uncomfortable with it too because instead of coming back to his apartment, she'd asked to be taken home.

Now, alone in the car, just the three of them, Peter's mother looked back at him from the passenger seat and smiled. "Carrie's such a nice girl. You two should spend more time together. You need each other to get through your grief about William."

He didn't dare tell them that he and Carrie had dated, before Lianne had come into the picture and lured him away.

One block more . . .

"Don't you think that would be a good idea, Peter?"

He put his hand on the door handle, his fingers tempted by the cool chrome. "You can just let me off. I'm really tired. I'll see you tomorrow at the funeral."

"We'll pick you up," his father said. "When do your morning classes get—?"

Peter opened the car door before his father had come to a complete stop.

"Peter! Careful!"

He got out of the car and leaned down to talk to them. "I'm not going to class tomorrow."

"But didn't you miss Friday too?"

Suddenly, Peter was too tired to lie. "I'm thinking of not going back at all."

"Quitting school?"

He hadn't meant to bring it up, nor had he ever, before that very moment, thought of it in such final terms. "Don't worry about it. I'm just tired. Pick me up at one." Peter shut the car door and ran inside.

Before he even closed the door to his apartment he called out, "Hey, William? You'll never believe the dinner I've just had with—"

He slapped a hand over his mouth.

Then, suddenly, he yanked open the door and ran into the hall. He couldn't stay in the apartment. Not tonight. Not the night before William's . . .

He ran out of the building and into the street.

Then he stopped.

Where should he go?

Carrie's.

He was stunned that his first thought was of her. And not Lianne.

There was only one solution.

Peter went to his car and climbed into the backseat. He pushed the old fast-food sacks to the floor, wadded up an old jacket, placed it under his head, and curled up as best he could.

But then, in the seat pocket in front of him, he spotted a Husker ball cap. It was William's.

He put it on his own head and lay back down. And tried not to think.

EIGHT

For even the Son of Man came not to be served but to serve others and to give his life as a ransom for many.

MATTHEW 20:28

The funeral at Billy's church was AJ's idea.

Or AJ's fault.

He'd caught Roman at his weakest, just hours after Billy died. When AJ had asked Roman if he could help make arrangements, Roman had mumbled, "Sure." His only stipulation had been, "No casseroles." AJ hadn't understood until Roman explained that when Trudy had died the people from church had inundated him with casseroles. That had been the extent of their usefulness. Not a single one had been able to explain to him *Why?*

After thirteen years he still had no answer. And now, with Billy's death another layer of *Why?* had been added. And not answered.

Roman had already arranged one funeral in his lifetime. It was an experience he'd vowed to never repeat, a task he'd accomplished out of respect for Trudy's parents. And his. But both sets of parents were gone now, and any remaining relatives had been relegated to sending each other Christmas cards splattered with jolly greetings. Ho ho ho.

Bah humbug.

Although AJ had left Roman's house in a huff the day before, he'd come back today, and together they'd driven to the church. Though Roman was wont to admit it, he appreciated AJ's ability to endure his abuse. AJ always sprang back and acted as though nothing was wrong. He was a true friend. The truest.

When they entered the narthex of the church, a pastor-type in a black robe approached. He seemed to know AJ and shook his hand before turning to Roman.

"I'm Pastor Miller. I'm very sorry for your loss, Mr. Paulson."

There was that word again. . . .

Roman nodded, and when the pastor turned his attention to AJ, he realized it just might be possible to go through the entire day without speaking to anyone.

It became his goal.

| | | | | | | | | | |

Peter tried to remember the last funeral he'd attended. Grandpa McLean had died when he was six, but other than that . . .

His parents had wanted to file past William in his open casket, but Peter had said no way. He wasn't sure how William would look, but he was fairly certain it wouldn't be a memory he'd want to keep.

While he waited for his parents to be through, Carrie came up beside him. "Hey." She leaned her head against his shoulder.

He wrapped an arm around her, pulling her close. "Do you want to go see . . . ?"

She shook her head vehemently. "I can't."

"Me neither."

Together they waited for his parents. Once his mother saw Carrie, she drew her into an embrace, murmuring kind words of comfort. She gently pushed Carrie to arm's length. "You look very pretty, my dear."

Carrie looked down at her pink flowered dress. "I know I should wear black, but William always liked this dress, so I—"

"Then you should wear it."

They found a pew and sat down. Peter had been asked to do pallbearer duty, but until then . . . He looked for William's father but didn't see him. He'd met Mr. Paulson only a couple of times. William wasn't tight with him; they'd drifted apart since he'd started college.

223

No. It had been later than that. Something to do with William finding God. Apparently his dad didn't like it. William hadn't talked about it much, and to his shame, Peter realized he hadn't asked. Honestly, he had trouble understanding such a thing. His parents had brought him up going to church and talking openly about God. To have *that* be a wedge between father and son . . .

Weird.

Not that he and his parents agreed about everything—or even much at the moment—but as far as the basics went, they were on the same—

"Hey, McLean."

Peter started as Lianne slid into the pew beside him. He moved an inch to his right, which caused a chain reaction down the pew through Carrie, his mother, and finally his father. They all looked down the row. They all saw Lianne. They all frowned.

"I'm sorry about William," Lianne said to Carrie.

"Thank you," Carrie said. She stared down at her lap.

Lianne looked past Peter, then leaned forward and stared directly at his parents. "Stop with the evil eye, Peter's mother. I'm leaving."

She kissed Peter on the cheek, then left the pew. He turned to see her walk toward the back of the church. She waved at a woman with gray hair and slid in next to her.

I should go after her. Apologize for my mother.

"Peter!" his mother whispered at him. "I did not give her the evil eye."

He nodded, though he wasn't sure. He hadn't seen anything pass between them. Yet he couldn't say it was beyond his mother to flash a look.

"Why didn't Lianne sit with you?" Carrie asked.

Peter made up an excuse. "She probably didn't want to intrude."

"She seems upset about something."

The music started. It was just as well. Peter didn't want to lie. Not again.

| | | | | | | | | | |

"Hey. Can I sit with you?"

Velvet was too startled by Lianne's sudden appearance to respond.

John, sitting on her other side, did it for her. "Have a seat," he said. Then he reached across Velvet to shake Lianne's hand. "Hi. I'm John Gillingham, an old college chum of Velvet's."

"Lianne Skala." She took another look. "You're the hundred-dollar man, aren't you? Change? At the game?"

"That's me."

For a moment Velvet felt as though her heart had left her body. It wasn't pounding, nor could she feel it beating at all. Time had stood still. Then she had the oddest notion, that God was looking down on them—father, mother, child—all sitting neatly in a church pew. And he was smiling.

Or laughing.

Or saying, "Gotcha!"

"Something funny?" Lianne asked.

"Shh. The service is starting."

| | | | | | | | | |

The sanctuary was packed, yet Roman didn't know but a handful of people. Three or four from work, plus William's roommate, Peter. And that girl who'd come to his house.

Except for Peter, the rest of the pallbearers were strangers: beefy boys who had no trouble lifting—

The knot in Roman's throat would not go away and he feared he would choke or faint dead away from suffocation. He tried to keep his thoughts anywhere but here. Detach himself.

It didn't work. His life revolved around Billy. And when he wasn't thinking about Billy he was at work. And work wasn't going well. The article—he couldn't allow himself to think of the repercussions of the article. Since Billy's accident on Thursday he'd had no contact with work and didn't care if he ever did. Work wasn't fun anymore. Or satisfying. And having to fire Maya ate away at whatever gratification he used to enjoy through being the boss. Billy's death had negated all feelings but pain.

The pallbearers placed Billy's coffin up front. A spray of mums covered the top.

Roman pulled his gaze away. *No, no, don't think about it. Don't think about your son being inside.*

The music stopped and the preacher took the podium. He said all the right words, which didn't make Roman feel any better, but he was glad they were said anyway. Glad something was said. Something *should* be said.

But then the preacher did the unexpected. "I'd like to ask people to come forward and share their special memories and thoughts about William. He was an extraordinary young man and I know we'd all like to celebrate his life." He opened his hands to the congregation.

To Roman's surprise a few people stood up. Once someone started toward the front, the rest sat down to wait their turn.

When he saw who was first up, he cringed. Coach Rollins. The man responsible for Billy's death.

The coach nodded his greetings, then began. "William loved. Those two words epitomized who he was. He loved the game of football, he loved his teammates, he loved college, he loved life, and he loved Jesus."

"Amen!" one of the pallbearers said.

The coach smiled. "Yet I have to tell you, it wasn't always so. When William first came to us he was a different person. In fact, he was known as Billy back then."

Finally, someone's calling him by his correct name!

"Billy was full of ambition, determination, and more than a little cockiness. He thought he was God's gift to football."

He was. He was more talented than any other—

"William wasn't alone in his high opinion. Many rookies come to the team with sass and brass. Not that he wasn't—not that the other rookies aren't—gifted. They are. We wouldn't take them if they weren't. But one thing they have to learn—that any great player has to learn—is that it isn't about them. Not specifically. Not exclusively. It's about the team. It's about giving as much as taking, acquiescing as much as demanding. It's about becoming the best you can be in the midst of finding your place in the bigger picture. It's about realizing the bigger picture includes God."

Great. Roman braced himself for the lecture. His heart started to beat double time, and he rolled the memorial program into a tube. This was his son's funeral. It wasn't a place for a sermon, and this man who'd hurt Billy—

He felt AJ's hand on his arm. "It'll be okay. I promise."

The coach continued. "Can a person live without faith? without knowing God? without accepting God? Certainly. But such a life is a life half-lived. And through the months that followed Billy joining the team he began to gravitate toward the players who had that something more, who believed in God, who believed in his presence in their lives—as well as in their own talent. None of us coaches make a habit of preaching at the kids about our faith, but when we see an opening and a longing, we address it. That's what happened with William. I will never forget the day he came to my office after practice. He sat in the chair in front of my desk and said, 'So, Coach. What's it all about—this God stuff I've heard about from some of the players?' With that one question, that one opening of a door, William let God in."

"Praise the Lord!" someone in the back shouted.

The coach laughed softly. "Indeed. Praise the Lord. William and I talked a long time that afternoon, but I left him with a Bible reference that some of you heard him mention many times since. I told him, 'The key is John 3:16, Billy. Believe that and the rest will fall into place.'"

One of the players stood up and headed toward the front of the church. "I must've heard him cite it a hundred times. 'John 3:16, Joe. John 3:16.'" The coach relinquished the podium to the ball player who stood a full head taller. "And William wouldn't quote it to me neither. I'd ask him what it meant and he'd say, 'Look it up,' and get this goofy smile on his face as if he knew a secret but wouldn't tell me what it was. And so I *did* look it up. At first I didn't understand what the big deal was, but then I read it again, and then again, and I realized how it was the key to everything. If I embraced those few words, then, like Coach said, the rest . . ." His voice broke and he gripped the edge of the podium until he regained his composure. "Soon after, he asked all of us if we would call him William. We thought it was kinda dumb, because Billy Paulson sounds more like a football star's name than William Paulson, but he said since filling out his life with Jesus he felt more grown-up, more of a man, and thought the name William sounded more grown-up." He looked out over the congregation, his forehead furrowed, his eyes glassy. "Do you know what the name *William* means? It means 'determined protector.'"

In spite of his resolve not to react, Roman gasped—as did most of the crowd.

The young man broke down and was helped back to his seat by the coach. While the service suffered this interruption, Roman repaired the battlement that had been breached by hearing the definition of Billy's name. As for the rest of it? Roman hadn't a clue. It was as though these people were talking about a stranger.

| | | | | | | | | | |

Maya glanced at her husband. Sal was crying. As was she, but . . . but Sal rarely cried.

They weren't alone. Throughout the congregation, people sniffed and dabbed tissues to their eyes. Although Maya had never met William, Sal had known him well. William had worked the entire summer on one of Sal's landscaping crews. A good kid. A good worker. Plus, Agata knew William from church. So when Sal had asked Maya to come to the funeral, she'd been willing.

But when she'd seen Roman there, being led up front as the father . . . she'd been shocked. She'd heard Roman brag about his football-playing son, Billy, but had never connected that his Billy and Sal's William were one and the same.

She'd made Sal sit near the back, not wanting to run into Roman. Surely he'd seen the newspaper article. . . .

But maybe not. He'd been busy. Losing his son.

Maya shivered. She couldn't imagine losing a child.

Or, having one.

Up front a little boy was being lifted onto a chair so he could see above the podium. Did William have a little brother? If so, why wasn't he sitting with Roman?

The man who'd accompanied him helped bend the microphone to the boy's level. "Go ahead," he said.

The little boy looked out at the audience and said, "That man—he saved me."

Sal grabbed Maya's hand and they exchanged a look. This was the boy from the picnic?

The little boy's composure crumbled and he began to cry. "I didn't mean to go too deep. I'm sorry. I didn't mean to make William die."

He fell into the arms of the man, who then carried him back to their pew. The man stroked the boy's hair, saying, "Shh, shh. It's okay, Barry. It's okay."

Maya began to sob. To see a child in pain . . . She longed to hold him and comfort him herself. Hug him tight. Make him understand he wasn't to blame.

"Sal . . . ," she whispered. "Oh, Sal . . ."

"I know." He pulled her under his arm.

On Sal's other side, Agata stood and sidled out of the pew. Was she going to go up front and say something too? It took Agata a while, but she made it to the podium. The preacher moved the chair away and readjusted the microphone.

"My name's Agata Morano. I've known William for two years now, ever since he started coming to our church. From the very first he struck me as an extraordinary young man because . . . because he'd talk to me." She smiled wistfully. "You don't understand how rare it is for a youngster to talk to us of plentiful years. Sometimes we feel quite invisible. Yet William always made a point of coming over to say hello. He had the prettiest blue eyes. If I'd been a couple hundred years younger . . ."

The congregation laughed softly.

"And when I got the cancer, William found out and called to

229

see how I was doing. When I told him I was having a few people over Thursday for a prayer circle, he wanted to come, but . . ." She lifted her chin. "But he couldn't because he was going to a picnic. To help some kids who needed him."

230   There were sounds of awe and surprise.

Agata raised a finger. "But—*but*—he told me he would pray for me on his own." She put a hand to her heart and closed her eyes, reciting. "'The earnest prayer of a righteous person has great power and produces wonderful results.' If William was praying for me—and I know he was—then I expect a miracle, for certainly there was no one more righteous than he. We need to remember: 'There is no greater love than to lay down one's life for one's friends.' Bless you, William. God's proud of you, and so are we."

A question surfaced in Maya's mind: Would she be able to do that? Lay down her life for someone else? Especially someone she didn't know?

When no others came forward to speak, the preacher took the podium once again. "I would like to close with an anonymous saying I embraced years ago—one that epitomizes the life and death of our beloved friend, William Paulson: A life of self is death, but the death of self is life." He looked to the heavens. "William? We know our Savior has welcomed you with open arms, and we look forward to seeing you again someday when we join you in paradise."

The organ began to play and Maya was overcome with a sense of humility—or the need for humility. All these people knowing God, doing good works, praying for each other. She'd been so caught up in her own problems that she hadn't allowed herself to look anywhere but at *self*.

A life of self is death. . . .

She certainly hadn't felt very alive lately. But how could she change that into the death of self?

Sal stood and offered her his arm. The service was over.
But the message remained.

| | | | | | | | | | |

Maya wasn't keen on going to the graveside. The church service
had left her drained, as if someone had pulled the plug holding
in her strength. When she'd agreed to go with Sal to William's
funeral she'd expected to coast through it, saddened but unin-
volved. She'd never expected to be moved.

Or changed.

Yet something *had* changed within her. As she stood among
the crowd in the cemetery there was an inner stirring, as if all the
atoms within her body had been shaken from their relative slumber and were bouncing against each other in anticipation of . . .

Of what?

Of something happening, something for the better.

But it wasn't a simple anticipation like being excited to go on
a trip or the anticipation that went along with waiting for a special celebration. It was deeper, richer, more intense, as though
something beyond her fathoming was possible if only . . .

If only what?

For she also had the feeling that *she* had to do something in
order for this amazing something to occur. But how could she
do it if she didn't know what was coming and didn't know what
she was supposed to do?

Just ask.

The words seemed so clearly pronounced that Maya looked
to Sal.

"What?" he said.

"Did you say something?"

"No."

She saw his eyes stray past her. Then he bumped her shoulder with his and nodded in that direction. The little boy, Barry, was being led to the place on the grass beside them. He looked up at Maya and she offered him a wistful smile. Then there was a bit of commotion as Roman was led to a chair by the grave.

"Is that William's daddy?" Barry asked his chaperone.

"Yes," the man said.

"He must be sad."

"Yes, I'm sure he is."

"William told us they used to play football together. He let us play with his very own football."

"That was nice of him."

The preacher took his place by the grave, ready to begin the final service.

Barry continued. "William's daddy . . . God lost his Son too. He understands what it feels like."

The man pulled Barry to his side. "That's right, Barry. I'm glad you remembered that."

Maya was stunned. She looked down at the boy. What he'd said was so utterly clear, so intensely profound. So beyond his years.

Barry looked up at her. "Do you have a son?"

"No. Not yet. I hope to someday."

Barry nodded. The preacher began to say something, but Maya didn't hear. Her mind was full of the simple words uttered by a wise little boy. Suddenly, she felt his fingers against hers, and his hand . . . his hand slipped into hers. His touch was as bold as a slap yet subtle as a kiss.

That inner voice returned with its instruction: *Just ask.*

And so she did: *What am I supposed to do?*

At that moment Barry squeezed her hand.

Her atoms stopped bouncing. They calmed.

She squeezed back.

And the world changed.

| | | | | | | | | | |

Standing before William's grave, Peter felt off-balance. He feared that if he leaned too far left or right, he might fall to the ground and shatter into a million pieces like a glass dropped on an unrelenting floor. He was already completely fractured inside.

233

William was dead. Lianne was pregnant; his parents hated her *and* hated his new major. His parents wanted him to take over the farm. If he wasn't sure about his future before, he certainly wasn't sure now that he was going to be a father and—

Carrie took his arm. She dabbed a tissue to her eyes. She continued to cry as the preacher prayed over William's coffin.

Once again, Peter let her in, encasing her with his arm. Unfortunately, he noticed Lianne watching him. She crossed her arms and shook her head.

Lianne, it doesn't mean anything. I'm just comforting her. I'm just—

Peter's mother took Carrie's hand, and Carrie moved away from him and toward her comfort.

Peter was relieved and looked to Lianne to show her he was free and—

Lianne was walking away, back toward the cars.

I should go after her.

But just as he felt the thought travel to his legs, his father moved beside him and held him in place with an iron hand on his shoulder.

He was stuck.

He was captive.

He was doomed.

| | | | | | | | | | |

"Lianne!" Velvet whispered after the girl as she suddenly walked toward the cars.

"What happened?" John asked.

"I don't know. One minute she was here and the next . . ."

234

Their discussion was cut short as the preacher led those assembled in the Lord's Prayer. "'Our Father, who art in heaven . . .'"

It had been a long time since Velvet had prayed that prayer, yet the words came back to her. *It's like riding a bike,* she thought as they all said amen.

"I should go and check on her," she told John as the gathering began to disperse. "It was nice of you to come to the funeral. I'm sure Roman was comforted by—"

"Have you told her yet?"

"Told . . . ?"

"Have you told Lianne I'm her father?"

Velvet had already fainted once in his presence. His newest words could have easily prompted round two, but as people began to file past, heading to their cars, she held fast.

John took her arm and said, "Shall we try to find her?"

Without making a scene, she pulled away from his touch. "No, *we* shall not try to find her." She wanted to say, *"This is none of your business"* but knew the words would catch in her throat. Not knowing what else to do, Velvet stormed off toward the cars, much in the same way Lianne had done moments earlier.

Like daughter like mother.

| | | | | | | | | | |

By the time Velvet got to the parking area of the cemetery, Lianne was driving away. Just as well. If only she could make the same clean getaway.

But she couldn't. She was blocked in by some latecomers. Oh, how she wanted to honk her horn and get people moving.

But then she spotted Roman and AJ walking toward the mortuary's limo. She had not had a chance to talk to him at the service.

He looked in her direction. She waved and blew him a kiss.

He looked awful. Gray. Shrunken. Withered.

John appeared at her window and tapped on it.

"Go away," she said.

"Not until we talk."

"Later. Not today."

"I'm flying home tomorrow. It has to be today."

The idea that he was leaving gave her courage. "Fine. Meet me at Valentino's."

He nodded and walked away.

But then she panicked. Valentino's had been their favorite restaurant when they were dating. What had she been thinking?

She wasn't. That was the point.

And the problem.

| | | | | | | | | | |

Peter and his parents rode back to his apartment. It was almost over—at least this part of his ordeal was almost over. When they left he might be able to think again. Work things through.

"Do you have homework tonight?" his dad asked.

Suddenly the thought of homework, of busywork, of any work was too much to bear. "I'm quitting school."

His father did a quick glance over his shoulder. "When you said that yesterday . . . I didn't think you were serious."

His mother looked back at him, her eyes concerned. "You're just upset about William. You shouldn't make any rash decisions."

Just *upset about William?* As if the act of attending the funeral could stop the pain? the confusion? the total feeling of drifting, of not being able to land on anything solid? "It's not just William," he said. "I have a lot on my mind."

"Maybe you need a trip home."

That was the last thing he needed.

His mother continued. "Your dad and I have to swing over to Omaha tomorrow, so you could have the farm to yourself for a few days. We've got Tommy Sedlacek coming over to take care of the stock, so you wouldn't even have to do chores. You know how being in the country calms you."

His mind changed. Maybe it was the exact thing he needed. The country *did* calm him. He also knew that being alone in the apartment without William made him cringe.

He'd go. Go home.

| | | | | | | | | | |

Roman and AJ entered Roman's house. They closed the door. The silence flooded in like a high wave, threatening to pull them under.

"I know you said no casseroles, but you could have had people over after the funeral."

"There wasn't anybody I wanted to see."

"That's not true."

Yes, it was. Roman rubbed his face. "I'm done talking." *I'm done.*

AJ didn't get the hint and sat in the recliner. "Actually, you haven't talked much at all. But others certainly did. Everyone had something nice to say about Billy." He clicked the footrest into place and leaned back, leaning his head on an upraised arm. "Did you know his name meant 'determined protector'?"

Roman remained standing near the door. "No, I didn't, but now I'd really—"

"And that kid . . . To hear that little boy go up there and apologize and thank Billy and—"

"Stop it!"

AJ sat upright, causing the recliner to return to its starting point. "What's got into you?"

"What's got into me? My son was buried today. If that's not bad enough, I had to sit in that church and listen to people talk about him. . . . It was like they were talking about a stranger. I didn't know *that* boy. I didn't know William. And worse yet, they made it sound like the kid named Billy wasn't a good kid to know. They called him cocky."

AJ latched the footrest and put his feet on the floor. "Face it, Rome, he was cocky. You and I made him that way. In our eyes the sun rose and set by that boy."

"They said he thought he was God's gift to football like it was a bad thing, and yet they talked about God this and God that. I don't see what was so wrong with his attitude. He *was* good."

"He was. But it's like the coach said about a lot of the rookies: At first Billy only thought about himself and his own ambition. He became a better player after he started to be a part of the team and became a better man after he started to be a part of God's team."

"Oh, please."

AJ looked to the ceiling as if he was searching for words. "'For I can do everything through Christ, who gives me strength.'"

"So we can do nothing without him?"

"Of course we can. Free will prevails. We don't even have to think about God if we don't want to, though personally I think we'd be rather stupid to ignore him."

"You used to ignore him."

AJ became engrossed in his fingernails.

Roman had hit a sore spot. He jumped on it. "I know the real AJ, and you're not so high and mighty," Roman said.

"I never said I was. Never, ever implied. And yes, I used to do a great job ignoring God; was rather proud of it too."

"See?"

"But Billy changed all that."

Billy? "Billy. Our Billy."

"Our Billy." AJ stood, put his hands in the pockets of his suit

pants, and looked out the front window. "He changed."

Roman let out a laugh. "You think?"

"All those times he tried to talk to us about what was going on in his life? All those times he mentioned going to church and tried to explain a bit of what Coach Rollins and the players were telling him? You ignored him."

"So did you."

"At first. I thought he was being an impressionable kid and it would pass. But then, when it didn't pass . . . The speakers at the church today mentioned Billy citing John 3:16 all the time. He did that to us too."

"It got annoying."

"Did you ever look it up?"

"Why would I?"

AJ let out a groan. "You and I are way too much alike, Rome. Or were alike. I used to think the same thing. 'Get over it,' I wanted to tell him."

"So you looked it up?"

"I did. And he was right. It's the key to everything."

Roman had to quell his first reaction, which was to roll his eyes. Nothing was the key to everything. Especially not some Bible lingo. And yet . . . he *was* curious. He asked the question but kept the contempt in his voice. "So what's it say?"

AJ shook his head. "I'm not telling."

Now he did roll his eyes. "Don't be difficult."

"I could tell you. I could shout it at you. I could write it and tear it into little pieces and make you eat it, but it wouldn't mean as much as it would if you took the time and effort to look it up yourself."

"You're being annoying."

AJ shrugged. "So be it. Everybody has a choice, Roman, including you. God could *make* you listen, *make* you believe in him, but he chooses not to do that. He doesn't want mindless robots; he wants people who have chosen him of their own free will." He pointed out the window. "Today you heard people share their stories about how Billy changed their lives, made their lives better, and in one case, even saved a life. You also heard that God was behind it all. If Billy were in this room he'd say that. If you want to ignore all you heard today, ignore the purpose and power behind Billy's death, then go ahead; but if you want to see what it's all about then—"

"'Purpose and power'? Billy's death had no purpose in it and has the power to cut me to the quick. That God may try to use his death for *his* own purposes . . . that's just selfish."

"You would know."

Roman couldn't believe what he was hearing. He needed comfort and empathy, not condemnation. "Get out."

"Again, that's your choice. But remember what the pastor said: 'A life of self is death, but the death of self is life.'"

Roman flipped a hand toward the door. "Let yourself out."

"As you wish."

As soon as the door closed, Roman headed upstairs. This parting in anger was getting to be a habit. It was God's fault. Ever since AJ started talking about how God had changed him, they hadn't had a decent conversation.

He headed toward his room but stopped short in the hall outside Billy's bedroom. He hadn't been inside since . . .

He stood in the doorway and reached his hand around the corner to flip the light switch. The room had no real decoration other than some sports posters on the wall. Decorating had been Trudy's department. Actually, nothing much had changed in this room since she'd died when Billy was seven. Even the blue and red wallpaper border showcasing various sporting equipment still ringed the room. A red comforter did little to disguise the less-than-smooth bed linens underneath. It had been aeons since Billy had slept here and yet the covers had remained as he'd left them. Billy had never been a good bed maker, and Roman had been the kind of dad who didn't press the issue.

Roman started to pull the corner of the comforter to better cover the pillow beneath it, but stopped the straightening and instead plucked the pillow free.

Billy's pillow.

He pressed it to his face and inhaled. *Billy!* He inhaled again and again, drinking in the scent of his boy.

He needed more.

He pulled back the comforter and sheet and climbed into bed, cradling the pillow under his cheek. With his free hand he pulled the bedclothes over his shoulder. Then he closed his eyes and let what was left of Billy enshroud him.

| | | | | | | | | | |

Velvet was glad Valentino's had a buffet. It meant she and John could come and go, to and from the food, and not have to sit and talk much. She filled her plate with lasagna, pizza, and salad, then dove in before John returned with his plate.

"I'm glad they still make the special. It's my favorite pizza."

Velvet's mouth was full, so she only nodded. Maybe if she *kept* her mouth full . . .

No such luck. After John's first bite he dabbed his mouth with a napkin and said, "Lianne's mine, yes?"

Velvet forced herself to swallow. "You're not going to give up on this, are you?"

"No. So you might as well tell me the truth."

"Fine. She's yours."

He sat back in his chair and breathed in and out a few times.

"Not what you expected, is she?" Velvet asked. "Not what you wanted."

"After all these years I guess I idealized the idea of a daughter. Pigtails with satin bows, and wearing little pink dresses."

241

"I doubt Lianne ever wore pink, and as far as pigtails with bows . . . Her tattoo has pink in it."

"Did she have a good upbringing?"

Velvet shrugged. "I assume so."

John lifted an eyebrow. "You don't know?"

"I only knew *of* her when she came to the stadium and applied for a job."

His mouth dropped in a gape.

"Your food's getting cold." To spur him on, she cut herself a big bite of lasagna.

He bit the tip of a slice of pizza, his head shaking even as he chewed. "You didn't know . . . ?"

"Nothing. I'd asked not to know. It was a closed adoption. I knew her parents' names, but that was it."

"Then how did she find you?"

"She didn't. She doesn't know I'm her mother."

John moved his hands to the side so quickly he nearly toppled his water. He caught it in time, splashing his hand. Velvet gave him an extra napkin. "But your looks, the gray stripe in your hair . . ."

She ran a hand along her hairline. "What stripe?"

He realized his mistake. "Then how . . . ?"

"The same way you figured it out. I saw the stripe in *her* hair. And then the last name of Skala. Of course her birth date clinched it."

"What did you do? I mean, to have her there, sitting in front of you . . ."

"I didn't—I haven't—done anything. Other than hire her.

Actually, she wasn't my first choice in employees, but somehow I couldn't let her fade away and disappear into the world. I'm still not sure I shouldn't have just let her go."

"But you didn't let her go. Which begs the question: when are you going to tell her?"

She stabbed some lettuce. "When I figure out whether I should."

"Of course you should. We should."

She put her fork down. "Should we? We gave her up. What right do we have to enter her life again?"

"We've already entered her life, or at least you have. It would be different if she were a child or a teenager. But she's a grown woman, out on her own and—"

"Pregnant."

"What?"

"She's pregnant." She enjoyed the shocked look on his face. "Déjà vu, huh?"

He shook his head. "We're going to be grandparents?"

Velvet choked and started coughing. She grabbed for her water.

"You okay?" he asked.

Not really. "I never thought of that."

"What?"

"That her being pregnant would make me a grandma."

John laughed. "That's how it works, you know."

She didn't like how easily he accepted the notion. "It's not like the title has been in my vocabulary, you know."

"But now it is."

Now it is. To travel from single woman to mother to grandmother in the span of a few days . . . She needed some time for it to sink in. And yet . . . "She might not be keeping it," she said.

"She can't have an abortion."

Velvet felt bad for upsetting him. "I don't know what she plans to do. I'm not exactly her confidante. Actually, when she told me, I confided in *her*. I told her I'd been pregnant and had given my baby up for adoption."

"You were talking *about* her *to* her."

"I know. Creepy, isn't it?"

"Miraculous."

243

Velvet dragged her fork through the cheese on top of her lasagna. It was getting cold and congealed. "Coincidence."

John shook his head vehemently. "There's no such thing. God arranged it."

She laughed. "I hardly think—"

"Why not think?" John said, pushing his plate aside. "What do you lose by believing God Almighty arranged for you to meet your daughter? What do you gain by believing that *nothing* was behind it except luck?"

"I would never think it was luck," she said. "Punishment maybe."

"Punishment?"

"Sure. After we make mistakes, life serves us up a dose of punishment. If God was involved at all, he sent Lianne here to punish and mock me."

"Do you think *I'm* here to mock you? punish you?"

She put her fork down. "Answer me this: *if* God had something to do with it, and it's this wonderful thing you say it is, why would he want us to meet? I haven't been one of his favorite little lambs all these years."

"How do you know?"

"Ah, come on, John. It's human nature to love the obedient child best."

"*Human* nature, not God's nature. He loves even those who hate him. And he never gives up on any of us. Ever. Over and over he arranges circumstances so we have a chance—a choice—to see him, to turn to him."

"Now you're sounding mystical."

"It can be mystical, but sometimes it's very practical. As practical as a young woman in need of a job."

He'd always been able to make her smile. "Do you do this often? See God in every nook and cranny?"

"I do now. But for years and years I didn't see him at all, even though he was all around me, waiting for me to notice."

"So God's been all around me, waiting for me to notice?"

"Yep."

"Prove it."

"Prove he *hasn't* been there." He gazed out over the restaurant. "You know, you haven't told me what you've been doing all these years."

With good reason. "I had Lianne, gave her up, moved up in my job, and voilà. Here I am."

He shook his head. "There has to be more than that."

"Well, there isn't. At least nothing I want to talk about." She refolded her napkin.

"Come on, Velvet. You can tell me."

"No, I can't. I've never told anyone."

"It can't be that bad."

Wanna bet? She set her napkin back in her lap and gave it a shot. "Let's just say after you left my life got a bit derailed and it was hard for me to get it back on track. I'm not even sure I ever did, not completely. I've never talked to anyone about it, never trusted anyone enough."

"You can trust me."

She would have liked to, but she couldn't. She'd spent her entire life being wary and guarded. He might have been comfortable displaying his mistakes to the world, but she was not. She needed to change the subject. "Now it's your turn. What have you done all these years?"

He put his fork down. "I messed around a lot, stirred things up some more, then came home and got my head together, found God along with my senses, went to seminary, was a pastor in a few good churches and a few so-so churches, then decided to write it all down. As you said, voilà. Here I am."

She was surprised to find that his short explanation was enough for her. What did it matter what had happened between then and now?

"We're good at the *Reader's Digest* condensed version, aren't we?" he said.

"I was always into Cliff's Notes myself."

His grin took twenty years off his face. "We were both into a lot of things back then."

She was shocked to feel herself blush. He could be *so* annoying. "Eat your pizza."

| | | | | | | | | | |

Velvet and John stood in the parking lot, her car door open, their time short. "So, you're finally leaving tomorrow."

"I wouldn't have to."

"I'm not sure you should stay," she said. "I'm not sure we should tell Lianne who we are. I don't know her well enough to gauge how she will react."

"But you *do* want to tell her, don't you?"

She gripped the top of the car door that stood between them. "Maybe."

"Which means you *maybe* want to see what God has planned."

"Trick question."

"Absolutely."

"The thing is . . ." She took a fresh breath. "You can't unring a bell."

"Point taken." He kissed her forehead. "Bye, Velvet. I do have to go home. But don't count me out of this. I will be back."

She stood outside her car and watched him walk away. Then, to her horror, she realized she missed him. Already.

If John was right—could he be right?—what was God up to?

246 | | | | | | | | | | |

Peter took the exit off the interstate and by habit turned off his radio. He'd started doing such a thing his first year in college. When he drove home and headed onto back roads, it had seemed almost sacrilegious to have music or talk radio or even noise accompany him.

There was something mesmerizing about the countryside, the stretches of hay and corn, and the creek beds marked by towering trees that no one had planted. Barns and houses dotted the hills, their long driveways offering a welcome yet keeping a distance between what was private and what was public, between blessed solitude and the commotion of the crowd.

As was also his habit, Peter rolled down his window and slowed his speed. It was as though there were a wall erected at the bottom of the off-ramp, a barrier that required a fee. It was a fee he gladly, instinctively paid. It was what kept him from telling his parents for 100 percent certain he would *not* take over the farm.

A familiar tan pickup approached from the opposite direction. Carl Swenson. As they passed, Peter lifted two fingers above the steering wheel in the traditional country wave. Belatedly, Carl recognized him and lifted his hand. The Swensons had been farming their land for over a hundred years. Many of the area's farms were legacies: the Swensons', the Machs', the Sedlaceks' . . . and the McLeans'. Pioneer stock one and all. Immigrants who cherished the land, nourished it, cajoled it, and worked it until it bore fruit.

There it was. The edge of *their* land. A few hundred feet

brought him to their mailbox that held no number, no street, just the name *MCLEAN* perched proudly—if somewhat precariously—on its peak. But as he drove up the gravel drive with the billows of dust marking his path, he realized he had never come to the farm when his parents weren't home. An odd feeling of unease squeezed his gut, like a kid being left alone for the first time while his parents went out for dinner and a movie. The bogeyman came out then. Every kid knew that.

247

Don't be stupid, he told himself and pulled in front of the house, quickly rolling up his window so the gravel dust wouldn't catch up with him and settle inside his car. He grabbed his gym bag and went to the kitchen door, fumbling for his key. He remembered a time when they never locked the place. Back then it was common for the neighbors to come and go from each other's homes, borrowing this, returning that, without benefit or need of a key.

But times had changed. Peter had been six when the Swensons' house had been burglarized and Grandpa Swenson had been hit over the head by the burglar. Ever since then the neighbors had locked things up when they left—though they all knew where extra keys were kept.

The house smelled of familiar spices. Peter took the lid off the cookie jar and found what he was looking for: molasses crinkle cookies. They were his dad's favorite and, as such, a staple in the family kitchen.

With one bite he was transported back to his childhood. How many meals had his mother served around this old maple table? How many math problems and spelling words had been written here after supper as Mom washed the dishes and Dad watched the news?

His thoughts flipped ahead to having his own family.

Lianne.

The baby.

He lost his appetite and returned a third cookie to the jar. The comforts of home competed with the crisis at hand. What was he going to do?

Peter heard a truck coming up the drive. It was Tommy Sedlacek, coming to do the evening chores.

Peter went out to greet him. And help him. Hard work would keep his mind occupied.

But not free.

| | | | | | | | | | |

Roman awakened with a start. He lifted his head from the pillow. *Where am I?*

He saw the moonlight reflect against Billy's sports trophies on the dresser.

He drew the covers aside and swung his feet over the side of the bed. How long had he slept? The numbers on the clock glowed: 3:16.

The verse. It's the same number.

Whatever.

He stumbled to his own room, to his own bed.

The clock in his bedroom now read 3:17.

He was more than a little relieved.

NINE

*"My thoughts are nothing like your thoughts," says the Lord.
"And my ways are far beyond anything you could imagine.
For just as the heavens are higher than the earth,
so my ways are higher than your ways
and my thoughts higher than your thoughts."*

ISAIAH 55:8-9

Peter opened his eyes and looked at the clock. Six thirty. Time to get up.

Early to bed and early to rise makes a man healthy, wealthy, and wise.

Peter wasn't sure if any of the saying was completely true, but upon starting his third day alone at the farm, upon starting his second day handling all the chores alone, he felt more . . . complete.

It was odd how he'd willingly taken on the chores that used to make him groan when he was growing up, telling Tommy Sedlacek thanks, but he could handle them until his parents got back.

It felt good to use his muscles again. Going to class and sitting around the apartment made him feel more tired than awake. He enjoyed the pull and strain of the farmwork and did not even mind the soreness that followed him to bed and awakened him in the morning. As his dad often said: "It's a good ache."

He pulled on his jeans and T-shirt and the old work boots he'd found in his closet and headed outside. He grabbed a couple of cookies on the way out but looked forward to the eggs and bacon he would make after the chores were through. At college he'd gotten used to skipping breakfast and living on a travel mug of coffee that he'd sip during his first class.

Class. He'd missed six days' worth, counting today. It would be nearly impossible to catch up. Doable, but . . . Was it something he wanted to do?

Ever since being on the farm he'd let his mind focus on country things. He'd been amazed how easily he had left the busyness of the city behind.

But not his problems.

Although he tackled the chores of the farm solo, he was far from alone. William, Lianne, and Carrie accompanied him. Thoughts of William made him question what he, Peter, had done with his life—or would do. William had saved a boy's life, sacrificed himself for a child. Peter had . . . Peter had . . .

Messed up a life, a bunch of lives. Because of his selfishness, his desire for instant gratification, he'd fathered a child. In finer circumstances that might have been a noble accomplishment, but considering he and Lianne weren't sure what they felt about each other, or what to do next, and considering Lianne was . . . Lianne . . .

He opened the barn door and flipped on the string of single bulbs that marked the horse stalls. He gave the animals some feed.

The image of Lianne mucking out a stall made him laugh aloud. Lianne in her long skirts, open-toed flip-flops, dangly earrings, and bangly bracelets. It was bizarre. Lianne would never fit here.

Actually, Lianne barely fit in Lincoln. The way she dressed, her attitude, her ideas . . . She was more suited to Soho, Berkeley, or Boulder. Someplace where the norm had wide, curving boundaries.

Suddenly, Carrie's image appeared. Peter stopped his work and let it take full root. He could easily imagine her in jeans and boots, her hair pulled into a ponytail, the tails of a plaid flannel shirt tied at her waist. Although she was a bitty thing, she would handle a pitchfork well, letting the straw fly, never once shooing it away from her face or pinching her nose against the smell of animals.

"Carrie would fit in here."

Peter tossed fresh straw into a stall. It was an absurd statement. Carrie wasn't his girlfriend. She wasn't the one carrying his child. Although they'd dated briefly before Peter met Lianne, there never would have been a child even if she had continued to be his girlfriend. She was saving herself for her spouse.

As I should have done.

Too late now.

He held his face against the cheek of his horse, Lindy. "What should I do, girl? Any suggestions?"

Lindy neighed, lifting her head as if nodding.

A ride. A ride would be the perfect antidote for indecision.

| | | | | | | | | | |

Peter rode hard across pastureland heading nowhere in particular. That was the best part of riding, not *going* anywhere. Not needing to go anywhere.

He gave Lindy free rein, keeping his thighs tucked tight against her back. His mom and dad never rode bareback, but it was his preference. Part of it had to do with his impatient nature. When he wanted to ride, he didn't want to take time to saddle a horse. He wanted to go. But most of it was the way this type of riding made him feel one with the horse, as if her muscles were his. Each stride resounded up her legs and through his, making his heart and lungs search for her rhythm.

Lindy turned toward an open gate and Peter let her go. The gravel road on the other side was poorly traveled and led to a good opening to the creek. But as they neared the fence opening, Peter spotted a lone car on the road, going slow, hesitating with stops and starts, stopping in the middle of a stretch, as if lost.

Then he recognized the car: a red VW bug.

He rode toward it, down the center of the road, claiming it as his own. The car remained stopped. Then its door opened and Carrie got out.

"Peter?"

"Morning, ma'am," he said, wishing he'd worn his cowboy hat for full effect. "You lost?"

"I was looking for you, for your house. But I got all turned around. There aren't any markings on these roads."

"You gotta know the lingo out here. Directions are told by way of landmarks. 'Turn left at the T and drive till you get to the red barn on your right.'"

She put her hands on her hips. "I stopped at one house and asked a farmer and he said that very sort of thing. But I still got lost."

"Not really. You found me, didn't you?"

"Actually, I think you found me. Whatcha doing?"

"Riding. Thinking. What are you doing?"

"Riding. Thinking. And looking for you. I hadn't seen you since . . . and a friend said you hadn't been at your classes, so I came to find you. To see if you're all right."

"How did you know I was here?"

"Your mother. She'd given me her number, so I called, and . . . here I am."

His mother the matchmaker. He should have been mad at her. Should have been.

"Come riding with me."

"On that?"

"It's called a horse, Carrie."

"I know. But I haven't been on a horse since I was a kid. And I've never been on one bareback."

"Then it's high time."

"What about my car?"

Peter gazed up the road. "Pull it in there, at that tractor turn-off. We'll come get it later."

| | | | | | | | | | |

"Don't let me fall, Peter."

"Never."

Carrie sat in front of him. Her legs were a vise around Lindy's shoulders, and she leaned forward, frantically gripping the mane, in the crouched position of a jockey at the starting gate.

"Let go," he told her. "Relax. Sit up straight."

"I can't let go; I'll fall."

"Let me hold on to you." He reached one arm around her waist. "Put your hands on my arm."

"Can you drive and hold me too?"

He pulled gently on the rein with his right hand. "One hand still free, see?"

She nodded tentatively. "Don't go fast, okay?"

"We'll go as slow as you like. Lindy's ready for a walk."

They walked toward his initial destination, down the road toward the creek. "See those trees? They edge a stream. It's pretty down there."

"It's pretty right here," she said. "I like the look of land—lots of land."

Peter laughed. "So do farmers."

"Where is your family's place?"

"There." Peter nodded to the west. "That land to our left—that's the easternmost boundary of it. Our house comes off a parallel road a mile west. You were almost there."

"I'm not so sure. I was completely turned around, so who knows if I ever would have found it. It's nice to have a private escort."

He prepared to turn Lindy off the road. "Hold on. We have to go down through the ditch." Carrie's grip on his arm tightened. Once on level ground again Lindy walked a little faster, knowing the way to Peter's favorite spot. When she reached the edge of the trees where the ground fell away toward the creek, she stopped. "Everybody off," Peter said.

"How do I do that?"

"Lean forward like you did at first, and I'll get off, then help you down."

He jumped to the ground, then held his arms out to her. With the faith of a child she slid down, into them. They lingered—but for only a moment.

Carrie turned toward the creek. "Show me your place."

Peter took her hand and led her over ground made uneven by the gnarled roots of the river trees. The first of the autumn leaves had begun to carpet the path. His path. For he didn't know of anyone else ever coming here. He led her to a large rock, his usual seat of choice. "Your throne, mademoiselle."

She got comfortable, bringing her knees upward, finding her balance.

Peter sat on a large root nearby, angling his body toward the water. And Carrie. "So. What do you think?"

"It's perfect."

"Hardly that," he said. "The ice storm last year broke a ton of branches, so the trees are kind of a mess, but—"

She shook her head. "But don't you see? In places like this, places away from people, the mess is part of the perfection, part of the composition. You'd have a hard time proving to me that that branch over there would look better a few feet to the left, or that bunch of leaves should rearrange themselves."

Peter saw the scene with fresh eyes. There *was* perfection in the disorder of nature, a satisfaction that it was exactly as it was supposed to be and there was no need to change it.

Carrie leaned her chin on her knees. "William would have liked it here."

"He *did* like it."

She sat upright. "You brought him here?"

"Yeah. Like when I came home for Easter last year. His dad didn't *do* Easter."

"I went to see his dad last Saturday. I brought him William's sign—the one he wanted me to hold up at the game. I just couldn't . . ."

Peter remembered William and Carrie creating the sign on the floor in the apartment. "Did Mr. Paulson say he'd do it for you?"

"He looked at me like I was crazy." She checked with Peter. "Do you think he'll hold it up?"

"He's pretty anti-God. William told you how his dad felt about such things, didn't he?"

"Only a little. It pained him." Her forehead furrowed. "I shouldn't have brought the sign to Mr. Paulson. I shouldn't have asked him to do it. He won't do it."

"Why *did* you bring it?"

"I told him it was because I was so upset I wouldn't be able to go to a game without William there, and I wouldn't be able to follow through with it."

"That wasn't the truth?"

"Not completely. I was plenty upset—still am—but I would

have taken it to a game. For William. Yet that morning when I woke up, I had this nudge to 'give it to the father' and so I did."

"We can always make a new one."

She considered this a minute. "It wouldn't be the same. The sign was William's idea. He made it. *That* sign needs to be held up at a game."

"I heard Saturday's game is going to be dedicated to William, that they're going to do something special for him during the pregame."

Her face brightened. "Then his dad will go for sure, right?"

"But will he bring the sign?"

"We need to pray he does." Without missing a beat she raised her face skyward. "Lord? Get Mr. Paulson to bring William's sign to the game." Then she turned back to Peter. "Do you want to go to the game with me?"

Her invitation caught him off guard. "I—"

"Oh. That's right. I'm sure you're going with Lianne."

He felt himself redden. "Lianne works concessions. She can't watch the game." She was waiting for him to say *they'd* go together, but he was uncertain. Not that he didn't want to spend time with Carrie, not that he didn't love spending time with her now but—

"Are you two still dating?" she asked. "At the funeral, Lianne sat with us, but then she left and . . ." She shrugged. "Your parents don't like her, do they?"

A laugh escaped. "They like you." Immediately, he wished he could take it back. Not that the statement wasn't true, but it implied . . . possibilities.

"And I like them," she said. "A lot. They make me feel like . . . like I'm home."

Peter sprang to his feet. "They shouldn't do that to you, to me; they shouldn't push us together. My mom's playing matchmaker; you know that, don't you?"

"I don't mind. Not really."

Neither did he. And yet . . . "I like you, Carrie. I like you a lot. But the timing is all wrong. William just died and you were his girlfriend, and—"

"I was your girlfriend first, Peter."

A bird paused on a branch overhead, then moved on.

Carrie pushed herself to her feet, balancing on the rock. "I shouldn't have said that. You and I had barely started dating when Lianne came along, and you went off with her, and I connected with William, and now . . . I admit it. I do feel guilty. William and I were heading for love, but we weren't there yet, and if he was still alive then it could have happened and—"

"If he was alive you and I wouldn't be happening. *We* wouldn't even be a consideration."

She stood on the rock, peering down at him. Her face was illuminated by the sun coming through the trees. She looked the essence of all that was good and bright and—

"Lianne's pregnant."

A leaf floated to the ground between them, landing without a sound.

"I don't know whether to say I'm sorry or congratulations."

Peter wasn't sure either. "It *was* a shocker."

"It was a consequence."

He was stunned. It was the most judgmental thing Peter had ever heard her say.

She jumped off the rock and went to him, touching his arm. "I'm sorry. That was unnecessary. It was mean."

But it's the truth. "You and William warned me; you talked about waiting, like you were waiting."

"Forget what I just said. What you need to think about now is the fact that there's a baby. *Your* baby. Are you getting married?"

"We probably should, shouldn't we?"

She bit her lip and looked out over the creek.

"I'm not sure I love her." He realized how horrible that sounded. "For a marriage to last, there has to be love, doesn't there?"

"Maybe you can grow into love? grow to love each other?"

"What if we can't?"

"Does Lianne want to get married?"

"Lianne doesn't even know whether she wants to have the baby."

Carrie's head shook in small bursts. "She can't abort the baby. The baby's not to blame. The baby is alive. It's a life."

"I've tried to discuss it, to call her. I've gone to her house but she won't talk to me."

"But she came to sit next to you at the funeral. That means she's ready to talk."

She might have been ready until she saw me with you. . . .

Carrie moved back to her place on the rock. "Is that why you've skipped class? why you've come back home? To figure this out?"

Peter threw a pebble into the creek. "I thought there'd be *the* answer waiting here for me. But all I've done is make myself more confused." He looked her way. "I'm not even sure if I should go back to class at all. I mean, what would I do with a sociology degree?"

"Then why is it your major?"

It was complicated. . . .

Comprehension bathed her face. "Lianne's a sociology major. You changed majors because of her?"

"Dumb, isn't it?"

"Very."

"Especially when I was an agribusiness major for two years."

When Carrie laughed, she leaned her head back, allowing the laughter free reign. "You changed from business to sociology? For a girl?"

"Partly. But I think I also did it because my parents were pressuring me to come back and run the farm. They've always assumed I'd do that. There was never much discussion about it, which isn't fair. Shouldn't I have a say in it?"

She spread her arms, encompassing the nature around them. "You'd really consider giving this up? selling this place to strangers? giving away your legacy because your parents had the audacity to trust you with it?"

"Well . . . not when you put it that way."

"What other way is there to put it? How many generations have lived here, worked this land?"

"Four, maybe five. A McLean homesteaded the place in 1873."

"And you're going to throw all that away to do something-or-other with a sociology degree?"

He scuffed a root with his toe. "You make it sound so stupid."

"I just want you to recognize what you have before you throw it away."

"You see things very clearly, don't you?"

"Some things. Others . . ." She shrugged. "I can't tell you what to do about Lianne and the baby."

They watched the water in the stream flow by. Unending. Unwavering. At peace.

Carrie broke the silence. "Have you brought Lianne here?"

"No. Never."

"Why not?"

Good question.

"Is she . . . Does she believe in God?" Carrie asked.

"I think she believes he exists."

"But your faith . . . You can't give up your faith. Not for anyone."

"She wouldn't expect me to."

259

"Are you sure? I mean, she already made you give up your mor—" She stopped midsentence, then waved her hands in front of her face. "I need to shut up."

"My morals. You were saying she made me give up my morals because we slept together."

"Well, yes."

"She didn't force me. I had a say in it. And I know plenty of Christian couples who end up having sex."

"I know," Carrie said. "Anyone can slip. And we all have the right to choose."

"I chose wrong. That's all."

"But that's not all." She stood for a second time, brushing off the back of her pants. "I shouldn't have come. I shouldn't be here."

"But I'm glad you came. It was nice of—"

"It wasn't nice." She pointed at her own chest. "I'm not nice. I came for selfish reasons because I missed you and wanted to see you."

"You were worried about me."

"But I was more worried about me. I like you, Peter, more than I should. And I'm not naive or blind. I saw the dynamics between you and Lianne. I didn't know the details, but I jumped into the cleft between you. I wanted you to dump her so you and I could have another chance together. That's why I came here. But now . . . with her pregnant . . ." She shook her head vehemently. "I have to go. You can't ask me for advice about Lianne because I'm prejudiced against her and toward my own interests. You need to do the right thing and you can't do that with me muddling your mind. I shouldn't . . ."

She scrambled up the embankment, past Lindy, and began running toward the road.

"Carrie!"

Too late. She was gone.

| | | | | | | | | | | |

"Thanks for seeing me on such short notice, Mrs. Graves."

"I think changing your major back to agribusiness is a wise choice, Peter."

261

"Me too."

"You're lucky classes have just started, but even so, you're going to be behind."

"I'll work hard to catch up."

Peter left his adviser's office knowing his hard work was just beginning.

| | | | | | | | | | | |

Barry, Barry, Barry.

The little boy Maya had seen at the church and stood next to in the cemetery, the boy William Paulson had saved from drowning, consumed her thoughts. Day after day she awoke with his name on her lips. The memory of his smile, his voice, and his touch was her constant companion.

How she'd wanted to share it all with Sal, and yet . . . she couldn't. Not until she was sure. She'd taken her husband on a roller-coaster ride the past few years and didn't want to hurt him any more by telling him something and then changing her mind.

Besides, Sal had been stressed for another reason. Some of his clients had seen the article about Maya and had lumped her and him together: if the wife was untrustworthy, then the husband . . . He'd lost three accounts this week because of her. No, indeed, she did not want to add to his stress level until she was certain about her decision. And to be sure about her decision . . .

She had to see Barry.

Although she knew her parents' opinion on the matter, a part of her also wanted to talk to them. She'd never *not* had contact for more than a few days. And yet, since they'd come to her house and yelled at her, since she'd yelled at them, there had been only silence between them, which was nearly unbearable. Her parents were the sort to call her often, at least a couple of times a week. The same with her sisters. Marta's and Marcela's silence indicated that a Castilla conspiracy was in place, or a punishment. Her parents had declared her unclean, persona non grata. Disowned.

At first, their shunning had been painful, and Sal had greeted her at the end of each day with, "Anything?" Meaning: *"Did they call?"* But after answering no for the fifth time, she found the strength to tell him, "Don't ask again, okay?"

He'd nodded and had abided by her wishes.

His simple act of acquiescence and support had moved her and made Maya realize how such acts had always been lacking from her own family. Any request—"call me" or "don't call me"—would have been ignored unless it fit within their own desires. Of course her parents would hone their desires according to what they deemed best, which—in shocking retrospect—Maya realized rarely had anything to do with what was best for anyone other than them.

Maya turned off the stove and poured the Alfredo sauce over the serving bowl of pasta. She tossed it a few times, covering each piece.

"That's quite a lunch you've made there," Sal said.

"I like to cook, now that I have the time."

She passed Sal the penne pasta and got to the subject that had been on her mind all morning. "I would never be a selfish parent."

Sal spooned pasta on his plate. "I'm sure you wouldn't be."

She withdrew her hand from the plate of garlic bread. "Why are you sure? Because I'm an unselfish person? an unselfish wife?"

He hesitated, then said, "I deem this unanswerable, on a par with 'Yes or no, did you stop beating your wife?'"

"See?" she said. "I am a selfish person. It's just who I am. But I would not be selfish with our children."

"Is there something you're not telling me?"

Maya closed her eyes and shook her head. She wasn't explaining this correctly.

Sal could obviously see her frustration. "Back up and tell me what started all this selfish-talk."

"My family doesn't give me what I need, but only what they want to give. That's not right. Doesn't real love involve looking to the needs of the other person and trying to meet them—even if they don't jibe with what *you* think they need?"

Sal stabbed a piece of penne, took it to his mouth, chewed reflectively, then said, "Yes? Garlic bread, please."

She handed him the plate. "I did wrong. I admit it. But I need my family's support. They can yell at me, tell me how stupid I was, the whole nine yards. But after they're through, shouldn't they forgive me and move on? Not ignore me completely as if I don't exist just because I made a mistake. I called them, but they aren't taking my calls, not returning my messages. They don't love me; they own me. Or disown me. What they're doing isn't right. It's not love."

"They do love you, Maya."

"In their own way. In a way that they choose, not in a way that I need."

He dipped his garlic bread in the sauce and took a bite. "Isn't that the way any of us love? In the way we are able? With an imperfect love?"

"You're defending them?"

"I'm saying none of us loves like we're supposed to love. 'We love each other because he loved us first.' But that doesn't mean we do it well." He put his fork down. "For instance, when you were so desperate to get the money for a third procedure, I should have found a way to make it happen. I should have started planning a way to get us through the winter months by scooping driveways or trimming trees. I partly blame myself for your mistake. You were driven to it by your desire to have a child. I should have loved you better and—"

Maya couldn't take any more. She leaned toward him and put her fingers to his mouth to stop his words. "I don't think loving means giving the other person everything they want. I was obsessed. It made me do things I shouldn't have done. It made me think things, want things, take things. . . . When we do have a child—if we have a child—are you going to give him or her everything they ask for?"

Sal looked to the ceiling, then said, "Pretty much."

She laughed. "No you won't. You'll be a wise parent and give them just enough—a nice mixture of what they want and what they need. But you'll let them know you will always love them, no matter what." Suddenly, tears appeared. Maya angrily brushed them away. "My parents' love is conditional, full of ought-tos and must-dos."

"Instead of love-yous."

Maya kissed him. How she wanted to talk to him about Barry.

But not yet. Not until she saw the boy again. Not until she *knew*.

| | | | | | | | | | |

Roman sat in his office, doing nothing, being nobody, feeling everything. He'd come back to work two days before, on Tuesday, the day after the funeral, but since then had accomplished little other than moving papers from one corner of his desk to another. A stack of pink telephone messages mocked him. He hadn't responded to a single one.

Luckily, most people in his office seemed content to ignore him. He was "grieving" and as such, most didn't know what to say, so most chose to avoid him.

He was fine with that because he didn't know what to say to them either.

He turned his chair so his back was to the door. He faced the window, but he didn't look outside. He closed his eyes. His biggest desire—his biggest need—was to sleep. For the most part, sleep had eluded him. He dozed in short snippets but most of the time lay awake thinking far too much.

Now, his radio played in the background. He let the words in. *"There was a ferry accident in Pakistan today. The overloaded ferry capsized. The death toll is 316."*

Roman jerked toward the radio. *316? Again?*

More proof he wasn't himself. Ever since the funeral the numbers 316 had appeared again and again. First the clock in Billy's room; then when he was back at work his boss had mentioned some sales conference next spring. "It would be good for you to go," he'd said. "Maybe it would be something you could look forward to. It's not until March, March 16."

Only after Mr. Moore left had Roman noticed what he'd jotted down on a pad of paper: *3-16.*

That evening at home, he'd picked up a book he'd been reading. The bookmark was on page 316.

Yesterday he'd had to make a sales call to a new client, and his secretary had written down the address: 316 Washington.

And now, the radio reporting 316 fatalities . . .

Enough of this nonsense.

He flipped the radio off. *You're not getting me to look it up. You're not.*

Sitting back in his chair, he realized how absurd it was for him to be having this battle with . . .

With whom?

No one. It was all a coincidence. A weird, bizarre, sick coincidence.

But what if it's not?

He sprang from his chair, then raked his fingers through his hair. "Enough!"

"Mr. Paulson, are you okay?" His secretary, Millie, stood at the door, holding some papers.

Suddenly, the truth overshadowed the quick answer. "No, I'm not okay. I'm horrible. I can't concentrate, I feel like crawling into a corner, I don't want to talk to anyone, I can't sleep but need to sleep . . . and I don't want to be here."

Millie clutched the papers to her chest. "I can't imagine how you feel, Mr. Paulson. None of us can."

You're darn right, you can't. He needed her to be gone. "Are those papers for me?"

She looked down at them, as if only then remembering they were there. "It's just some sales stats. I thought it would cheer you up to know sales are up 316 percent this month."

Roman froze. "316 percent?"

Millie looked confused. "No, 3 percent." She offered a little laugh. "316 percent—now *that* would be cause to celebrate." She put the papers on his desk. "FYI," she said before leaving.

I'm going crazy.

Roman started to return to his chair but stopped before sitting down. A new thought interrupted his action. *Quit.*

He grabbed on to the word as if it were a lifeline.

Then, instead of sitting down, he left his office.

He had something to do.

| | | | | | | | | | | |

Mr. Moore leaned back in his chair and let his hands drop into his lap. "What are you doing, Roman?"

"The right thing."

"Quitting is not the right thing. You've worked too long and too hard in this company to throw it all away on a whim."

Roman crossed his legs. "It's not a whim. I've thought about this for a long time."

Mr. Moore sat forward. "You've thought about it this week, since Billy died. This is a reaction to *that*."

"Everything I do from now on, for the rest of my life, is a reaction to that."

"I know. Or I don't know. I can't imagine losing a child."

"My only child." Roman thought of something else to add that might aid his case. "And my wife."

It worked. Moore's eyes widened, revealing that he *had* forgotten the extent of Roman's loss over the years. But then Roman saw his boss's face take on a practical facade. "Does this have anything to do with you having to fire Maya Morano or that awful article about her?"

"Sure." It was a better explanation than to tell Moore his resignation had to do with a little voice telling him "Quit."

Moore's eyebrows lifted.

"You expected me to deny it?"

"Actually, yes. Maya isn't the first person you've had to fire, Roman."

"But she was the first person I had to fire after she did exactly what I asked her to do."

It was Roman's day to shock his boss. This time, Mr. Moore was rendered speechless.

Roman didn't wait for him to recover. He moved to the edge of his chair and explained. "At this company we stress sales. We have seminars to give the salesmen pointers, have conferences to inspire them, send memos to spur them on, and hold contests to pit them one against the other."

"Hold on there. You're not being fair."

"I'm being more than fair; I'm being honest. And to be honest, I will admit that selling *is* our business. If we didn't sell our goods, the company would not exist."

"Exactly."

"But our focus seems wrong, and I was the head cheerleader. 'Sell, sell, sell!' I used every bit of my own experience to push our people toward higher numbers. My experience, which was often just as on-the-ethical-fence as Maya's was. The difference is, she got caught. She had to pay the price with her job. But then that horrible reporter started snooping around. Did you know Brian called him and gave him the tip that ignited the article?"

"I didn't know that."

"But do we fire Brian? Should we fire Brian? These past few days since I've been back at work, I've heard the gossip about Maya. I've seen the glee with which her old coworkers are gloating over her rise and subsequent fall."

"Surely you don't condone what she—?"

"No. But I understand it. She needed money. Everybody needs money. But the reason behind her need should elicit some compassion. She didn't need money to pay off gambling debts, or because she bought too big a car or house, or any result of ultraconsumerism—at least that we can see. She wanted a child. Perhaps she was too desperate in her desire, too driven, but having just lost a child . . ." Roman's voice broke. He swallowed, needing to finish this. "You say that my resignation is the result of Billy's death. Yes, it is. Because I'm tired and weary and overwhelmed and . . . and I'm needing something different in my life. Something good and hopeful and . . ." He couldn't even explain it to himself, so how was he ever going to explain it to Mr. Moore?

"I'm done." He stood and offered Mr. Moore his hand. "Nice knowing you, George. Have a good life."

| | | | | | | | | | | |

Roman was as surprised as anyone that the first person he thought about calling was Velvet. Velvet was his need-a-distraction person, not his go-to person to share life's ups and downs. Yet, considering nothing much made sense anymore, he went with his instinct and called her.

"Can we talk?"

"It's nice to hear from you, Roman. I've been hoping—"

"Are you busy? Now?"

"Uh . . . no. I'm free. Do you want to come to my office?"

"Fine. I'll meet you there at three."

Once he hung up, Roman had second thoughts. What good would it do to tell Velvet his troubles? Yet what did he have to lose?

| | | | | | | | | | | |

As soon as he neared the stadium—the football stadium that housed Velvet's office—Roman realized it was a mistake for him to come. The stadium was Billy's world. To enter it, even to remain in the space surrounding the actual seats and playing field, was a test he wasn't sure he was ready to pass.

If he'd ever be ready.

But he couldn't *not* show up. Velvet was making time for him. *He*'d asked *her* to meet.

Nearing the entrance, he began to give himself a pep talk. *Buck it up, Roman. It's just a building.* He had just put his hand on the doorknob when he heard—

"Mr. Paulson!"

He turned and saw Coach Rollins running toward him. He was the last person Roman wanted to talk to. Or see. Ever.

Since Roman didn't care for the man, he didn't care if he was rude, so he continued opening the door to enter the building. Maybe the guy would get the hint.

No such luck. Rollins followed him in, out of breath. "Wait! Please."

270

Reluctantly, Roman stopped walking and faced him. He offered no greeting.

"I've been trying to get ahold of you all week. I've left messages."

I don't want to hear whatever it is you have to say.

The coach continued. "This Saturday, during the pregame, we are going to dedicate the game to William. We're going to have a little ceremony in his honor. And I . . . I wanted to make sure you were at the game. We would like you to be on the field, as his father, to . . . We would like you to be there."

Roman's anger, his antipathy toward this man, pulled up short. "You want to honor Billy?"

"We do. Not just because he died, but because of who he was for the team, for you, and for everyone he met. Fans know about his death, but they might not know about his life. We want to see that they do."

Suddenly, Roman's anger left him and was replaced with the sorrow that was always lurking close by. Roman placed a hand over his eyes, trying to hold back the tears.

Rollins put a hand on his shoulder. "He was quite a man, your son. Will you be there?"

How could he miss it? Roman nodded.

"Go to Gate 1 on Saturday, an hour before game time, and tell them who you are. I'll have someone waiting for you."

Roman nodded again. It was all he was capable of doing.

| | | | | | | | | |

Roman knocked on the door to Velvet's office.

"Come in."

He opened the door.

"You're late," she said.

"What time is it?"

She looked at her watch. "It's 3:16."

He stopped halfway through the doorway.

"What's wrong?" she asked.

Should he make a list? He sank into a chair.

"Roman? You look like you've seen a ghost. What's wrong?"

"316."

"The time. Yes."

"No, the number 316. It's everywhere."

"What are you talking about?"

Roman went through the odd occurrences of the number that had dogged him all week. "It's the number of the verse Billy cited all the time."

He saw recognition in her eyes. "The one at the funeral."

"That's the one. 3:16 in John."

She cocked her head oddly. "John."

"John 3:16."

"The other day I was dogged by Johns, seeing the name John everywhere until I realized the John I was supposed to pay attention to was John Gillingham, an old friend from college and—" She stopped her recitation and waved a hand, brushing her words away. "That's not why you're here. You're here because you keep seeing the numbers 3:16?"

"Not exactly. I'm here because I quit my job and—"

"Why?"

"Why not?"

She played with a pencil on her desk. "You shouldn't be hasty, Roman. You're in no frame of mind to make life-changing decisions."

"But maybe I'm in exactly the right frame of mind to make life-changing decisions. The foundation of my life has been ripped away. What better time to wipe the slate clean and start over?"

She tossed the pencil aside. "Have you looked it up?"

"No."

"Because you're scared?"

"Of course no—" He couldn't finish the disclaimer. "Maybe. Probably. What if it's something about fatherhood? What if it condemns me?"

"Billy wouldn't quote that kind of thing. You're reading too much into it."

"Probably."

"If I had a Bible here, I'd look it up for you. You *will* look it up now, won't you?"

He wasn't sure.

She slapped her palm on the desk. "Roman. What does it take? Neon numbers shining above your house?"

He smiled. "Maybe."

"Don't be so stubborn."

He knew it was one of his worst traits. "What did *you* do when you kept seeing all the Johns?"

"I accepted the nudge. I went to see John. The John I knew from college, who was in town."

"And it turned out okay?"

She hesitated, but only a moment. "Pretty good actually. I'm glad we met up again."

"Was he a boyfriend?"

She blushed. "I guess you could say that."

"Are the old feelings returning?"

"No. No, of course not."

"Methinks the lady protests too much." Yet even as Roman teased her, he felt jealousy intrude—which was unfair. He and Velvet were not an item. Not like that. If this John fellow cared about her . . .

Velvet looked at her watch. "I'm sorry, but I have another appointment and—"

He stood. "Thanks for seeing me. I don't quite know why I
came, but . . . I guess I'm glad I did."

"Go home and look it up, Roman."

"I will."

"Promise?"

"Promise."

| | | | | | | | | | |

Velvet stared at the doorway. Roman had just left.

She'd lied to him. She didn't have another appointment,
but when their conversation hadn't gone the way she'd expected . . .

She'd heard Saturday's game was going to be dedicated to Billy
and there was going to be a pregame memorial. That had been
the main reason she'd been eager to see Roman. She hoped he
would say something to her about it, maybe even ask her to be
there on the sidelines with him.

But he hadn't said a thing. Hadn't extended an invitation. Had
not included her. Had he even thought about including her?

Probably not.

And then it hit her, like a wave of cold water splashing her in
the face, making her wake up: Roman was not in love with her.

And even more than that, she was not in love with him.

"Duh," she said aloud.

She laughed at her reaction, and yet that one stupid word
was an apt assessment. They'd never proclaimed their love
for each other. They'd dated. They'd even kissed. They talked
about . . . stuff—mostly meaningless stuff. But they'd never
made plans for a future together—though Velvet *had* thought
about it. Vaguely.

Thank goodness they'd never slept together. She'd kept her own promise about *that*.

Velvet tapped a pencil in a frantic rhythm, waiting for her emotions to catch up to reality.

274 Nothing happened. No tears. No flip of her stomach or catch in her throat.

Her pencil stopped tapping. *Oddly enough, I'm okay with this.*

And beyond being okay she was relieved. Although it didn't say much for her strength of character, Velvet wasn't comfortable with the thought of dealing with Roman's grief. She had no experience with such a thing and she'd long ago hardened herself from feeling anything so deeply. If she was in love with him, surely she would step up and be supportive, be willing to sacrifice her time and energy to give him whatever he needed to get through this tough time.

And if they were that close, shouldn't she have told him about Lianne and John and . . . ?

Instead, she was handling things on her own and glad he was doing the same. Didn't she have enough problems with Lianne? Not only her worry about the girl's pregnancy but the constant worry about the secret of her parentage. Should she tell Lianne she was her mother? And that John was her—

John.

Velvet realized she was smiling.

At the thought of John she smiled, and at the thought of *not* being closely tied to Roman she felt relief? What was going on?

Velvet looked at the phone. It was not the first time since John had flown home she'd considered calling him. Yet to call him was to invite him back into her life. Into Lianne's life.

Talk about complications.

She pushed the phone aside and got back to work.

| | | | | | | | | | |

Today was the day. After three days in limbo, Maya had taken action. She'd called the First Hope Children's Home and asked if she could come volunteer. Today. Right now, if they didn't mind.

She would not have been surprised if they'd seen through her feeble ruse, but she didn't care. It's not like she was going to grab the kid. She just wanted to see him, be with him, study him. . . .

Nate Blackmore welcomed her with a handshake. She apologized up front. "I'm sorry if I sounded so impatient, but I . . ."

"You're feeling a nudge?"

She looked at him, incredulous. "Is that what it is?"

He smiled. "'God moves in a mysterious way, his wonders to perform.'"

"So I've heard," she said.

"So you're living," he said. "Come on. The kids are busy with an art project. You any good at cutting and pasting?"

"I really don't know."

Nate laughed and pointed her down a hallway. "On your left. The door marked *Art*. I'll join you in a bit."

Maya walked along the hall, seeing doors marked with construction paper signs: *Music, Library* . . . Finally, on her left was a door with a piece of red construction paper taped to its glass.

It was blank.

Maya looked back at the other doors with their own construction paper signs—signs with words on them.

She turned to the red sign. It was no longer blank. The word *Art* glared back at her.

She rolled her eyes. Blank red signs. She was getting used to them.

Just then a woman came to the door and opened it for her.

"Are you Maya?" she asked. "Nate said you were coming, that you wanted to help."

"Just tell me what you need," Maya said.

"Help the kids when *they* need it. That's about it." The woman led her into a classroom set with four tables of elementary-age children busy with construction paper and scissors. They were cutting out leaf shapes and gluing them on a picture of a tree. Intent with their creations, the children did not acknowledge her. She scanned the children's faces, looking for—

There he was. Sitting at a table near the window. Maya edged her way to Barry's table. A little girl looked up at her and said, "I can't get the leaf to stick." As she talked, she held her fingers wide. They were covered with glue.

Maya spotted a sink nearby and dampened a paper towel. "You've got too much glue." Maya wiped off her fingers. Once the little girl's hands were clean, Maya handed her the glue stick. "Try putting the glue on the page and press your leaf into it."

The girl did as she was told and lifted her hands from the paper, victorious. "It worked!"

"Can I have a paper towel too?"

It was Barry. "Of course you can." She retrieved another damp paper towel and took his outstretched hands in hers, gently stroking them clean.

He looked up at her with deep brown eyes. "Thank you." Then he did a double take. "Hey, you're the lady from the grave place."

"I am. And you're Barry, right?"

"He drowned," the glue girl said.

"I did not," Barry said. "A man saved me. His name was William."

The girl shrugged and continued her work. Another boy showed off his messy fingers. "My hands are sticky too."

Not wanting to be left out, the other two kids at the table decided they wanted their hands cleaned too, which kept Maya busy until—

"Maya?"

She looked up to see her sister coming into the room with a stack of construction paper. "Marcela? What are you doing here?"

"Same to you, sister."

Maya stepped away from the kids, lowering her voice. "I came to volunteer. I met a child the other day and—"

"I've been volunteering here for two years," Marcela said.

This did not make sense.

Her sister explained, "I wanted to adopt, but when that didn't work out . . ."

Maya turned her back to the children and lowered her voice. "You have two teenagers."

"I wanted more children. But Craig . . . he wasn't sure, and so time sped by, and now Brian is in high school and Maria in junior high . . ." She shrugged. "So I come here and help when I can." She looked over Maya's shoulder, checking on the kids. "But you, Maya . . . you're trying to have your own."

"Things aren't working out," she said simply. "And the other day I met one of the kids from here." She shook her head, confused again. "I don't know if I should pursue this or not. I don't know if it's the right thing or—"

"Giving a child a home, two parents, and lots of love is always right, Maya." Marcela slipped her hand around her sister's arm and turned her toward the tables. "Which one?"

At that moment Barry looked up at them and smiled. Maya gave him a little wave.

"Barry?"

"Uh-huh."

"He's a feisty one and was even kind of difficult—until he nearly drowned last week. I've noticed he's mellowed since then. I think the whole thing really moved him."

"Being saved will do that," Maya said softly. *Saved for me?*

"Maybe he was saved for you."

A shiver coursed down her spine. And up again.

Maybe.

| | | | | | | | | | |

On her way home from the orphanage, Maya's thoughts were like a hundred pennies thrown into the air. She had no control over where one would land, nor how it would land: heads or tails.

When she found herself on the edge of Agata's neighborhood, she knew her mother-in-law was perhaps the only person in the world who could help her.

"Maya! What a nice surprise."

Although Agata's greeting was genuine, Maya felt a self-imposed condemnation. Agata was going through her own hard times, and Maya wasn't doing her part to offer support. And now, *she* wanted support and—

"What's wrong, dear?" Agata asked as soon as the door was closed.

With those three words of concern, it popped out. "I want to adopt a child."

"Good for you." With a wave of her hand she offered Maya a seat on the couch and headed to her olive chair.

"You don't seem surprised," Maya said.

"It's that boy at the funeral, isn't it? Larry?"

"Barry. Yes, he's the one who got me thinking about it."

"He seems like a very nice boy. I'm sure you and Sal will make—"

"Sal doesn't know. I don't know. I don't know for sure. How do I know for sure?"

"Have you been praying about it?"

"I went to the orphanage today and—"

"Maya. Answer me. Have you been praying about it? asking God for his direction?"

Oh. That. "No."

"Why not?"

279

It took her only a moment to pinpoint her reason. "What if God says no?"

Agata rocked back and forth a few times. "So you only want to consult God if you'll get the answer you want?"

"I'm certainly not seeking an answer I don't want."

Agata hesitated a moment, then laughed. "No, I suppose you're not. I suppose none of us does."

Maya felt better, a small part vindicated.

"The thing is, Maya, God knows best. He knows what he's doing because he sees the big picture. We may think we know what's best for us, or even for others, but he *knows*. That's why it's best if we let him do the choosing for us."

Maya didn't like the sound of that. "Then why pray for anything specific? If you're just going to let God do what he wants anyway, then why ask?"

Agata smiled. "We don't *let* God do what he wants. He just does it."

"I repeat, why ask?"

"Because above all else he wants us to turn to him, communicate with him. That's what prayer accomplishes. And it does yield results. 'For everyone who asks, receives. Everyone who seeks, finds. And to everyone who knocks, the door will be opened.'"

"But I have asked. Maybe not recently, but I have asked."

"For . . . ?"

"A child."

Agata spread her hands.

"But I want a baby."

"Perhaps you will still have a baby. But maybe this child, Barry, is also part of God's answer to your prayers. Or perhaps he is *the* answer to your prayers."

Maya stroked the shoulder strap of her purse. "My parents are against adoption, stringently against adoption. And even Sal isn't gung ho about it."

"Sal will come around. And I do admire your concern with your parents' opinion, but although we are to honor our parents it doesn't mean they're always right. Loving doesn't mean always giving the other person everything they want."

Maya's mind sped back to her lunch discussion with Sal, when *she* had said very much the same thing.

"But adoption will take effort," she said. "Barry won't fall into our lap from above. How do I know if God is behind this? if we should even pursue it? I don't want to cause pain for Barry, or Sal, or even myself, by starting something that shouldn't be started."

"Remember what I asked you first thing?"

"Whether I was praying about it?"

"Exactly. Pray, Maya. Share your heart with God, but also tell him you are willing to accept his answer, his will, and his plan."

"And then?"

"And then be patient and keep your eyes open. God has already placed Barry in your life, in your mind, and even in your heart. If he is supposed to be your child, things will fall into place."

"But what if I misread the signs? What if I run ahead *thinking* I'm doing the right thing, but it's not?"

Agata leaned her head against the back of the chair and nodded knowingly. "If you're truly trying to do God's will and you get on the wrong road, he'll pull you back onto the right one. Just keep looking for his direction. It's not a one-shot deal, Maya. 'We can make our plans, but the Lord determines our steps.' So step out in faith and let him lead the way."

"That's hard."

"Never said it wasn't. But in the end, you'll be pleased. God's got you, Maya. And Sal. And Barry. 'Trust in the Lord with all your heart; do not depend on your own understanding. Seek his will in all you do, and he will show you which path to take.'"

281

Maya went to Agata and leaned over her chair to give her a hug. Only when she stood upright did she realize she hadn't asked . . . "How are you feeling? With the chemo and all?"

"I'm doing just fine." She pointed skyward. "He's got me."

| | | | | | | | | | |

Maya sat in her car in front of Agata's house, hoping her mother-in-law wouldn't notice she hadn't driven away and worry about her. But she didn't want to drive yet. She didn't want to do anything that would distract or dilute.

Maya gripped the steering wheel and lowered her forehead to her hands. "Please, God, I know I haven't come to you as often as I should. And you have every right not to listen to me now. But please help me do the right thing. I want a child. Is Barry that child? If so, give me a clear yes so I do this your way. And help me stay *out* of the way. I know I tend to push things, rush things, force things. Let me let *you* . . ."

She sat that way a few moments, letting her words resonate within the car and within herself. She knew she could pray more, could say things differently, but she also knew she would be saying the same thing over and over. Since God knew her heart he could take her less-than-eloquent words and make them pleasing to his ears. If she trusted him on the one thing, she had to trust him on that too.

She started the car and repeated her final plea. "Let me let *you* . . ."

| | | | | | | | | | |

Roman sat in his living room with a Bible in his lap. He was in the antique chair by the window, the chair he'd never sat in. He figured since he was about to enter foreign territory, it was fitting.

He held Trudy's Bible. He'd found it on a shelf by the fireplace. The cover was red leather, and the edges of the pages gold. He closed his eyes and let himself remember his wife holding this book, reading it with a pen clenched in her teeth to mark in it. *"Hey, listen to this one, Roman."*

The sound of her voice made his eyes shoot open. She'd read to him from the Bible?

She'd read to him from the Bible.

He'd forgotten that, just as he'd forgotten many of the details surrounding her illness, purposely shoving them into a locked closet in his mind.

Roman ran a hand over the cover, finding the cool texture of the leather appealing. As Trudy's illness had progressed, this Bible had become a staple beside her bed. In her bed. In her lap.

And when she got really, really sick . . .

Roman sucked in a breath as a memory appeared: the sight of a seven-year-old Billy, sitting at Trudy's bedside, this Bible open in *his* lap, with his soft child's voice reading to her.

Why didn't I read to her?

More memories gushed from the opened closet. She'd asked him to read to her, but he couldn't. Wouldn't. His bitterness toward God had started even before her death. And so their son—who was new to reading—stepped to the plate and fulfilled his mother's wishes.

Roman drew the Bible toward his chest and bowed his head in shame. Even if he'd been mad at God he should have done what she asked, anything she asked. He shouldn't have caused her more pain by being difficult.

Selfish.

Suddenly the old pain of her passing rushed to the surface and joined the fresh pain of Billy's death. Roman began to cry, embracing the Bible as he wished he could embrace his wife and son.

Another memory forced him to stop. The memory of Velvet making him promise to look up the verse.

He'd delayed long enough. He lowered the Bible to his lap, wiped his face with a swipe of his sleeve, and took a cleansing breath. He opened the pages, having no idea where the book of John was located. The margins of the opened page were full of notations in Trudy's gentle cursive, with some words and phrases underlined and others starred.

He turned the Bible so he could read one of her notes: *Something good comes from dark times. Share it!* He turned the book straight again and read the words that were underlined: *What I tell you now in the darkness, shout abroad when daybreak comes. What I whisper in your ear, shout from the housetops for all to hear!*

Roman whispered, "Oh, Trudy, even then you were thinking of others."

He read it again, his wife's words, then the underlined passage. *Something good comes from dark times. . . . What I whisper in your ear, shout from the housetops. . . .*

The times couldn't get any darker. Roman couldn't imagine wanting to share anything from these times.

Uncomfortable with these thoughts and uncomfortable in the antique chair, he needed to move, and so he pulled the opened book to his chest and moved to the recliner.

Something fell from the Bible. When he bent to pick it up he saw it was a small sealed envelope. With his name on it.

To my dearest Roman

He nearly missed the recliner but caught himself before he ended up on the floor. He stared at the note. The note his wife obviously thought he would find. Hoped he would find—if only he would have opened her Bible during his time of grief.

But he hadn't sought God after her death. Only now, after the death of their son, was he finally holding it in his hands—and even this he'd done reluctantly.

Reluctant or not, he was there now, open Bible in tow, holding a note written thirteen years previous, from the love of his life.

His hands shook as he broke the seal and pulled out the note. A warmth spread over him as he recognized her writing.

> *Dearest Roman,*
> *If you're reading this, I will assume God finally got your attention. Good. Because as I write this, I will be leaving you soon. You are angry. I was angry.*
> *But I am past that now. I do not understand the reason God is taking me away from you and Billy, but I accept it. He knows what he's doing. Please set aside your bitterness and remember the love we shared. Take care of Billy and raise him to be a great man of God. I see the spark of God within him even now. God has important things for him to do. For you to do. Say yes to God as I have.*
> *Love never dies, darling husband. I am with you always.*
> *As is he. Remember: John 3:16.*
>
> *Yours always,*
> *Trudy*

Roman's heart stopped and only by the sheer tenacity of his body's will to live did it start up again.

The verse. Waiting over thirteen years' time, intertwining with the same one heralded by their son.

Had Billy seen this note? Was that why he'd chosen John 3:16 as his own?

Roman turned the envelope over in his hand. Had it been sealed or opened when he found it?

He remembered breaking the seal with a finger. Billy had *not* seen this note.

And yet he had chosen John 3:16 of his own accord.

Roman shivered. *It's God's doing.*

As were all the 3:16 references. It was not coincidence. It was not luck or chance. It was God working in *his* life, trying valiantly to get him to read what had meant so much to his wife and son.

It was time.

Roman flipped through the pages of the Bible, searching for John.

There it was, about three-fourths through. He saw the chapter numbers and turned the wispy pages to number three. He pulled his finger over the lines until it landed on number sixteen—which was underlined by Trudy and starred. In the margin were two words: *THE KEY!*

Roman finally read the words: *For God loved the world so much that he gave his one and only Son, so that everyone who believes in him will not perish but have eternal life.*

His one and only son.

God had given his one and only Son. His one and only Son had died.

My one and only son has died.

Roman looked up from the Bible and whispered, "He understands."

As if by command, an excruciating weight was pulled from his shoulders. He was not alone in his grief. There was someone who understood his suffering.

God.

TEN

A knock on the kitchen door. A pause. More knocking.

A moment later the phone rang. And rang.

Then stopped.

A key in a doorknob.

Footsteps.

"Roman?"

AJ came into the living room from the kitchen and looked up the stairs. "Roman? You up there? We're going to be late for work."

"I'm here," Roman said softly.

AJ spun around, his hand to his chest. "You scared me!" He moved to an end table and turned on a lamp to supplement the early morning light. "What are you doing in the dark?"

"Sitting."

"I can see that. . . . I saw your car in the drive, but the house was completely dark like you weren't up yet, and I got . . . I was—"

"You were worried about me." Roman didn't recognize his own voice. It was so . . . mellow.

"Yeah, I guess I was. Still am. What gives?"

Roman put a hand on the closed Bible in his lap. "I've had a revelation."

288

AJ's eyes followed Roman's hand. "Is that . . . is that a Bible?"

"Trudy's Bible. She left me a note in it." He removed the note from inside the front cover and gave it to his best friend.

AJ read it. When he looked up, there were tears in his eyes. "Wow."

Roman was done with tears, had shed all he had. "The verse."

AJ looked at the note again. "John 3:16." Then his eyes lit up. "It's Billy's."

Roman nodded once—twice would have been beyond his strength. "God's been trying to get me to look it up since Billy died."

"God's been . . . ?"

He didn't want to go into it. "I looked it up."

"It's a good one. It sums up the whole gospel message."

"God's Son died. My son died. Both were sacrificed so other people could live."

AJ sank onto the couch as if needing its support. "You got it; you finally got it."

Roman extended his hand, palm up. AJ returned Trudy's note, which Roman safely tucked away. "I've been an idiot. An arrogant know-it-all who knew nothing." The wasted years haunted him.

"I was slow coming to the truth too," AJ said. "Billy was the one who got me to finally wake up. Actually, I always believed there was a God, even believed Jesus was his Son, but I didn't accept the personal stuff—how he died for *my* sins—until Billy started talking about him."

A twang of guilt attacked Roman's heart—again. "He talked but I wouldn't listen. I got mad at him for talking about God and Jesus. I refused to let him talk about them in my presence. I pushed him away. I lost precious time with him. I . . . He'll never know how his death led me to finally understand."

With a nod AJ's gaze found the floor, then slowly made its way upward again. "He'll know, Roman. I truly believe God lets everyone in heaven know when another person finally believes—especially because of them." He smiled. "In fact, I think they have a party to celebrate."

Roman managed his own wistful smile. "Billy always loved a good party."

"You bet he did." AJ stood and gave Roman the once-over. "Weren't you wearing that shirt yester—? Have you been sitting here all night?"

"What time is it?"

"7:20. Go change your shirt. You're going to be late for work."

"I quit."

"Quit?"

Roman felt an inkling of regret, but it passed quickly. "It was impulsive, and knowing what I know now, I realize it was probably stupid, but—"

"Go in today and ask for your job back. They'll give it to you. They'll understand you were only reacting to the grief."

He *could* go back. AJ was right. Yet beyond the logic, Roman sensed a calming hand on his shoulder. A call to wait. He'd spent too many years rushing ahead, thinking too much, not feeling enough. This time, he vowed . . . Suddenly, he felt a tingle surge through him, a shiver of anticipation as if something else was on the horizon, something better.

"I'm not going back," he said with a brand-new conviction. "It's a good thing I quit. There's a reason for it—somewhere. Somehow."

AJ laughed. "God got you good, didn't he? He took out the big guns and is working on you with both barrels blazing."

That's exactly what it felt like. "I guess he is."

"You seem pretty calm about it. Almost serene. And let me tell you, I have never, ever seen you serene."

Roman tested a deep breath. AJ was right. He'd never felt like this before. And it wasn't playacting; this serenity was not contrived or put on. It came from the inside out. "I think I am serene. Peaceful."

AJ pointed to the Bible. "There's another one in John I like." He cleared his throat. "'I am leaving you with a gift—peace of mind and heart. And the peace I give is a gift the world cannot give. So don't be troubled or afraid.'"

Roman smiled. "That's it. That's what I feel."

AJ held out his hand. "Let me shake the hand of a new brother in Christ."

But when Roman held out his hand, AJ pulled him to his feet and into an embrace. "Welcome to the club, Roman."

| | | | | | | | | | | |

Soon after AJ left, Roman experienced a surge of energy. He set Trudy's Bible in a place of honor on the coffee table, took a shower, got dressed and shaved, and made himself a breakfast of bacon and eggs. And coffee. Lots of coffee.

Feeling revived, he began to clean his house—which had been completely ignored for over a week. As he vacuumed the living room, he spotted something against the wall near the antique chair.

He pulled it out. It was the rolled-up sign Billy's girlfriend had brought over.

"There you are again," he said to the words.

Billy had made this sign; Billy's own two hands had cut this red vinyl and painted the bold white letters.

Then Roman remembered that before tomorrow's game they were having a memorial for Billy.

The girlfriend's voice came back to him: *"Where else do you have eighty thousand people gathered together, facing each other?"*

At that moment, Roman knew what he was going to do. What he had to do. 291

| | | | | | | | | | | |

Velvet sat on the floor just outside the open closet. A box of old pictures sat front and center, its contents divided between the nos, tossed on the floor, and the maybes, yet to be gone through. She held a stack of twenty-some snapshots in her hands, flipping through them, looking for the *one*.

She did a double take on a picture of herself in a knee-length knit top over leggings. The shoulder pads made her look like a linebacker. But it was the hair that screamed the eighties. Her gray streak was accentuated against her dark hair by ridiculous amounts of hair spray. She looked like a cockatoo with head feathers. How had John ever been attracted to her? Love was certainly blind.

She moved on, still needing to find—

"Aha!" She held on to her prize and let the other pictures fall away. There he was, his own hair fluffy and swept to the side, like Tom Cruise in *Rain Man*—though John's twinkle in his eye and smile had Tom Cruise beat. She'd been a sucker for that twinkle and smile. The photo had John standing next to Velvet, his arm draped around her shoulder. Her head leaned toward his, proclaiming their intimacy.

Velvet ran a finger across the curve of his face, suddenly wistful that he wasn't present so she could exercise the same gesture in person, on his person.

This thought surprised her. How could she have fallen for

him again? She wasn't searching for love. She'd long ago given up on such a notion.

At the bottom corner of the photograph was a date: *SEPT 12, 1984*. Velvet did the math. . . . *I was two months pregnant with Lianne.*

She looked at the photo with new eyes. Although her left hand was hidden around John's waist, her right hand was spread a bit oddly across her abdomen, as if even then protecting her child.

Was this the last photo they'd taken together? For it was only two weeks later that she'd told him the news. A week after that he'd left.

He was sorry about that. He'd said as much the other day. But was he as sorry as she was?

"We might have eventually gotten married if only . . ."

I hadn't gotten pregnant.

That crisis had cut short the possibility of them. Too soon they'd been forced out of romance and into reality. "I've been alone ever since."

A crowd of male faces flashed through her mind, challenging her statement. She shoved them away. They didn't count.

She stroked John's face once more and focused on good thoughts—thoughts full of possibilities. . . .

| | | | | | | | | | |

The first thing Velvet did at work was to place the photograph of her and John on her desk, wedging it into an existing framed photo of Longs Peak in Colorado, taken ten years ago during a vacation. Although the photo would have fit *into* the frame, she wasn't ready for that. Its temporary status on the outside of the glass was enough.

For now.

She pushed the frame to the far corner of the desk. Enough

nostalgia—and wishful thinking; she had to get to work. Tomorrow was another game day and—

"Knock-knock."

Velvet was surprised to see Lianne. "You're up bright and early—a day early. The game's tomorrow. So, what's up?"

"I need a job."

Velvet didn't understand. "You have a job."

Lianne took a seat in the guest chair. "I need a full-time job."

"Won't that interfere with school?"

"Completely. Which is why I'm quitting school."

"Whoa there, girl. Back up. What's happening?"

"The baby is what's happening."

Velvet was very relieved there was no more talk of abortion. Her grandchild would be born. "You can still go to class and be pregnant. As you yourself stated, this isn't the fifties. You will not be shunned."

"I know that, but since the father doesn't want anything to do with me, I'm going to be responsible and—"

"He won't marry you? He rejected you?"

"He's made it clear enough that I'm not number one on his chick list."

"I'm sorry to hear that."

She shrugged. "Actually, I'm not entirely sure I'm going to keep the baby—I've never thought of myself as the mother type. I had big plans to go to Africa or Asia, work in the Peace Corps, change the world."

Velvet nearly choked. She couldn't believe what she was hearing. She'd had similar dreams when she was in college. Dreams quashed by a baby and the life she'd chosen as her punishment.

"It's not that bizarre," Lianne said. "Lots of people want to change the world."

"Some people," Velvet managed. "And some say the words but

don't have a plan. At least you have a plan. That makes it an admirable goal."

"Maybe," Lianne said. "But I can't go if I have a baby. Actually I could go if I *have* the baby but don't actually *keep* the baby, but . . ." She suddenly leaned her elbows on the top of the desk and pushed her fingers through her hair. "To say I'm confused is an understatement."

Her movement caused some files to inch to the right, bumping into the photo frame, which made the new addition fall from its temporary stand.

"Oops," Lianne said, reaching for it. "Sorry."

"It's—"

Lianne's eyes locked on the picture. Then she looked at Velvet, then down at the picture again. "This is you."

Velvet put her hand out to take the picture back. "A long time ago."

"You have a gray streak in your hair."

Velvet's insides crashed. She withdrew her hand. This was it. *The* moment, appearing without announcement or fanfare. "I did. When I was young." She swallowed hard and was surprised to realize she wanted to complete the sentence with *just like you.*

Lianne returned her attention to the photo, staring at it. "Is this that man you were with at the funeral?"

"John. Yes."

"Were you married?"

"No. But we might have. If only . . ."

Lianne looked up, her eyes intense. "You told me you had a baby once. Out of wedlock."

There was a surreal feeling to the moment, as if it had always been sitting within time, waiting for actual time to catch up to it. "I did."

"Was it his baby?"

Velvet's heart threatened to come out of her chest. "Yes."

"You put your baby up for adoption."

"Yes."

"*I* was adopted."

Velvet lost her ability to form a word. She just sat there, hoping her silence would speak for her yet afraid it would do just that.

"What's your baby's birthday?"

Velvet felt her composure begin to crumble like a building shaken by an earthquake, with little bits of brick and mortar falling away from their once-stable foundation. Any minute she risked turning into a worthless pile of rubble. And yet . . . this moment was too important to let it be engulfed in an unrestrained tumble of emotion.

She cleared her throat. "What's yours?"

She watched Lianne suffer a slow swallow. "April—"

"Tenth. Nineteen eighty—"

"Five."

They took a deep breath, in concert, as if it were directed. Velvet wasn't sure what to do next, say next. The truth floated in the air between them, theirs for the taking. Would it be completely real until one of them said it out loud?

To make it so, she took the next step. "Yes. It's true. You are my daughter, Lianne. I am your mother."

Lianne let out a long breath, as if she had been saving it for days. For years. "This is . . . this isn't . . . You didn't invite me to come to this place in order to meet me. I came here to apply for the job—by chance."

Velvet shook her head vehemently. Although she'd never been one to ascribe divine intervention to life's happenings, in this case . . . "It was not chance. It just couldn't be. You were *brought* here, led here. By . . . by God? That's where the evidence points. We were brought together."

Lianne looked at the picture again. "After all these years."

"After all these years."

Lianne looked up. "Did you search for me? Or did you know where I was?"

Velvet's sins of omission stepped into line. "I knew you were adopted by a family in town. I knew their last name. But I didn't . . ."

"You didn't want to see me."

Velvet was just about to admit as much, but suddenly the acknowledgment seemed false. *Had* she wanted to see Lianne?

She'd pretended she didn't care, didn't want to know about her child, but now . . . flickers of memories materialized, sheer seconds from her past that were heavy with longing, envy, concern, and ache for the child that was no longer hers. She *had* wanted to know about Lianne, but she hadn't dared pursue it. Giving her up once had been hard enough, but giving her up over and over and over . . .

It would have been unbearable.

Suddenly, what had seemed like an act of strength was now revealed for its true core. "I was a coward, Lianne. I cared about you. I loved you. But I didn't dare have contact—even if it would have been allowed. It would have hurt too much to see you, hold you, talk to you, and then watch you go back, again and again, into another mother's arms." Velvet's voice broke and she struggled to keep the tears contained. "You were my child and yet, I knew I couldn't . . . I loved you so much that I had to give you up, so you could be happy." Yes, that had been her goal. Her child's happiness had driven her.

"You could have taken care of me as a single mother."

On this point Velvet could be adamant. "No, I couldn't have. I may have had the instinctive love of a mother, the good intentions of a mother, but neither of those pays the rent or keeps a baby fed. And to my own shame . . ." She sighed. She hated to admit this next but had to get it out in the open. "Neither of those things—love or good intentions—could overshadow *my* big plans." She sighed and looked around her office. "I never, ever expected to still be working *here* after all these years."

"What were your plans?"

"I . . ." She shook her head, knowing how contrived it would sound. How convenient. "I wanted to travel the world with . . ." She needed a fresh breath to finish it. "I wanted to join the Peace Corps."

Lianne's eyebrows rose. "No. No way."

Velvet nodded. "When you told me your dreams of the Peace Corps I nearly choked at the irony of it."

"The destiny of it."

Yes. That too.

Suddenly, Lianne pegged a finger to the photo. "If this is the baby's father, then he's *my* father."

"His name is John Gillingham. He's a . . ." She thought about what occupation would make Lianne think best about him. "He's a writer." She spotted the copy of his book under a pile of papers and pulled it out. "He wrote this book."

Lianne turned to the back cover, to the photo. "He's handsome. More handsome now than in the picture."

"He's aged quite well."

"I have his eyes."

"Yes, you do."

Velvet waited while Lianne read the back cover—his biography.

"It says here he's a pastor."

"Well, yes."

She considered this a minute. "*That's* ironic."

"Why?"

"Because I think church is hooey."

"That's a little strong."

"Do you go to church?"

Velvet fingered the corner of a pile of papers, making them come into line. "I don't think church is hooey." And she went to church last Sunday. Did that count?

Lianne moved on. "It doesn't sound like he ever married."

"He's been busy."

She pointed to the title. "Making mistakes."

"We all make mistakes."

"Were we a mistake to him? Was I a mistake?"

Velvet wanted to lie, and she *hadn't* read the book yet. But John had implied their situation was mentioned. "Our story is in the book—disguised, but there. I haven't read it yet but—"

Lianne pulled the book to her chest. "Can I read it?"

If only Velvet knew what it said . . .

"I need to read it."

"Go ahead," Velvet said. "At your own risk."

Lianne put the book back on the desk and let her hand linger upon it. "I'll buy my own copy. You need this one."

Velvet wasn't so sure.

Lianne bit her lip, thinking. "It said he lives in San Diego. But he was here. With you. Has he moved here? Are you back together?"

"He was here for book signings and for a speaking engagement." She nearly added, *And to find you,* but quickly decided that was John's point to make. "He went home Tuesday."

"Will he be back?"

"I don't know."

"Do you want him to come back?"

"I don't know." Velvet hated that she'd said that. She *did* want him back. Why was it so hard for her to admit it?

"I want him here," Lianne said. "I want to talk to him. I want to find out why he wouldn't marry you."

Velvet came to John's defense. "He was young, Lianne. Immature. He made a mistake." Velvet pointed at the book. "Mistakes. He told me he's sorry."

"He needs to tell *me* he's sorry."

"He wanted to but I—"

Her eyes grew wide. "So he knows I'm his daughter?"

Velvet ran a hand along the edge of her own hair. "The streak. He recognized it too."

Lianne sat very still, staring at her lap. "Was he disappointed finding . . . was he disappointed it was me?"

Velvet hedged. She didn't want their relationship to start on lies, yet she also didn't want to hurt her daughter. "He wants to meet you and get to know you."

Suddenly, the tough girl that was Lianne melded into an insecure little girl. "Really? You're not just saying that?"

"Really."

"Would you call him? ask him to come?"

"Now?"

"Now." She was a child, begging for her heart's desire.

Although Velvet pretended to drag her feet, inside she was excited to have an excuse, a reason, a chance to call John.

"You have his number, don't you?"

Velvet retrieved a business card he'd given her. On the back was his home number.

Lianne reached for the phone, handing it to her mother.

"You are a pushy thing, aren't you?"

"Like mother like daughter."

What a wonderful saying.

| | | | | | | | | | |

Velvet was surprised John answered on the second ring. "Hi, John. This is—"

"Velvet! I'm so glad you called."

Really? "Actually, I'm calling for someone else . . . well, actually for me too, but . . ." She was muffing this.

"Just tell him," Lianne whispered.

"Lianne knows I'm her mother and you're her father and she wants to meet you."

Silence on the line.

"John?"

"How's today at 5:27 sound?"

"Why 5:27?"

"My flight to Lincoln. That's when it gets in."

"You were already coming?"

He hesitated a moment "I . . ."

"What?"

"I hesitate to say this because I don't want to scare you off, but I missed you, Velvet. I need to see you. And now . . . now I have more reason to come. Will you pick me up?"

Velvet knew she could answer for the two of them. "We'll be there." She hung up. "You'll never believe it."

That God. He was really something.

| | | | | | | | | | |

This is getting to be a habit.

Peter sat in his car in front of Lianne's apartment.

Waiting.

For her.

They had to talk. He had to tell her about changing his major back, about his decision to be a farmer. But he also had to convince her to get married. For the baby. He'd provide well for them. He wasn't sure exactly how it would work while they were both still in school, but at least it was a plan. Or part of one.

Just when he'd nearly given up, her car pulled up front.

He got out and hurried toward her. "Hey," he said, swinging her car door wide.

"So you still exist."

"Of course I—"

She got out of the car, brushing past him. "I figured you'd run off with Mama's choice and I'd never see you again."

He was a little confused. "Carrie?"

Lianne headed up the front walk. "At the funeral all of you made it very clear she was acceptable, and I was . . ." She stopped and faced him, a finger to her chin as though thinking. "Scum? White trash? A freak with a tattoo and a nose ring? You discarded me like a fast-food wrapper." She turned away and entered the building. "And pouncing on your best friend's girlfriend—at his funeral. Tacky, McLean. Very tacky."

The door nearly hit Peter in the face. "We—I—didn't discard you. I wouldn't do that. Why do you think I'm waiting for you?"

Lianne took the steps to the second floor two at a time. "I'm sure I wouldn't know. Or care." She put a key in the lock and went inside but barred his entrance. "Go away, McLean. I've got it handled."

She started to close the door the rest of the way, but Peter grabbed it within an inch of his knuckle's sacrifice. He pushed the door open but did not enter. "Stop this," he said.

She hung her purse on a wobbly hall tree. "Why should I?"

"Because this isn't your problem; it's our problem."

"This isn't a problem at all. It's called a baby."

Her statement flooded him with relief. "So you are going to have it?"

"Call me stupid."

"I call you courageous. And good."

She laughed and headed to the kitchen, getting herself a glass of water. Peter entered the apartment and shut the door behind him. He waited for her to throw him out.

Instead she leaned against the counter and drank the water. "So. Now that you know I'm not doing the nasty deed, that the baby's safe with me, you can go."

He kept his distance but for a single step toward her. "I'm glad you're having the baby. Very glad. But I'm not going. I can't. I'm the father."

"How do you know?"

He lost the step he had gained.

She poured the rest of the water into the sink, opened a cupboard, and took out a jar of peanut butter. "You're not the only fish in the sea, Peter McLean, nor the only interested party. You may have been a virgin when we had sex, but I certainly wasn't." She got a spoon out of a drawer, then studied him. "You don't look relieved. I thought you would look relieved if I implied you were off the fatherdom hook."

She was right. Shouldn't he feel relieved?

Lianne set the spoon aside and swabbed a finger through the jar of peanut butter, as if this were the way she'd planned to eat it all along. "Could it be you want this baby?"

"No. I mean yes, I want you to have it, but I certainly would never have chosen this, and . . ." He wasn't making himself clear.

Could he make himself clear? Were his thoughts clear? He decided to tell her what he came to tell her. "I've been out of town, at the farm. Thinking."

"Woo-hoo. Let's have a party to celebrate."

He kept going. "You'd like it out there; I know you would. It's incredibly peaceful and beautiful and—"

She put the jar of peanut butter on the counter. "And what makes you think I would ever—ever—enjoy life on a farm?"

Actually, he didn't think that, but he had to say something. "You like . . . you're kind of a back-to-basics kind of person."

"Because I . . . do what?"

He looked around her apartment, which was a studio with one big room and a tiny bath. "Because you like to live simply. You don't require things."

She shook her head incredulously. "I don't have things because I can't afford things. But even if you're right—which you might be—doesn't mean I want to be stuck out in the country in some dilapidated farmhouse."

"Our house may be old, but it's not dilapidated."

She rolled her eyes. "You're missing my point. I want to see the world. I want to change the world, McLean. I want to provide faraway people with some of the basics we take for granted."

He'd heard her talk about joining the Peace Corps before, but he'd always thought it was just talk, an exaggeration, the symbol of her wanting to escape anywhere else when things weren't going her way.

And yet . . . if she wanted to leave the country . . .

"You can't take the baby with you."

"You're right. Which is why I'm going to put the baby up for adoption."

"You're going to give the baby away?"

"To let someone else raise it. Yes. That's the way it works, you know."

"But—"

"By the way, I found my birth mother."

Peter put a hand to his forehead, trying to assimilate her words. "What?"

"Velvet Cotton. My boss. She's my birth mother. And my father is a famous author." She got her purse off the hook and pulled out a book. "See? He wrote this book—which I really need to read if I'm going to know what he's all about before Velvet and I pick him up at the airport at five thirty." She opened the door. "You need to go. I've got a lot to do."

This was happening too fast. "You found your birth parents? Just like that? How did it—?"

She pushed him into the hall. "Go."

For the second time, Peter stopped a closing door with a hand. "But how did it happen?"

She looked at him a moment, then smiled wickedly. "Here's an answer for you: God did it. Ciao."

He got his hand out just in time.

| | | | | | | | | | | |

"Thank you, Ms. Morano. We've had quite a few applicants . . . but we'll get back to you."

No, they wouldn't. Just like the other five places where she'd applied for a job. Two had blatantly asked if she was related to that woman in the news, one had raised their eyebrows when they'd seen her name, and another had asked about the gap in her resume—there was no way she could put down her latest company as a reference, so there was a two-year blank spot in her credentials.

When one of the interviewers asked about it, Maya had answered his query with an awkward, "Let's just say I did not leave my last employment on the best of terms."

Oh yeah. That impressed them.

Only one employer—the head of the sales department at an auto parts store—seemed completely ignorant of her reputation and didn't blink at the gap in her job history. Goody.

If Sal weren't so firmly entrenched with his landscaping business, she might have suggested a move—to someplace far away like Rhode Island or Timbuktu.

Yet employers anywhere would have the same issues. She'd been such a fool. A shortsighted fool. *A wise man can see more from the bottom of a well than a fool can from a mountaintop.*

She'd hit bottom all right. As far as being wise? *That* was a

full-time job. She'd prayed about wisdom, asking God for it.
And she supposed that facing reality was a part of being wise.
Accepting responsibility for her own stupidity. There *was* wisdom in that.

But it still hurt.

| | | | | | | | | | |

Maya was just leaving her last interview to go to another one
when her cell phone rang. She looked at the caller ID and answered. "Marcela. Hey."

"So?" Marcela said. She got right to the point. "Are you and
Sal adopting?"

"I told you yesterday I was *thinking* about it."

"You say *I*. What does Sal think about it?"

"It's complicated."

"But if you can't have your own . . ."

"I know. It *is* like a door has opened, or at least been pushed
ajar."

"Don't let it bang shut on you."

"I'll try not—"

"I never asked you, but . . . did you do those things you got
fired for?"

The question made Maya bobble her phone. *Now* her sister
wanted to know? After a week of family silence, *now* she asked?
"I did."

"Wow," Marcela said. "You *were* desperate for a baby."

"I was, but now . . . I'm trying not to be desperate; I'm trying
to let it all fall into place without me pushing so—"

"Maybe you getting fired was a good thing."

Maya stopped at the edge of the parking lot. "What?"

"If you are supposed to adopt Barry, then it's not like a
pregnancy where you have nine months to wait before the

child is here. He would need you now. And though you *could* work outside the home, wouldn't it be nice to be home with him, at least for a while?"

Suddenly, the bad became good, the negative, positive.

"Maya? You there?"

"I'm here. I was just thinking . . . what if you're right?"

"I am right. I am always right."

Actually it wasn't just bragging. Marcela did have a knack for homing in on the truth. She'd been the one to wisely tell Maya *not* to date Harry Klammer in high school; to definitely buy the pink lace dress for prom that still made Maya feel like a princess just thinking about it; and to quickly marry Sal, before some other woman grabbed him first.

"Yank that door all the way open, Maya, and close all the other doors you may still have open. Commit to this and see what happens. Gotta go. Bye."

Maya got in her car and sat there, letting her sister's wisdom settle in around her. Her old job had required her to work fifty to sixty hours a week. She and Sal had talked about her quitting while the baby was young, so the fact she had been forced to leave the job early . . .

Close all the other doors you may still have open.

What did that mean? What doors were still open, letting her peek into her past, keeping her from fully facing the new door that was opening?

And then she knew, and marveled at how God *had* given her wisdom—through her dear sister.

She started the car.

| | | | | | | | | | |

Maya walked toward the office building, trying to keep her courage intact.

I have to do this. I have to do this. I have to . . .

Fueled by a deep breath, she entered the building and headed to the elevators and pushed the Up button. She noticed that one of the four elevators had a red sign taped to its doors. But instead of saying Out of Order, the sign was blank. Maya shook her head at the sight of it. *Not another one.* If only God would give her a bit of wisdom about these stupid signs . . .

A man came close, pushed the Down button, and began to wait. She saw him glance at the elevator's sign, then look away, as if it was nothing.

Does he see words? Or a blank— "Excuse me," she said. "What does that sign say?"

He looked at the sign, then at her. "What do you mean, what does it say?"

"The red sign. On the elevator."

"Can't you read?"

The bell of an elevator dinged, and the doors opened. "Never mind," she said. She went inside with her question still unanswered.

But as the doors closed and the elevator ascended to the third floor, she realized it *had* been answered.

"Can't you read?" he'd asked.

Which meant there *were* words on the sign. Other people saw words.

Which didn't explain why she did not.

The doors opened on three. Blank sign or not, the time had come for Maya to wipe her past clean and close all its doors.

As best she could.

| | | | | | | | | | |

Maya's nerves stood at attention. People looked up from their desks when she passed. A few said hello, though most looked back to their work as if they hadn't spotted her. She thought about leaving but forced herself to keep going. She had to finish this—and finish it right.

She approached her boss's office, hoping Roman was back at work. Upon seeing her, his secretary, Millie, looked up and blinked as if Maya were an apparition, then said, "Maya."

"Is he in?"

"Mr. Paulson?"

Of course, Mr. Paulson. "I know about his son. I'll only take a minute, I promise. I just want to leave him some—"

"He's not here. He doesn't work here anymore. He resigned."

"Because of me?" The words spilled out before she could stop them.

Millie made no attempt to deny it. "I think it was a lot of things. We're all hoping he comes back. Eventually."

Maya reached into her purse and retrieved the plaque that had lived in her briefcase since the day she'd been fired. "I'd like to leave this here."

Millie studied the award. "It's got your name on it."

"But I didn't deserve it."

"Why don't you just throw it away?"

"I . . . I need to return it. If you want to throw it away, that's fine. But please let me leave it here. Please."

Millie set it on the credenza behind her—facedown. "Anything else?" she asked.

"No. I think that's it."

Millie picked up her pen and went back to work. Maya turned away, but before she could take two steps, Millie said, "I'm sorry about the baby, Maya. I do understand—at least that part of it."

It was something.

Next.

| | | | | | | | | | |

Maya approached Brian's cubicle, feeling like a felon walking a gauntlet. Once again some of her old coworkers looked at her with open curiosity, some looked away, and some put their heads together and whispered. No one approached her with a friendly hello. Not even Susan—who wasn't at her desk.

309

Brian *was* at his desk. He was busy at the computer with his back to her.

"Hi, Brian," she said.

He whipped his chair around, his eyes wide. "Maya."

"Yeah. It's me."

"Are you back? I mean, were you rehired or—?"

"No, no. I'm still persona non grata. Still guilty as charged. Which is why I'm here." She took a step closer, hoping the entire office wouldn't overhear. Though she noticed the noise level of the main room *had* lessened since she'd passed through.

So be it. Let them listen.

"I came to tell you how sorry I am for what I did. I was wrong. I hope you'll forgive me."

His eyebrows formed two awnings above his eyes. "Uh . . . I guess so."

That's all she needed.

Let the gossip mill begin.

Yet there was still one more door to close. . . .

| | | | | | | | | | |

Maya felt more nervous standing at Roman's front door than she'd been entering the lion's den of her old workplace. She'd considered going home after apologizing to Brian but knew if she was going to do this right . . .

She rang the doorbell. Her heart pounded a double rhythm. *Maybe he's not home.*

The door opened. "Maya."

"Hi, Mr. Paulson. I don't mean to bother you, but can I come in?"

He hesitated—but only for a moment. "Sure."

She entered the house and sat in the chair he offered. Roman had lost weight and not in a healthy way. His face was drawn. He had circles under his eyes. He seemed *less* than he was before.

One son less.

"What . . . why . . . ?" He stumbled, obviously not knowing what to ask.

"I've come to apologize, both for my unethical behavior and for damaging the reputation of the company. I was wrong and . . ." She placed her hands on top of the purse in her lap. "I'm so sorry for that, and for your son."

"I saw you at the funeral. Thanks for coming."

"Sal always spoke highly of William."

"Sal?"

"My husband. William worked in his lawn-care business all summer."

"Oh. I didn't know. Small world."

Maya suddenly didn't know what else to say, so she stood. "Anyway, that's all I wanted to do, to say, so I'll be—"

"Wait. Sit. I've got something to say to you too."

Maya wasn't certain she wanted to hear it and braced herself.

Roman folded his hands on top of his knees. "You were wrong in your methods, Maya, but I was also wrong because I pushed too hard, stressed sales above all else, and perhaps gave you the impression that anything goes."

She couldn't believe what she was hearing. "I don't know what to say."

He shook his head, looking as though the weight of the world had made a dent upon his shoulders. "Sometimes it's hard learning a person isn't always right, doesn't know everything, and there are other ways of thinking and doing things. Other ways to live." His gaze was far away. He may have been talking about work—partially—but it was obvious his son's death had caused the biggest change in him.

He stood. "Anyway, I appreciate your apology, I accept it, and I wish you all the best. Perhaps if I had been a different sort of boss none of this would have happened. Both of us are good people who made bad choices."

Roman saw her out, and as she heard the door shut behind her . . .

She smiled.

She was free—finally free to look ahead.

| | | | | | | | | | | |

Velvet turned into the airport parking lot, found a place, and shut off the car. She sat a moment in the sudden silence. "This is weird."

"I vote for bizarre," Lianne said from the passenger seat. "What are we going to do with John when he gets here?"

Velvet hadn't thought of that. The last time John was in town he'd stayed at a fancy hotel and had book signings and speaking engagements and work to occupy his time. For him to return for personal reasons . . .

For her. For Lianne.

They headed into the terminal and up the escalators to the bridge that spanned the building. It was five thirty. His plane had landed. In just a few minutes he'd be there.

Lianne broke the silence that had accompanied them all the way from the car. "Is he going to stay at your place?"

"No, of course not," Velvet said—although she had no idea where John was planning to stay.

"Do you regret me?"

A man ran past them, obviously late for a flight. The sound of his footfalls and the wheels of his roller bag intruded loudly, then faded away. But the question would not fade away. Its intent and its desire for the truth shouted.

Velvet adjusted the purse on her shoulder, needing to do something, anything, to stall.

Lianne looked up at the antique biplane that hung from the ceiling. "You don't have to answer that."

Good. A way out.

And yet . . . didn't her daughter deserve *some* explanation? Lianne, who was facing the same sort of situation with her own baby? Lianne, who had lived the consequences of Velvet's decision?

Velvet said, "You deserve an answer although I'm not sure I can express it well or even know exactly what to say."

"Anything." Lianne's voice was soft.

"I do not regret *you*. A life was created. Your life. It's not up to me to question that. And I don't think I regret giving you up, but maybe I do—" Velvet angled toward her daughter—"and yes, I wish John and I would have married and raised you and lived happy ever after. But I'm not sure that would have happened. And yet . . . look at me. I'm still working at the stadium. I have no impact on anyone's life other than to make sure they get their popcorn and nachos. I'm unmarried. I never had any other children, never . . ." She sighed, not able to go *there*. "I work, go home to an empty house, and go to work again. I have friends, I have hobbies, and I am . . . some sort of happy. But happy isn't the same as fulfilled, is it?"

Lianne's face was serious. "I don't think it is."

Velvet nodded, just once. "Yet if I'd done things differently, who's to say John and I wouldn't have gotten divorced. And then, instead of living with two loving parents you would have had to go through that pain. And maybe with John being around me all the time—a woman who's never been into God or faith—would John have become who he is? Would you have become who you are?" She twisted the handles of her purse. "Regret you? No, I don't regret you. But I do wonder, 'What if?' I regret not being *better*. Not being *more*."

313

They looked at each other, so close, shoulder to shoulder. Then Lianne said, "Maybe this is more. You and me here, now. Maybe *this* is more."

Velvet's eyes filled with tears. She reached out and tentatively moved a hand toward Lianne's face. To Velvet's relief, the girl did not jerk away but let Velvet's fingers touch her cheek. *I haven't touched this cheek since the day she was born.* Lianne placed her fingers on Velvet's and for a moment the time between then and now was erased.

Then a commotion drew their attention as a new group of travelers entered the area.

Velvet withdrew her hand. "He's here."

Lianne stood. "He's here."

Velvet's stomach clenched. John wanted to see Lianne, and she, him. All was right with the world.

And yet . . . Velvet sensed the world was changing for all of them. Forever. She wasn't sure if she was ready for it. She'd done nothing to prepare herself for such a change. Her life had been all about beating back change, beating back memories, not accepting change or embracing the past.

Lianne grabbed Velvet's arm. "There he is!"

John saw them and waved, and there was no time for more nervous what-ifs. When he was close, he hugged Velvet but hesitated with Lianne. He extended a hand. "Hi again." Then he laughed. "Can you tell I make my living with words?"

"I'm not sure there are any words for this situation," Lianne said.

"Or perhaps there are thousands."

"What do you think?" Velvet asked Lianne.

"I think I'm not prepared for this."

Velvet slipped a hand around her arm. "None of us are, Lianne. None of us."

"So," John said. He pointed at his rolling suitcase. "This is all I've got."

"So," Velvet repeated. "Are we ready to do this?"

"First things first," John said. "Food. We need food and lots of it. I'm buying."

That would work.

| | | | | | | | | |

John dipped another chip in the salsa and ate it. Lianne did the same. Then Velvet. Dip, crunch, chew. Dip, crunch, chew.

Going to a Mexican restaurant was a good idea. The free chips served before their meals gave them something to do. They'd already devoured one bowlful.

Yet something had to stop the rhythm. Someone.

Velvet pushed the bowl of salsa away. "No more. If this keeps up I won't have any room for my real food."

John raised his hands in surrender. "You're right. Self-control."

Lianne sat back in the booth, also relenting. "'My fault, my failure, is not in the passions I have, but in my lack of control of them.'" She wiped her mouth with a napkin. "You said that. In your book."

"Wow. Good memory," Velvet said.

"Great memory," John said, "but actually, that's a quote from Jack Kerouac. I used it in my book because I believe it's true. I was not a role model for self-control."

"Are you now?" Lianne asked.

"Is anyone? Completely?"

Lianne straightened her silverware.

Velvet thought of another quote. "Didn't Shaw say, 'Youth is wasted on the young'?"

315

"It doesn't have to be, does it?" Lianne asked. "We *can* get it right. It's not inevitable we make stupid choices."

Considering Lianne was pregnant and unmarried, Velvet thought the statement revealed one of the main problems of youth—cockiness. Or the false sense of invincibility. She couldn't let Lianne get away with it. "Are you implying you chose to get pregnant? that you think it's a good idea?"

To her credit, Lianne blushed. "It just happened."

"By magic?" John asked.

The way Lianne rolled her eyes made her appear even younger than her years.

"So you knew what you were doing."

Lianne hesitated. "That's a trick question."

"How so?" John sat up straighter and Velvet remembered this particular glimmer in his eyes, his I've-got-you-now look.

Lianne curved her hair behind her ears, readying for battle. "If I say I didn't know what I was doing by having sex, then I come off as an ignorant youth, but if I say I did know but chose to ignore the possible consequences, then . . ."

John lowered the flat of a hand to the table, quietly, but firmly. "Then you reveal your lack of self-control."

Not wanting a conflict to come between them so early in their knowledge of one another, Velvet stepped in. "That happens a lot. We know what *could* happen but choose to go ahead anyway."

John nodded. "We lose our self-control and we mistakenly believe—even for a minute—that we are immune from the consequences."

Lianne pulled her hands into her lap. "So my birth was a consequence, evidence of a lack of self-control on both your parts."

John moved his hand toward her, as if he wanted hers. But she made no move to take it. "Consequences are inevitable. No one is immune. And for my mistakes, I am sorry, and for the mistake I share with Velvet, just know I suffered consequences having nothing to do with you." He looked at Velvet. "I was weak and didn't do the right thing; I left your mother alone to deal with everything. It was a cowardly thing to do."

Velvet was touched. "But we might *not* have ended up married anyway."

"We'll never know, will we? Maybe that's the biggest consequence of any action: wiping out what could have been with what must be."

Lianne's hands became mobile again, as did her face. "I know a solution. Marry her now. Make up for lost time."

Velvet drew in a breath.

"Isn't that why you're here?" Lianne asked. "Because the flame is still smoldering?"

Velvet cleared her throat. "Lianne, you're jumping to conclusions. John came back for you, not me."

"Don't *you* jump to conclusions," he said quietly. To Velvet. Directly to Velvet.

A warmth surged through her—and their food came.

Good timing.

ELEVEN

*No eye has seen, no ear has heard,
and no mind has imagined
what God has prepared
for those who love him.*

1 CORINTHIANS 2:9

"Good morning, sunshine."

Maya opened her eyes and saw Sal coming toward her with a breakfast tray.

"Sit, sit," he said. "Breakfast is served."

She pushed herself to a sitting position, rearranging the pillows against the headboard. Sal placed the legs of the wooden tray around her own. There were pancakes and syrup, a bowl of cantaloupe, a glass of orange juice, and a carafe of coffee.

She rubbed her eyes, trying to force herself to full wakefulness. "I love pancakes."

He drew a cloth napkin off his arm and into her lap, then stepped aside like a butler with a completed mission. "Au contraire, madame, you love syrup." He waved a hand over the food. "Eat, eat. Don't let it get cold."

Maya poured the beloved syrup, delighting in its amber flow. She took a bite, then exclaimed. "Chocolate chips!"

"Although I continue to *not* share your taste for them in pancakes—" he bowed—"your wish is my command."

She finished chewing, her mind finally awake enough to be wary. "It's all very nice, but . . . why? What's going on?"

He reached forward to turn the handle of her coffee mug for easy pickup, then stepped back. "I could say 'no reason' other than I love you, but . . ."

"But there is a reason you're buttering me up."

He nodded. "I want you to go to a football game with me."

She remembered it was Saturday. "Today?"

"One o'clock. Nebraska."

"Since when do you have tickets?"

"Since yesterday."

"I know you like to go to games once in a while, but you usually go with one of your buddies. Why me?"

When he sighed, he looked like a little boy. "I . . . I've felt separate from you lately, as if we've each retreated into our own corners. I know you're still upset about the job and the article—"

"And the fire in the lab."

"And that. But I miss you. I miss us. We used to go to ball games. . . ."

It was true. They'd always enjoyed baseball, basketball, and football games, but since Maya had become so consumed with her job, they'd stopped going. Then she thought of another reason she should go to today's game: she'd been wanting to have a serious talk with Sal about adoption. Maybe after a fun day together he'd be more receptive.

She stabbed at a wedge of fruit. "I'm in."

"You are?"

"As long as I get a Runza *and* popcorn."

He made a face. He'd never liked this Nebraska creation of cabbage and ground beef in a bread pocket. He leaned over the bed to kiss her, nearly spilling her coffee. "I'll go find our Nebraska stuff."

Go Big Red.

| | | | | | | | | | |

The doorbell rang—which surprised Velvet greatly. No one came to her house on a game day morning. They knew better. And she was already running late.

She headed down the stairs, buttoning her red shirt. "Coming!"

She undid the dead bolt and opened the door—and saw John.

"Top o' the morning to you, Ms. Cotton."

"What are you doing here? We agreed to meet after the game. I'm already late for work and—"

"Work is why I'm here." He stood at attention and saluted. "John Gillingham, at your service."

It took her a second. "You're offering to work for me? Selling concessions?"

"Whatever you need," he said. "Hey, it's either sit around doing nothing while I wait for you to be free or make myself useful. I choose the latter."

"What if you don't have the job skills to handle the work?"

He smiled slyly. "I'm a fast learner."

What a charmer. For the first time Velvet noticed he was wearing a long-sleeved Husker T-shirt. "Where did you get that?"

"The store in the hotel. I could have bought Husker earrings but thought that might have been too much."

"Just a tad."

"So?" he said.

"What if I don't pay the wages you want?"

"Oh, don't worry. I'll find some way for you to compensate me."

Oh yeah. It was a deal.

| | | | | | | | | | |

Behind the concessions counter, Lianne did a double take. "What are you doing here?"

"Why do people keep asking me that?" John said.

Lianne looked to Velvet for an answer. "He's your coworker today."

"He's working with me?"

Velvet shrugged. "What can I say? The price is right. He's working for free."

John bumped into her, whispering near her ear. "Nothing is free, my dear."

Velvet enjoyed a swell of goose bumps.

John bypassed both of them and approached the two other workers. "Hi, my name's John."

Velvet watched him make himself at home. This might be fun.

| | | | | | | | | |

Peter flipped open his cell phone and began to punch in the number.

He flipped it shut. He wasn't sure he should do this, yet he wanted to do it. And he could even rationalize doing it if he—

His phone began to play its song and vibrate in his hand. He checked its display before answering. *No way.* "Carrie. Hi."

"I'm so sorry to be calling, Peter. I promised myself I'd leave you alone, but when this morning came around I . . ." She sighed. "Is it all right I called?"

"Of course," he said. He did not add that he was glad to hear from her, nor that he'd just been struggling with wanting to call *her.* "How have you been?"

"Fine." Then suddenly she added, "No, not fine. After seeing

you at the farm and seeing your special place, and then . . . then
this game today with the memorial to William . . . I'm . . ."

"Me too."

"Really?"

"Totally."

"Are you going to the game?" she asked.

"I am." He wanted to ask her but hesitated. A part of him
wanted to leave it alone and see if it played out without him.
Wouldn't it mean more that way? As if it was meant to be.

"Can . . . could I go with you? I wouldn't ask but . . . with it
being William's day, I'm not sure I can handle . . . I could use
the support."

Bingo. "I'll pick you up."

| | | | | | | | | |

Roman walked toward the stadium. Two hours before the
game and the Nebraska campus was already an undulating
mass of red.

AJ walked beside him. "You're not saying much."

"Because I'm feeling too much."

AJ nodded. "It is a nice thing they're doing."

Roman wouldn't argue with him. Yet nice or not, it was hard.
Hard now, in anticipation, and harder still once he got out on
that field and—

He shook the thought away. He'd make himself crazy thinking about it. Worrying about it. For once in his life he had to
live a moment at a time. Not a moment past, not a moment
future.

As they approached the southwest corner of the stadium,
Roman looked up and noticed the words carved into the stone
walls: *Not the victory but the action; not the goal but the game; in
the deed the glory.*

AJ must have noticed the direction of his gaze because Roman felt a hand on his shoulder. "Billy lived those words."

But have I?

He pulled the rolled sign from under his arm to his chest. Maybe he could live them. After today.

If he got through it.

| | | | | | | | | | | |

"It'll be just a few minutes now," said the woman who would escort Roman onto the field. *Mindy, Mandy, Mary?* She'd introduced herself, but Roman had lost her name the moment it had been given. He nodded and waited off to the side of the tunnel that would lead him onto the playing field that meant so much to his son.

And to him. He'd be the first to admit that Billy becoming a Husker football star was *his* dream as much as Billy's. Maybe more so. Was that wrong? Or did most parents look for satisfaction and fulfillment in what their children attained? Did kids offer their parents a second chance to be somebody?

A man approached them, a child in hand. Roman's escort beamed. "Welcome, Mr. Blackmore." She leaned down to address the child. "And you, Barry. A big welcome to you."

It took Roman a moment, but then he recognized them. This was the man and boy from Billy's funeral. This was the boy Billy had saved from drowning. He hadn't known they would be here. If he had, would he have come? Wasn't this going to be hard enough without having to be reminded . . . ?

"I'm sure you three know each other," the woman said.

Know of *each other.*

Blackmore offered his hand to Roman. "Nice to see you again, Mr. Paulson. I'm glad we could be here today to honor your son."

AJ knelt next to Barry. "How you doing, kid? You ready to go wave at all the people?"

Barry's face was serious. "This is William's team."

AJ stood. "Yes, it is. Do you want to play football someday?"

"If William did it, I want to do it too."

AJ glanced at Roman, and Roman knew *he* should be the one asking these questions, connecting with the boy. Yet he couldn't seem to do it, to say or do the right thing.

The woman bit her lip, then said, "It'll be just a few minutes now. Just a few minutes." She took a few steps to the side, talking with someone on her walkie-talkie, leaving the four of them alone. Leaving the right-thing hanging between them.

Come on, Roman. Say something to the kid. Say anything.

But before Roman could push himself out of his reserve, Barry moved directly in front of him. "You're William's daddy, aren't you?"

Roman cleared his throat. "I am."

"He saved me."

"I know."

"He died."

Roman cleared his throat. "I know."

"I'm really sorry." Barry tentatively touched Roman's fingers.

And then Roman got it. This wasn't about him anymore. It wasn't about his loss, his sorrow, his regrets. Today was about Billy and *his* victory. And the boy . . . Today was about showing this boy to the world as evidence of that victory. Somehow Roman moved past his reticence and took the boy's hand in his own. The boy smiled up at him, as though a weight had been lifted from his tiny shoulders. Roman knew the feeling because a weight had also been removed from his own. Physically connecting with the boy, knowing that William had also touched him, had lifted him back toward life. . . . Roman's knees buckled and he let the weakness take him into a kneeling position beside the boy . . . where he drew him into his arms.

Suddenly, the years fell away, and this boy was *his* boy.

| | | | | | | | | |

"*. . . We have his father with us today, as well as the boy William saved. Please welcome Roman Paulson and Barry.*"

"Go," the woman said. "And wave."

Roman took a deep breath, took Barry's hand in his, and said, "You ready?"

Barry nodded.

They walked onto the field. The people in the stadium applauded. Rose to their feet. It was overwhelming. Roman had never been on the field when the stadium was full. The scale of the stands rose around him; the vast sweep of red and the constant swell of the people as they clapped and cheered filled every space of his being, every breath, every heartbeat.

They clapped and cheered for him. And the boy. But mostly for Billy.

His chest tightened and he wanted to retreat. He looked down at Barry. The little boy's eyes were wide and a bit frightened.

Roman squeezed his hand. "It'll be okay." He remembered their instruction to wave. "Shall we wave?"

They both waved, but as Roman raised an arm he quickly withdrew it. It seemed wrong, like he was accepting Billy's glory. Billy deserved the applause, not him.

And then he remembered the sign—Billy's sign. A few more steps . . . Once in the middle of the field he knelt beside Barry. "I have a sign here. A sign my son made. Do you want to help me hold it up?"

Barry nodded.

"You take this end." Barry held one end of the red banner while Roman unrolled the sign. "Hold it high," Roman said.

Barry held his end of the sign above his head and Roman held his end chest-high, making it straight. He had no idea what kind of reaction the sign would get. He'd never thought twice when he'd seen such a sign.

To his amazement, the crowd roared anew. Barry's look of surprise mirrored his own. "Let's turn around in a circle," Roman suggested.

Barry beamed and nodded. Together they slowly made a 360—to the crowd's approval. Were people clapping to be clapping or did they know what the sign meant?

When they reached their starting point, Roman knew their time—Billy's time—in the spotlight was over. He rolled up the sign and reached for Barry's hand. Instead, Barry raised his arms to him.

Roman complied, lifted Barry off the ground, and together they exited the field.

AJ and Mr. Blackmore met them. "That was great!" they said.

"That was amazing," their escort said. "The fans loved it."

Oddly, Roman didn't care if the fans loved it.

Barry must have felt the same because he said, "I sure hope William got to see it."

Roman agreed. Surely God allowed his son this glimpse to earth. This one glimpse. "I'm sure he did."

| | | | | | | | | | | |

Maya couldn't believe what she was seeing on the field. "It's Barry," she said.

She and Sal stood shoulder to shoulder in the crowd, clapping with the rest. Sal took her hand and pulled it toward his heart.

"It's the little boy William saved. I'd heard he was coming to the game today—for the ceremony honoring William."

Maya's heart raced. Was this a sign? She hadn't come to a game in years, and yet now . . . today . . . to come and see the boy—the boy now singled out in front of eighty thousand fans . . .

"What are they doing?" Sal asked, pointing to the field.

They watched while Roman unrolled a sign. He and Barry were facing away from Maya and Sal, but then they slowly turned, making sure every fan in the stands saw the sign's message.

A red sign. A red sign whose message would be revealed to Maya any moment.

She grabbed Sal's arm with her free hand. "It's a sign."

"I know it is," Sal said. "It's why I wanted you to come. It's . . . oh. Now we get to read their sign." He held her hand tighter. "John 3:16." He looked to Maya, his face alight. "It's William's John 3:16. How perfect."

Maya stared at the sign. Her sign—her red sign that was *not* blank. And yet its message was cryptic to her. "What does it mean?" she asked.

Sal recited it. "'For God loved the world so much that he gave his one and only Son, so that everyone who believes in him will not perish but have eternal life.'"

Maya's mind focused on one word. The word that had consumed her thoughts the past week. "Son," she said aloud.

Sal angled his body toward hers, forming their own private space, even amid the crowded bleachers. "I want to adopt a son, Maya. Adopt Barry."

She was glad he was holding her hand because she would have fallen. "You? You want to adopt Barry?"

"I know, I know," he said. "I've been against adoption, but when I saw him at the funeral and then again at the cemetery, and when I thought about William—my employee—saving his life . . . I don't believe in coincidences, Maya. We haven't been able to conceive. Maybe there's a reason for that. Maybe Barry was saved for *us*."

Maya grabbed her husband's face and kissed it, then wrapped her arms around his neck. All the pain, all the confusion, all the discouragement fell away as God answered their prayers for a child. "Yes, Sal. Yes."

A man standing in the row behind them tapped on their shoulders. "Hey, save the celebration for a touchdown."

Maya grinned. "No way." Then she kissed her husband again. And again.

| | | | | | | | | | |

Velvet stood off to the side of the concessions counter, needing to watch the ceremony in Billy's honor. Luckily, quite a few people had turned toward the monitors mounted in the concourse around the food stands, so customers were few.

"What are you looking at?" Lianne asked.

"They're dedicating the game to Billy. My friend Roman is his dad. Roman's going out on the field now."

John joined them. "Who's the little boy?"

"It must be the boy Billy saved from drowning."

John squinted his eyes. "It is. I recognize him from the funeral."

"I still can't believe William died saving somebody," Lianne said. "That kid has a lot to make up for."

It was an odd way of putting it. "A lot to live up to, you mean."

Lianne shrugged. "They're unrolling a sign. What's it going to say? 'Hey, William, wish you were here'?"

"Lianne!"

"What? It's what we all think, isn't it? All I'm saying is that that kid has to do a lot to make up for William's sacrifice. To earn it."

What she said was true, but Lianne's tone, her way of saying it was almost accusatory. There was little empathy there. What had happened to her to make her react this way?

The sign turned around so they could read it. "'John 3:16'?" Velvet said.

John laughed. "How perfect is that?"

"I don't get it," Lianne said. People around them started to clap. "Now I really don't get it. What is it? A secret code?"

"*The* code," John said. "But it's hardly secret."

"It's from the Bible," Velvet said. When John looked surprised she said, "I do know something about the Good Book."

"It's everything rolled into one," John said. "'For God loved the world so much that he gave his one and only Son, so that everyone who believes in him will not perish but have eternal life.'"

"What does that have to do with football?" Lianne asked.

John thought a moment, then smiled. "If you want to win the big game, make Jesus your coach."

"Oh, please," Lianne said.

Velvet couldn't take her eyes off Roman, out on the field, displaying a religious sign for all to see. "But Roman doesn't believe in God."

"He does now," John said.

Velvet remembered Roman coming into her office, his face pulled with sorrow and confusion over a string of 316 numbers appearing in his life. She'd made him promise to look it up. Obviously he had. And obviously it had touched him enough to want to share it.

She was happy for him. But she felt left out.

She tried to remember the words John had just recited, but they were gone from her memory. Something about God and Son and eternal life.

"Ma'am?" said a customer at the counter. "Can I get some popcorn here?"

She couldn't think about it now. Maybe later.

| | | | | | | | | | |

Carrie laughed and cried at the same time. "He did it! He held up William's sign."

Peter looked around the stadium. People were clapping and cheering. Were they reacting to William's sacrifice or to seeing his father with the boy? or to the John sign? Or were they joining in to merely be one of the crowd?

He clapped with the rest of them but leaned toward Carrie. "Do people even know what John 3:16 is?"

Carrie stopped in midclap and stared at him, and for the first time, looked at the crowd. "Sure they do. Some of them do. And maybe some of them will go home and look it up."

"Do you really think so?"

"You need to think like a farmer, Peter. That sign's sowing a seed. Some will brush it away but some will plant it and nourish it so it can grow." She looked back to the field where William's dad was rolling up the sign. "He did a brave thing out there."

Mr. Paulson and the boy walked off the field. The applause pittered away and people sat down. When they were seated, Carrie put a hand on Peter's knee and nodded toward the field. "What are *you* going to do with it, Peter?"

The band started playing the Nebraska fight song and the crowd stood once more.

Peter joined them.

| | | | | | | | | | |

"What are you going to do with it, Peter?"

Carrie's words hovered around him despite touchdowns, fumbles, penalties, and field goals.

Peter stood when the crowd stood, sat when they sat, clapped when they clapped, yet wasn't there for any of it. His thoughts were with the sign.

He remembered the day William and Carrie created it. . . .

He'd come home from class to find the two of them kneeling on the floor beside the coffee table, the red plastic of the sign spread in front of them. They had the *John* part painted and William was carefully painting the first curve of the *3*.

"Whatcha doing?" Peter had asked.

William kept painting. "Changing the world. Want to join us?"

Suddenly, the memory of Lianne's words interrupted the image of William. *"I want to change the world, McLean."*

Lianne and William, two friends as different as yes was to no, black was to white. Yet they shared a common goal.

"I wonder what Lianne thinks of the sign."

"What?" Carrie asked.

He hadn't meant to say the words aloud. "I'll be right back. Want something to eat?"

She shook her head, her eyes intent. "Tell Lianne hello."

| | | | | | | | | | |

The concessions stand where Lianne worked wasn't busy enough to scare Peter away but he did let a few people go in front of him. He wanted to be the last in line so he could talk to her—if only for a minute.

She saw him but acted as though she hadn't—until it was just Peter in line.

"May I help you?" she asked, her voice bland.

"Don't," he said.

"What do you want, McLean? I'm tired of rehashing the same things over and over. Besides, I'm working."

He looked right, then left. There was only one customer, and she was being helped by another worker. "Did you see the 3:16 sign—William's sign?"

"I saw it."

That's it? "Wasn't it cool for William's dad to do that? Wasn't it brave?"

331

She made a face. "Brave? To hold up a sign? Give me a sign, I'll hold it up. It's no big deal."

"But it's from the Bible. It's important. It's William's verse."

"William's, no one else's."

"But his dad put his faith on the line. In front of everyone."

"He was pushy. I don't like pushy people."

Peter found that ironic, considering Lianne was one of the pushiest people he knew. He wasn't willing to let it go. Not yet. "That sign could change people. Challenge them."

Lianne rolled her eyes. "If you're waiting for me to say the sign made me see the light, that the heavens opened and God spoke to me, you might as well put on some long johns and a parka, because you're in for a long wait." She wiped the counter with a damp towel. "So William's dad held up a sign? Whoop-de-do. In case you haven't noticed, I have problems that no words from the Bible are ever going to solve."

"But in a way the words are the answer—the answer to all problems, everybody's problems."

She shrugged. "You're talking mumbo jumbo, McLean, like it's magic. What do I have to do, say it three times while standing on my head and my life will be perfect?" She tossed the towel into a sink on the back wall. "Give me a break."

"The verse in itself doesn't have power, but the content does. If we believe what it says, we tap into huge power. God's power."

"God hasn't done me any favors so far, so why should I believe he will make everything right if I take it on?"

It was a hard question. An important question. "Because he said so."

She put her hands on her hips. "It says that?"

"It promises eternal life—in heaven."

"But what about the mess down here on earth? *That's* what I have to deal with. Today. Heaven's a long way off."

"Not necessarily. What about William? One minute he's here, the next he's—"

Her laugh was sarcastic. "If you're trying to win one for the Gipper, you're not doing a very good job, McLean. If that verse was William's and God let him die, thanks but no thanks."

Two people got in line behind him. He was out of time.

He leaned on the counter, confidentially. "Good things will come from William's death—have come."

"Don't ever be on a debate team, McLean, because you'd lose." She looked past him and waved him away. "Now, if you'll excuse me? I got customers."

Peter stepped aside, feeling hollow. He'd only made things worse. He and Lianne were on separate banks of a wide river and there wasn't any way across.

He stuffed his hands in his pockets and headed back to his seat.

"Hey! Lianne's friend? Hey, you!"

Peter stopped walking and saw a middle-aged man rushing toward him. He'd seen the man behind the concessions counter.

"Forgive me, but I overheard your conversation with Lianne."

Great. "Yeah? Well?"

"Just because she's a hard nut to crack doesn't mean we should give up on her."

We? "And you are?"

"I'm John Gillingham. I'm her birth father."

Peter felt his eyebrows rise. "She said she found you."

"I found her, actually. I've been wanting to meet her for a long time."

The thought of this man wanting to meet his daughter and finding out she was someone like Lianne . . . "She's not as bad as she pretends to be," Peter said. Then he realized how horrible that sounded. "I don't mean she's a bad person, but she's—"

"Difficult. Opinionated. Independent."

Peter laughed. "You learn fast."

"She is her mother."

Peter glanced back to the concessions stand. "Lianne said her mother was her boss?"

"Small world, isn't it?"

"That's strange."

"That's God."

The man spoke of God. Maybe he could be an ally. "I'd hoped the John sign had some effect on her, but it didn't."

"Not today," John said. "Sometimes it takes a while, takes a long while for people to let him in."

"And not everyone does," Peter said.

"No, sadly not everyone does." John sighed and looked to the side, as if remembering specific people who'd said no to God. Then his eyes returned to Peter. "I just wanted to encourage you not to give up on her. She's got to go from zero to one hundred to find him. Although sometimes it happens dramatically, most times it happens over the long haul. The seed has been planted, but now it needs to be fertilized, pruned, and weeded."

Peter smiled. Carrie had mentioned the seed. . . .

"Thanks for the pep talk," Peter said. "I won't give up."

"And neither will I."

| | | | | | | | | | |

During the game Velvet's thoughts were like balls in a pinball machine, bouncing off the flippers and bumpers, propelled up, back, and side to side. Unfortunately she didn't feel as if she was earning any points. Since seeing Roman hold up the John 3:16 sign . . . What compelled him to do such a thing? Roman was a man who bristled at all things God. If anything, since Billy's death she'd expected him to dig his heels in even deeper against God. Something big must have happened.

And she wasn't a part of it.

It made her sad. Roman gave all appearances of having gone through a huge metamorphosis from skeptic to believer in less than a week. Sure, he'd come to her office with his confusion about all the 316 incidents, but she'd sent him on his way with his promise to look it up. But as far as what had led from that to this?

John's voice intruded, adding another ball to the game. "Enjoy your hot dog," he told a customer.

The man nodded, then did a double take. "Hey, John. I didn't know you were still in town."

"Pastor Evers." They shook hands. "I wanted to tell you how much I enjoyed your church's hospitality when I spoke there."

"We were glad to have you." The pastor scanned the concessions area. "What are you doing here?"

John pointed at Velvet. "Velvet's a good friend. She runs this place."

The man nodded in Velvet's direction. "Your friend here gave quite the sermon. People are still talking about it."

Velvet nodded, glad the pastor didn't recognize her as the woman who'd fainted. She wondered if people were still talking about *her*.

She noticed Lianne watching them as she filled a cup with Coke.

John must have seen the direction of her gaze because he looked at Lianne, then swept an arm toward her. "And this—this is my daughter, Lianne."

Pastor Evers looked confused. "I didn't think you had any—" His eyes lit up with recognition. "Oh. Is she *her*?"

Lianne brought the Coke to the counter and took the customer's money. "Yep. I'm the one, the big mistake of his youth." She looked directly at Velvet, as if challenging her to also own up.

John shook his head once. "Now you are the joy of my middle age."

335

Lianne looked as though she was trying to think of a comeback.

In an instant Velvet's thoughts fell into place. *I should say I'm her mother.*

But before she could do the right thing another customer needed Lianne's attention.

"Well then," the pastor said, "nice seeing you again, John. And nice meeting you, ladies."

"Small world," John said when he'd left.

Lianne finished up with her customer. "You didn't have to do that, you know. Acknowledge me as your daughter."

"Why wouldn't I introduce you like that?"

Lianne passed Velvet a scathing look and Velvet realized she'd not told anyone Lianne was hers. To the world she was just an employee.

Lianne glanced at the back shelves. "We're nearly out of cups." She left for the storeroom.

Forget any ricocheting thoughts. The game was over. The clock had ticked to zero. It was done. And she'd lost. "I should have said something to the pastor," Velvet told John. "I should have said something to someone. I haven't introduced Lianne as my daughter to anyone."

"You just found out."

"So did you, but you've already jumped in and claimed her publicly." Velvet pressed her fingers against her forehead. She felt a headache coming on. "It's good I was never a mother. I stink at it." Her thoughts of Roman intruded. "I'm not even a good friend." She pointed at the TV. "Roman's out there, holding up that sign, and I had no idea he was going to do it, that he'd found God, that he . . ." She sighed.

John lifted the hinged counter that accessed the public area. "Go find him. Talk to him now."

"I can't *now*," she said. "The game is on, I have work to do, and—"

"Then write a note telling him you'll meet afterward. Do you know where his seats are?"

"Pretty much."

"Then write it. I'll be your courier."

"John . . ."

He looked under the counters and found a yellow pad and pen. "Here. Now. If I've learned anything from my mistakes it's to act ASAP to make things right."

Velvet knew he wasn't going to let up until she did it. She wrote Roman a note and folded it into fourths. "Section three, about halfway up."

"Gotcha."

And he was off.

| | | | | | | | | | |

The stadium was nearly empty and Velvet's work was wrapping up when John cleared his throat and nudged her arm. She looked at him, but he pointed elsewhere.

And there he stood. "Roman."

"I got your note." He looked at John. "You came to my house before the funeral, didn't you?"

John nodded.

Roman nodded back.

They waited. It was Velvet's turn but she didn't know what to say. "I . . . I saw you. On the monitors." She searched for the right words. "I never expected . . ."

"Neither did I. I never dreamed I'd do something like that."

Velvet looked toward John. She really needed to talk—

"Go on. We're almost through. I'll wait for you here," he said.

She and Roman walked out of the stadium. The area was far from still, as victorious fans gathered to make plans or to offer their take on the game's best and worst plays. There was no place for privacy, nor would there be for quite some time. And so Velvet made a decision. She sat on the steps, claiming a space—private or not. Her legs and back appreciated the break. Roman sat beside her. "So," she began. "What happened between me sending you off to look up the verse and you proclaiming it to the world?"

"Everything."

"Can you be a bit more specific?"

"After we talked in your office, I did what you said. I looked it up."

"And that was enough?"

"That and a note from Trudy that I found stuck in her Bible. It was written shortly before she died."

"A hidden note?"

"Hidden in plain sight." He pushed a peanut shell away with the toe of his shoe. "In it, she asked me to bring Billy up to be a man of God." His voice broke. "I didn't do that." He leaned his arms on his knees and looked to the ground. "I always said I would do anything for my family, but when I look back I realize I didn't give them what they wanted, what they needed, what I should have given them."

"I'm sure you did the best you could."

He looked at her and his eyes glistened. "I didn't. I was so angry when Trudy got sick. And in those last days, when she asked me to read to her from the Bible, I wouldn't even do that. Billy read to her."

"That's nice. I'm sure she liked—"

337

"But she asked me and I wouldn't do it!"

A group of students nearby looked up from their conversation. Velvet shot them a get-out-of-here look. They moved on.

Roman lowered his voice. "I couldn't get past my stupid anger to give her what she wanted, what she needed." He pointed in the direction of his house. "Her note has been lying in that Bible for thirteen years, unread. I have not picked up a Bible in all that time. And because of that I didn't raise Billy to be a godly man because *I* wasn't a godly man. It took some coach to reignite the faith his mother planted. And when Billy wanted to share it with me, I refused to listen. Refused, Velvet. What kind of man refuses to listen when his kid wants to talk about something that means that much to him?"

His words had come in a rush, his face contorted with pain. Velvet put an arm across his shoulders. "So that's why you held up the sign? I heard a lot of talk about it. People thought it was a neat thing to do. They admired you for doing it."

"No one should admire me for anything. I'm no preacher, and I have no clue what I'm doing, but that verse was Billy's. It's full of hope. It's a promise." He touched her knee. "After all these years, I finally got it—got what my wife and son already knew. If I believe in Jesus like Trudy and Billy believed in Jesus, then I will live forever in heaven—where they live. I want to see my wife and son again, and if this is what I have to do to see them, I'm doing it."

There seemed something odd about his motivation. But who was Velvet to question—

"I know how strange it sounds. And selfish." He laughed sarcastically. "I can't even do a good thing without thinking of what I get out of it. But so be it. I'll leave it up to God to work out the details. I'll do the believing and let him do the rest of it."

Now *that* was impressive. Velvet pulled back to get a better look at him. "Wow."

"There's no wow to it. 'It's about time' is a better reaction."

She moved close again and linked her arm through his, resting her cheek against his shoulder. "I'm very proud of you, Roman. I may not understand what you've been through, but I can see how important it is to—"

"Mr. Paulson?"

They looked up to see a young woman wearing a red blazer. Velvet was just about to tell her to move along when Roman said, "Mindy, is it?"

"Mandy."

Roman explained. "Mandy helped me know when to go out on the field today."

"I'm the PR liaison," she told Velvet. Then she looked back to Roman. "Speaking of PR, there are a few people from the media who've been asking to talk to you about the sign. I wasn't sure how I'd ever find you, but I guess it's fate you're still here. Will you come talk to them?"

No, he will not come talk to them. Give the man some space, Mindy-Mandy. The press never did anyone any favors and they'll eat him alive if they get their claws—

"I don't know," Roman said. "I'm exhausted, and I don't really have anything else to say. It was Billy's sign. I just—"

"This is another chance for you to talk about your son." Mandy smiled. "Maybe . . . do it for him?"

Roman looked at Velvet and she could tell that Mandy had hit his soft spot. And maybe, somehow, it would be good for him. Maybe—by some miracle—the press would be understanding and kind and—

"What do you think, Velvet?" he asked.

She could see he wanted her to tell him to do it. "Go on. Do it for Billy."

He hesitated. "I'll go . . . if you'll go with me."

Me and my big mouth.

| | | | | | | | | | |

"A few people from the media" turned out to be a roomful. And not just print media but TV, with cameras and lights. Velvet regretted saying yes to accompanying Roman. She was dressed in her work clothes, covered with popcorn butter, pop, and ketchup. Because of this, she quickly relegated herself to supportive bystander, letting Roman take the spotlight alone.

"Sit by me," he'd whispered.

"I'll be right over here. This is your time. And Billy's." She also didn't want to explain their relationship to the press. It was too complicated. And what if they asked her what *she* thought about John 3:16? Her ignorance would ruin everything.

Once the lighting was set and the microphones were in place— all at Mandy's direction—the interview began.

"So, Mr. Paulson, the sign. Would you like to explain its meaning?"

"It was a sign my son created. He'd asked a friend of his to hold it up at a game. But then he . . . he died. The friend was still upset so she asked me to do it for her."

"She? Was it a girlfriend?"

"A friend."

Another reporter chimed in. "The sign references the Bible, yes?"

"Yes."

"What does the verse say?"

Velvet's stomach clenched. Roman didn't know his Bible. And even if he'd read the verse, to be able to recite it on cue . . . She didn't want him to be embarrassed.

"I don't know it word for word but it basically says that God sacrificed his Son—for us. If we believe in him, we'll go to heaven."

A woman reporter looked confused. "What does that have to do with a football game?"

"Nothing. At least not specifically. I suppose you could stretch it and say the words talk about the game of life."

"Why this particular verse?"

"It was Billy's favorite. Apparently he used to cite it often."

"Apparently?"

Roman fidgeted. "He and I were somewhat estranged when he died."

The reporters perked up and Velvet's stomach wrenched. They'd found the dirt.

"Why were you estranged?"

Roman looked at Velvet as if he wanted to be rescued. She couldn't help him, not without making things worse.

"My son . . ." He grappled for words. "To put it plainly, he found Jesus. He talked to me about it, about what was going on in his life, but I wanted nothing to do with it." Roman clasped his hands on the table. "Ever since my wife died I haven't been too keen on God." He took a fresh breath and looked at the reporters. "I wouldn't let Billy talk about his faith. Ever. I cut him off and he pulled away. I was wrong."

Velvet was shocked by Roman's confession. Roman was not the kind of man who admitted he was wrong. Ever.

He continued. "I've made a lot of mistakes and held on to bitterness for a lot of years, wasted years that I could have more fully shared with my son."

A reporter who didn't look old enough to drive stood. "Speaking of your mistakes, you were recently mentioned in the news regarding the firing of one of your employees for unethical behavior. What do you have to say about that?"

Roman's jaw tightened. So far he'd been calm and measured with his answers. Velvet hoped he wouldn't blow it now and give the media an enraged rant. They would eat it up, and all the good Roman had done would be relegated to secondary news.

Roman's chest heaved, in and out, as he struggled for control. His head shook back and forth, his eyes on the table in front of him.

Then, with an expulsion of breath, he looked at his audience. "Our society celebrates success and achievement. What my employee did was wrong. But if we're honest with ourselves we've all pushed too hard, taken shortcuts, and misplaced our common sense in the quest for success. It's people like my son who remind us that *taking* is not the answer. *Giving* is. *Sacrificing* ourselves for others is the only way to make a positive difference."

His shoulders lowered and he seemed calmer. "I am here today to honor my son's sacrifice. He gave his life to save another life. Today he was recognized as an extraordinary person. The team played for him. They won the game for him. I held up the sign—for him. As far as having faith or expressing faith, I am a student. He was the teacher. If only I had listened to him sooner. Would it have changed the outcome? No. Billy would still have gone to the picnic. He would still have saved that boy. But maybe, if I had been more involved in his life and faith, I might have been there too. Would I have been able to save him? I don't think that was an option. In some way beyond our understanding, Billy needed to die so that others could be changed by it."

His voice cracked and he took a moment to contain himself. Velvet held her breath, hoping no one interrupted.

The reporters waited. Surprisingly respectful. Expectant.

Roman wiped a sleeve across his eyes, sniffed, and held his chin high. "The fact is this: if Billy's friend had held up the sign during a game from within the stands—as Billy had asked her to do, and as some have done before—a few people would have seen it. A good thing. And yet . . . today, because of Billy's death, because of the inspirational details of his sacrifice, because of this game dedicated in his honor, tens of thousands of people saw

Billy's sign and will hear about him through the stories you write and report out of this interview. I only ask that you don't back down from the facts of Billy's death, nor the facts of the sign and its content. I know it's not politically correct to talk about God, or especially mention Jesus, but I ask you all—I beg you— to take a stand and let the message of Billy's death be told. John 3:16, ladies and gentlemen. John 3:16."

Roman stood and looked to Velvet, and they exited the room out a back way. Once in the hallway, his knees buckled and she caught him on the way to the floor.

Together they slid to seating. Roman began to sob.

Velvet joined him. She had never been so proud . . . so proud.

And humbled. He'd changed so much.

And she?

| | | | | | | | | | | |

Velvet stumbled back to the concessions stand where she had left John. Her legs barely moved and felt as though she'd run a marathon.

She'd been away far longer than she'd intended, and she expected John to be gone.

But he was there, sitting on the counter, his legs dangling. "I thought you'd run away and joined the cir—" He let his smile go and jumped down. "You look horrible. What happened? Was Roman that upset?"

She shook her head and pointed to the counter. "Sit. I need to sit." She put her hands in place, intending to hop up, but couldn't find the energy.

Without saying a word, John lifted her into place, then joined her. He took her hand and rested it on his knee. "Talk to me."

Velvet ended up telling him everything. John listened well

and offered only a few comments that led her deeper into the telling.

When she was through, she sighed. "All that. I never planned on telling you all that."

"*All that* has obviously affected you deeply."

"Roman is so changed. I still see the old Roman in there, the one who needs to be in total control, yet that Roman has been beaten back."

"Or maybe he surrendered?"

Surrendered? Roman? "It's too much. Billy's death, then the verse and . . ." She turned to see John's face. "Roman took a risk holding up that sign. He took a stand."

"Indeed he did."

Finally, she realized the source of her anguish. "I've never done that." She waited for him to disagree.

He didn't.

Were her shortcomings that obvious? A hint of her old defensive nature started to rise, but she shoved it back. Now was not the time to get testy. She'd come this far; she had to see this thought through—wherever it led. "Roman talked about seeing his wife and son in heaven someday. That seemed to give him a lot of comfort."

"As it should."

Here was the point—the point she had to get out in the open. "I have a daughter *here*." She looked away. "Lianne found me by some miraculous intervention, and I haven't even acknowledged her. Today you introduced her as your daughter. Just like that. I had the chance to chime in, but I didn't. Why didn't I? Why haven't I claimed her?"

John remained silent.

Velvet hopped down, faced him, and repeated the question. "Why haven't I claimed her as my daughter?"

"She's not the stereotypical dream daughter."

"Which is . . . ?"

"Beautiful, smart, poised, classy, and elegant, with an inevitable future full of grand things."

Velvet's laugh was heavy with sarcasm. She looked up and down the corridor, just to make sure Lianne wasn't still around. "She's an eccentric, smart-mouthed girl, wearing vintage hand-me-downs as she complicates her life with an unwanted pregnancy and lofty plans to change the world."

345

John gripped the edge of the counter and extended one leg toward her as a pointer. "Sounds like another girl I once knew."

Velvet froze.

"Gotcha."

He was right. One hundred percent right. She batted his foot down, then pressed her fingers to her temples. "She's me. I'm her."

"Two of a kind."

Velvet stepped away from the counter, turning in a circle, her fingers still pressed to her head, trying to keep the thought from escaping. Once she had done a complete 360, she let her hands fall to her sides. "No wonder I'm not rushing to claim her. She reminds me of myself, at a difficult time in my life."

"She's forcing you to think about it, relive it."

Velvet pointed at John. "Your sudden appearance isn't helping matters."

He shrugged. "Maybe it's time to deal with it, accept who you were."

"And what I did."

John jumped off the counter and put his hands on her shoulders. "You had a baby, Velvet. You gave her up for adoption. Like the words in John said: God gave his child out of love. So did you."

She felt some of a weight being lifted—but not completely. John didn't know the half of what she'd done. No one did. But maybe . . . was now the time to change that?

She took his hands and moved them off her shoulders, holding them in the space between them. Looking down at their hands, clasped, gave her strength. "Getting pregnant and giving Lianne away is only the beginning of what I need to deal with and accept."

A veil of worry shadowed his face. "What are you talking about?"

After all the years of not trusting anyone enough, it was time. Yet she couldn't tell him and be so close, so she moved away, putting the counter between them. "I was so angry and confused after you left, and sad and confused after I gave up Lianne. I was alone. But . . . but not for long."

"You had another boyfriend?"

"I had boys. Men. Football players. And they had me. As many as would take me. I made myself available for their . . . their use."

"Oh, Velvet, I'm—"

She stopped his words. "No. Don't give me sympathy. I knew what I was doing. I hated myself, I hated you, I hated anything having to do with the football game you played, and so I jumped into a life of self-punishment."

John pressed a hand against his chest. "Because I left."

She couldn't let him take the blame. "Don't give yourself all the credit, John. I did my part messing up my life. And I kept doing my part." This next would be the hardest to say, but since she'd opened the Pandora's box of her sins, she had to continue. "I got pregnant. Twice."

"You had two more child—?"

"No. I had no more children. I aborted both of them." Her throat tightened and she had trouble continuing, for this was the sword that had been permanently held above her head, ready to take its revenge. "I killed my babies."

John didn't move for a moment, and her first thought was

as selfish as her entire life had been: *I've lost you because of this, haven't I? This is just another punishment being played out in grand style. I fall for you and then God takes you away from—*

But then John took a step around the counter to comfort her. His face was so sympathetic, so kind, it shocked her, and even as she wanted to fall into his arms, she found she couldn't. She didn't deserve his kindness. Especially when he still didn't know the worst of it. She raised her arms, holding him away. "No! Don't come near me. I'm not through."

He froze, his kindness being tainted by apprehension.

"The last abortion went wrong, and I was injured internally, so much so that I could never get pregnant again. I killed my babies, and God punished me by taking away any chance that I could ever have another one."

The apprehension was replaced by compassion. "I . . . I don't know what to say."

Her voice came out in shattered pieces. "There's nothing to say," Velvet said. "That's why I never got married, nor even got close to marriage. How could I ask a husband to love someone who'd done all that? someone who had ruined her chances to ever be a mother?"

He hesitated and looked to the floor.

Indeed. What more could he say. She'd lost him forever now. Her sins had piled, one upon the other, until they'd become an insurmountable barrier between them. His next words would certainly be, "I can't deal with this now, Velvet. I have to have time to think." And when he said those words, she would know for certain that it was over, the final punishment of all punishments. For having him back in her life had allowed her to think positively about the future. Now there would be no future. Not with her past piled between them.

"Say something!" she said. *Hate me. Yell at me. Walk away from me.*

347

John finally looked up from the floor and said, "Did you stay at this job to punish yourself too?"

A bitter laugh escaped. That was it? That was his worst? It took her a moment to adapt from her imagined scenario of him storming away to the reality of him still standing before her, waiting for an answer.

"Of course," she said, and even smiled at the irony of it. "I hate all things football, so working here was a perfect punishment."

John looked pensive; then he said, "Is that why you befriended Roman? Because his son was a player? Because football is so important to him?"

Velvet stopped smiling and nearly stopped breathing. That there was yet another layer to her vendetta against herself . . . "I . . . I didn't think of that." She began to pace behind the counter. "I used to go after the players, but when I got too old to be attractive to them . . . did I subconsciously choose Roman because . . . Oh, that's horrible. That's sick." She stopped pacing and faced him. "You need to go home, John, back to San Diego. You need to run away from me as fast as you can. I'm no good for you, no good for anyone."

But then, in a scene that had not even registered in her mind as a possibility, he came to her and took her into his arms. At first she fought against him, thinking, *No, you can't do this. You can't care for me anyway.*

"No one cares about your past, Velvet. Or mine. It is what it is. The big question is who are we now?"

She pushed away from him. "I'm no better now than I was. Look at what I did to Roman."

"You didn't do anything to Roman except be a friend to him. You didn't hurt him. You didn't hurt his son. If anything, you were punishing yourself, but they didn't suffer from the association."

Maybe. Maybe what he said was true.

John continued. "You need to forgive yourself and ask God to forgive you too."

A bitter laugh escaped. "God? Forgive me? And me, go to him? Why should I seek him now? Where was he while I was messing up my life? Why . . . why didn't he stop me?"

John's eyebrows rose. "You can't blame God for your choices."

She felt a pang of uncertainty but continued the argument anyway. "Sure I can. If he's so all-powerful, then why didn't he—?"

"Velvet . . ."

She let out a sigh. She knew she was being unfair, and childish, and wrong. It's just that she was so incredibly weary. "Forget I said that. I know he wasn't to blame. I'm the only one to blame. I made the choices. I wanted to punish myself. I accept responsibility for all of it. And I'm sorry for all of it."

"And because of that, God will forgive you." He clapped his hands once. "There! It's done. God has forgiven you."

John looked so happy it was almost comical. So certain. "Just like that?"

"No, not just like that. Jesus suffered and died on the cross; *he* took the punishment we all deserve. *That* act made forgiveness possible. Peace. Grace. New beginnings."

Suddenly, Velvet felt an inner stirring. *New beginnings? Is such a thing possible?* She placed both hands on her heart, wishing she could capture what was going on in there, draw it out into the open so she could be sure. Certain.

Yet could it be true? Could she truly let the entirety of her horrible past go?

John's voice was soft. "Now is what matters, Velvet. What about *now*? How can you move on with your life from this moment? How can you show others a bit of the love and forgiveness God just extended to you?"

Now. The past didn't matter. Now mattered. And now included . . . "You're here. Lianne's here," she said.

"Exactly. And trust is here. I appreciate your telling me your story. It means you trust me. I don't take that lightly, Velvet."

Neither did she. But it felt good to have it out, to share the burden. And yet . . . *now* was still filled with uncertainty. Even if she could let the past go, it didn't mean she had suddenly morphed into a loving, caring person. A mother. "How . . . how can I love Lianne now? As she is."

"You love her by forgiving her for being imperfect. And then you remember this—" John held out his hands and waited for her to take them—"'Love is patient and kind. Love is not jealous or boastful or proud or rude. It does not demand its own way. It is not irritable, and it keeps no record of being wronged. It does not rejoice about injustice but rejoices whenever the truth wins out. Love never gives up, never loses faith, is always hopeful, and endures through every circumstance.'" He grinned. "There. That should cover it."

She shook her head, smiling back at him. "How do you do that? Quote stuff like that."

"You read a truth often enough it finds a place inside and takes up residence. It becomes yours."

Velvet once again looked at their hands, clasped together. It seemed so right to see them like this, to feel the power in their shared surrender and strength. *Surrender.* John had said Roman had surrendered. Was this what it felt like to give in, to let go? to let another person take and give and be a part of her? She'd never done that—or hadn't since John had last been in her life. "You're too good for me."

He brought her hands to his lips and kissed them. "Nah. Just good enough."

She hadn't felt the safety of his arms for over twenty years, and yet . . .

As she stopped fighting against him and let his arms encase her with love and care and warmth . . . it was like coming home.

| | | | | | | | | | |

351

Roman came out of the kitchen, wiping his hands on his jeans. "Pizza's in the oven. What movie do you want to watch?"

AJ looked through the shelves of DVDs. "Do you want a manly-man movie, a too-stupid-for-words comedy, a bad-team-wins-the-big-game movie, or a boy-gets-girl romance?"

Roman turned on the TV. "I don't own any romantic movies. Do I?"

AJ pointed a DVD at him. "Actually, you don't. Which speaks volumes for why you have no love life. Women like a man who can tap into his sensitive side."

The advice, coming from AJ, who wore baggy sweatpants and a fly-fishing T-shirt, held little persuasive power.

AJ made his own decision. "*Saving Private Ryan*. A classic."

"Fine with—"

Suddenly, glass shattered. Something flew through the living room window. Roman instinctively protected his face.

He heard a car zoom away.

AJ ran to the window. "What was that?"

Roman spotted a rock under the coffee table. There was a note tied around it.

"A rock? Someone threw a rock at your window?"

"*Through* my window." Roman released the note and read it aloud. "'Keep God to yourself.'"

"Nice," AJ said.

"I've had a few phone messages too. One threatened me."

"Just because you held up a sign."

"A sign about God."

"You pushed somebody's button."

"I thought if people weren't interested, they simply wouldn't notice. I never expected people to be so . . . angry."

"It goes with the territory."

"What goes?"

"Persecution. The Bible warns us we'll be persecuted if we are his."

"Nobody told me that."

"It's in the fine print."

Roman weighed the rock in his hand. If either of them had been in its path . . . "I didn't sign up for this. I didn't want to upset people."

"If you would have held up a sign saying, 'Eat Chocolate!' you would have upset somebody." AJ set a newspaper on the floor and began placing shards on top of it. "Since when have you cared what people thought?"

Roman got a wastebasket from the corner. "That's not nice."

"Ah, come on, Rome. It's me you're talking to."

AJ was right. Roman had always waved his opinions as a banner—before setting a chip on his shoulder, daring people to disagree. The habit had cost him with Billy, with potential girlfriends, with . . . most everyone.

He used a magazine to shove shards from the windowsill into the wastebasket. "I did get a few nice phone messages. And a lady stopped me in the grocery store and said she'd seen me on TV and the sign had spurred her to start praying again. She'd gotten out of the habit."

"See?" AJ said. "Grab on to the good that sign did and shake the dust off your shoes for the ones who don't get it—or refuse to get it."

"Dust?"

"That's what Jesus told his disciples to do when they'd done their best and people wouldn't listen. There's only so much you can do. God appreciates your effort. He'll take up where you left off. Do your best and move on." AJ transferred a paper full of shards into the wastebasket, then arched his back. "Billy would be proud of you. Hold on to that."

That *had* been the one image he'd held on to, that somehow God had allowed Billy to see the stadium today, and he'd seen his dad hold up the sign and had heard him talk about God at the press conference. If Billy was proud of him . . .

If God is proud of me . . .

It was odd to think of such a thing, or especially to strive for such a thing, but Roman would give it a shot.

For Billy.

353

TWELVE

*He saved us, not because
of the righteous things we had done,
but because of his mercy.
He washed away our sins, giving us a new birth
and new life through the Holy Spirit.*

TITUS 3:5

Roman placed an empty box next to a bookshelf in Billy's apartment. Cleaning out his son's belongings was a horrible job, but one he felt he should do sooner rather than later. Peter had told him to take his time, but Roman knew for budgetary reasons Peter needed to get a new roommate—sooner rather than later.

The bottom shelf held the usual batch of textbooks, kept from past years because they were worth next to nothing in resale, along with a batch of Louis L'Amour Westerns that Billy had been addicted to as a kid.

The top shelf was full of books Roman never would have expected but that spoke to his son's depth of faith: *My Utmost for His Highest*, *The Confessions of Saint Augustine*, *Mere Christianity* . . .

Roman leafed through *Discover God* and found the pages covered with his son's notes, underlining, and highlighting: *"God's love is a gift to all who will receive it by faith; he offers it to us freely. Nothing we do will make God love us any more; nothing we do will make him love us any less. He loves us because he is gracious, not because of who we are, but because of who he is."*

The quote was connected by an arrow to some words Billy had written in the margin: *"I wish Dad would love me like this—and understand God loves him. I pray for him."*

He was praying for me? I wasn't praying for him. Maybe if I had prayed for him . . .

Roman pressed his fingers on the words his son had written. Why hadn't he listened? Why had he shut the door? He'd always bragged that he would do anything for his family, and yet . . .

"I only did what *I* wanted."

He turned the pages and read more notations from Billy: *"I wish I could make God proud of me. . . . God loves me, but what is my purpose? How can I love him more? . . . I'm here, God! Send me! Help me love my father better. . . .*

"Mr. Paulson?"

Caught. Roman brushed the tears away. "Yes, Peter?"

"Are you okay?"

"Fine; I'm just . . ." He shook his head. Enough playacting. He was sick to death of pretending to be strong, knowledgeable, and in control. "No, I'm not fine. I found this book and it has markings Billy made, and he . . . he was praying for me."

"He was," Peter said. "He asked me to pray for you too."

Roman was incredulous. "Both of you?"

"Carrie too."

Roman didn't know whether he should feel like an idiot for needing the prayers of these young people or feel humbled that they'd thought enough of him to care.

"You did a good thing holding up that sign the other day, Mr. Paulson."

"You saw it?"

"I was in the stands with Carrie. It made me think. . . . It made me realize I need to do more, speak out more, live like William lived so people know—they just know—God's going on inside."

Roman liked that: *God's going on inside.*

Peter shuffled a foot against the carpet. "You want some help in here?"

357

"No, thanks. I need to do this myself. It's helping me know Billy—know William. Know the kind of man my son had become."

Peter nodded and left him alone to his quest.

Too bad Roman's interest was later, rather than sooner.

| | | | | | | | | | |

Maya got out of the car and joined Sal at the sidewalk leading up to the First Hope Children's Home. Although Sal was the one who sought her hand, she was glad to give it. "Are we really doing this?" she said.

"Apparently." Sal took a deep breath. "It does seem a little surreal. A few weeks ago we were worrying about where to get the money for another procedure, and today we're going to see the boy who might become our son."

"Instant family," she said.

He pulled her to a stop. "Are we ready?"

"Is anyone?"

"We don't even have a room fixed up for him."

Doubts slid between them and began to pry apart Maya's resolve. "What if he doesn't like us? What if he cries and runs away and says, 'No! I won't go with *them*!'"

"He wouldn't." Sal's forehead furrowed. "Yet . . . he doesn't know us. There's no guarantee."

This wasn't doing either of them any good. Maya knew how easy it was to talk herself out of something good and into something bad. She hoped to eventually learn to do the opposite, but it would take a lot of practice.

Starting now.

Maya faced her husband, taking his hands in hers. "We have to stop talking ourselves out of this, thinking the worst. Haven't we discussed how much of a God thing this is—which means it's a good thing, something we *are* supposed to do. We wouldn't have come this far if it weren't for him nudging us to do it. All those blank signs I saw . . . and then seeing Roman's sign. You were the one who told me that was God."

"It was God. This is God's doing." His voice was stronger, his face lost its doubtful edge, and he offered her a brave smile. "Let's do it."

Onward, Christian soldiers. It was time to claim their son.

| | | | | | | | | | |

Maya and Sal sat on an alphabet carpet with Barry playing between them. He made car noises and pushed a red truck up and down the L on the floor. Sal did the same with a blue car. "Vroom, vroom," Sal said.

"Mine goes fast," Barry said. He stopped the car in front of Maya's leg and looked up at her. "Do you want a car too, lady?"

"Okay." Maya dug into the toy bin. "I pick a green bus."

Barry began singing, "'The wheels on the bus go round and round . . .'"

Maya had heard her nieces and nephews sing that song. She joined in, "'Round and round . . .'"

Sal joined too. "'Round and round. The wheels on the bus go round and round, all through the town.'"

Barry grinned like they'd done something profound.

Maybe they had.

| | | | | | | | | | | |

"I like 'ghetti best of anything."

Maya put another spoonful on his plate. "That's why I picked it." She'd asked the people at the children's home about Barry's favorite things. Although this time they were spending together was a part of the introductory phase, although the adoption was not fully approved, she wanted to make Barry feel at home. And happy.

It was odd to have someone besides Sal to please—to love—and yet, Maya found it surprisingly easy, as if there was some limitless source available, one that had been patiently waiting for her to tap into.

"Want me to cut it into smaller pieces?" Sal asked the boy.

Barry shook his head. "I can do it."

Watching Sal watch Barry, Maya was shocked at the wave of emotion that swept over her like a soothing blanket. This was right. And it was good.

Once Barry was through, he put his fork down and looked at Sal, then at Maya, as if waiting. . . .

Sal understood first. He took Barry's hand and then Maya's. Barry held his hand across the table to Maya, forming a circle. Then Sal prayed, "Thank you, Jesus, for this meal and for this time we have together." He looked at Maya. "Do you want to add something?"

She was taken aback. She'd never prayed aloud before. And though she was certainly grateful for a lot of things, for Sal to put her on the spot like this, in front of the—

Barry said, "I'll go." He closed his eyes and bowed his head again. "Thank you for saving me for Sal and Maya. I like them and I like it here. She made me spaghetti." He hesitated just a moment. "Thank you, God, for spaghetti."

Sal squeezed Maya's hand, a gesture that expressed a thousand words between them. Maya suddenly forgot that she didn't pray aloud. Words born from their clasped hands and this boy's heart wove together and found release. "Thank you, God, for giving us a son."

She opened her eyes to see Sal and Barry looking at her.

"You agree?" she asked them.

"Yes, yes," Sal said.

They both looked to Barry. He did not speak—with words— but left his chair and moved into the space between them.

Filling the space between them.

| | | | | | | | | | | |

Roman piled the boxes from Billy's apartment in the garage. He had no idea what he would do with them. Those were decisions for another day.

This day had been full: full of to-dos, now completed, but more so, full of emotions and ponderings, never completed.

Peter's phrase had stuck with Roman all day: *God's going on inside.* Billy had lived such a life, a witness to others in spite of Roman's ignorant objections. Billy had left behind a legacy.

What was Roman's legacy?

He closed the garage door and entered the house, tossing his keys on the counter. But as soon as their rattle ceased, the silence slammed against him, as substantial and unrelenting as if he'd run into an invisible wall.

A wall between this moment and the future.

Roman froze. His breaths became short bursts, and his heart beat double-time, as though on high alert.

It was the oddest feeling, as though this house were different from the house he'd left this morning before going to Billy's apartment.

That was absurd. It was the same house. Nothing had changed. The box of Life cereal still sat on the kitchen table, as did his

dirty cereal bowl and spoon. The newspaper was in a haphaz-
ard pile nearby. The sink was stacked with dirty dishes from last
night's dinner of Dinty Moore beef stew.

Nothing had changed.

No thing had changed.

God's going on inside.

Roman drew in a new breath, forcing his lungs and heart out
of their alert mode and into a moment that was new and fresh.

Was God going on inside *him*?

He put a hand on his chest and breathed in and out a few
times, trying to gauge . . .

It was subtle and perhaps not even tangible. An X-ray or MRI
taken before and after might not have detected the alteration,
but Roman knew something had changed between this morning
when he'd left to go to Billy's and now, when he had returned.
He felt . . . fuller. Something had been added to who he was, giving him a sense that he could be something more and *was* something more even now. It was as if an inner door had been opened
and he was on the verge of passing through it. On the other
side were promises of amazing things beyond his comprehension. His entire being tingled with an anticipation that his own
future—which he'd never belabored, which he'd pretty much ignored—was something he wanted to touch and hold and run
through and absorb.

Is this you, God?

In return for his thought, there was no booming voice from
heaven—which was a relief—but Roman did feel a renewed
sense of *more*.

And because of that, he wanted *more*.

He moved to the kitchen table and took his usual seat. He
pushed the breakfast debris aside, needing a clear space, then
spread his hands on the table and with the smallest trace of trepi-
dation whispered, "Okay. I'm here. So now what?"

Now what swelled into a bevy of thoughts and images pertaining to work. His job. Or rather, his lack of a job. He tried to rein in the thoughts because they didn't seem very ethereal—and shouldn't thoughts at such a time seem ethereal?—but they persisted.

He'd quit his job. He needed a new one. The bills didn't care if he was having a God moment or not.

Roman noticed the newspaper. He pulled it close, finding the want ads. Yet despite his intentions, he couldn't get his mind to focus on any of them. He read the words but not a one of them registered any meaning.

He pushed the paper away and looked upward. "If you want me to do something, you're going to have to be plain about it."

The phone rang, making his heart jump. He laughed. If God was on the line he was going to be very impressed.

It wasn't God. It was Velvet.

"Are you busy?" she asked. "Could you stop over to my office and talk to me?"

"Is something wrong?"

"Actually, something's right and it's scaring me spitless."

"Now there's a way to pique my interest."

"Good. I'll be waiting for you."

Roman hung up the phone. Any message from God would have to wait.

| | | | | | | | | | |

Roman approached Memorial Stadium with his neck hunched low in his collar, his hands in the pockets of his jacket. The fickle weather of autumn had turned the afternoon blustery and cold. A gust of wind burst between the campus buildings, making leaves and litter execute a frenzied dance. He hurried toward the entrance that would lead to Velvet's office, hoping she had some hot coffee available. The wind played tug-of-war with the door, but Roman won, letting it blow shut behind him. He took a moment to shake the chill away.

"Mr. Paulson!"

Roman looked to his right and saw Coach Rollins. The old feeling of dread was intercepted by a nudge to be civil. Things had changed since the last time they'd talked. He'd changed. "Hi, Coach," Roman said. As an afterthought he offered his hand.

Coach Rollins seemed a bit surprised but shook it eagerly. "I'm so glad you're here. Did you read my mind today, or what?"

"Read your—?"

The coach brushed the question away. "Do you have a minute?"

Roman thought of Velvet but knew she'd wait—a minute.

"Let's sit." Coach Rollins led Roman to a sitting area off the entrance. Once Roman sat, the coach took a chair nearby. "I have a business proposition for you."

"For me?"

"For you."

This I gotta hear.

"I was very impressed by what you did for William's dedication at the game last weekend. Holding up the sign like that . . ." Rollins shook his head. "You surprised me. When we'd talked before, you didn't seem very open to God things and—"

"I wasn't. But . . ." He wasn't sure how to say this. "Let's say he got my attention."

The coach beamed. "That's good to hear. And that's perfect for what I want to talk to you about. In fact—" he gathered a new breath—"in the past few days your name kept coming to mind. And then, when the coaches started discussing the advantage of having a noncoach mentor for the players . . ."

Mentor?

Rollins leaned forward. "Let me get to the point. When

kids come here to play for the team they quickly become over-whelmed. It's a big program and they have dreams and ques-tions and classes and roommates and . . . and they have to do a lot of adapting, fast. They need guidance. Not just team or academic guidance but life guidance. Your son exemplified the type of young man we want this program to nurture and de-velop. We want them to leave here better men than the boys they were when they came. That's why the idea of a mentor came up. Someone to be a buffer between their teachers, us coaches, and life. Someone who loves the team but who's also experienced some of the ups and downs of juggling real issues and problems. A godly man who can guide them in whatever way they need to be guided." The coach stopped talking and waited.

Surely, he's not . . . Roman shook his head, incredulous. "Surely you can't mean me?"

"Surely I can."

Roman waved away the words. "But I'm not a godly man, at least I haven't been, and it's too soon to say if I ever will be. I made a ton of mistakes with Billy, with being a father. And I know next to nothing about God. It's like we've just been intro-duced and are sizing each other up."

Coach Rollins laughed. "Sounds interesting."

"That remains to be seen."

The coach sat back. "Actually, that's perfect because we don't want a preacher or somebody who wears God on their sleeve. We need someone who's been on the nonbelieving side, who un-derstands the doubts and fears of *not* being his. And your new faith, no matter what level it's at right now, is of use to these boys. Because you are a bit uncertain, because you realize you don't know all the answers, you'd be approachable. We think boys will relate to where you've been and to the journey you're on right now. And this would be a chance for kids to hear about William and his sacrifice. Between the two of you, we hope to inspire the boys to be . . ." He searched for a word, then found it. "Be more."

More. It was the same word that had come to mind back in his kitchen just an hour before. His desire to be more than he was. To know more. Understand more.

"Are you interested? I know we're asking a lot, because you have a job and—"

"I quit my job."

Coach Rollins smiled. "Well, well. It looks like God has been setting things up for us."

Roman had never thought of it that way, and yet the timing was hard to ignore. He'd had the job at Efficient for five years. For this new job offer to come on the heels of leaving the other job behind . . .

"I . . ." Roman cleared his throat and knew what he was going to say, even though common sense told him he was crazy to say it. "I think I'm interested."

"You're saying yes?"

"I guess I am."

| | | | | | | | | | | |

Roman didn't wait for an invitation to enter Velvet's office. Propelled by what he had just done—what he had just agreed to be and do—he went in, walked up to the edge of her desk, and said, "You'll never believe what I just did."

In response to his aggressive entrance, Velvet rolled her chair back a foot. "You climbed Mount Everest."

He laughed. "Figuratively, yes."

She took hold of the desk and pulled herself back into place. "Tell me more."

He told her about his chance meeting with Coach Rollins. "I said yes, Velvet. I told him I'd do it."

"You hated that man. I remember you detailing—on more than one occasion—exactly what you planned to do to him and it involved pain, humiliation, and other nasty things."

Roman remembered his tirades with shame. "To be honest, I'm the one who drove Billy away. The coach didn't do anything wrong."

Velvet caught her breath and raised her eyebrows. "Who *are* you?"

He sank into a guest chair, suddenly exhausted. "I'm not sure. Lately, I'm not quite *right*."

"Actually, maybe now you *are* right. Maybe now you are finally *right*."

He didn't know what to say. Velvet had always seconded his opinions and let him wallow in his moods. "If I'm right now, that means before I was . . ."

"Wrong." She sighed. "Both of us, wrong."

Now it was his turn to be incredulous. "Ms. The-World's-Done-Me-Wrong is admitting *she* was wrong?"

Velvet shrugged. Then she eyed him strangely. "There are a few things I haven't told you about, Roman. New developments."

"Such as?"

She reached for a photo on her desk and handed it to him. "This sweet young thing in the photo is me, aeons ago, and the man next to me is—"

Roman recognized him. "John. The man who came to my house and watched videos of Billy, the man who brought me the note from you in the stands."

She put a finger on her nose. "Development number one is his reentry into my life."

Roman tried to remember some of the scant facts she'd told him about her past. He took a guess. "Was he the one who left you in a lurch? ran out on you?"

"One and the same."

"And now he's back?"

"Him, and—" she took a new breath—"our daughter."

"Your—?"

"Her name's Lianne Skala, and she applied for a job here at the concessions office, and I hired her, and . . ." Velvet added details, leading Roman in an incredible journey from then to now. "So," Velvet concluded, "they are the reason I've changed, or am trying to change, or am thinking about wanting to try to change." She slumped in her chair. "Being wrong is exhausting."

367

"Admitting you're wrong is exhausting." He sighed. "I know."

She held out a hand, wanting the picture back. Once she had it in her possession, her expression changed. Softened.

"I've never seen you like this, Velvet. You're . . . softer."

She laughed. "I think there's a cut in there, somewhere amid the compliment."

"We were both hard. Too hard. Too angry."

"We egged each other on—in a bad way."

He let her words sink in. Was she right?

Velvet returned the photo to its place and spread her hands on the desk. "We kept each other angry, Roman, by ignoring what was really bothering us. We kept the fire blazing. We never helped each other quench it. We never helped each other move on. We let our anger fester."

It was a blow. He'd always considered Velvet a good friend. But did friends conspire to keep each other miserable? "Were we bad for each other?"

The speed at which Velvet nodded indicated she'd already thought about it. "It makes me sad," she said. "What could our friendship have been like if we'd helped each other out of our moods? helped each other be happy?"

Roman shared her sadness. He'd never had a relationship like the one he'd had with Velvet. Maybe that was a good thing. "I do like you, Velvet."

"I like you too. But I think I like the new Roman better. What you said during that press conference . . ." She shook her head. "Never in all our years spending time together did I meet the man who said those words. Where was he? Was I partly responsible for keeping him hidden away?"

He had to stop her. "No, Velvet. Don't say that." He reached for her hands on the desk. "I am responsible for me. I've blamed other people and other things. I've blamed God for all my troubles. Not that it was my fault Trudy or Billy died, but it was my fault for being difficult and cold. What did I gain by it?"

"As much as I gained by being mad about *my* past."

He squeezed her hands before letting them go. "Look at us. Two middle-aged people learning lessons we should have learned years ago."

"Better learned now than later."

He thought about his new job with the football team. "I have the feeling our learning curve is just beginning."

She rose and came around the desk, her arms outstretched. They lingered in an embrace.

"I'm sorry, Velvet."

"Me too."

Roman let her go and noticed tears in her eyes. "Keep in touch, yes?"

"Maybe we can have dinner and catch up on all the good stuff going on in our lives."

"It's a date."

| | | | | | | | | | |

Roman paused at the exit from the stadium, taking time to zip his coat and raise the collar against the wind.

And yet . . . as he went outside he immediately noticed the

sun was shining and the wind had exchanged its bitter bluster for a gentle breeze.

He laughed, lowered his collar, and let the tension fall from his shoulders. There was no need for it.

For any of it.

When he rounded the corner of the stadium, the sun reflected off the facade, showcasing the chiseled words he'd noticed last Saturday: *Not the victory but the action; not the goal but the game; in the deed the glory.*

Today the motto had special meaning. Roman didn't know what the future held. He never would. All he could do was act, execute the next play, and hope for a victory.

At least now he knew he wasn't alone.

| | | | | | | | | | |

How odd.

To feel free.

After embracing Roman—in a final embrace?—Velvet returned to her desk and found herself feeling lighter in a way that had nothing to do with pounds and ounces.

They'd shared a confession: they had *not* been good for each other. Why hadn't she ever realized that before? They'd been going out for a couple of years, filling their time with chitchat and gripes, never addressing their innermost thoughts beyond quick mention, never allowing themselves blessed release or a chance at healing. Velvet had worn her bitterness like a coat, buttoning it tight against any hope or happiness. She'd lived in a perpetual winter, encumbered by the heavy covering of her past.

Until now.

Needing to expand the feeling of *new*, Velvet drew a new breath into her new lungs within her new body. Oddly, there seemed to be more space inside. She pointed at the picture of her younger self and said, "You really messed things up, kid. But I forgive you for it." Her eyes strayed to John. "You too, Johnny-boy."

The old photo suddenly felt out of place. She needed a new one.

John's book still held court on the corner of her desk, so she set it upright, the author photo of John smiling out at her.

One down.

Lianne. She needed a picture of her daughter.

Then she remembered. . . .

Velvet rushed to the file cabinet and found the Employee Badges file. She pulled out two copies, took them to her desk, and carefully cut the extraneous information away, leaving her with a not-too-bad photo of Lianne and one so-so picture of herself.

With a piece of tape to the backs, she added the pictures to John's book cover, Velvet on his left and Lianne, his right.

"There," she said.

And yet it was a slipshod arrangement. Hardly good enough for a proper family.

But easily enough remedied.

| | | | | | | | | | |

Peter took his jacket off the hall tree in the entry of the McLean farmhouse and zipped it up against the fall day. Then he kissed his mother on the cheek and hugged his dad. "Thank you for listening to me, for offering . . . I mean it. You two are amazing."

His mother had tears in her eyes. "Let us know," she said.

| | | | | | | | | | |

On his drive back to town, Peter prayed for courage—and practiced what he would say to Lianne.

If he didn't chicken out.

He couldn't chicken out. This was the only way.

He pulled in front of her apartment building. Her car was there. She was home.

It was time.

He headed to her apartment, mentally repeating *help me, help me, help me* in sync with his steps.

He knocked on her door.

Lianne swung it open—wide—which surprised him, as last time she'd nearly nipped his knuckles. "Well, well. Where have you been the past few days?"

"Home. I mean, my parents' home. The farm." He finally let the nuance of her question connect. "Were you looking for me?"

"I was. Come in. I've made a decision about the baby."

"Good. So have I." Peter was surprised at how resolute his words sounded. Strong. He didn't feel strong.

She led him into the living room and climbed into a round rattan chair, tucking her feet beneath her long red skirt. Peter sat on the futon couch. "I—"

She stopped his words with a hand. "No. Let me go first. The point is, I don't love you, McLean. To be truthful, you were an afterthought."

"What?"

"I was after William, not you."

He had no idea what she was talking about. "*After* William?"

"None of my plan had anything to do with love. It was about revenge. Payback."

She was pushing him further and further down a side road. "Payback for what?"

"For my parents' deaths."

Peter stopped breathing as her words slammed into the moment, cracking what was real—or what he thought was real. "You never said your parents were dead."

"Yeah? Well, they are. And William's dad killed them."

Peter raised his hands on either side of his face. "Stop."

"No, I will not stop. It's all gone wrong and I'm tired of it. And so I've made a decision."

Peter shook his head. Although he wanted to hear her decision . . . "Rewind. Tell me about your parents and you being *after* William . . . and tell me what you're talking about."

She sighed dramatically. "A few years ago my dad and William's dad worked for the same company. But Mr. Paulson—Roman—he rooked my dad out of some sales by being unethical and making my dad look unethical. But Dad hadn't done anything wrong. Roman had. But Dad got canned. And Roman didn't."

"I'm sorry."

She pulled her knees to her chin. "Soon after that, Mom got sick with cancer and because Dad didn't have a job, we didn't have health insurance and we didn't have any income and Mom didn't get the treatments she needed." She lifted her chin—set it free from her knees. "She died."

Peter knew he was repeating himself, but . . . "I'm so sor—"

"Dad blamed himself and lost it. In that state of mind, he couldn't get a job and . . ." She raised her eyes above Peter's head. "And then he died. He just faded away. I'd heard of couples doing that, the remaining one dying of a broken heart, but I'd never believed it could really happen." She glared at Peter. "It happened. And Roman Paulson was to blame."

Unfortunately, from what he'd heard William say about his father, Peter could believe it was true. "When did all this—?"

"Five years ago. I was all set to go to college, but after they died, I didn't go. I couldn't. My dad had a life insurance policy that paid off the medical bills, the funeral, and gave me a little to live on until I got my head together." She smoothed her skirt over her knees. "But then things got worse. I was going through my parents' stuff and found my adoption papers. Adoption papers! They'd never told me I was adopted."

Peter let his mind glance across the what-if of his own parents keeping such a secret. To be betrayed like that . . . "They should have—"

She put her bare feet on the floor and pointed at him. "You bet they should have. And then I found a diary where my dad wrote about all the Paulson stuff. He was a broken man, McLean. I was mad at them for not telling me I was adopted yet sad for all the horrible things they'd gone through." She looked into the air between them. "If you asked me what I did during that year after they died, I couldn't tell you. I was eighteen and alone. I lived in the family house awhile. I did a lot of wandering, room to room. But then it became this coffin to me. I couldn't breathe; I couldn't live there." She shook her head, as if ridding herself of bad memories. "After a year of zombie hell, I finally sold it." She looked around her tiny apartment. "This is enough for me. It's my place. No one else's."

Peter felt new empathy for her. No wonder she was so fiercely independent. Aggressive. Bitter. She'd been burned—in so many ways.

Her anger dissipated; she pulled her feet back into the folds of the chair and tucked her skirt around them. "That's why I'm behind in school. Why I'm older," she said. "Last fall I used the money from the sale of the house to pay for tuition. I went into sociology because . . ." Her face suddenly softened as if her mask had accidentally slipped. "The reason will sound dumb," she said. "But every month Mom and Dad sent money to some kid in Thailand. I remember that. They sent letters too. Even when they didn't have the money for Mom to go to a doctor, they kept sending money to help that kid. And so I thought I'd get a degree in social work and go help some other kid somewhere." She cleared her throat. "For them, you know?"

"They'd be proud of you for that." He'd never seen her like this. Sensitive. Vulnerable.

She shrugged, and with that one action dispelled any hint of vulnerability to the past. "But then I met William in one of my classes and found out his dad was Roman Paulson, and my noble thoughts about doing good got sidetracked. I decided revenge was the way to go. It was much more satisfying than mooning over some fantasy about changing the world."

"Helping kids is not a fantasy. It's a good—"

She glared at him, stopping his words. "Are you going to let me finish or not?"

"Sorry. Go on."

"*Anyway*, I started hanging around with William. When I found out he was a Jesus freak and didn't believe in sex before marriage, I got the grand idea that I could be the one to break him, seduce him away from his lofty ideals. It was going to be *the* perfect revenge against his father."

Except that . . . "Mr. Paulson wasn't into God. Only William."

"I know that. Now. At first I didn't know his dad was anti-God like me. Or that they weren't close."

"When you found out, why didn't you back off?"

"I did, eventually, when William wouldn't give in to my charms. But by then . . . then there was you." She smiled. "You were sweet and nice to me and above all, interested. What can I say? I was in need of some comforting arms, and you were ready to supply them. And more."

Anger swelled his chest. She was so matter-of-fact, so calculating. And he'd been gullible enough to fall into her trap. "So you had fun tempting another virgin, huh? Using me for your own amusement?"

"Comfort, McLean. I needed to feel comfort and love. Because you weren't one to sleep around, I knew if I got you to have sex it would mean something—at least to you."

A new wound opened. "But not to you."

"I didn't love you, but I did care about you. Do, I suppose. Do care."

He'd been a complete fool. An idiot. "But you cared about yourself more."

375

"Guilty." She let her legs loose and put her feet on the floor. "And because I do care about me first, and as far as I know will always care about me first, I've decided to have this baby and give it up for adoption. I'm going to quit school and join some charity organization overseas right away." Her gaze landed on a book on the coffee table. Although the title was covered, Peter could see the word *Mistakes* in the title. "Who knows?" she said. "Maybe I'll find what I'm looking for by helping some kid a world away."

Her pronouncement made him remember why he'd come. "You don't need to put the baby up for adoption. I want it."

She laughed. "You're going to raise it? By yourself?"

"Not by myself. I went home and told my parents everything. They were shocked and disappointed, but after all that, they offered to keep the baby at the farm until I finish school. I'll only have one more year after it's born, and then I can move back to the farm too and be a real father to it."

"Him. It's a boy."

"You know that?"

"I feel it."

Peter liked the idea of having a little boy. He'd get him a pony and they could go riding through the fields, and he'd show him his special place by the creek. . . .

They sat silently, neither looking at the other. Peter was numb for one breath and agitated the next. He was glad to have learned more about Lianne and understood her better now. But the bottom line was he wanted their baby to be brought up with *his* family—perhaps now more than ever.

Lianne broke the silence. But her mood had changed. Her shoulders were slumped, her hands clasped, her arms locked between her knees. "There's good reason your parents don't like me, McLean. They're a good judge of character—or lack of character. I'm sorry I hurt you. I was wrong."

Well, well. Let the earth stand still.

"I appreciate that," he said. He knew how hard it was for her to say it. And in spite of the sting of his humiliation, he found it easy to accept her apology. After all, she'd suffered too. The key was to make sure their son didn't suffer. "What about my idea? Having our son grow up on the farm?"

She looked pensive. "At least I'd know where he was, who had him."

Relief bathed him with a luscious warmth. He'd expected her to argue because she always argued. But maybe she was done arguing. "You can come visit him anytime."

She shook her head. "We'll see."

Lianne's cell phone rang from the kitchen. She got up to answer it. After listening to the caller he heard her say, "You're kidding," then a few moments later, "Fine. I'll be there."

She flipped the phone off. "I have to go. That was Velvet—my birth mom. She's got it in her head to have a family photo taken."

Peter stood, readying to go. "That's a nice idea."

Lianne shrugged. "We'll see."

| | | | | | | | | | |

The session with the photographer was over and the results were . . . interesting.

Lianne had come to the appointment wearing a red Indian-print skirt, a beaded caftan blouse, and lace-up boots. Velvet was not completely certain if the girl had even run a comb through her hair for the occasion.

John must have sensed Velvet's reaction because he'd pulled at her hand and whispered, "Let it go."

And so, somehow, she had. The result was a picture of a professional-looking man wearing a blue and white striped shirt and khakis, a slightly overweight woman in black pants and a red sweater that covered her midsection if she held in her stomach, and a hippie-bohemian girl with a striking gray streak in her hair. They were an odd-looking trio. At least the reds coordinated.

At least it was done.

Afterward, Velvet had hoped Lianne would appreciate the symbolism of the picture: Velvet's public recognition that Lianne was her daughter. But the girl seemed oblivious. They walked toward their respective cars in the parking lot. "We're over here," Velvet said, pointing to her car.

Lianne pointed in the opposite direction but paused. She nodded to John. "I finished your book."

"How did you like it?"

"It kept me reading." She looked toward her car as though she was wrestling with wanting to tell them something else. "I'm going to join Kid Help International. As soon as the baby is born."

The baby. Velvet jumped in. "What are you going to do with the—?"

John interrupted. "Kid Help International?"

"Yes."

Velvet looked from one to the other. Something was going on between them that she didn't understand. "Will one of you fill me in?"

"Chapter five," John said.

Lianne nodded. Their eyes were locked.

377

Velvet waved a hand between them, trying to break through. "Hello?"

John pulled his eyes away. "After running out on you when you were pregnant, I joined Kid Help."

And now Lianne was joining the same organization?

"But I'll do better than you did," Lianne said.

Velvet was appalled. "Lianne, that's rude."

"Not really," John said. "I want her to do better than I did. While I was in Kenya I made one of my mistakes. A big one."

"I won't make the same mistake," Lianne said.

"I'm glad."

Velvet stepped between them. "I haven't read the book. I'm in the dark."

John dug his hands into the pockets of his jacket. "I wanted to run away from here and thought Kenya would be far enough. But I wasn't ready. I was a spoiled brat who complained about the living conditions, the work, the heat, the people."

"He was sent home," Lianne said.

"I was sent home. They were glad to be rid of me. It was best for the kids I didn't try to help them—not when I couldn't even help myself."

"I won't be sent home."

John reached out and touched his daughter's arm. "I'm sure you won't be."

Velvet felt like a fool. Why hadn't she read John's book? She knew so little about what had happened to him in the past twenty years. She'd thought she knew enough, but now, after spending more time with him, suddenly she wanted to know more. Much more.

"Peter's taking the baby," Lianne said. "His parents are going to raise it until he graduates. They live on a farm not too far away." Lianne got her keys out of her purse and started walking away. "I've got to go. Thanks for the pic—"

"Stop!"

Lianne turned around and suddenly Velvet realized she had no idea why she'd stopped her.

"Yes?"

And then she did know. "I'm . . . I'm going to be a grandma."

Lianne gave her an odd look. "Isn't that old news?"

Yes, it was, which added another layer to Velvet's faults. In addition to not recognizing Lianne as her daughter, she'd never allowed herself to publicly acknowledge her grandchild. Velvet shortened the space between them. "You're leaving the country, and you inform us that the father of the baby is going to raise it."

"Yes."

"I'd like a say in this. You're talking about my grandchild."

"Our grandchild," John said.

Lianne looked surprised. "I didn't think you were interested. You've never said a word."

No, she hadn't. But at the thought of the child being brought up elsewhere, away from her . . . "I want to be a part of its life."

"So do I," John said.

Lianne let out a puff of air. "*I* may not even be a part of the baby's life, yet you two want to be involved?"

Velvet looked at John, and together they nodded.

"Well then," Lianne said. "I'm sure something can be arranged so you can see him, have him over for cookies or whatever grandparents do."

"Him?" Velvet asked.

"I have a feeling it's a boy."

Velvet smiled. Yet she knew that boy or girl, it didn't matter.

"I'll move here," John said. "So I can be close too."

Both women looked at him. "You're going to move here?" Velvet asked. "From San Diego?"

"It's a little hard to get married and live in different cities. Different states."

A laugh escaped. "Married?"

He took Velvet's hands in his. "We both acknowledge God brought us together. And what God has brought together let no man put asunder, right?"

Oh my goodness. Mother, grandmother, and wife? The order may have been wrong, but . . .

This wasn't happening.

And yet it was.

Velvet threw away restraint—and the past twenty-three years—wrapped her arms around his neck, and kissed him.

More than once.

EPILOGUE

Maya pulled into her parents' driveway and shut off the car. She'd already had a long day, training to be a para—a teacher's assistant—at Barry's school which started next month. She couldn't believe he was going into the first grade. Big-boy school. They'd had him only nine months, but it seemed like forever. They couldn't imagine life without him.

Her parents had agreed to keep him today, as they were in between research projects. Egypt during the reign of Alexander the Great had been completed. Next, they were hoping to dive into Cleopatra's rule. Actually, Maya was early. She just wasn't feeling well. She hoped she wasn't coming down with something.

She rang the doorbell and expected Barry to be the one to answer it. He loved answering the door. Instead, she was surprised to find her sister Marcela.

"Hey, sister," Marcela said, checking her watch. "I thought you weren't going to be here until noon."

They headed back to the kitchen. The house was way too quiet. "I'm not feeling well. Where's Barry?"

"Out back with the other archaeologists in the family." Marcela took a seat at the kitchen's bar, two recipe file boxes in front of her. "Do *you* have the recipe for Grandma Castilla's fontina chicken?"

382   Maya took a seat at the bar to wait. "That dish with the mushrooms?"

"Yeah."

"No."

"Oh."

"Why aren't you at the university?"

"I was. But I'm having a dinner party tomorrow night for some of the faculty and got that particular recipe in my head, but now I can't find it."

"Make something el—" Suddenly, Maya felt green. She leaped off the stool and ran into the bathroom. She barely made it.

Marcela followed her. "I hope you're not getting the flu." She dampened a washcloth and wrung it out for her.

Maya flushed the toilet and wiped off her mouth. "Me too. Not with school starting."

Marcela put a hand on her forehead. "You don't feel feverish. Do you have body aches? a cough? sore throat?"

Maya hated being fussed over. She pushed past her sister and went back to the kitchen. "I'm fine. It's no big deal. Mostly queasiness. It passes."

"Queasiness that passes?"

Maya opened the refrigerator. Maybe a Sprite would make her feel better. "As the day wears on, I usually feel better." She grabbed a can.

Marcela gripped her arm and turned her around. "Queasiness only in the morning. Maya . . ."

Maya stared into her sister's eyes and saw their excitement. And realized the meaning behind their excitement. She let her jaw drop. "No. It couldn't—"

"But it might—"

"I can't—"

"But you could—"

"We adopted—"

Marcela pulled her into an embrace and swung her around, doing a little dance. "You're pregnant!"

Maya stopped the dance and shushed her. "We don't know that."

"*I* know," Marcela said. "And you wouldn't be the first couple to adopt and then find themselves with child."

Maya had heard of such a thing. More than once. She popped open the Sprite and took multiple swigs. "But Dr. Ruffin said it would take a miracle."

Marcela spread her hands. "Ta-da!"

Maya leaned against the counter, attempting to let the possibility be born.

Born. A baby of her own, born . . .

They both turned their heads toward the backyard when Barry and her parents laughed aloud. "You can't say anything to them, Marce. Nothing, you hear?"

Her sister made a zipping motion over her lips. "But only on the condition that I'm the second—no, make that third—to know."

Maya agreed with a nod, finished off her Sprite, and headed to the backyard to pick up her son.

Her child. Her oldest—of more than one—child?

Her mind boggled, her heart raced, and her prayers soared.

| | | | | | | | | | | |

"Mommy! Come see!"

Under the shade of massive maple trees at the back of the lot, Maya found Barry and her parents sitting on the ground. In the dirt. Digging.

Barry popped to his feet, his knees and legs speckled with dry soil. He carefully came toward her, something balanced on the palm of his hand. "See what I found?"

It looked like a shard of something. "What is it?"

Barry looked back to his grandmother. "It's pottery from the twenty-ninth dynasty, right, Grandma?"

"Exactly right."

"Where did you get it?"

"In the dirt! We dug it up. It's been buried there for a zillion trillion years."

"Or since yesterday," Maya's father said under his breath.

Barry left the shard in his mother's hands and jumped back into the dirt. He lifted up two items. "See these? This is a brush and this is a sieve. I used the sieve to shake the dirt away, then the brush to clean off the rollics real careful-like."

"Relics," his grandma said.

"Relics," Barry repeated.

Maya's father stepped around the edge of the dig and sat on a step stool. "We've had a very productive afternoon. Barry can repeat the rulers of Egypt's twenty-ninth dynas—"

Barry stood up, as if needing room for big names. "There's Nepherites, Psammuthes, Hankor, and another Nepherites."

"Not Hankor," his grandmother explained, "Hakor."

"Hank or Hak, I'm impressed," Maya said. "How did you ever learn those hard names?"

"While we were digging for re—" He looked to his grandma. "Relics."

She ruffled his hair. "This boy has a real talent for archaeology."

"A real love of history," her father added.

Their words made Maya smile. "It must be in the genes," she said.

Her parents did a double take, then nodded.

It was an unnecessary jab. Her parents had warmed to Barry—

he, the adopted child of unknown genes—with an amazing speed and grace that Maya could only attribute to God's intervention.

And Barry's charm. For who could fail to fall in love with a child who loved unconditionally and only asked to be loved in return? And now . . . would there be another child to love?

Her mother stood and brushed off her khaki capris. "Who wants lunch? Maya, you're here early. Is everything all right?"

"Everything's grand. I just wanted to have lunch with my favorite archaeologists—all three of them." She held out a hand to her son.

Barry jumped up, pottery shards forgotten. "Grandma and I made oatmeal raisin cookies for dessert."

"You can dig *and* cook?" Maya said. "My, my, you are talented."

Barry took his mother's hand on one side and his grandma's hand on the other, and together they walked to the house.

"Everybody wash their hands," her father said, leading Barry to the sink. He looked over his shoulder. "Where's Marcela? She was going to join us."

"Her purse is gone," Maya said.

"She probably had to run an errand," her mother said. "She'll be back. She can't resist my egg salad."

| | | | | | | | | | |

"I'm back."

"See?" Maya's mother said to the others. She held up a tray of sandwiches. "Egg salad. I told you she wouldn't miss it."

Marcela came into the kitchen and plunked her purse and keys on the counter—along with a white plastic sack from a nearby drugstore. Before anyone could question her, she said, "Maya, I got what you needed at the store."

"What I needed?"

Marcela shoved the bag into her hands and took a pitcher of iced tea to the table.

Maya looked inside, having no idea—

Until she saw it. A pregnancy test.

"What is it, Mommy?"

Marcela answered for her. "Just some mommy stuff. But I got you some Skittles you can have for your afternoon snack."

"Yay!"

"Come on, Maya," her father said, already seated. "We're starved."

Maya stuffed the bag into her purse and sat down with her family. Her stomach was queasy again.

Out of excitement.

| | | | | | | | | | |

"Don't go yet." Maya's mother handed Barry a napkin for his milk mustache. "We have more digging to do, treasures to find."

Maya was already cleaning up the counter, needing to get home. She wasn't sure if the pregnancy test had to be taken at a certain time of day, but she knew for a fact she couldn't do anything here. She used an excuse that was only a slight exaggeration. "I'm still not feeling normal. But I want to thank—"

Her cell phone rang. It was Sal. Agata wanted to see them. "Now?"

"Now," Sal said. "I hope it's not bad news."

If only she had some good news to add to the day.

Not yet. One thing at a time. "We're coming."

She flipped her cell phone shut. "We have to go," she told Barry and her parents. "Agata needs to see us. Now."

Maya's mother offered Barry a cookie to go. "Her . . . ?" She mouthed the word *cancer*.

"I don't know. I hope not."

Her father took a couple of plates from the table to the sink. "Maybe Barry should stay here."

Maya removed her own plate and glass, shaking her head. "She specifically asked that he come too."

"Oh dear," her mother said.

"What's wrong?" Barry asked.

The adults exchanged a glance; then Maya smiled for his benefit. "Nonna Morano wants to see us. Your daddy is going to meet us there. Are you ready to go?"

"Will she have cookies too?"

"Grandmas always have cookies."

Maya hugged her sister good-bye. "Call me," Marcela said, her eyes full of meaning.

Maya nodded, then gave her parents a hug good-bye. She was amazed at this—the Castillas suddenly hugging the past few months—but she didn't question it.

"Good luck," her mother said. "I hope it's nothing."

At Agata's? Yes. *Nothing* would be good.

But at home . . . Maya was definitely hoping for a very big *something*.

| | | | | | | | | | |

On the drive to Agata's house, Maya was glad for Barry's monologue about his archaeological dig because it enabled her to insert an occasional "Oh really?" or "That's nice" and still worry about what was going on with her mother-in-law and wonder about whether she could possibly, maybe miraculously, be pregnant.

But that joy was for later. Now she had to be there for her mother-in-law. Agata had been through a lot the last year. Chemo and radiation and doctor visits had weakened her physically. But not mentally, and certainly not spiritually. If anything, Agata's faith seemed even stronger. Maya had come to a few of her prayer gatherings, listening more than talking, watching, ever watching, trying to figure out this strange phenomenon of prayer.

Sal and Barry came too, and Maya learned an amazing amount about faith from watching their little boy pray and praise. Barry didn't argue about the finer points of faith, or even know what he was doing. He just believed. Maybe the key was as simple as that: to have faith, have faith.

"Yay! We're here." Barry pointed to Sal's car in the drive. "And Daddy's here too."

Barry ran ahead to the front door—which was opened by Sal, who scooped his son into his arms. "Hey, bud. What did you do today?"

"Don't get him started," Maya whispered, "unless you want a list of Egyptian pharaohs."

Agata negated the warning by calling to him from her chair in the living room. "Come here, Barry-boy. Come give Nonna a big hug."

While the two of them were busy, Maya whispered to her husband. "Any clues?"

He shook his head and led her into the room. "So, Mom. The gang's all here."

It was Sal's normal greeting, which today, considering their summoning, seemed too flip.

But maybe that was best. Act normal.

Maya took her place on the couch. "Is that a new blouse, Agata?"

"It's blue," Barry said. "I can spell blue: b-l-u-e."

"Very good," Agata said.

"Barry, come sit by me," Maya said. *Leave Nonna alone. She has something important to tell us.*

Agata let him go—reluctantly—making Maya regret taking Barry away from her. Maybe she wanted him there for comfort?

Maya was just about to send him back again, when Agata spoke. "I have news. News I needed to share with my family."

The turn in Maya's stomach was reminiscent of her queasiness this morning. *Oh no. Here it comes.*

But then Agata smiled. "The prayers worked."

At first Maya didn't understand, but then Sal jumped off the couch and ran to his mother's side. "Oh, Mama. Really?"

She accepted his embrace, nodding. "The doctor said the tumor is gone. *Andato, sparito.*"

Maya rose to her feet. "You're . . . you're cured?"

Barry stood beside her. "Nonna, you're all well?"

Agata held out her hands to both of them. "God is good. God is merciful."

They gathered around her, hugging each other. Laughing. Crying.

When the initial celebration subsided they returned to their seats—except for Barry, who sat on the corner of Agata's chair, her arm keeping him close.

"Tell us what happened," Maya said.

"God happened." She pointed at each of them. "Your prayers happened."

Barry looked at his grandmother. "I prayed too."

She gave him a squeeze. "I knew it. I could feel it."

Maya was in shock. "But the doctors had said your chances were—"

"My doctors could only go by the facts they had in front of them," she said. "Apparently God had other plans."

"He listened to us!" Barry said.

"He most certainly did."

Maya was in awe. And feeling shame. Ever since learning about Agata's cancer she'd been bracing herself for the worst.

"Maya, you look troubled," Agata said.

How could she say this? Should she say this? "I . . . I never believed you'd be cured. I prayed, but I really didn't believe it would happen. So my prayers—they didn't help."

Agata smiled and nodded. "'I do believe, but help me overcome my unbelief!'"

Maya didn't understand.

Agata pulled Barry onto her lap. "God instructs us to pray. You prayed. You were obedient to him."

"But I didn't believe—"

"You went to him. That's the most important thing. There are no magic words. None of us know exactly how prayer works—only that it does. God knows your heart. He knows mine. He knows everyone's."

"Mine too?" Barry asked.

She kissed his cheek. "Especially yours." Agata continued. "Who's to say whether your prayer—even steeped in unbelief—wasn't the prayer God was waiting for before implementing his will?"

Maya laughed. "I assure you, my prayer did not change God's mind."

"No one's prayers change his mind," Agata said. "God does not change his mind. But I do believe he sometimes waits until after one of us prays to showcase his answer. He doesn't change. We change. Through prayer."

The idea of God waiting for her prayers . . . She began to cry. And then she remembered the pregnancy test in the car. Would God answer that prayer too?

She suffered a wave of doubt. No. He wouldn't give her two miracles. It would be too much, and she was a nobody. Agata deserved a miracle, but Maya . . .

She felt like a fool and covered her face with her hand. "I'm sorry. I know this isn't about me but—"

"But maybe it is about you, Maya. Maybe my sickness was a vehicle to get you to pray more often, to think about prayer."

"So you suffered because of me?"

"I suffered because he needed me to. His thoughts and ways are far beyond anything we can imagine."

Sal spoke up. "But now you've been granted a miracle—because he wanted a miracle."

"You're exactly right. It was a miracle." Agata pulled Barry close. "Another one."

In the excitement she'd forgotten that she'd already received a miracle in Barry. She pushed the hope of a pregnancy away. Three miracles? No. Two were more than generous. She couldn't even think about three. That would be greedy. She braced herself for the worst; she couldn't be sad when the pregnancy test came out negative. She wouldn't. God knew what he was doing.

If only *she* did. Maya had so much to learn about faith, about prayer, and about being a mother.

| | | | | | | | | | |

"They can't make me."

Roman had heard it before—variations of *stubborn* coming out of the mouths of young men whose minds were consumed with football glory but who were unprepared for the work involved, the waiting, the highs and lows of achievement, and the basic challenges of college life.

Desmond Wilson was no different. He was a kid from the East Coast who'd moved to the middle of the country after being a high school football star. He would be redshirted this year and maybe next year too, giving him time to mature as a player—and as a man. He'd been asked to give glory a wait.

"Actually, they *can* make you," Roman said. "Or they can create consequences if you don't follow the rules."

"I hate rules."

"Tough."

It was not the answer Desmond expected. He lifted himself out of his slump enough to lean on the table that separated them. "Hey, I know there's stuff to think about, and you want me to get involved with the other rookies and do good in class, and Coach Rollins talks about helping in the community and all, but the truth is, all I want to do right now is play football. That's why I'm here, you know? I can't spend my time worrying about all that other stuff. I gotta think about my future."

Was that an opening, or what? Roman took a pen from his shirt pocket and wrote on a piece of paper. He slipped the note to Desmond. "Here's the scoop about your future, Desmond, *and* why you're here."

Desmond looked at it, clearly confused. "'John 3:16'? What's that?"

"It was my son's favorite Bible verse."

Desmond made a face and pushed the slip of paper back toward Roman. "No offense, Mr. Paulson, but I don't need no Bible junk. I'm here to play football."

"Indeed you are. But there's so much more than that going on. Important stuff."

"Like what?"

"Like . . . let me tell you a story about my son and some words that were very important to him. . . ."

| | | | | | | | | | |

Peter stood at the mudroom sink and wiped off his freshly cleaned hands and forearms. His dad splashed water on his face, also making himself presentable after working in the field all morning.

They had guests.

Not guests. Family.

Carrie popped her head into the room. "Come on, you two. Velvet and John are here."

"Coming." Peter tossed a towel to his dad. "Come on, Grandpa. I smell fried chicken."

"If you grab all the legs, you'll be needing two new ones yourself."

They walked through the kitchen, where Peter's mom stood at the stove, making chicken gravy in a sizzling frying pan. "About time," she said. "We were going to eat without you."

Peter's father plucked a piece of crispy batter from the serving plate of chicken. "The wheat is ready to be planted and seeds need to be sown, fried chicken or no fried chicken."

Velvet came into the kitchen, carrying four-month-old Ethan. "Can I help?"

"You could put the mashed potatoes in the serving dish," Peter's mom said.

"I'll do that," Carrie said.

John followed his wife into the kitchen. "Hey, men. Hot enough for you?"

"I've seen hotter," Peter's dad said.

"I bet you have. The crops coming around like they should?"

"They're getting there."

Peter's dad and John wandered into the dining room talking about farming. Peter rubbed his nose against the nose of his son while he lay in Velvet's arms. "Are you a happy baby with Grandma?"

The baby smiled and Peter beamed. Smiles were a recent accomplishment for the boy.

"He's getting so big," Velvet said, rocking him in a grandma rhythm.

Carrie finished spooning out the potatoes. She added a large dollop of butter on top. "He can sit up. Kind of."

"If we prop a thousand pillows around him," Peter said.

"My, my," Velvet said, "before you know it, he'll be walking."

Peter's mother turned off the burner and poured the gravy into a server. "He'll be walking in time for the wedding—or if he's anything like his daddy, he'll be running. Peter ran every-where."

Velvet bounced the boy in her arms. "How are the wedding plans coming? What's the final date?"

"May 22. The weekend after I graduate," Peter said.

"I picked out a dress," Carrie said. She beamed and looked mischievous at the same time, a feat Peter was still trying to fathom. It was something in her eyes. . . .

"What's it look like?" he asked—knowing the question would get him nowhere. Carrie was being very secretive.

"Curiosity killed the cat." She brushed her arm against his as she took the potatoes into the dining room.

"And drove many a groom crazy," Peter's mother added.

"The dress is always a secret," Velvet said. "Your job as the groom is to show up on time and smile adoringly at your bride."

He could handle that.

"John and I made sure we'd be in town the entire month of May to help."

"How is the speaking circuit going?" Peter's mother asked. "Are you enjoying being a part of it?"

"John's helped me slog my way through it. I'm not used to speaking to a crowd but we've had good response from people who've heard my story. Who knew my mistakes would help any-one else? Punishment to peace."

Peter's mother handed him the platter of chicken. "Everyone likes to hear stories of victory over hard times."

"Over stupidity."

"That too."

They all moved into the dining room amid the swell of laugh-ter and family chatter.

| | | | | | | | | | |

The dinner was nearly over. People sat back from the table, their stomachs full.

Peter's mother got up. "Who wants peach pie?"

Everyone moaned and "later" was the consensus. His mother had started clearing the table when she sidestepped and looked out the dining room window. "It's Ned, the mailman. He never comes up to the door unless he has a package." She looked at her husband. "You expecting anything?"

"Not me."

She moved to the door. "A package for me, Ned?"

"Nope. But there's another letter from Africa, for Peter. I'm afraid it got a little mangled, like it's had a hard journey, so I wanted to bring it up to the house and make this last part easy for it. And it's . . . it was supposed to be Express Mail International, but obviously it's been delayed. Sorry 'bout that. Have a good one."

She brought the letter to Peter. It was a mangled thing, looking like a dog ate it.

"It's from Kid Help International. It must be from Lianne," he said. But then he checked the postmark. "Sent on the sixth."

"That's ten days ago. That is *not* Express Mail," his dad said.

Carrie gathered some dirty plates. "I have a gob of photos of Ethan to send to Lianne."

"Did you make doubles for me?" Velvet asked.

"Of course."

"Baby pictures," his father said. "We could wallpaper a room with them."

"Hmm," Peter's mother said. "That might be an idea."

"Don't even . . ."

Peter had the envelope open and pulled out a letter—and a snapshot.

Carrie looked over his shoulder. "It's Lianne with a little girl, probably one of the kids she's helping." Peter passed it around the table.

"She looks happy enough," John said.

"I think she is happy," Velvet said. "Her last letter practically burst out of the envelope with excitement. She really loves teaching the kids songs and drawing with them. There's one little girl she especially loves. Her name's Diabra—or something like that. I wonder if this is her."

Peter opened the letter, expecting to see Lianne's messy cursive. Instead was a typed letter on Kid Help letterhead.

Dear Mr. McLean,
We are extremely sorry to tell you that . . .

Peter's eyes skimmed ahead and landed on *accident*. "What?" He shook his head back and forth, unwilling to allow the words on the page to land. "Lianne's been in a car accident."

"Is she okay?" Velvet asked.

He got back to the letter and decided to just read it aloud. "'. . . sorry to tell you that Lianne was in a car accident on the fourth and—'"

"Nearly two weeks ago!" Carrie said.

He put up a hand, needing to finish it. "'. . .and she's been in the hospital here. A broken leg and arm, and some other injuries that—'"

"Other injuries?" Velvet said. "More than two broken limbs?"

John put a hand on hers. "Shh. Let him finish."

Peter read the rest through and summarized it. "She's being sent home for medical attention and recuperation—they mention 'to her mother's house.'" He looked at Velvet.

"Don't look at me. I know as little as you. But that's fine. That's good. She doesn't have an apartment here anymore. Of course she can stay with us. The point is she's coming home."

"But she needs more medical attention," Carrie said. "Which means they can't handle it."

Velvet bit her lip and then gripped John's hand. "And the letter's old. How is she now, today?"

"And when is she getting here?" Carrie asked.

"And why didn't anyone call?" Velvet asked.

Peter couldn't answer Velvet's question but had an answer for Carrie. "She's being flown into Lincoln on the sixteenth. Flight 2580, arriving at three fifteen."

Suddenly, Velvet stood, nearly toppling her chair. "Today's the sixteenth!"

Peter looked at the date on his watch. "It is." Then the time. "It's one thirty."

Velvet rushed for her purse. "We have to go."

Peter took Ethan out of his infant seat and gave him an extra hug. "Your mommy's in trouble, buddy. Let's go make her better."

He hoped "better" was a possibility.

| | | | | | | | | | |

I shouldn't think this way.

Peter stood on the large balcony dividing the security checkpoints leading to two gates. Lianne's plane had arrived. In a few minutes he would see her for the first time in nearly three months. And more than that, she would see Ethan.

Their son.

Would her motherly instincts kick in? Would she suddenly want to be an active part of Ethan's life? Would the tidy little world Peter had created for himself, Carrie, and Ethan be complicated or, even worse, destroyed by her presence?

Once again the realization that he shouldn't think this way intruded—and he was convicted anew. Lianne was hurt. She was home to recuperate. He had to think of her needs too.

"There! There she is!" Velvet said.

Lianne came out of the security area—was pushed out in a wheelchair. Her leg was in a cast, as was an arm. Her head hung low, nearly touching her chest.

Velvet rushed forward, offering her an awkward embrace.

Carrie gripped Peter's arm, whispering, "She looks awful."

Peter's mom put a hand on his shoulder. "She's had a hard trip, hard for a healthy person to endure. She's going to need some TLC."

Peter glanced at her. His parents had not warmed to Lianne before she left, for Lianne had continued to do a good job of being bristly enough to keep them at arm's length. Now, to hear true compassion in his mother's voice . . .

His mother caught his look. "What? The girl will need help. We'll all need to help her."

"Thank you."

She pulled his forehead to touch hers. "Some people are hard to love, but that doesn't mean we shouldn't do it. I feel bad I wasn't nicer."

Peter was moved by his mother's confession. "She didn't make it easy."

"Which does not excuse me in the least." She let him go, nodding toward Lianne. "Show that baby to her. Seeing her son should make her feel much better."

Peter stepped forward, sitting Ethan facing outward in his arms. "Hey," he said.

Lianne looked up at him, her complexion pale and punctuated by blotches of multicolored bruises. Her eyes brightened and she smiled at the baby, reaching her good hand toward him. "Hey, big boy. How you doing?"

Ethan kicked his feet over the shelf of Peter's arm and put his fingers in his mouth. Then he let out a wail, surprising them all.

Lianne pulled her hand away and looked appalled. Carrie

stepped forward, a bottle in hand. "He's just hungry, that's all. Come on, sweetie." She took him from Peter and expertly cradled him as he fed, swaying gently to soothe him.

Peter looked at Lianne, wondering how she would react. He'd told her he and Carrie were getting married, and she'd written back that she was happy for them, but to actually see Carrie taking care of *her* son . . .

Lianne took a deep breath and said, "I'm really tired. I need to get to sleep." She looked to Velvet and John.

John took control of the wheelchair. "And we're off. Before you know it, you'll be settled in."

They all headed to an elevator to make their way to the baggage claim below. Lianne looked up at Carrie, still feeding Ethan. "You're a good mama to him. Thanks."

Peter sucked in a breath, pushed the Down button . . .

And thanked God.

| | | | | | | | | | |

"Thanks," Lianne said.

Velvet smoothed the covers, then adjusted the blinds of the guest room so the sun wouldn't bother her daughter's rest. She began to unpack Lianne's suitcase. "These top two drawers are empty, but I can make more room if we need—"

"Stop," Lianne said.

Her voice was not demanding but held a foreign softness that Velvet had rarely heard from her. Velvet put the final shirt away and shut the drawer. "You're right. You need to sleep," Velvet said. "I can finish—"

"Will you bring me something from my carry-on, please?"

"Sure." Velvet found the bag by the door.

"In the outer zipper there's a pocket Bible. I'd like to have that here, with me."

You're kidding.

Velvet must have made a face because Lianne laughed, then grimaced and held her ribs. "I know, I know. But a lot has happened the past three months."

Obviously.

Velvet brought the Bible to her, but Lianne put up a hand. "Open it to the bookmark and read the words underlined in red."

Velvet opened the Bible and saw them. Her throat tightened, but she read aloud. "'For God loved the world so much that he gave his one and only Son, so that everyone who believes in him will not perish but have eternal life.'" She closed the Bible and looked at her daughter. "The verse."

"The verse." She held her hand out for the book and set it against her chest, her good hand holding it there protectively. "The words *did* affect me, Velvet. It took a while, and I fought them, but . . ." Lianne shrugged. "God got me. Got to me. And I let him in. After all, we both gave up a son."

Velvet put a hand on Lianne's. "Oh, my dear girl."

Lianne let her head sink deeper into the pillow and closed her eyes. "I have to sleep now. Would you sit with me awhile?"

"Of course I will." Velvet made one last adjustment to the covers and pulled a chair closer to the bed. In just a few minutes, Lianne's breathing settled and slowed.

And she was asleep.

Velvet looked upon her, then reached out and touched the blanket as if making sure this was real. Could this really be . . . ?

Yes. This was her daughter. Blood of her blood. Heart of her heart.

Speaking of . . . Velvet felt her heart swell. The feeling surprised her, the sudden fullness. The odd ache. The pull that was poignant and bittersweet and very, very real.

With a sudden rush she realized *this* was what it felt like to love—love like a mother.

God was good. Very, very good.

| | | | | | | | | | | |

Maya sat on the toilet lid in the master bathroom. It was three in the morning.

The pregnancy test had suggested that the most accurate test was taken in the morning when the pregnancy hormone was the most highly concentrated.

So what constituted morning? Six o'clock? Seven?

Was three good enough?

It had to be because she wouldn't get any sleep until she *knew*. And so, a few minutes ago she had tiptoed into the bathroom and taken the test out of its hiding place at the back of the linen closet. She'd already read the directions multiple times. She knew what to do. Step one. Step two.

Now she was well into step three: the waiting part.

Maya held her watch in her hand, vowing not to look at the results until the time was legally up. She pressed her forehead against her hands, letting the latest of multiple prayers wind their way to heaven. *Please, please, one more miracle, Lord. One more miracle. . . .*

She checked the watch again and was shocked to see it was five seconds beyond *time*.

Maya sat upright and pressed a hand against her throbbing heart.

This was it.

She attempted a breath to calm herself, then took the test stick in her hand and . . .

Gasped.

It was a +.

"I'm pregnant!" she whispered. And then she began to sob, letting her head drop to her knees. "Thank you, Jesus. Thank you, Lord; thank you—"

"Maya? Are you okay?"

402 Maya leaped to her feet and yanked open the door. She threw her arms around Sal's neck, and shocked by her sudden onslaught, he held her tight against him.

"Hon? What's wrong?"

She realized the panic he must be in and let him go. She felt the pregnancy stick, still in her hand. "Here," she said.

He stared at it. Then looked up at her. "A pregnancy test?"

"A positive pregnancy test."

He gaped at her, then looked at the test, then at her again. "But we can't—"

"'Humanly speaking, it is impossible. But not with God. Everything is possible with God.'"

Sal shook his head, incredulous. "'Anything is possible if a person believes.'" He took her hand and brought it to his lips. "We prayed for this."

"We did."

"And God answered—he gave us a miracle."

"Another miracle," Maya said, pulling him close enough to kiss him on the lips.

Then together, without need for discussion, they sank to their knees and gave thanks.

| | | | | | | | | | |

Faith is the confidence that what we hope for will actually happen; it gives us assurance about things we cannot see.

HEBREWS 11:1

SCRIPTURE VERSES IN *JOHN 3:16*

CHAPTER 1:   Pride/Psalm 123:4

CHAPTER 2:   Wicked/Psalm 10:11
Temptation/Matthew 26:41
Temptation/1 Corinthians 10:13 (paraphrased)

CHAPTER 3:   Approval/Galatians 1:10
God's provision/Psalm 121:3

CHAPTER 4:   Plans/Proverbs 19:21
Purpose/Jeremiah 1:5

CHAPTER 5:   Pain/Psalm 69:29
Unity/Matthew18:20

CHAPTER 6:   Hope/Psalm 130:5-6

CHAPTER 7:   Wisdom/James 1:5-6

CHAPTER 8:   Sacrifice/Matthew 20:28
Prayers/James 5:16
Sacrifice/John 15:13
Lord's Prayer/Matthew 6:9
Strength/Philippians 4:13

CHAPTER 9:   God's ways/Isaiah 55:8-9
Love/1 John 4:19
God's ways: Isaiah 45:15 (paraphrased)
Prayer/Matthew 7:8

Nancy Moser

Plans/Proverbs 16:9
Trust/Proverbs 3:5-6
Sharing/Matthew 10:27

CHAPTER 10: Renewal/Psalm 51:9-10
Peace/John 14:27

CHAPTER 11: Plans/1 Corinthians 2:9
Salvation/John 3:16
Love/1 Corinthians 13:4-7
Persecution/2 Timothy 3:12 (paraphrased)
Moving on/Mark 6:11 (paraphrased)

CHAPTER 12: Renewal/Titus 3:5

EPILOGUE: God's signs/Job 33:14
Faith/Mark 9:24
God's mind/1 Samuel 15:29 (paraphrased)
God's ways/Isaiah 55:8 (paraphrased)
Possibilities/Mark 10:27
Possibilities/Mark 9:23
Faith/Hebrews 11:1

404

DISCUSSION QUESTIONS

1. Have you ever seen someone hold up a John 3:16 sign at a sporting event? What did you think about it at the time? Did you know what the verse said/meant? Why is the message of this verse important?

2. In Chapter 1, Maya says she is striving to be the person she wants to be. Is this goal common to all people or are some people content with who they are? Which is better: to strive for change or to be okay with who you are?

3. Maya followed her boss's instructions toward success but went too far. Do you think she should have been held more or less responsible than she was? Have you ever experienced a situation at work where a coworker cut ethical corners? What were the results?

4. What do you think of William and Carrie's vow to stay pure until marriage? Is this feasible in today's world?

5. At Billy's funeral, Agata says William was praying for her and cites a verse: "The earnest prayer of a righteous person has great power and produces wonderful results." What constitutes being a "righteous" person? Who, in your life, would you deem righteous?

6. Peter gets seduced away from the foundation of his life. When have you or those you loved been lured away from your foundation? What came of the experience? Are you better now for having gone through it?

7. Roman put all his hopes and dreams into his son. Is this inevitable for parents? Is it a good or bad thing?

8. In Chapter 10, Maya tries to close the doors on her old life—her past mistakes—so she can continue on a new path. When have you closed such doors? Did it help you move ahead? Or did it matter? What doors should you close today?

9. Velvet imposed punishment on herself for past sins. How do you think her life would have been different if she'd forgiven herself for her past and moved on sooner? What do you need to forgive yourself for?

10. Maya and Sal were obsessed with having a child. Their prayers were answered—though not as they expected. What prayer of yours has been answered in unexpected ways?

11. What is Lianne's true personality, i.e. is her tough-girl number genuine or a front? Are other characters pretending to be something they're not? Maya? Roman? Peter? Velvet?

12. What do you think of Lianne's decision regarding her child?

13. Velvet and Roman decide their relationship was not healthy. In what way? How can you identify healthy or unhealthy aspects of your own relationships?

14. John Gillingham wrote a book about his mistakes and what he learned from them. How is your life better—or worse—for the mistakes you've made?

15. Maya is affected by her parents' view of adoption. How have you let your parents' opinions affect your decisions? What were the results?

16. Agata believes that sometimes God waits to grant an answer to prayer until one particular person prays. What do you think about this?

17. Many of the characters receive nudges: the multiple "Johns," the red signs, the number *316* . . . What nudges have you experienced? What happened when you followed them? Or when you didn't?

18. In the end, the characters discover their true purpose. Have you discovered yours?

ABOUT THE AUTHOR

Nancy Moser is the best-selling author of seventeen novels including *Solemnly Swear*, *The Good Nearby*, *Mozart's Sister*, and the Christy Award–winning *Time Lottery*. She also coauthored the Sister Circle series with Campus Crusade cofounder Vonette Bright. Nancy is a motivational speaker, and information about her Said So Sister Seminar can be found at www.nancymoser.com and www.sistercircles.com. Nancy and her husband, Mark, have three grown children and live in the Midwest.

A NOTE FROM THE AUTHOR

Dear Reader,

If someone held up a John 3:16 sign right now, how would you react?

I have to admit that years ago, when I first saw such a sign at a game, my first reaction was, "Huh?" My second reaction was to figure the verse had something to do with victory. Only years later did I actually read the verse and remember the sign and go, "Oh . . . that kind of victory." Better late than never.

In this book I wanted to showcase characters who were given multiple chances to say yes to God but for a variety of reasons told him "No" or "Not now." We all have a tendency to believe there's always another day to dig deeper into our souls and commit. We can pray a little harder later, when we have more time. Like Scarlett O'Hara always said, "I'll think about that tomorrow . . . after all, tomorrow is another day."

Sometimes. But not always. Because time does run out.

I am guilty of all the excuses listed above—and more. I'd like to rationalize that it's normal and human nature, but so is eating too much at Christmas and vegging out in front of TV, neither of which is good for us. Making our relationship with God number one on our daily to-do list is a goal we need to strive for—over and over and over again. He appreciates the effort and blessedly understands and forgives the failures.

This book is also about lives that intersect. Some call it coincidence. I call it destiny. Some may say, "But to have so many lives intersect is implausible."

Is it?

There's a game about Kevin Bacon that points out how most Hollywood stars can be traced back to some connection with

410

Kevin Bacon. Is that because Bacon is that important or special? No. The same exercise could be executed with other actors who have been around awhile.

Why can't the same exercise occur between unfamous people? We all know dozens, if not hundreds of people and come in contact with hundreds more. Is there a thread connecting us, pulling us together? I believe that's how God works, binding us, weaving our lives into a fabric of being. Why has God created us to live at this particular time, together? Why do we live where we do? Why do we have the jobs, the families, the organizations, the hobbies we do? To bring us into contact with others. Sometimes that contact is trivial, but sometimes . . . if we look closely, we can see the warp and weft, we can see the stitches, the knots, the mistakes of the weaving. Perhaps from far away, we can see only a block of color. Unimpressive. Ordinary. Yet, when we get close and really look . . . we just might see a purpose in it. A plan.

On a less lofty train of thought, the other reason this book combines these people in amazing ways is that I want it that way. I'm certainly not interested in writing about people's lives that have nothing to do with each other, and I bet you aren't interested in reading such a bit of prose, either. And so . . . I had great fun in discovering the connections, the possibilities, the *aha!* moments of the plot, where A could add to B and get C. And I want to thank my editor, Denise Little, for helping me dig deeper into their heads and hearts in the process.

So forgive me if I've annoyed you by my weaving. My intent was to inspire and to open your eyes to the weavings going on around each one of us. Take up a thread and dive in. Become part of this amazing fabric of life God has created for us. John 3:16, people; John 3:16.

Blessings,
Nancy Moser